BY THE SWORD

a novel

AN AMBER ROBBINS MIDEAST THRILLER

MIKE YORKEY RICK MYATT

BY THE SWORD

a novel

NASHVILLE, TENNESSEE

Printed in the United States of America

13-digit ISBN: 978-0-8054-4073-7
10-digit ISBN: 0-8054-4073-9

Published by Broadman & Holman Publishers,
Nashville, Tennessee

Dewey Decimal Classification: F
Subject Headings: ADVENTURE FICTION
MIDDLE EAST—FICTION

1 2 3 4 5 6 7 8 9 10 10 09 08 07 06

To Nicole and Laurie, the loves of our lives

1

Friday, April 7
2:46 A.M. local time
Jerusalem

Kareh Bottstein groaned softly and turned to her side. Her fingers pushed against her tight abdomen, and a baby's foot, or perhaps an elbow, shoved back. Despite the middle-of-the-night hour, nature was calling . . . again. With only three weeks left in her pregnancy, regular visits to the bathroom were the norm. She kicked the fluffy ivory-colored duvet off her bare legs and pushed her bulging torso to an upright position. Glancing at the ruby-red numerals of her clock radio, she yawned and ran her fingers through the brown hair that fell in thatches across her face. Then she waddled toward the apartment's single bathroom.

As she stepped inside the W. C. and flipped on a light, Kareh realized she wasn't the only one awake. Sounds of an ancient city journeyed through the open window. Traffic echoed off the cobblestone streets of old Jerusalem, and in the distance, a police siren reverberated somewhere within the Walled City.

She had just flushed the toilet when the sound of a muted voice halted her. After standing frozen for a moment, ears perked to the slightest sound, she relaxed. Must be Alev mumbling in the next room. For someone so skilled at keeping government secrets, he sure did talk in his sleep a lot.

She trundled back to bed. Gathering the warm duvet over her body, she leaned over and kissed her husband's cheek, then lay on her side, her hand resting on his muscled chest. As she closed her eyes, images of the night's Passover meal replayed in her mind.

"Come, lay down," Aunt Sora had urged, whipping off her wedding ring and searching for a string. "I'll tell you the sex of your babushka."

Soon every woman in the room was settling her down on the couch.

"Relax," Aunt Sora ordered. "It's painless. All I have to do is dangle my wedding ring above your navel. If the ring spins clockwise, then you'll have—"

"I don't believe in those old wives' tales," Kareh protested. "Besides, I don't think Benjamin cares if he has a brother or sister. That's why I told the doctor doing the ultrasounds not to tell me. I don't want to know."

"I do! I do!" Benjamin, their three-year-old son, jumped up on the couch next to his mother.

Aunt Sora giggled to the other ladies. "So, we won't tell you. We'll just tell the father. Anyone working for the Zahal can keep his mouth shut."

Alev sampled from a dish of olives with an amused grin. "I don't think I'd be very good at keeping that information a state secret," he said.

Kareh smiled at the memory, but more noises from the hall rose above the rhythmic breathing of her sleeping husband and disrupted her thoughts.

How can men sleep so soundly? Kareh shut her eyes and allowed her fatigue to wash over her. Then she heard another thump from somewhere in their apartment building.

Louder.

Closer.

Perhaps it was Tirov. The army officer next door did keep odd hours. Maybe Tirov had invited colleagues from the night shift to celebrate a late Passover with a glass of wine.

No, there was more to it than that. Kareh sat up. She heard grunting, along with a heavy object being dragged down the hall.

"Alev." She shook her husband's shoulder. "Someone's making a terrible racket."

"Probably Tirov," he moaned. "It's nothing."

"You're not getting up?"

"It's nothing."

Tirov never makes such noise. She slipped out of bed and wrapped a bathrobe around her, the belt barely fitting around her bulging abdomen. Hurrying into the living room, she turned the corner and flipped on a light. A scream caught in her throat at what she saw.

Two men, dressed in black and wearing hoods with eye slits, stood in her living room, fanning their machine guns from side to side. The shorter of the two raised a thick finger to his mouth.

Kareh gripped her stomach then spotted the other weapons attached to their black leather belts. Her eyes darted around the room. *Should I run? Wake Alev?* Through the open front door she saw two more black-hooded men lugging a footlocker down the hallway.

"Who are you?" she asked in Hebrew. "What do you want?"

When they failed to respond, Kareh asked the same questions in English. The steely glance between the men told her they understood.

"Not to know for you," the tall, lean intruder on the left said in an accent that showed Kareh, a part-time English teacher, that these men spoke Farsi or Arabic.

Alev's voice carried from their bedroom. "Bubbeleh, come back to bed."

The stout man skulked toward Kareh, his cold eyes piercing hers. He touched his swarthy index finger to her lips. A sick shiver shimmied down Kareh's spine.

"Kareh?" Alev's voice was louder this time.

"Attackers!" she cried out in Hebrew. "Alev, hel—"

Her assailant wrapped his beefy arm around her throat and squeezed. She clawed his arm, fighting to breathe.

Kareh's fingers dug deeper into the man's arm. She thrashed and wrestled with all her might, but she was no physical match.

A gloved hand squeezed her mouth. Kareh bit as hard as she could, gnawing a fat finger. The intruder reared back and slammed her to the ground. She rolled, hugging her stomach to protect the life of her unborn child.

Alev stumbled through the doorway.

"No!" she managed to choke out.

Too late.

A silenced burst from a compact submachine gun raked her husband's chest, pinning him against a wall. Alev struggled for several seconds to remain upright, then slid to the floor, leaving a trail of blood.

Kareh scrambled on her hands and knees, lunging toward her husband. The tall one stepped in her path, his sidearm targeting her midsection. "Always have I wanted to kill a pregnant Jew."

"No, not my baby!" Kareh darted past the man's legs but stopped when she felt cold metal pressed against her forehead. She slumped against the back of the couch as horrified sobs shook her body. Slowly he redirected the tip of the barrel toward her expansive belly.

"No, no, no . . . ," she pleaded. "Don't shoot my baby! Not my baby!"

Screams and panicked outbursts from throughout the apartment building interrupted Kareh's plea, yet the intruder's soulless eyes remained locked on her.

"One way you save yourself," the hooded man said as he bent down. He spoke the Question into her ear.

Her eyes widened. "I can't! I could never do that!"

"Then by the forces of Islam, you and your child will die."

"No!" Kareh lunged at the intruder. He tripped, hitting his head hard against the corner of the wall. Kareh trampled over his body toward the door, but he grabbed one leg and wrestled her back to the ground. She tumbled to the hardwood floor and felt a pistol tip plunge into her abdomen.

She jerked her torso in one last valiant attempt to escape, but the force of the bullet tore into her flesh. She screamed—not for herself, but for the unborn child she would protect to her death.

"Search the rest of the apartment," the triggerman and commando leader barked. "You know our orders: unless they convert, everyone dies."

Several minutes later, two comrades dragged an unconscious man—dressed in black from head to toe—into the Bottstein apartment. At the same moment, another intruder emerged from the master bedroom.

"Did you find the gun?" the commando leader inquired.

"In his nightstand, as you predicted."

"Lot of good it did him. The stupid infidel. Allah deals with him now."

The commando leader directed his comrades as they hauled the drugged man into the hallway and slumped him on top of Alev's bullet-ridden body. A gloved hand passed him an Israeli army pistol, which he placed into Alev's clammy right hand, carefully wrapping the thumb and forefinger around the firing mechanism. The leader then lifted Alev's dead hand up and brought the handgun to the back of the unconscious man's head, quickly squeezing the trigger. Blood gushed from the head wound.

As they turned to leave, one of the attackers could not resist a final indignity—a swift kick to the man's groin. The intruders regrouped and exited the front door where the commando leader opened the footlocker, revealing a screwdriver, two gallons of paint, and four paintbrushes.

"Here, take this," he said, lifting a paint can and screwdriver out of the box. With two or three quick motions, he popped off the lid. The paint was a deep, crimson red—the same color as the blood that now stained the Jews' apartments. "Watch this."

With elated satisfaction, he brusquely dipped the brush past the bristles into the can, then jerked it out, allowing gobs of paint to drip onto the hallway rug. The commando leader swathed the doorjamb in red paint as the others gawked.

"What are you waiting for?" he yelled to a pair. "Paint!"

The two men's Mac-10s clattered to the ground as they grabbed paintbrushes. They swashed the Bottsteins' doorjamb, the smell of paint mingling with the acrid odor of gunpowder. The commando leader smirked as they slathered blood-colored paint over the *mezuzah* scroll blessing the doorpost.

Within minutes they'd painted the doorjambs of the other three units on that floor, mirroring the actions of fedayeen elsewhere in the building.

"The Angel of Death has surely visited our enemy." The leader's voice exuded confidence. "I can assure you that this is only the beginning."

The commando leader spoke rapidly into a radio securely fastened to his sleeve. "Go now," he called to his men, assured his instructions had been followed according to plan. As the men scrambled down the stairs to the getaway vehicle, he hung behind. One final job awaited him—the front entrance. Working quickly to avoid being seen, he sloppily swabbed the jamb outlining the glass doors in bright red paint. "Dirty Jews. Rest you will not find."

When he had finished his final painting chore, the commando leader vaulted into the passenger seat of the van. "*Allahu Akbar!* God has granted us victory over our enemies!" he called to his comrades. *Yes,* he thought, *everything as planned.* All that remained was to exit the country, but he expected no problems there.

2

Friday, April 7
6:10 A.M. local time
Jerusalem

As much as Amber Robbins hated rising at dawn, the sight of a brilliant orange sun bursting above the Judean foothills and their orchards of olive trees made the pain worth the gain. She finished tying her Nike running shoes and grabbed a small wallet from her purse. She clipped a cell phone to her waist then zipped the jacket of her white Adidas warm-up suit, which completely covered her arms and legs. This was a concession to living in the Middle East; black spandex shorts and a sports bra didn't cut it in this part of the world.

Amber stretched her hamstrings at the stairwell of her apartment building then windmilled her arms to boost circulation. Her body, dormant just twenty minutes earlier, was ready for an endorphin boost.

Amber pushed the panic bar on the door and stepped onto a sidewalk bordering Ben Gurion Boulevard. Soon the summer sun would scorch the countryside, making jogging nearly impossible, but today's spring air was cool with a hint of cherry blossoms in the breeze.

Even at this early hour, Friday morning traffic moved briskly in all four lanes. Amber jogged slowly but purposefully in a northerly direction. After a minute or two, she settled into her seven-minute-mile pace. Amber liked dawn patrol because she didn't have to contend with as many buses and trucks belching noxious fumes. After four blocks, she turned left at Damyon Street, the gateway into the Harish neighborhood, where influential bureaucrats and intelligence types lived in government-financed housing tracts.

Amber breathed in and out gently, enjoying the solitude of Harish. A shop owner washing down the sidewalk with a green hose directed the spray to his left, so as not to wet Amber's ankles and running shoes. "Thank you," she huffed as she jogged past. Amber concentrated on her running cadence, finding just the right stride as her feet pounded the stone sidewalk. When she turned onto Zigzo Street, she lowered her head and increased her gait. Amber glanced at her Ebel watch to see whether she was making good time—

"Halt!"

Amber didn't have time to break her stride. Her body propelled into the arms of a uniformed man with a thud. He forcefully pushed her away, and she hit the unforgiving sidewalk on her tailbone. Her hands weren't quick enough to break the fall.

"Hey!" Amber cried out, pushing back strands of brunette hair from her face. She was about to launch into a tirade when she noticed his Israeli corporal's uniform. He pointed an M-16 assault rifle directly at her face.

Amber sucked in a breath then shielded her eyes from the rising sun. The soldier backed up quickly and took a position behind a parked sedan. He yelled something in Hebrew and waved the rifle at her chest.

"American! American press!" she screamed in English, hands raised.

"Against the wall! Now!"

Amber jumped to her feet and faced the wall, raising her hands higher above her head.

"Lift up your shirt!"

"What?"

"Lift up your shirt now or I shoot!"

Amber understood. He thought she was a suicide bomber. This was no time to stand on modesty. She swiveled her head toward him and rolled up her loose-fitting jacket, exposing her back.

"Turn around and keep your arms up."

Amber slowly pivoted and faced him. The soldier circled his rifle at her abdomen. Amber lifted her training top, exposing her stomach but nothing more.

Satisfied, the solider lowered the gun and approached her.

"Identification, please."

Amber reached into her back pocket and pulled out a slim wallet. She handed him her international press card.

"You're a reporter for the *Washington National*," the soldier said, stating the obvious.

"Yes, I've been stationed here two years."

"You may go."

"Wait a minute." Amber retrieved her wallet from his hand. "What's going on?"

"We have an incident." He jerked his head up the street.

Amber peered over his shoulder. "Can I take a look? For my job, you know."

He nodded then stepped aside. Amber cautiously moved toward the yellow ribbon outlining the crime scene. Several emergency vehicles blocked the streets where Israeli soldiers swarmed like angry hornets. No press yet.

"What the—" she began, catching sight of the door of the nearest apartment building. Red paint had been roughly brushed along the doorjamb.

A voice surprised her from behind. "What's the word you Americans have for something like this? 'Bizarre'?"

Amber pivoted to face the voice. "Colonel Levi?"

The Israeli officer offered a wan smile.

"What's going on?" she asked.

Colonel Leonard Levi tamped a Marlboro cigarette a couple of times, lit it, and took a long drag. He had briefed Amber more than a dozen times for various situations since she'd arrived in Jerusalem. They'd hit it off—unusual considering the adversarial relationship between the Israeli army and foreign journalists.

"Miss Robbins, our nation must bear another tragedy." He glanced at the building and exhaled a ring of smoke. "A half hour ago, one of our corporals on routine patrol noticed the red paint around the front entrance." He pointed toward the glass doors. "The soldier stepped inside and immediately called for backup. They arrived ten minutes ago. I just got here myself."

The colonel's radio squawked.

"We're coming down the hallway now," said a disturbed voice. "Looks like a whacked-out Picasso did some painting in here too. Wait a minute. We have an open door . . ."

Amber and the colonel waited.

"Two bodies in the main bedroom. Dead. Shots to the back of the head." Silence. Then boots trampling and soldiers shouting at each other.

"We're in the next apartment." The man's voice was raspy. "The body of a young woman is in the living room. She was shot in the stomach. Looks like she was pregnant. Hold on. I have a pulse. Get medics up here now! Second floor!"

A pair of paramedics listening to the same transmission sprinted into action, hustling a backboard and medical kit through the front entrance.

Colonel Levi and Amber continued to listen.

"I need somebody to stabilize this woman! Got her? Good. I'm investigating now . . . I see two more bodies . . . one of them looks like a perp. Someone must have popped him. What a bloodbath."

Amber spoke up. "If you don't mind, Colonel, I'd better call this in."

"By all means, Miss Robbins." He excused himself and hustled toward an approaching military jeep.

Amber reached for her cell phone and speed-dialed a number in Washington, D.C.

"Hello, Amber," said a deep voice. "It's awfully early where you are. What's up?"

"Listen, Evan. How much time do we have before deadline?"

"Let's see, it's just after 11:00 P.M., so ninety minutes," replied Evan Wesley, the foreign desk editor of the *Washington National* newspaper. "Why?"

"There's been another terrorist attack. This one's bad."

"Nothing's come across the wires."

"I'm the first Western journalist on the scene. Heck, I'm the first journalist period. I was out jogging this morning when I came upon it. I'm in the Harish neighborhood with Colonel Levi."

"Well, we have a little exclusive. How many did you say were killed?"

"I have no idea, but more than one."

"Another car bomb?"

"No. An apartment building was attacked. They're finding dead bodies all over the place inside the apartments. We could have a massacre on our hands. The sickos even painted the doorjambs red before they split."

"Why would they do that?"

"Evan, don't you know what Passover is?"

"Passover?"

"Listen, I don't have time to explain." Amber watched as more emergency vehicles circled the building, their sirens muted. "When word gets out that terrorists desecrated a crime scene like modern-day Angels of Death, the news will infuriate the Israelis."

"They know who did it?"

"They're not saying. Maybe it's the handiwork of Hezbollah. Or perhaps the Palestinian Liberation Front decided detonating suicide bombs on buses wasn't killing Israelis fast enough. Bottom line, I'm not sure who's involved."

"See what you can find out," Evan instructed. "I need eight hundred words in forty-five minutes. Can you do it?"

"I guess I have to."

After hanging up, Amber borrowed a notepad from Colonel Levi and interviewed him for ten minutes. Updates arrived regularly from the soldiers inside. The underground parking garage had become a makeshift morgue. Amber flipped the notebook closed just as a CNN camera crew pulled up. A cameraman jumped out and filmed paramedics hurrying a stretcher into a waiting ambulance.

Time to go. Amber jogged two blocks and hailed a taxi. "Twenty-seven Avenue Promenade," she said to the driver, jumping in. By the time they passed two stoplights, Amber had already written the third paragraph on her borrowed notepad.

Back in the apartment house on Zigzo Street, military investigators discovered a bloodstained piece of stationery where Kareh Bottstein had been found on the living room floor. The letters MB had been written in blood.

"She obviously tried to write a message," one of the army officers said to his colleague. "But in her own blood?"

"Brave woman," a major said. "What do you suppose she was trying to say?"

"I don't know. Maybe Mossad can figure it out."

3

Friday, April 7
2:15 P.M. local time
Tehran, Iran

One thousand miles to the east in the windowless Iranian intelligence compound in Tehran, Mohammed Faheedi sipped a mocha coffee. CNN International flickered on the thirteen-inch TV resting on the corner of his desk. Reports of a terrorist strike on a Jerusalem apartment building had launched the global network into its breaking-news mode. Anchor Wolf Blitzer's face scrunched, eyebrows appearing as one, as he spoke of "high-ranking Israeli sources" placing the death toll at more than seventy people.

Mohammed's phone rang.

"Faheedi."

"Briefing in twenty minutes. Room 42," a clipped voice said.

"Yes sir." His superior was speaking of an off-site conference room in the basement of the Sepahsalar Mosque, the biggest mosque in Tehran.

Mohammed hung up then dialed the motor pool.

One of the few perks, he thought. That and Starbucks beans blended in an Italian-made espresso machine in his office. Mohammed had acquired the taste for café mochas during his trips to Washington and Geneva. Drinking Starbucks coffee in Tehran was cool, he decided. There was no way to translate that English word into Farsi, but it certainly fit.

Mohammed donned his coat and grabbed his hefty briefcase. A service elevator dispatched him to the basement where a car and driver waited.

Mohammed slid his lanky, six-foot-two frame onto the rear seat of an older four-door sedan cloaked in layers of dust. He exhaled and rubbed his burning eyes.

"Tired, sir?" The gray-haired driver, maneuvering the car into the sunlight, appeared old enough to be Mohammed's father.

"I'm doing all right. Thanks for asking."

"I'll get you to Sepahsalar by the third bells, sir." The driver punched the gas as he joined the chaotic traffic flow on Tehran's main artery, the Via Asr. A mixture of beat-up and well-maintained sedans, imported from Germany and Japan, jockeyed for space on the wide, unmarked boulevard against hulking trucks loaded with goods destined for the open-air markets. Mohammed's driver zipped through a crowded intersection where two women shrouded in full-length *chadors* stepped in front of the car—then immediately retreated.

"Khange khodah!" the driver swore and then looked into his rearview mirror to see how his pronouncement played with the officer in the backseat. Mohammed kept his thoughts to himself.

"I apologize if I upset you, sir," the driver said. "These women do not understand the law of the road."

"Maybe not," Mohammed allowed.

The driver seemed to relax. "Have you always been in intelligence?"

Mohammed glanced at the chatty driver in the rearview mirror. "No, I started in the service of Islam by joining the air force. I wanted to be a pilot."

"An air force pilot? You look like one."

Mohammed smiled. He didn't know whether he had just been complimented for his rugged good looks or typecast as one of those cover-boy pilots heralded as the "best of the best" in his society.

He remembered well the day his letter of acceptance for flight school had arrived. It had been less than two months after graduation from *hamsayeh*, or high school. His father boasted that his son was destined to fly fighter jets, not work in the family stall, haggling with old ladies over the cost of a kilo's worth of potatoes.

Mohammed couldn't wait to experience the rush of adrenaline and stomach-grabbing g-forces that modern jet fighters produced. Once in flight school, however, he had to overcome the prejudice of those who thought the air force was exclusively for the sons of the religious elite. If his counterparts received an 80 percent on tests, Mohammed had to score at least 90 percent, which he did. After two years, this son of lower-class parents qualified to fly Iran's most advanced fighters.

Given the backward state of the air force, "advanced" was a relative term, Mohammed learned all too quickly. Still, the quickest way to get ahead was in the bucket seat of a fighter jet. After six months and only one hundred hours of flight time, however, he realized the dreams of youth didn't always match up with the realities of adulthood.

He'd distinguished himself in the classroom and in the physical training arena, but there was one area he couldn't master—airsickness. Each time the Mirage trainer broke free from gravity and lifted into airspace, nausea overwhelmed him.

Flying while airsick was no fun, nor was piloting planes older than he was. Ever since the shah had been overthrown in early 1979, Iran had lost easy access to current military hardware. Although Iran had cajoled a handful of modern MiG-29s out of the Soviets—bribes in Yankee dollars and gold bullion still opened doors—those fighters were reserved for a privileged few. Pilots like Mohammed were stuck flying the aging MiG-23s and -25s. Piloting a Russian aircraft, vintage 1971, against the latest generation of American fighters—based in Turkey and Saudi—tipped the odds against surviving.

Mohammed's thinking was confirmed by what happened to Saddam Hussein's air force when American and British forces stormed Iraq. The Iraqis never pushed their air assets out of the hanger against Coalition forces because satellite-guided bombs destroyed Iraqi command-and-control capabilities early in the invasion. He assumed that Iraq's pilots had found reasons *not* to confront superior American aircraft and pilots anyway.

"We're here," the driver said, pulling into the square at Sepahsalar Mosque. "May your work be done for the glory of the Prophet."

"Of course," Mohammed said as he stepped out of the vehicle. "For the Prophet."

Amber regarded the e-mail missive from her boss, Evan Wesley: "Nice work—the copy desk got your story to page makeup in time for today's edition. We'll want an update for the Web, but we don't need that until midmorning our time, so you've got a few hours."

Amber sighed. Ever since the *Washington National* had gone online in the mid-1990s, there was no rest for reporters in the field, as the newspaper's Web site promised Web surfers fresh, updated stories every few hours—"when news happens as it happens."

Still, Amber loved her work and had earned her acclaim in it. Even her Mideast beat competitors working for the *Washington Post* and *New York Times* admitted—over nursed beers at the Jerusalem Hilton's Pompano Beach room—that the daughter of the *Washington National* owner, Jack Robbins, had compiled a solid reporting record in less than three years.

How could a preppie-born boss's daughter beat out accomplished journalists? The answer lay in Amber's ambition to work harder, develop more sources, and bring more dead-on perspective to her writing than her journalistic rivals. Amber had goals—goals of one day covering the White House or Congress. If that meant cajoling her father into letting her prove herself in Jerusalem—well, here she was.

Mohammed Faheedi strode into the Sepahsalar Mosque, a bit awed to enter Iran's most important house of worship. The faithful were summoned to pray five times a day from one of the eight minarets ringing the distinctive mosaic dome.

In his reading on the West, particularly America, Mohammed had frequently come across the term "politically correct." How ironic a similar concept was at work in his country. Not only did political correctness matter but so did religious correctness. Mohammed had faith, sort of. He believed that Allah existed and was the Creator of all. He suspected that the Qur'an contained considerable truth. What bothered him was the rigid fundamentalism controlling his nation. Not that he *ever* hinted such thoughts to anyone. His mother raised no foolish children. To survive and succeed in Iran, one needed to give every appearance of being the most devout Shiite to ever lay his mat down in a mosque. And Mohammed acted the part—even as he entertained questions in the privacy of his thoughts.

Though Mohammed had attended just a handful of meetings at Sepahsalar Mosque, he knew the way to room 42—the conference room located down a series of steps in the dark catacombs. Guarding the door were two Revolutionary Security Forces officers holding automatic weapons. A captain checked ID badges.

Mohammed's heart rate soared when, upon entering the room, he saw Ayatollah Ali Hoseni, the leader of the Islamic Revolutionary Council, seated sternly at the head of the ornate mahogany table. What was the most powerful man in the country doing there?

Six generals, including General Abnuma, the head of Iranian intelligence, joined the clerics seated around the table. Mohammed's rank did not merit a place among the elite. He took a seat in one of the chairs positioned against a wall and counted heads. All told, eighteen of Iran's most powerful men—representing the Islamic government, cleric association, and military—were gathered.

A briefing colonel stood next to Ayatollah Ali Hoseni, clutching several sheets of paper.

"Is your report ready?" asked the Great Leader.

"Yes, Your Excellency." The colonel bowed and held the deferential pose for several long seconds.

"Very well. You may begin."

"At approximately 0300 hours today, 7 April, an undetermined number of assailants arrived in a fifteen-passenger van outside 18 Zigzo Street in West Jerusalem and entered an apartment building. The murder squad has since been estimated to have involved at least ten attackers. Investigators found a witness who saw a white van parked outside the building at 0330. Other witnesses stated that it had not been there prior to 0230.

"Beginning on the top floor, the perpetrators broke into the apartments. Using silenced automatic weapons, they methodically executed the inhabitants. They attempted to kill everyone in the building: men, women, and children. We hear reports, though, that one woman survived. As far as investigators could determine, the assailants suffered only one casualty, which I will cover shortly."

The briefing colonel drew in his breath and continued.

"The intruders policed their own empty shells, apparently in an effort to make tracking them more difficult for investigators. However, stray bullets were dug out of the walls and furniture. Investigators identified the weapon type—Mac-10s—by interviewing the survivor, but they recovered no definitive fingerprints. Once finished with the killings, the intruders splashed red paint on the apartment's doorways. We suspect the paint was intended to mock the Jewish Passover. Then the attackers escaped in a rental van. According to an eyewitness out walking his dog, he noticed a Budget Rent-a-Car sticker on the bumper of the van, but nothing has developed from that lead.

"The Israelis don't know where they are, but investigators are checking with border crossings and exit points. They are not optimistic that any leads will be produced. Obviously, the usual suspect in this investigation is Hezbollah, but the Israelis are clearly rattled since this departs from the usual suicide bomber pattern."

"Could it be one of Osama's sleeper cells?" asked one of the generals as he poured tea from a service set.

"Doubtful," the briefing colonel answered, "but anything said about al-Qaeda at this point would be total speculation, so let me return to the facts. Apparently one of the victims, a military officer in counterterrorism, lived in the building. He kept a gun in his apartment and fired off several rounds before he was killed. One of his rounds found a mark, killing his assailant with a headshot. Something must have hurried the intruders at that point because they failed to recover the body of their fallen colleague. The murdered intruder has been identified as Barzin Shirazi, the head of the al-Aqsa Martyrs Brigade."

A murmur swept through the room. Mohammed ran his finger around his starched collar. He watched as another general lit a filterless cigarette and exhaled a long stream of smoke into the room.

Mohammed searched his memory for information about this group. He knew the Martyrs Brigade was the name of an Islamic guerilla movement that had started as a splinter group of Yasser Arafat's Fatah group following the death of the Palestinian leader. As pressure grew from America's war on terrorism, they had found sanctuary and support in Syria. The Martyrs Brigade concentrated on mounting attacks against Western assets, especially American ones, in parts of the Middle East and Europe. They had experienced their share of successful operations, which made Mohammed wonder why the sudden change with this attack in Jerusalem.

One thing was for sure: the "Passover Massacre" insured that the Martyrs Brigade would become a household name in the Western world. If Mohammed remembered correctly, Barzin Shirazi was respected as a careful planner, brilliant strategist, and charismatic leader. Over the years, his cell had conducted timely "disruptions" against Western companies, embassy diplomats, and, on occasion, isolated military personnel. These were never highly publicized in the West but were closely watched by the CIA.

"Are you absolutely sure it was Shirazi?" inquired General Abnuma. "He's Syrian."

The briefing colonel quickly nodded. "Investigators have concluded the obvious: the Martyrs Brigade *was* responsible for the massacre. This was confirmed by another mistake found at the scene. Evidently they were sloppy with the pregnant wife of the military officer. She survived the shooting and is presumably telling Israeli authorities what she saw."

At this point the ayatollah interrupted the briefing colonel. "Where did you get this information? It has not been released to the public."

"Sir, we have an operative inside the Jerusalem PD. He received copies of the reports from the investigation team."

"How reliable is this operative?"

"He has always yielded high-quality product, Your Excellency. We rate him as highly reliable."

"What information are the Israelis releasing?"

"Just the major details. Fifteen minutes ago, Fox News reported that the Mossad has linked Shirazi with the Martyrs Brigade."

"Very well." The Great Leader waved off the colonel.

"How will the Israelis respond?" interjected a robed cleric.

The briefing colonel rocked on his heels then leaned toward the cleric. "Usually the Israelis respond within twenty-four to forty-eight hours by sending helicopter gunships into the West Bank or strafing training camps in Lebanon's Bekaa Valley. Syria presents a different problem because of its military capabilities. I suspect the Israelis are determining a plan of action at this moment."

The discussions of the last five minutes satisfied most of the men sitting around the table, but not Mohammed. He'd witnessed scores of briefings such as this one, where the participants sat as mute as a collection of rocks, nodding their heads whenever Ayatollah Hoseni spoke. Normally, it didn't matter much, but something about this briefing left Mohammed with a nagging sense of doubt. This bold attack was uncharacteristic for the Martyrs Brigade. He just couldn't imagine them mounting such an ambush on their own.

Mohammed was tempted to ask a question—he even raised his arm partway before he quickly brought it back down. *No, you need more information.*

Friday, April 7
3:06 P.M. local time
Ashdod, Israel

The freighter *Atlantis*, a hulking and rusting container ship, moved at turtle speed, breaking free from its moorings at the Israeli seaport of Ashdod. Sailing under the distinctive white and azure Greek flag—the two colors symbolizing the blue of the Greek Sea and the whiteness of the restless Greek waves—the 40,000-ton ship moved at a pedestrian three knots in the afternoon sun. The freighter encountered little traffic as it sliced through Mediterranean waters toward the harbor exit. After entering the open sea and heading west, the *Atlantis* would reach its ultimate destination of Istanbul, Turkey, in three days.

The *Atlantis* cargo hold was filled to the brim with fourteen-meter steel containers holding cardboard boxes of Jaffa oranges, Benik avocados, and romaine lettuce harvested from the fertile fields of the Jordan Valley. Loaded onto wooden pallets, these boxes of Israeli fruit and produce were destined for Turkish markets.

One of the last of four hundred containers to be lifted onto the ship was not filled with foodstuffs but rather a Renault fifteen-passenger van from Budget Rent-a-Car. There would be no drop-off return for this vehicle; it was destined for Turkey's black market auto bazaar. At that moment, the van's driver puffed on a cigarette in stateroom 6, which he shared with the commando leader.

The driver sucked a long draw of nicotine-rich smoke into his lungs. "We can relax. Everything happened as you said it would."

"Allah was with us," the leader grunted. "Our enemies suffered great harm, praise be to the Prophet."

"Where did you get that idea to write 'MB' in her blood?" the driver asked. "Clever, if you ask me."

The commando leader picked at his teeth with a wooden toothpick. "I can't take credit for that."

"Then who?"

"You don't want to know," he replied in an icy tone.

The driver shrugged his shoulders, letting the matter go.

The commando leader recalled their early morning getaway. After leaving the apartment house, their van drove quietly through the Harish neighborhood before turning toward an industrial part of the city and into an auto repair shop. The driver steered the van into the building, slowly maneuvering up a ramp into a steel-lined shipping container mounted on the flatbed of an eighteen-wheeler.

When the container's steel doors finally enclosed the van the lights came on. Everyone remained silent as the lorry engine roared to life. They soon felt the truck turning around and exiting the building. Within two hours, they arrived at Ashdod and experienced a slight roller-coaster ride when a large crane lifted their container off the flatbed and deposited it into the ship's hold. Within minutes the container doors opened, and the fourteen men were escorted to their staterooms to relax.

The commando leader was too hopped up to rest. Killing infidels released adrenaline into his system like a spigot, and he was elated after sending so many Jews into the hereafter—especially that pregnant Jew woman. Allah had a special place reserved in hell for those cursed people.

Besides, they all had their chance, he thought. *They all said no.*

4

Friday, April 7
3:30 P.M. local time
Jerusalem

"So it's not Islamic Jihad or Hezbollah. Who's Martyrs Brigade?" inquired Evan Wesley, speaking from the *Washington National's* foreign desk in the nation's capital.

Amber adjusted her headset, glad her boss couldn't see her eyes rolling. "The Martyrs Brigade is an Islamic terrorist organization operating out of Syria."

"Right, but I need details. You got more?"

"Are you telling me you need a refresher course on Terrorists 101?" Amber teased. "Hold on, let me pull up my file." While she waited for her Apple PowerBook to boot up, she peered out the window of her second-story studio apartment. The sidewalk teemed with Israeli mothers corralling their rambunctious children on their way home from school. When her CRT screen came to life, Amber opened a file named "martyrsbrigade.doc."

"Let's see. Here's what my notes say. The Brigade is an Islamic revolutionary group led by a Syrian named Barzin Shirazi. He's smart, determined, and hungry—or was anyway. Shirazi was the one they found dead in the apartment. The group's never operated in Israel before, and they haven't pulled off anything of this magnitude either."

"So why did Shirazi and his Brigade kill all those Israelis?"

"Nobody knows. The military is still trying to piece together the crime scene. As for Shirazi, he apparently got overpowered and lost his gun. He was shot at close range, disfiguring his face."

"How did the Israelis ID him?"

"They ran his fingerprints. Perfect match."

Friday, April 7
4:30 P.M. local time
Tehran

As the meeting droned on in the mosque basement, loudspeakers broadcast the third *azan* of the day. Mohammed looked at his watch—afternoon prayer time. His thoughts turned to the religious functions taking place above him. The Qur'an was clear on the absolute necessity for every good Muslim to pray if he desired paradise, but the mind-numbing repetition! "Ilaha illa Allah. Muhammad rasul Allah," the muezzin chanted over and over—"There is no God but Allah. Muhammad is the messenger of Allah." Sometimes, though, the ritual of falling to his knees, leaning forward, and prostrating himself before Allah comforted him, especially when he considered how Allah saw his faithfulness and would surely reward him for his religious virtue.

But more often, Mohammed wondered—really wondered—if Allah had grown tired of listening. He certainly never felt his presence. In Islam, prayer was all about adoration, not asking Allah to do something or heal somebody in pain. The more he thought about it, Mohammed couldn't think of one occasion when Allah answered his entreaties. This type of thinking wasn't religiously correct, and religious correctness affected every area of his life, even his work.

Mohammed considered Abbasi, a fellow student in flight school. In one mock exercise staged in the valleys of the Surren Mountains, Abbasi was supposed to role-play an American pilot who sneaked into Iranian airspace. Several Iranian MiGs circled above, then swept in for the "kill." Abbasi's superior piloting and clever evasions reversed the war game situation. He "lit up" all three Iranian fighter jets with the distinctive beep-beep, signaling *they* were in his sights, not he in theirs. Was Abbasi promoted to major like the three pilots he bettered in the air? No, because he was found several times in his barracks studying his pilot manual when he should have been in the mosque, prostrate with his fellow pilots.

The Great Leader interrupted Mohammed's unlawful thoughts. Robust for his sixty years, the ayatollah suddenly stood and gathered his clerical robes around him. In unison all present rose in respect. Mohammed understood: a bathroom break. Everyone filed out of the meeting room into a larger chamber, where a banquet table was draped with a white tablecloth. In the middle of the table, an oversized silver plate was stacked with *boulani*, a savory pastry stuffed with garlic chives. Mohammed set three on a plate and poured himself a cup of tea mixed with saffron.

"Three boulani might not be enough."

Mohammed spun around and regarded a tall, angular colleague with a clean-shaven face. He looked familiar. "You could be right," Mohammed said with a smile. "I'm sorry. I forgot—"

"Ganji. I work in the Western Europe section. You're Faheedi, right?"

"Yes, I am." Mohammed offered his hand.

"Greetings." Ganji shook Mohammed's outstretched hand then stabbed four boulani with his fork and landed them on his plate. "Listen, whatever happened to Colonel Heen? It seems like he was around the last time we met here at Sepahsalar."

Colonel Jammar Heen. Mohammed remembered the savvy communications specialist. *Had it been a month since the rumors began?* "I'm not sure where he is—or if he is alive."

"Oh?" The intelligence officer arched an eyebrow.

"Yeah, the talk around the office is that Colonel Heen kept a backstreet apartment with a young woman not his wife. The morals police picked him up."

"And you haven't seen him since?"

"No. It's like he never existed, which is a shame, because I wouldn't have this position if it weren't for Colonel Heen. When we expanded the intelligence operations after the Americans invaded Iraq, he recruited me out of the air force."

"That was good timing for you."

"Yes. I've lost several good friends whose aircraft nose-dived into the ground for unexplained reasons." Mohammed set down his untouched boulani and picked up a sweating glass of water.

"I've heard about you, Faheedi. Colonel Heen told me you have an uncanny knack for gathering isolated facts and coalescing them into a coherent picture."

"Well, he's kind, but ever since Colonel Heen disappeared, I've been shuffled into an intelligence side alley. Not to complain, of course." He took a long drink of his water. "I'm grateful to serve my country in any way they would request."

"Of course," Ganji nodded.

They exchanged another handshake. Mohammed watched the analyst refill his cup of tea, reminding himself that if he discovered more information than the next person, his options increased. In revolutionary Iran, it was never a bad idea to have options.

When they reconvened, General Abnuma continued his questioning in room 42 of Sepahsalar Mosque, grilling the briefing colonel as to why on earth the Martyrs Brigade would target an apartment building in Jerusalem.

"Apparently, there was a military officer involved with Israeli counterterrorism," the briefing officer said. "We suspect he was close to compromising the Martyrs Brigade and thus had to be taken out."

"Are you telling me they killed seventy-five people to cover up the murder of one counterintelligence officer?" General Abnuma asked.

Sweat beads dripped from the briefing colonel's temples. "Well, uh, sir, I agree. None of this makes any sense," he stammered. "Maybe Shirazi lost his mind."

Mohammed's unsettled feelings were growing stronger. The more he considered the details, the more out of focus the picture became. The Martyrs Brigade's stated purpose did not include taking on the state of Israel so directly.

Mohammed aligned the facts like ivory dominoes on a table. Barzin Shirazi was a mastermind behind most of the Brigade's operations, but he was not a triggerman. Then there was the problem of weapons: the warriors of the al-Aqsa Martyrs Brigade brandished cheap AK-47s obtained from the stockpiles of former Soviet bloc nations, never expensive Mac-10s. And why would they have taken the time to police their own shell casings but not take Shirazi's body with them?

The briefing officer opened a folder and extracted six black-and-white glossy photos and passed them to his right. As the photos worked their way around the conference table, Mohammed saw knowing glances exchanged among his colleagues. Several pointed to particular aspects, while others registered smugness. No love lost for dead Jews among this crowd.

When the official police photos from the Passover Massacre reached Mohammed, one stood out to him: the image of the pregnant woman lying on the floor with a piece of paper next to her. A large "MB" had been inked in her blood. How would she have known that the Martyrs Brigade was responsible? Most likely all she saw were men in black hoods.

The briefing colonel was saved another embarrassing question by a commotion in the doorway. A blindfolded prisoner, dressed in a torn khaki uniform of the Iranian intelligence service, was unceremoniously jerked into the room. An infantryman maintained a firm grip on the nape of the man's neck, keeping the prisoner's head bowed. Another soldier grasped the man's right arm.

"We will come back to the Martyrs Brigade, but for now, I see our wayward colleague has arrived," the Great Leader announced.

Mohammed, standing behind the table, noticed meaningful looks launched around the table, but they were flashes of fear, not puzzlement. He strained his neck to identify the handcuffed prisoner, but the bloodstained rag around the eyes prevented recognition.

The Great Leader stood up and dramatically smoothed the mustache leading to his graying beard.

"Welcome, Colonel Heen, to our little meeting." The ayatollah's tone was not at all welcoming. All movement froze as three-dozen sets of eyes locked onto the disheveled prisoner. Streaks of blood were caked under his nose and around his jowls, a sure sign of torture. From the odorous smell, the colonel had either been forced to swim in a tub of sewage or wear clothes dipped in human waste.

"I'm pleased you joined us today." The Great Leader sent a wicked smile toward the prisoner before directing his attention to those around the table. "You may be wondering why our colleague has arrived late to our meeting or why he's in such a . . . state of disarray. Two weeks ago, a close aide of mine discovered Colonel Heen attending an underground Christian gathering. It was not the first time we had seen him entering and exiting a certain apartment. After we arrested the colonel, we questioned him. We wanted to know whether he was merely infiltrating a heretical sect on his own or if there was something more to his, shall we say, unusual interest in the blasphemous religion that defames Allah and his messenger Muhammad."

As if on cue, a swarthy bearded man stepped out of the shadows and pulled a Glock from his waistband. Mohammed, frozen as the rest of the attendees while the man snapped a metallic clip into the pistol's handle, noticed a large scar on the man's left cheek. With three purposeful steps, the scarred man placed the Glock's muzzle against the left temple of the prisoner, who stiffened. Both guards standing behind the captured intelligence officer maintained vise-like grips on the prisoner's arms.

"Colonel Heen, are you aware what our holy book, the Qur'an, says about Christianity?"

The prisoner shook his head. The ayatollah picked up a Qur'an and quickly found the page he was looking for. He reached for a pair of reading glasses on the table. "In the Surah, chapter 4, verse 171, it reads: 'O People of the Book! Commit no excesses in your religion; nor say of Allah anything but the truth. Christ Jesus the son of Mary was no more than a Messenger of Allah. . . . Do not say "Trinity": desist: it will be better for you: for Allah is One God: Glory be to Him: far exalted is He above having a son.'"

The Great Leader took off his reading glasses. "Prisoner Heen, our sacred text is also quite clear what we leaders should do to those who dare blaspheme the exalted name of our Holy Messenger. We are in the midst of a righteous jihad against our enemies, especially those who would attempt to convert the faithful. There is no blasphemy higher! Those who prey on the weakest must be eliminated!"

Heen's shoulders slumped while a stream of urine pooled at his feet. The guards repositioned their feet but continued to grasp the prisoner tightly. Meanwhile, Mohammed's lunch of lamb kebab felt unsettled in his stomach. He was glad he hadn't eaten those pastries.

"Prisoner Heen, I will give you one chance, so think carefully. Will you renounce the heretical Christian religion and tell this body that you believe Allah is the true god and Muhammad is his messenger?"

"No, I will not," the prisoner replied with a firmness that surprised Mohammed. "I place my trust in Jesus Christ, who died for me and rose again on the third day, so that I might have eternal life."

"In hell you will." The ayatollah nodded to the scarred man holding the Glock. He reached into a pocket and retrieved a four-inch silencer, which he slowly screwed onto the end of the pistol. The metallic screeching in the otherwise absolutely silent room increased Mohammed's tension as the seconds passed.

One guard reached down and spread the prisoner's feet while the other pushed Heen's upper torso slightly forward. The man with the scar then pressed his Glock against the back of the prisoner's skull. One second, two seconds, three seconds . . . and a muffled *poof* emitted a bloody mist into the air.

Mohammed closed his eyes. Someone was sending a message that those who don't recant their Christian religion will be violently killed, and he knew who that someone was.

Sunday, April 9
11 A.M. local time
Jerusalem

"And this is our maternity ward."

Colonel Levi shepherded Amber through the antiseptic-smelling Ein Karem Hadassah Hospital in Jerusalem. "Our medical staff has more physicians who performed their residency at Johns Hopkins than any of your hospitals in the States, including New York Presbyterian."

"Impressive." Amber followed the Israeli officer down a hallway that gleamed with linoleum in a palette of colors that mimicked quarried rock. The walls of the maternity unit, sponge-painted in a sand-colored fresco, presented an image of hearth and home.

"And here we have the Golda Meir Nursery, named after our beloved prime minister."

Through a large plate-glass window, Amber observed two nurses in starched white hats tending to a dozen incubators, each warming an infant. One nurse lifted a baby boy and gently patted his back. The little guy responded by burping formula onto her shoulder, which was draped with a nursing towel.

"Which one is Baby Bottstein?"

"Sorry, state secret." Levi tilted his head toward a male dressed in sterile whites standing in the right corner.

"Armed?"

The Israeli nodded.

"I still can't believe the baby survived."

"The doctors couldn't believe it either."

"Poor little munchkin," Amber remarked. "Someday he'll ask where his father is, and his mother will . . ." She let the thought trail off as she imagined Kareh Bottstein reliving a night of unspeakable horror. "He had a brother too," she added.

"Meanwhile, the living must carry on."

That must be how everyone in this part of the world copes, Amber thought. *Otherwise, you'd never get through the day.*

"Is Mrs. Bottstein ready to see us?"

"Let me see." The colonel spoke into a lapel mike, but Amber couldn't make out the guttural Hebrew.

"I have two guards posted outside the room," he stated. "Mrs. Bottstein's available now."

"Thanks for arranging the interview. I owe you one."

"I think Mrs. Bottstein is waiting," he said.

Amber didn't know what to expect, but it wasn't seeing Kareh Bottstein sitting up in bed, chatting with nurses while sipping a Coke through a straw.

Colonel Levi made the introductions and then spoke in Hebrew with Kareh. If Amber read body language correctly, he seemed to be telling Kareh that Amber could be trusted.

"Thank you for agreeing to see me today." Amber gazed at the woman's smooth olive skin, strong yet feminine jaw line, and deep black eyes. She noticed the blankets lying over Kareh's level stomach. "Before I get started," Amber began. "I want to say how sorry I am for all you went through. I can't imagine how horrible that must have been."

"Thank you."

"It's a miracle you survived."

Kareh smiled softly. "Yes, it is."

Amber set a tape recorder on the bed stand and opened a notebook. "I'm eager to tell the world how this miracle happened."

"You may not be able to tell everything," Colonel Levi interjected.

Amber nodded. "I know, but my editor in Washington won't like it."

Kareh's eyes perked. "Washington, D.C.? I lived there once."

"You did?"

"Yes, I was an au pair for the Israeli ambassador and his family. They had two preschoolers I looked after. I loved your America and learned English while I was there. Great memories . . . so carefree . . ." Her voice trailed off.

"What are some of the things you remember?"

Kareh's face brightened. "Oh, that's where I was introduced to Alev. He was some sort of attaché to the Israeli embassy, but he said his job was so secret that he couldn't tell me what he did."

"What was Alev like?"

"Warm, considerate, the type who brought home flowers every payday. He loved getting on the floor and playing with little Benjamin. He loved me so . . ." Kareh's voice cracked, and her lips quivered.

"I'm sorry," Amber reached for Kareh's hand. "I'm so sorry about what happened."

Kareh dabbed her eyes with a handkerchief. "You'll have to excuse me. This is hard. I know you have questions to ask."

Amber gently guided the interview toward Passover night. "Tell me a little about your Seder. How many did you invite for Passover dinner?"

Kareh described the events with surprising calm. A smile returned to her face when she described Aunt Sora's antics before dinner.

"Thank you for letting me talk," she said, finishing a long story about her aunt's determination to find the sex of the baby. "The investigators never let me just remember." She looked away. "They always interrupt with questions. I am tired of questions." She smiled at Amber.

"I understand." Amber set her pen down and waited while Kareh took another sip of her soft drink. "Do you think you can tell me what happened after you went to bed?"

Kareh's lips curled downward, and her eyes glazed with tears. She described crawling back into bed with Alev and later confronting the commandos.

"When he pointed the gun at my navel, all I could think about was saving my baby. I wrestled with him, and the gun went off. The pain knocked me out, and I must have hit the floor in an unconscious state. Several minutes probably passed before I heard a commotion."

"A commotion?"

"This man was saying something that sounded like 'Yasus Christus, Yasus Christus' under his breath, but the attackers kicked him each time he said it. I could hear them dragging him toward our bedroom, and since I was facing that way, I opened one of my eyes. I watched them put a gun in my dead husband's hand and shoot the man in the back of the head."

"Wait a minute," Amber interjected. Too much information was flying around. "What was the man saying?"

"'Yasus Christus.' I think he meant Jesus Christ."

Now Amber was confused. Colonel Levi's face revealed the same bewilderment.

"We're talking about Shirazi, the terrorist who got killed?"

Kareh nodded.

"Why would he be saying the words 'Jesus Christ'?"

"Perhaps he was praying," Kareh suggested.

"Why would he pray to Jesus Christ?" Amber asked. "Isn't he Muslim?"

"Definitely," the colonel stated with authority. "But I'm going to ask that this part of the interview be off the record." Amber had never seen the Israeli officer so serious. "You cannot print this information at this time, do you understand?"

"Of course. You set the ground rules." Amber needed time to collect herself. "What else happened?"

"Well, the terrorist asked me an interesting question."

"Mrs. Bottstein, I'm afraid I must stop you here," Colonel Levi said as he stood up, signaling the interview was over. "We're not prepared to release that information."

Sunday, April 9
10:30 P.M. local time
Jerusalem

Amber leaned back in her chair, rubbed her eyes, and reread her story for the fifth time:

> Kareh Bottstein, the only adult to survive the Passover Massacre, said that her attacker pressed the tip of his gun to her navel with the intention of shooting her unborn son and killing her simultaneously.
>
> In an exclusive interview with the *Washington National,* the twenty-nine-year-old Israeli mother said she instinctively grabbed the attacker's pistol when he aimed it at her abdomen, setting off an intense struggle. Moments later, the gun discharged, causing the bullet to strike her in the lower groin. "That's what saved my life and the life of my child," she said yesterday at Ein Karem Hadassah Hospital in Jerusalem.
>
> The miraculous story of this Passover Massacre survivor has resonated throughout Israel as the country struggles to return to normalcy following another shocking terrorist attack. Emotional pictures of the young mother cuddling her bundled-up newborn were splashed across Israel's major newspapers, giving this beleaguered citizenry something to feel good about.
>
> Mrs. Bottstein, who teaches English part-time at a local language school, said she played dead after she was shot to fool the attackers, a ruse that successfully saved two lives. Her decision meant, however, that she could not come to the aid of her husband, Alev, nor save her three-year-old son, Benjamin, whose lifeless, blood-soaked body was found in his bedroom. The two of them were among the seventy-four victims, who included fifteen children under the age of six.
>
> "I'm still grieving for my husband and my little son,"

> Mrs. Bottstein said from her hospital bed before bursting into a torrent of tears. "How those animals could point a pistol at my unborn baby was inconceivable. Fortunately, the bullet missed little Dylan."
>
> Meanwhile, as more details of the Passover Massacre emerged, further outcry was sparked among the citizenry. Israelis visited the Wailing Wall yesterday in droves, say local authorities. The *Jerusalem Post* carried two pages of e-mail messages expressing outrage against the attack, and a popular radio talk show, *Moshe Bayer Live,* added three hours of programming to give Israelis "a chance to vent their frustration," host Schlomo Glickstein told reporters.

She had read enough. Amber closed the file and attached it to an e-mail to Evan. Fifteen minutes later, he called. "Very good piece. Her survival puts a face on this terrible tragedy. That sells papers, you know."

"Thanks, Evan, but I'm not trying to boost circulation rates. People need to know about Kareh Bottstein. To be shot when you're eight months pregnant and survive is something beyond my comprehension."

"And it was amazing that the bullet didn't hit the fetus."

Amber couldn't believe his choice of words. *Fetus* sounded so . . . clinical.

"Did you say 'fetus'? A baby was born several days ago, Evan. A baby with two legs and two arms and two beautiful eyes—not a fetus."

"OK, OK, stop the sermonizing."

"I'm not preaching. Just speaking in facts."

"But he wasn't born yet, so he really wasn't a baby."

Amber knew better than to argue with fools, so she let it pass. "I hope you aren't planning to bury this story on A22."

"Don't worry. We'll give it the play it deserves."

Sunday, April 9
11:33 P.M. local time
Jerusalem

Amber walked through her Jerusalem flat with the disinfectant scent of the hospital on her skin and the words of Kareh Bottstein nagging her senses. Her ears perked up for the slightest noise. She slowly made her way through the apartment, ensuring that all doors and windows were locked tightly. Not that it would help. She could picture Alev Bottstein doing the same not too many nights prior, peeking in at his sleeping son one last time before settling in next to his pregnant wife.

Amber plunked her lithe frame on the couch and rubbed her temples. Sure, there would be the requisite follow-up stories in the days ahead: police and military leads, forensic evidence, grieving relatives, and speculation if and where Israeli F-15 Eagles would retaliate. But how did the revelation that Shirazi said "Jesus Christ" fit into the picture? And what was that question Kareh heard from the terrorist?

Amber knew this story would not die. Not to her, at least. This was more than just another killing spree. Something bigger was happening here, and she had to know what that was. Perhaps solving the Shirazi aspect would point her in the right direction. She was starting to take the Passover Massacre personally.

5

Monday, April 10
7 P.M. local time
Tehran

Few families in the southern quarter of Tehran could afford to live in what Americans would call a single-family home. Only oil-rich scions and the ruling elite could support the sizable estates separated from the streets by whitewashed, three-meter-high walls. The masses were relegated to vast housing blocks that butted up to each other in tired-looking five-story increments. Most Iranian working-class couples with children leased threadbare five-room apartments that came with the basics: a small kitchen, dining area, toilet and tub, and two bedrooms.

Davood Rashee searched two years before finding a ground-floor apartment within walking distance of a major transportation depot. The price was right—500,000 rials a month (worth U.S. $75 on the black market), or about 30 percent of his take-home salary from the auto repair shop where he worked. His three children—nine-year-old Maree, six-year-old Caleb, and Ruthina, his two-year-old toddler—shared one bedroom. They didn't complain about the cramped conditions, nor did his wife, Mrna, who expressed relief that she no longer had to carry groceries up five flights of stairs.

The apartment had one other invaluable feature: a backdoor entrance into an alley. *You can never be too careful,* thought Davood. *Make a mistake, and it'll be your last one.*

A few minutes after seven o'clock, several people arrived at Pastor Davood Rashee's back door. The women were dressed from head to toe in their black chadors, and even the men wrapped themselves in black shawls. Every few minutes, another couple slipped inside.

To rendezvous like this was dangerous. A nosy neighbor, a suspicious friend, or an attentive policeman would be enough to prompt a call to the Islamic authorities, triggering a middle-of-the-night roundup. "Justice" from the ruling council was always swift; their sentence always brutal. Fortunately, the stone masonry walls muffled noise.

By 7:20, the apartment was filled with a dozen guests. Many carried black sacks containing their most prized possession: a Bible translated into Farsi.

"Let's start with a song." Davood slowly strummed a guitar, the familiar chords driving the melody of "Heart of Worship." Only in this place, it was sung in Farsi.

When the last chord faded into silence, Pastor Davood bowed his head, his dark hair falling across his forehead. "Lord, we pray for the safety and well-being of all your children gathered in this room tonight and our dear brothers and sisters who could not be with us. We pray for your merciful protection, in Jesus' name, amen."

Nearly a dozen heads lifted in unison, expressions of hope flickering from each.

Pastor Davood cleared his throat and opened his Bible. "Tonight, I would like to encourage you from the Book of Hebrews," he began. "Hebrews 10:35–36 was written to some brothers who happened to be Jewish—brothers who were suffering for their faith much as we are today. Listen to its challenge, 'So don't throw away your confidence, which has a great reward. For you need endurance, so that after you have done God's will, you may receive what was promised.'"

Davood paused to allow God's Word to sink in. "My brothers and sisters, how truly this passage of Scripture speaks of us. Certainly we have every reason to compromise, to give up, because of the heavy price we could pay for standing firm in our faith." Davood peered around his living room, gazing intently into each face.

"But you have not thrown your confidence away. God truly is pleased. Remember you are not alone."

The Christian Iranians murmured in agreement.

"My friends, I have news of our courageous brother, Gul." His voice rose slightly.

"Excuse me, Pastor," an older man who'd been to the study only a few times broke in. "Who is Gul?"

Davood smiled at the gray-bearded baby Christian. "I'm sorry, please let me explain. Gul was arrested for sharing his faith in our Jesus with an interested neighbor. He was charged with and convicted of defaming the prophet Muhammad. The judge sentenced him to death by firing squad."

The gray-bearded man shook his head. "Ah, if they only knew the truth."

Davood cleared his throat and continued. "But our brothers inside the jail, at great personal risk, managed his escape."

"How did this happen?" a young mother asked.

Davood broke into a smile. "My dear ones, I cannot talk more, but our brother no longer has a date with the firing squad."

The room erupted in joyful thanksgiving. Once everyone quieted, Davood continued. "We have reason to be grateful, but the ayatollah will not let this pass easily. He has issued a *fatwah* ordering his assassination. Posters have been displayed in markets around Tehran, calling for his death. Gul continues to live in hiding to this day."

Davood paused, prompting a comment from the floor. "I don't think I could be as brave," a young woman said. "Where does he find the strength?"

"Brothers and sisters, that strength can only come from the Lord Jesus Christ. I can tell you the same thing our brother Gul has told others. Even in a prison, separated from family and loved ones, our Lord is faithful to strengthen, encourage, and comfort. As you walk through the valley of the shadow of death, truly you need fear no evil, for he is with you."

Davood eyed Mrna and his children sitting to his right.

"Yes, this is a difficult time to be alive. Bitterness taints our lives, and we face opposition everywhere we turn. But in Christ we can stand firm. Each of us will someday rejoice that we could suffer for our Lord's name. We must remember what the writer of Hebrews promised: if we do not throw away our confidence, we will be richly rewarded."

The pastor finished his study from Hebrews 10 and closed his Bible.

"Please, Pastor, don't stop," one of the students said.

A robed man joined the plea. "Yes, won't you read something from the apostle Paul or Jesus' words?"

Davood sighed. "No, my friends, it is late. If we stay much longer, we run the risk of being noticed. Let us spend a few minutes praying together before returning to our homes."

After a closing prayer, the people offered warm embraces to one other, whispering, "The Spirit of God go with you." Mrna carefully parted the curtains. After thoroughly checking in both directions, she turned and nodded to two men by the back door. They quickly slipped outside then walked up the alley in the direction of the nearest bus stop. In pairs or one by one, the guests left the apartment in one-to-two-minute intervals, heading various directions.

Only one woman came without her spouse that night.

"Good night, Rida." Davood gently pumped her hand. "Thank you for coming. Is your husband still working late every night?"

"Yes, he is." Rida Faheedi lowered her gaze. "Sometimes I think he's more married to his job than to me, but he's a good provider. It's just that I sometimes wish . . ."

"I know. Our thoughts and prayers are with you," Davood said and bade her good-bye.

Rida closed the door to her two-room apartment and slumped into her favorite chair. The weariness she felt was much deeper than mere physical fatigue. Yes, much deeper. Rida was weary of facing evenings alone. Weary of having so little closeness with her husband. She knew he was faithful, but she also knew she wanted far more from her marriage. In just five years since their wedding, they'd drifted apart. Other things seemed more important to him—especially his work in the military intelligence section. Not that she knew one scintilla of what Mohammed did all day. He would no sooner tell her what he was working on than he would call the editor of the *Jerusalem Post* and allow himself to be interviewed regarding Iran's military readiness.

The pain of that loneliness was amplified by the isolation imposed by her society. Women were not seen as having much value—especially if she did not produce a male heir, and that hadn't happened yet, though from no lack of trying. In moments of honesty, she also had to admit that living as an underground Christian made Rida wearier than any amount of rest could ever relieve.

She recalled the peace and joy she felt when she prayed with Pastor Davood and received Jesus into her heart, but as the weeks passed by, the reality of living as a Christian in Iran troubled her. She wondered if she had made the right decision, but now that she knew Jesus, she couldn't imagine going back to her old life. Yet figuring out what a "life in Christ" meant without confiding in her husband sapped her energy.

Her thoughts wandered to Mrna Rashee, the pastor's wife and her part-time maid. She certainly did not envy Mrna's place in life, for she knew the Rashee family struggled mightily. They were extremely poor. Yet Mrna seemed so . . . what? Happy? Yes, happy. Rida had hired Mrna to clean her home once a week. How cheerfully she went about her work. A friendship had formed, and when Mrna sensed Rida's bouts of despondency, she asked her to join their "meeting."

"It would be an honor if you could come one evening," the maid had courageously said. "You would meet some very nice Christian people."

Having found contentment nowhere else and desperate for companionship, Rida took the risk and said yes. Their unconditional love made her painfully aware of the emptiness in her heart.

In subsequent meetings, Mrna's husband, Davood, explained how Jesus Christ was the only true God, and that he came upon this Earth so she might have eternal life through him. The concept of having a personal relationship with a God who knew her and cared about her was radical in her society. God loved *her?* In the Qur'an, no such statement could be found. Islamic teaching affirmed that Allah *hated* sinners, but something fluttered in her heart when Pastor Davood opened his Bible to Romans 5:8.

"Let me read the following verse to you," the pastor said. "'But God proves his own love for us in that while we were still sinners Christ died for us.'" Davood closed the Bible. "Compare what's said here with the Qur'an, which says in Surah 2:190 that Allah 'loves not transgressors.' Jesus Christ not only loves you, but he wants to have a relationship with you. He's knocking at the door of your heart. He loves you in ways you cannot imagine, and he's just waiting for you to let him in. Will you?"

Rida lowered her gaze. The question frightened her, but not enough to keep her from saying yes to Jesus.

6

Tuesday, April 11
10 A.M. local time
Tehran

One by one the men filed out of the teak-paneled conference room. General Abnuma watched impassively, arms crossed. With a tilt of his chin, he motioned to Ayatollah Hoseni. The Great Leader of the Islamic Revolutionary Council raised his eyebrows in understanding. As the last cleric exited, Abnuma stood up to stretch before taking two strides toward the ayatollah.

"May I have a few more moments, sir?" The general made a slight bow to the Great Leader.

"Of course, General. You have concerns. I can see them written all over your face." The Great Leader sat forward in his leather chair and poured each of them a cup of tea from a sterling service. His eyes met Abnuma's as he passed a cup.

"Yes sir, I do." He sipped his tea and returned it to the table. "It will not be long before someone in Israel has serious questions about Syria's involvement with Martyrs Brigade. When that happens, there could be some significant problems concerning our plan."

Iran's leading cleric dropped a sugar cube into his tea. "First of all, General, I have no doubt the Israelis smell something foul in their investigation thus far. Part of the reason for inviting so many officers to our briefing several days ago was to gauge their response. Many believed without question."

"But Great Leader, if I may say, military discipline requires following orders—"

"Enough! They are too used to parroting the latest party line. And, if I read body language correctly, one fellow kept raising his hand but was not called on. If he can figure it out, so can Mossad." His voice grew stern. "But it doesn't matter. The global media has framed the story as we wish, and now the West blames the Martyrs Brigade. Everyone knows this group operates out of Syria, which leads me to believe that the Israelis are already planning their retaliation against Damascus."

"Correct," General Abnuma interjected. "The government in Israel is under enormous pressure from its citizens to do something." The general leaned back as a sense of satisfaction came over him. "Still, even with these few concerns, it seems the mission went off as successfully as we hoped."

"I agree. We struck a devastating psychological blow against our greatest enemy, and we also signaled that any infidel who does not accept Muhammad as the Prophet faces severe consequences. As for the Israelis, if they show some backbone and retaliate inside Syria's borders, we will make it look as though they are up to their usual reactionary violence. The Western media will report it our way, just as they have in the past."

"We could have problems along that front."

"Oh?" The Great Leader refrained from taking another sip of tea.

"Yes. We have been monitoring the reporting of a *Washington National* correspondent based in Jerusalem. "She—"

"A woman?"

"Yes, an American woman. Over the last year, she has broken stories that have not, shall we say, put our holy cause in the brightest light."

The Great Leader considered the general's words for some time. "But she can be dealt with, right?"

"Truly, you are wise, Holy One. We have options."

"Fine. Then put the next phase of our plan into operation. Immediately."

Tuesday, April 11
9 P.M. local time
Tehran

"Hello, Rida, I'm home."

Mohammed Faheedi ducked inside the front door of their apartment in Tehran's *cherim* district. The once-modern apartment had been built with the shah's oil money back in the mid-1970s when the country was flush in petrodollars. Zellweger AG, the German construction firm hired to modernize Iran's living conditions, had not skimped on materials or craftsmanship. While Mohammed's apartment house could use some stucco work and a coat of whitewash, the four-story apartment block stood proudly in a park-like setting, a sturdy reminder of what might have been.

"Oh, there you are!" Rida stepped out of the bedroom, dressed in a beige lacy-ribbed tank and white roll-up shirt from Christian Lacroix—an ensemble Mohammed had purchased on a trip to Paris. Her stone-washed jeans from the Gap were several years older—a tangible reminder of Mohammed's first intelligence-gathering trip to Washington, D.C. Like many modern Iranian women, Rida often dressed in Western clothes behind closed doors, safely away from the prying eyes of the morals police.

Mohammed kissed her. "I'm sorry I had to work late again."

"I hope it was nothing serious."

"No, just a long meeting."

Rida regarded her husband. "Serious enough to keep you out at this hour?"

"Well, I guess 'serious' is an appropriate term."

Her narrowed gaze told him she wasn't pleased with his secrecy. Mohammed knew she wouldn't give up until he told her *something*.

"OK, OK." Mohammed lifted his palms. "It seems the Israelis have a problem on their hands."

"You mean those killings in that apartment block? It's all over the news. Horrible, those men breaking into the apartment and shooting people, even children."

"Yes, but what we need to know is what happens next—what Israel's response will be."

Again Rida paused, as if waiting for more. This time Mohammed refused to cave.

"Very well," she said finally, turning toward the kitchen. "I can still put together something for you to eat. You must be famished."

"I am."

"Give me a few minutes. It'll only take me a moment to reheat your meal."

Mohammed walked into their bedroom and unbuttoned his tunic, which he hung in the small open closet. He was about to drop his undershirt into a rattan hamper when he spotted the corner of a book underneath yesterday's underwear and shirts.

What? Mohammed reached down and grabbed the large volume from the hamper. It felt heavy in his hands. A dark foreboding caused his breathing to quicken when he realized what he had found.

It was the Bible. A black, leather-bound Christian Bible translated into his mother tongue.

Mohammed's mind swirled. *Where did she get this? And why? Do its contents mean anything to her?* He was hurt and afraid. After witnessing Colonel Heen's demise, he knew what it meant to be a Christian in Iran.

Mohammed leaned his head back against the doorframe and closed his eyes. His curiosity turned to concern as his intelligence training came to the fore. He knew what to do. He would detach himself emotionally and treat this situation as just another job assignment. There was no reason to confront her now. He had the element of surprise on his side.

Tuesday, April 11
9:51 P.M. local time
Jerusalem

Amber sat at her computer, staring at the story she was working on. She reread her lead for the third time:

> Israeli military sources remained tight-lipped today regarding reprisal raids following the Passover Massacre, which authorities now believe took the lives of seventy-four men, women, and children in the predawn darkness.
>
> "We are studying our options," Colonel Hafar Bamar said at a press briefing. "While it appears the Martyrs Brigade is responsible for this murderous attack, we don't want to rule out other terrorist groups acting in concert with these international outlaws. There is a possibility that other terror groups could be involved."
>
> Upon further questioning by Western journalists, Colonel Bamar admitted that the Martyrs Brigade killing dozens of innocent people "doesn't add up," since the terrorist group generally operated outside Israel.
>
> "Whether Martyrs Brigade alone was responsible for the Passover Massacre is something we're still investigating," the Israeli colonel said.

Amber liked where her story was heading but wondered what other journalists were saying. She hopped online and clicked on BBC Worldwide News. She scanned the headlines and noted that reporter Charles Stammer had hung the same lead—Israeli reprisals—on top of his story as well.

She slipped over to Reuters, another quick-off-the-mark wire service. Yup. The prevailing storyline was whether Israel would issue reprisals, followed by the official outpourings of grief from Jewish leaders worldwide. Print journalists would be marching in lockstep on that score, and she was among them.

Amber reveled in her ability to come up with unique angles—angles that other journalists missed—but tonight her weary mind lacked original thinking. She tossed the facts around one more time in her head: Why would a Syrian-based terrorist organization, successful in their attacks on targets outside Israel and America, steal their way into Jerusalem? Why would they deviate from their M.O. and slaughter innocent families in such a gruesome manner? Amber looked around her apartment for inspiration. When nothing came, she closed her eyes and prayed. *Wait,* she felt something inside tell her. *Just wait. The answers will come.*

She was too tired to argue, so Amber finished her story—similar as it was to the others—and sent it electronically to the Washington foreign desk.

Chocolate, I need chocolate. She stood up and walked to her refrigerator, where she had plenty of hundred-gram bars of Frigor chocolat noir on hand, thanks to her last shopping trip in Geneva. She unwrapped a bar, broke off a three-section piece, and returned to her chair. She took a languorous bite, allowing the Frigor to melt in her mouth and release theobromines into her brain.

Revitalized by several bites of Swiss chocolate, Amber returned to her computer screen, where two news items on the Reuters home page caught her interest because they involved Christians:

> **Missionary Detained for Protesting against Blasphemy Laws**
>
> (Karachi, Pakistan) Thomas Neeley, a missionary and member of the Human Rights Commission of Pakistan, was among the 150 protesters arrested in Karachi following a demonstration calling for an end to Pakistan's notorious Blasphemy Laws. The protestors were expressing outrage after a 14-year-old boy was executed for allegedly writing derogatory remarks about the Prophet Muhammad on the walls of a mosque.
>
> "The boy was singled out because he had become a Christian," Neeley said. "They fabricated a story that

he had written negative things about Mohammed on a mosque wall, and that was all Islamic authorities needed to sentence the poor boy to death. We are absolutely heartbroken over this tragic event, as is his family."

The second was equally heartbreaking.

Forced Conversions to Islam to Continue

(Jakarta, Indonesia) A growing body of evidence confirms reports that Christians in Indonesia's Maluku Islands have been forced to convert to Islam under the threat of death, although Muslim clerics deny the claims. Indonesia is the world's most populous Muslim nation, where 85 percent of the country's population of 210 million is Muslim.

Christian refugees, church representatives, and even government leaders are troubled by the accounts of forced conversions, which reportedly have included circumcision of both males and females as part of the conversion "process."

"We are hearing reports that there is a systematic effort by Islamic extremists to convert Christians to Islam," said Indonesian president Abdurrahman Wahid, a Muslim scholar known for his message of tolerance. "This is not right."

Interviews with Christian refugees forced to flee their homes revealed that they were coerced to convert at gunpoint. Others reported being circumcised and having their heads shaved. Some of those interviewed said that they did not wish to end up like two Protestant teachers, James Curtin and David Bartholomew, who were killed earlier this month for failing to comply.

"I only said yes to save myself," one refugee stated.

Forced circumcision for men *and* women? What a horror for those poor souls! The news report sobered Amber even further.

She picked up the phone and dialed Washington, knowing Evan Wesley had arrived at the foreign desk.

"Your story was fine," Evan said.

"Thanks. I guess I was looking for a dose of reassurance. But I can't help wondering why those innocent families were slaughtered."

"The 'why' comes up continually in our business. Sometimes we find the answers, other times they elude us. Don't worry. It'll come."

"Maybe so, but the Passover Massacre was more than just a message to Jews."

"Could be, but I have an editors' meeting I have to run to. Stay on top of it, OK?"

Amber set the cordless phone onto the handset. She was about to turn off her computer for the night, but out of reflex or boredom—she wasn't quite sure—Amber checked her e-mail again. Six messages had arrived in her inbox. One was from Dad, who encouraged her to keep digging into the Passover Massacre story. The remaining e-mail messages were spam, except for two. One was from a colleague—the Fox News reporter based in Jerusalem—who had forwarded an e-mail joke making the rounds in cyberspace. It was titled "The al-Jazeera TV Guide":

Monday
8:00 Survivor: Saddam's Last Episode
8:30 Mad About Everything
9:00 Everybody Loves Muhammad
9:30 Allah McBeal

Tuesday
8:00 Wheel of Misfortune
8:30 The Price Is Right If Osama Says It's Right
9:00 Veilwatch
10:00 No-Witness News

Amber chuckled. *OK, I've seen enough.* She deleted the message and opened the last item in her inbox—a message that froze her smile and would keep her from falling asleep that night.

Eight hundred and sixty-three miles to the southeast of Amber's apartment, Sam Teymour adjusted his red-and-white-checked *keffiyeh* and logged onto a top-of-the-line computer at the Easy Everything store along King Fahd Avenue, a pleasant boulevard that teemed with shoppers and businessmen. EasyEverything was one of the new cyber cafés recently opened there in Riyadh, the capital of Saudi Arabia. With more than four hundred outlets worldwide, EasyEverything had become a global purveyor of computer access for tourists. Sam was no tourist, but he found the cyber café an efficient way to check for clandestine messages without leaving evidence on his personal computer.

Sam typed in his account name and sipped the half-decent cup of coffee while he waited for the browser to come up. He then typed in a URL address, which connected him to a special server. Two password entries later, a single message waited in his inbox.

"Tomorrow night, 1900 hours, meeting point 3."

7

Wednesday, April 12
6:55 P.M. local time
Riyadh, Saudi Arabia

Tourists and evening shoppers packed the wide sidewalks in Saudi Arabia's proud capital of Riyadh. Two women in black *abaayas*—their eyes peering out through narrow slits—passed Sam Teymour as he sat at the outdoor table in front of an unpretentious coffeehouse on King Fahd Avenue. As he calmly drank his coffee—black, no sugar—Sam listened to the heavy fabric of the women's robes swoosh with each step. He set the white china cup on its saucer, allowing the warmth of the April twilight evening to settle over him. Sam carefully opened his copy of *al-Bawaba*, the local newspaper, keeping his eyes on cars passing his location, also known as meeting point 3.

In these early evening hours, Sam looked like any normal countryman: cobalt gray slacks, tasseled loafers, a white button-down dress shirt, and a red-and-white-checked keffiyeh. Meticulous in every detail, Sam had adopted a half-Western, half-Saudi look that rendered him completely unremarkable, a fact essential to his continued existence. Were his activities to become known to the royal family, or any of their minions in the government ministries, his life would most certainly be forfeit. He preferred to wear the cloak of anonymity, his only hope of continued safety.

Sam was careful to hide not only his activities, but also his true beliefs. He was a loyal—some might even say fanatical—

Shiite Muslim in a land ruled by Sunnis. The differences between the two sects might seem minor to an infidel, but to Sam—and to a Sunni—they were of great significance. The Sunnis recognized religious leaders—or caliphs—who were *not* related to the Holy Prophet, Muhammad. The Shiites believed their caliphs had to be descendents of the Prophet. Over this difference, Sunnis had slain innumerable Shiites down through the centuries. Sam knew he had to be careful.

In Saudi Arabia, he appeared to be simply another faithful Sunni as he went about his trivial life, reporting promptly to his job at an electronics store each day and returning home to a sparsely furnished studio apartment. Only in the nighttime hours did he dare carry out his clandestine activities.

Sam flipped a page of the newspaper as he stealthily perused the passing traffic. There, a half block to his left, he spotted a white Mercedes stopped at the traffic light. For the briefest instant, the car's bright lights flashed as though the driver had bumped the toggle by mistake. Sam checked his watch—6:58, close enough to the 1900-hours check time. The make and model of the car also matched. The meeting was on.

Sam swiveled his neck ever so gently as he watched the car proceed a block down the street and change into the left turn lane. This happenstance told him that the meeting had been moved to the second alternate site. Had the white Mercedes continued down King Fahd Avenue, he would have traveled to the original site. Such complicated tradecraft seemed foolishly cloak-and-dagger, but Sam felt more comfortable observing these precautions.

After fifteen minutes had passed, Sam paid his bill and began his circuitous route to the meeting. He took a cab to the Hotel Intercontinental on al-Ma'ther Street and walked around to the rear. Spotting a door marked Employees Only, he boldly opened it and bounded down the stairs to the hotel basement, where the maintenance staff and offices were located. Pretending to be a vendor who knew his way around, Sam passed several uniformed workers, careful not to make eye contact. He quickly found the correct door that opened to the loading dock behind the hotel—just a few steps from a bus stop frequented by hotel employees. His timing was perfect. Five minutes later, bus 24 arrived. He boarded, dropped the correct change into a fare box, and settled into a seat near the rear.

As the bus rumbled through the Suleimaniya district, where Riyadh's business class lived, Sam cast his eyes about the half-filled bus. No women were on board, which didn't surprise him. Women weren't allowed to ride unless accompanied by their husbands or fathers. Nearly all the passengers were foreign workers headed for Riyadh's outskirts after a long day of toil. If Sam had to hazard a guess, the construction worker seated across from him was Iranian.

"How are you?" Sam asked in Farsi.

"Tired." The man's faded beige work uniform was caked in dried cement.

"Guest worker?"

The Iranian shot Sam a glance.

"Oh, pardon me." Sam held up his hands in mock surrender. "Why else would we find ourselves in a 'paradise' like Riyadh?"

The Iranian smiled. "What's your story?"

Sam normally didn't like this type of question but sensed that the construction worker was harmless.

"I'm working in an electronics store. The pay's good."

Wasn't that why they all were in Saudi Arabia? Guest workers—mainly Indians, Filipinos, Vietnamese, and a few Iranians—traveled to Saudi Arabia because jobs paid five or ten times as much as the same work in their home countries. Sure, Saudi Arabia was a blazing inferno nine months a year, and its people snobbish if not rude. But if you could hack it, there was plenty of money to wire home at the end of the month. Workers just had to minimize their living expenses—like sharing a one-bedroom apartment with five others.

The bus arrived at his stop, and Sam stepped off alone and watched the diesel bus expel black smoke as it pulled away. He used the occasion to cough several times while turning his head from side to side. No cars or pedestrians were in sight; he had not been followed. Sam stepped inside the lobby of a nearby apartment building. He climbed two flights of stairs and located the correct apartment. He knocked twice, and the door immediately opened. Now he was in al-Shanoosh's territory.

Once inside, he spotted al-Shanoosh, which meant "the Hammer" in Farsi, seated at a grimy kitchen table. The air stank of old sweat and cigarette smoke. As expected, one of his henchmen was perched at a front window, keeping watch below. Sam knew very little about the Hammer except for two things: he worked for the Iranian government, and he paid well. That was enough for him.

"Good evening, Mr. Teymour." The bearded man's penetrating dark eyes contrasted with his disconcertingly soft voice. "I trust you were vigilant and cautious in your approach."

Momentarily observing the Glock in al-Shanoosh's waistband, Sam replied, "Yes, Your Kindness. Allah was with me, and I can assure you I was very cautious." Sam fought the urge to wipe his sweaty palms on his pants. It never ceased to amaze him how the Hammer could somehow make him feel threatened, even while uttering the simplest and most innocent of words. Sam found himself anxious to end this meeting with the scarred man, just as he had on every occasion they had met.

Al-Shanoosh smiled with a slight upturn of his mouth. For all Sam knew, this was probably the height of merriment for the chieftain. "It is never wise to let down our guard. Please remember that, my friend."

How is it possible to make the words my friend *sound like a threat?* Sam wondered to himself. "Your words will always be heeded, holy sir." Sam understood it was time to get to business. "How would His Kindness instruct me?"

The Hammer glared at him with hooded eyes before picking up two manila envelopes then indicating the first one. "Our operatives in France collected this report on the activities of two Saudi royal princes who recently visited Paris and the Côte d'Azur." He spread several photos on the table like a hand of cards. "You will see that they have availed themselves of the services of women of the lowest character. They were observed drinking liquor and using drugs in nightclubs, and they have attended 'shows' more degraded than I care to describe. They also cavorted on yachts in broad daylight with infidel women. It's all here in the photos." Al-Shanoosh paused. "I want you to disseminate these copies among your cell leaders. Understand?"

Sam nodded.

"Now, we both know that no newspaper in Saudi Arabia will touch these lurid photos. That is why I suggest you meet with your contact at that German magazine, *Stern*. Is he reliable?"

"Yes sir. He is committed to our cause."

Both men knew that once *Stern* published the shocking photographs of the Saudi princes sailing on yachts with partially clad blondes and clinking martini glasses in dimly lit discos, the images would spread through the European continent like a prairie fire. The British tabloids—the *Daily Mirror* and the *Sun*—would gladly knock the royal family down a notch or two, as would *Paris Match* and *Il Journo*. The next domino to fall would be the American scandal sheets: the *National Enquirer, Star,* and the like, luring readers at supermarket checkout stands.

"I want you to smuggle thousands of these magazines and newspapers into Saudi Arabia." He lifted one finger. "But don't distribute them until I tell you. These unprincipled princes are lackeys of the West, unworthy to be entrusted with leadership of the faithful. Until these magazines arrive, you should prepare your cells for timely demonstrations against the royals."

Sam lifted his chin. "As you have instructed, it shall be done."

The chief hardly acknowledged Sam's words. "This second packet should be even more useful," he continued. "In it you will find a dossier on an American couple. The man works for a satellite communications firm here in Riyadh. He and his wife are secretly spreading their heretical, Christian message and are even converting some of the faithful to their blasphemous religion. For the past year, they have led a Bible study among guest workers in this area.

That was bad enough. But now they have begun similar meetings among the faithful at their apartment. They are very careful, but not careful enough. The dossier presents all the details of their activities and schedules. When the time is right, I will give you a signal, as described in the packet. You will need to have people ready to catch them in the act of baptizing traitors to the Holy Prophet. Be prepared to foment a riot. Do you understand?"

"Yes sir. It will be accomplished."

"But there's one more request: the Americans must not survive the uprising."

Sam nodded solemnly, as if he had received an oracle from the most learned man west of the Euphrates.

"Do not fail me." The Hammer's voice was barely more than a whisper.

"Yes, Your Kindness."

Sam exited the apartment. As soon as the door shut behind him, he leaned against the wall and heaved a heavy sigh. Urging his heart to stop its wild beating, he took out a handkerchief and mopped the sweat off his forehead. Then, as if nothing had happened, he ambled toward the bus stop for his return trip home.

8

Wednesday, April 12
7:15 P.M. local time
Tel Aviv, Israel

Amber coasted her two-door white Fiat Uno past the U.S. embassy on Hayarkon Street, where a local gendarme motioned for her to fall into a queue inching its way toward a dusty parking lot one block north. The last time any vehicles were allowed to park *inside* the U.S. embassy compound, Amber thought, had to have been before she was born—in Nixon's time. A sweaty lot attendant directed her to a tiny space between a sleek Mercedes CLK 500 and an imposing BMW 7-Series sedan. In contrast to the European luxury cars, her boxy Uno had the word *nondescript* written all over it. In this part of the world, it was better not to be too showy, especially for a young American woman.

Amber cut the engine and flipped down the sun visor, which had a slender mirror mounted on the back. She reached for a hairbrush in a cup holder and swiped it through her mid-length brunette hair, styled by Yves Fignon on once-a-month weekend trips to Geneva. The mascara around her hazel eyes looked fine, as did the hint of rouge on her high cheekbones. The one glaring imperfection was a sizable pimple that had surfaced overnight near her chin but was now covered with Lancôme foundation. Amber was sure her breakout was related to the stressful Passover Massacre story.

Stepping out of the car, Amber straightened her form-fitting, azure evening dress from Louis Féraud before falling in with other invitees—men dressed in black blazers and women in evening gowns of various hues—walking purposefully toward the gated embassy entrance. As with any public event in Israel, everyone had to pass through a security checkpoint. Amber patiently waited her turn and thought about what the next several hours could bring. Tonight's embassy affair, a cultural reception in honor of several leading American celebrities visiting Israel, was sure to attract the country's glitterati. Harrison Ford was rumored to be among the stars in attendance, and later that evening James Taylor would perform a forty-minute set.

This was an A-list invite for Tel Aviv. Scores of wealthy businessmen and social climbers used their behind-the-scenes influence to wrangle invitations. As for the reason she was there, it was simple: the power of the press.

"Your turn, ma'am," said the U.S. embassy Marine, an African American who looked no older than twenty. She passed through the metal detector without incident then handed over her Hermès handbag, stepped on a square-meter carpet, and raised her arms to shoulder level while another Marine passed a wand over her.

"I'm glad I put on deodorant tonight," she joked with a smidgen of nervousness.

"Me too." The Marine grinned and motioned that they were done.

Another line awaited her—into the embassy itself. This one didn't come with red carpet, but red velvet rope had been strung to separate the invitees—and celebrities—from the paparazzi. Suddenly, a dozen flash strobes went off and a battery of videocams charged the rope line. Harrison Ford was making his entrance. The local media jostled for position, shouting questions at the Hollywood film star. An Israeli entertainment journalist—dressed in red like Joan Rivers, no less—poked a microphone in the actor's face and asked what he thought about the land of his forefathers. Few knew Harrison Ford was one of the leading Jewish actors in the Hollywood community.

This event probably wouldn't be newsworthy to anyone other than the local equivalent to the E! Channel, but Amber had an ulterior motive for being there. The Passover Massacre was like munching popcorn—once you started digging in, you couldn't stop. There was far more to the story than the few kernels she had uncovered. Perhaps this evening she'd pick up some new nuggets of information.

Chief among the guests Amber planned to mingle with was the senior attaché at the American embassy, a fellow in his forties named Robert Turner. Amber had been told by more than one source that Turner was the local CIA station chief. Aside from Turner, she hoped to run into several high-ranking Israeli officials from the military and law enforcement side. They might prove to be valuable sources or reveal an insight into the motives behind the atrocity in the Harish neighborhood.

Like a tide ebbing into the Mediterranean, the paparazzi backed away from the velvet ropes after a beaming Harrison Ford waved good-bye.

"Ticket, ma'am?"

"Oh, yes, right here." Amber fumbled with her purse. The Marine guard, dressed in formal blues, waited with his white-gloved palm up. When she placed the chit in his hand, he nodded her forward. With a smile, Amber proceeded past the tall, highly polished mahogany doors into the elegant dodecagon-shaped ballroom. The walls were paneled in dark cherry wood and accented by glow globes. At the far end of the ballroom were two sets of French doors, painted in eggshell white, leading to a garden courtyard. Although the crowd blocked her view, Amber recalled that the garden was accented by a circular pond and salmon-colored gravel paths trimmed with pink roses and tidy hedges.

The American reporter gazed at the massive crystal chandeliers hanging from the ceiling three stories high. Then she turned her attention to the cacophony of conversations arising around her. Most were conducted in English, but she picked up a smattering of Arabic, Russian, and French from the foreign diplomatic corps.

"Bonsoir, Mademoiselle Roebeens, comment-allez vous ce soir?" inquired a Moroccan diplomat.

"Je vais très bien, merci," Amber replied in a Swiss-French accent learned from her mother. "Et vous, Monsieur Ambassador? Et comment va votre famille?"

The ambassador smiled, happy to talk about how his family was doing. They continued chatting for several minutes while Amber surreptitiously scanned the room. Functions like this were all about meeting the right people, but this Moroccan ambassador was not on her list.

Wednesday, April 12
7:19 P.M. local time
Tehran

Davood Rashee was used to making house calls, but something told him this would be his most difficult visit yet. Two church elders accompanied him as he stepped out from the elevator of the fourth-floor landing.

"What number did you say her apartment was?" the underground pastor asked one of his colleagues.

"I believe 4B. I was told to take a left out of the elevator."

The floor creaked. Davood strained his eyes in the hallway illuminated by a solitary sixty-watt light bulb. He knocked twice on the front door and then straightened his posture.

A young woman opened the door, and before he could say anything, she fell into his arms, weeping. Her shoulders heaved in his embrace as Davood's white dress shirt grew damp with tears. The pastor patted her back as the two elders walked to her side and gently placed their hands on the woman's shoulders.

Minutes passed before the woman stepped back and blew her nose with a well-used handkerchief. "Excuse me," she mumbled, pointing inside. "I haven't even invited you in."

Inside the apartment, Davood took both her hands in his. "I'm so sorry about your husband, Mrs. Soltani."

His formal offer of condolence triggered another round of wailing. Mirza Soltani blew her nose again before she finally composed herself. "Sayed was powerless, was he not? He was like a lamb led to slaughter."

"Yes, we knew his life was in mortal danger once our brother was spirited away. We were praying for his safety."

Mirza reached for a plate of rice cookies and offered her guests a sample. "After Sayed was baptized two months ago, we knew life would be dangerous, especially since he was a physician at the state hospital. Still, my husband remained vigilant, especially with his co-workers. He greatly enjoyed the meetings at your house, Pastor. He longed for that fellowship."

"It's what keeps us going," Davood offered. "And your cookies are very good."

"Your wife made them." Mirza's eyes crinkled with appreciation for an instant before grief returned.

"Please, sit." She motioned to a plaid upholstered sofa and two wicker chairs.

"Anyway," she continued, slumping into the sofa next to Pastor Davood, "a few days ago, while we were shopping together in the market, three men came up to him and said someone at the hospital needed to see him. He was whisked away in a government car."

"Was that the last you heard of him?"

Mrs. Soltani nodded her assent, prompting another round of sobbing. Davood patted her back, an act that would have merited a beating from the morals police had he done it in public.

"I think we have some answers for you." Davood nodded toward one of the elders, who stood up and opened the front door.

Standing in the doorway was a menacing man in gray work clothes. He hadn't shaved in a week, and large stains marked his underarms. He managed a weak smile before looking out of the corner of his eye toward the elevator.

"Omeed, please join us," Davood directed. "Thank you for coming here on short notice."

"This isn't going to take long, is it?"

"No, no, not at all. We understand the danger you're in. Please sit."

"I'd rather not."

"So be it." Davood turned to Mirza. "Mrs. Soltani, may I introduce Omeed? That is not his real name, however."

"Who . . .what . . . ?"

"Omeed is a believer at one of our other underground churches. He works at the prison where Sayed was held and says he has information about what happened."

Mirza's chin quivered as though she would cry again, but she held it in check.

"Omeed, please tell us what you witnessed this week."

The burly prison guard scratched his head and exhaled. Then he raised his gaze and looked Mirza Soltani directly in the eyes. "Your husband was arrested for treasonous behavior and driven to the prison where I work," he began. "For two days and nights, an interrogation squad questioned him about his involvement with Pastor Davood's church. They had pictures of him leaving the pastor's apartment before and after your meetings."

Mirza turned to her pastor. This time it was Davood's turn to fight for composure. "You mean—" he began.

"Yes. They have pictures. Of all of you. The authorities know a Christian group has been meeting in your apartment."

Davood walked away from the group as he processed this information. "Go ahead," he said, returning.

"I witnessed several of Mr. Soltani's interrogations. They blasted him with questions. One would knuckle his head and shout inches from his face. 'Is it true that you're a Christian!' He never wavered, though. 'Yes, I believe in Christ,' he said. I heard him quote Matthew 10:32–33, in which Jesus says, 'Everyone who will acknowledge me before men, I will also acknowledge him before my Father in heaven. But whoever denies me before men, I will also deny him before my Father in heaven.'"

"Oh, praise the Lord," Mirza whispered.

"He was quite brave, this husband of yours. Because of his answer, the four guards spent the next twenty minutes taking turns beating him, but I've seen worse."

"Oh, my Sayed, my love."

"They let him recover for twenty-four hours," Omeed continued. "But for the next round of questioning, he and two other Christians were dragged back to the interrogation room and thrust into seats at a wooden table. In front of them were documents stating that they were renouncing Christianity and returning to the one true faith of Islam. The three men were given fifteen minutes to decide whether their brains or their signatures would be on those pieces of paper."

"This is unbelievable," the pastor said.

"But true," assured the prison guard. "At the end of fifteen minutes, the interrogating team returned to the room. Your husband and the two others sat in their chairs, perfectly still, and held hands. They hummed 'Amazing Grace' while they were given one last chance to renounce the Lord. When they kept humming, the colonel in charge shot the first man in the back of the head. Seconds later, the second man. Tears ran down Mr. Soltani's face, yet his humming turned to singing. 'I once was lost but now am found, was blind, but now, I see.' He bowed his head as the gun was placed against his skull—and click! No shot was fired. He fainted, and when he came to, he was told he would be made a public example because of his prominent position at the hospital."

Davood felt queasy.

"My Sayed." Mirza's right hand clutched her stomach. "I can't take this."

"Are you all right?" the pastor inquired.

"No, I'm feeling sick, but I need to hear this."

"Then I will continue, but I can't stay much longer." The prison guard wiped away a bead of sweat that had dripped into his bushy eyebrows. "Sayed was thrown into a cell with other believers. All night, just like Paul and Silas, they prayed and sang. Your husband gave courage to those men, Mrs. Soltani.

Yesterday afternoon, their earthly songs were silenced. Your husband was executed at a public square in Tehran. I can assure you, he died a martyr's death, and he sings with Jesus now."

Omeed's hands were trembling.

"Thank you, Omeed," Davood muttered.

"You're welcome, and I'm truly sorry," the prison guard said. "I'm afraid I have to go." After gently shaking Mirza's hand, he rumbled down the hallway.

Amber had chosen to attend this evening's soiree without an escort. She was here to work the room, not socialize. Besides, it had been awhile since she felt attracted to anyone. Unless you count that dashing fellow back in Switzerland, but that puppy-love thing was over years ago. Or was it? She had received that mysterious e-mail from him in her personal inbox. He asked Amber to meet him in Geneva as quickly as she could get there. How did he find out her electronic address?

Amber willed her wandering thoughts back to the present. Right away she spotted a general in the Israeli Defense Force standing by the bar, sipping Chardonnay. He coolly acknowledged Amber upon her approach.

"Good evening, General Herzog. I was curious if you had a moment—"

"The last time I talked to an American reporter at an embassy reception, my words made the front page of the *New York Times*." The two-star was clearly agitated.

"Don't worry. I know the ground rules. Anything said here is unofficial and can't be used for attribution. I'm just looking for some leads with the Passover Massacre story." Amber flashed a friendly smile, knowing it couldn't hurt her cause.

The general exhaled. "I'm sorry to be gruff with you, Ms. Robbins. You've treated me fairly in the past. It's just that a *New York Times* reporter burned me a few weeks ago. I'm afraid I can't help you at this time, however. I wish I could, but we're still in the middle of the investigation."

"Any leads that look promising?"

The general raised his glass to his lips, pretending he didn't hear the question. Amber understood. Their conversation was over.

"Well, thank you for your time, General," she said as the pair shook hands. Amber excused herself and withdrew.

She glanced around the ornate reception room and its equally ornate inhabitants. Robert Turner, the local embassy attaché and CIA station chief, was nowhere to be seen.

"Hello, Ms. Robbins! Shalom," boomed a heavily accented voice. Amber turned to her right to locate the source of the thunderous baritone. A large, rotund man bore down on her. She immediately recognized the gray, curly hair belonging to the florid face of Moishe Lebov, whose hefty wife, Hannah, followed in his wake. Moishe Lebov was the owner of one of the largest publishing houses in Israel. He and Hannah were longtime family friends and one of the most cheerful couples Amber had ever known.

"Moishe, Hannah, how wonderful to see you. And since when am I 'Ms. Robbins' to you?"

Moishe opened his palms, as if to say, *Hey, I know, but . . .*

The grandfatherly friend spoke with a conspiratorial air. "Well, we must give the impression that you are a professional and I am a professional, must we not?"

Laughing, Amber tapped her friend on the forearm. "I appreciate your efforts on my behalf, Moishe, but I'm afraid I can't stand so much formality with two of my favorite people. I guess I'll just have to let my work speak for itself and hope for the best."

Hannah Lebov enveloped Amber in a motherly hug. "Sweetie, you look lovely tonight. What a delight to see you! How are your mother and father?"

"They're in Switzerland now at the family chalet in Villars."

"Villars? Oh, yes, that ski resort near the Lake of Geneva," Hannah said. "I forgot momentarily that your mother is Swiss."

"Don't worry. My parents are spending half their time in Switzerland these days. I try to get over once a month to see them."

"Please say hello from us. And I know you hate it when I ask, but I must. Is there anyone in sight yet? Moishe and I are so worried for you. A girl at your age . . ."

Heat rose in Amber's cheeks. "Mom and Dad are doing great, as usual. And no, there is no one in sight—not yet anyway."

"Well, my dear, I am just going to have to take a more active role in solving this problem. You are too full of life and too beautiful to let it all go to waste. Now, I have a number of gentlemen in mind that you just might appreciate meeting—"

"Oh, Hannah, leave Amber alone," Moishe interrupted. "The last thing this American flower needs is a Jewish mother hovering over her. She's mature enough to determine her own future."

"So Mister Big Guy, you care nothing about affairs of the heart?" Hannah pinched her husband's bicep then turned back to Amber. "Seriously, my dear, I do worry, but that's my job. Why don't you come over to our house soon for a bowl of my homemade matzo ball soup so we can make a plan of attack?"

"I'm not so sure about the plan of attack, Hannah, but I would love to spend some time with you both and catch up on the latest family news."

"No! No!" Moishe exclaimed. "Amber, you must not get my wife talking about her grandchildren. We will spend the rest of the evening looking at pictures and getting more details of those terrible toddlers than a sane mind can possibly bear. Why don't you tell us what you are up to instead?"

"Well, I am working on several stories. The one that has me most curious, though, is the apartment massacre story."

"Terrible, wasn't it?" Moishe's bright face darkened. "The times we live in—who can explain?"

"I don't know whether anyone can, but I'm giving it a try. The Martyrs Brigade plot feels like a setup. It's my opinion they had nothing to do with it."

"You really think this?" Moishe asked.

"I do. Some details don't fit, however. For instance, the perpetrators mounted an attack inside Israel's borders—with Israel's incredible security, this is not an easy task—but then they were so sloppy that they left an identifiable body behind? It also bothers me that I don't hear officials talking about the problems this case presents. It seems that someone is not talking."

Moishe's gaiety had long disappeared. His voice grew serious. "Amber, there *are* people who suspect something is amiss. I have friends who, well, let's just say they are very knowledgeable. They tell me that investigators are puzzled. So you are right in your suspicions. But please heed the advice of your old friend." He engulfed her hand in his. "Let the experts handle it. Whoever is behind this has killed many times before and would have no problem killing again—especially a journalist who is, how you say, 'digging too deep.' Do you understand?"

Amber nodded, hoping Moishe didn't realize she had no intention of stopping her investigation now.

9

Wednesday, April 12
7:57 P.M. local time
Tel Aviv

Though Amber loved talking to the Lebovs, she was glad to zero in on the one person she really wanted to corner. Robert Turner was standing with a small group of three men and two women about fifteen feet from her. One of the brunettes was Turner's wife, Natalie. One of the men was a deputy minister from the Israeli foreign office whose name Amber could not recall. The other woman appeared to be his wife or date.

Amber also recognized the second man as an official from the U.S. embassy. The entire group seemed to be listening intently to the third, a U.S. military man (his slate blue uniform and white sidewall haircut gave him away), tell some story. Amber wondered how she could interject herself. As her dad would say, "He who hesitates, hesitates," so she made her move, approaching the group as the military man gestured with two hands, demonstrating a flight maneuver. The way he swooped his hands told Amber he belonged to the fraternity of fighter pilots.

A clearer look at the man confirmed her observation. He wore U.S. Air Force dress blues with golden wings pinned above his left breast pocket. His insignia indicated captain. He was tall, at least six feet two, and well built with close-cropped sandy hair and chiseled features. His deep-blue eyes communicated amusement and intelligence, but Amber had discovered that eyes were not always an accurate barometer of character. Eyes could deceive.

Amber positioned herself on the fringe of the group as the military man finished his story. "So then one of the rookie pilots screamed over the radio, 'Man, I'm totally fouled up,' but he used a different word than *fouled,* if you know what I mean. As the commander, I needed to know who this screwup was, so I said, 'Identify yourself!' There was a long pause, then a tentative voice came back, 'Sir, I may be fouled up, but I'm not so fouled up that I'd tell you who I am.'"

The group broke into laughter, and Natalie Turner spotted her.

"Amber, how are you?" She gave her a quick hug. "I haven't seen you in months."

"Wonderful to see you, Natalie. I think the last time we were together was at the symphony last fall. Robert, good to see you too."

Robert Turner smiled at her. "Good evening, Amber. Let me introduce you to everyone."

The fighter jock didn't seem flustered to lose his audience. "By all means, Rob."

Turner proceeded. "Everyone, this is Amber Robbins, reporter extraordinaire with the *Washington National*. She was one of the embedded journalists during the Iraqi war. She wasn't with any of the frontline units, but I heard you had quite an adventure, Miss Robbins."

"Really, this is not the—"

"No, I think these people would like knowing the full story. Perhaps you should enlighten everyone."

Amber felt all eyes on her. "I can't. I just happened—"

"What Amber is trying to say is that she was assigned to the 507th, the rear-echelon supply unit that departed Kuwait shortly after hostilities began."

"Wasn't that the unit Jessica Lynch and Shoshana Johnson were in before they were captured?" one of the men asked.

"Yes, but Miss Robbins here did not get captured. She escaped with some of our fine men and women, and from what I understand, performed heroically under fire. Even took up arms against those Fedayeen Saddam."

Everyone's attention focused even more intently on Amber, who wished she could slip away. One of the ladies even let out a little gasp. Amber could almost feel another pimple rising to the surface. "It was either me or them, and I didn't want to die," she offered as a way of explanation.

"Miss Robbins's modesty is appealing but unnecessary." Turner squeezed her shoulder. "The battlefield report said Amber and her company came under withering fire. The soldier designated to escort her got hit. At that point, it looked as though their position would be overrun. Amber grabbed the fallen man's M-16 and opened fire. We believe two Iraqis were KIA. We don't know why, but the Fedayeen Saddam gave up their attack and withdrew."

"Very impressive, Miss Robbins," the man in the military uniform said, raising his water glass as a salute.

"And you are . . . ?"

"Amber," Turner said, "this is Captain Luke Mickelson, the son of an old college chum. Everyone calls him 'Divot.' He's currently on loan from the United States Air Force."

Luke "Divot" Mickelson came to full military attention. "Miss Robbins," he intoned in a grave voice and with a slight bow. "It's infinitely more than a pleasure to make an acquaintance with such a gallant and brave reporter as you."

His audience chuckled. Once again Amber was caught off guard. She didn't appreciate becoming the center of everyone's attention. "Tell me, Captain, how is it you came to be called Divot?"

"Yes, tell the reporter," Robert Turner grinned.

The brawny captain situated himself, then took a deep breath. "Well, a few years back, I was doing some cross-service training at Miramar. I was rotating in an F-15 Eagle when the engine flamed out on me. You know where Miramar is, don't you, Miss Robbins?"

Amber felt as though she had walked into a pop quiz. "Sure, I do. It's in San Diego and was home to the Top Gun school back in the eighties."

The answer satisfied the pilot. "That would be correct, Miss Robbins. The pilots take off toward the west, just a few miles from the coastline. At any rate, on this training run, I was no more than thirty seconds in the air when I flamed out. I didn't quite reach the Pacific before I punched my ticket and ejected. Fortunately, I was over the Torrey Pines Golf Course, not a populated area. The plane nose-dived toward the seventh hole of the North Course. Nobody was hurt, although the plane left a huge divot in the fairway; hence, my nickname."

"That's quite a story, Divot." Amber flashed a smile.

The pilot grabbed a water glass from the tray of a passing waiter. "Not as good as yours, I'm afraid."

"Divot is underestimating himself," Turner declared. "He's here to show the Israeli pilots a thing or two in the sky."

"That's right, ma'am. I'm here as part of an exchange program with the IAF. My task is to pass on the latest tactical information we've gleaned and to learn all that I can from the Israelis. It's all pretty mundane, though."

"I hardly see how you can call flying supersonic fighter jets mundane." Amber squinted her eyes skeptically.

"Really, my duty here is nothing out of the ordinary. We are doing these kinds of exchanges with friendly countries on a routine basis."

"Well, it seems to me you're here during momentous times. I think everyone is holding their breath waiting for the other shoe to drop after recent events."

"You mean the Passover Massacre?" Turner asked.

Amber held back her enthusiasm. She could not have asked for a better opening.

Thursday, April 13
7:47 P.M. local time
Tehran

A half-moon rose above the minarets outlining the Tehran skyline, casting an eerie shadow over the metropolis. Davood Rashee stood in the doorway of his small apartment, shaking hands with a few men and nodding with respect to the women as they passed into his home. *If they only knew how brave they are*, he thought. He periodically glanced up and down the neighborhood avenue while being careful not to draw attention to himself. He wondered how long he could maintain an air of normalcy.

A pair of university students arrived at his front door, a bit out of breath. "Good evening, Pastor," said one. "I hope we're not too late."

"No, not at all," Davood said, smiling. "Some of the others are enjoying refreshments while we're waiting to start." He pointed toward their only table, where Mrna stood beside a pewter plate piled high with triangles of pita bread arranged like an Egyptian pyramid. She reached for a stone bowl filled with yogurt-and-cucumber hummus and offered the small repast to the students.

"Please, take two," the pastor said. "I don't think we'll have a large turnout tonight. Besides, Mrna has prepared another plate."

The students lingered around the table as the pita pyramid dwindled. Pastor Davood glanced at his watch—8:10 P.M.—and cleared his throat. "Let's be seated," he announced. "I don't think we can wait any longer."

The young pastor mentally counted his flock—ten people, leaving plenty of elbowroom in the modest living room.

"Greetings, my fellow saints. Thank you for coming on short notice."

His depleted congregation sat down on floor pillows as Davood rocked back and forth on his feet, knowing what he had to say would be difficult for his sheep to hear.

"I'm afraid I have bad news to share with you this evening. We can no longer meet in my home." Murmurs rose among the guests.

"What happened, Pastor?" The question came from a clearly surprised man in the rear.

Davood shook his head. "I don't know how to explain this, but a reliable source informed me that the secret police have been keeping tabs on our meetings."

The two university students stopped eating. "What does this mean?" one asked.

"It means our lives could be in danger. I've talked to other pastors who've told me about sudden disappearances from their churches."

"Disappearances?"

Davood lowered his gaze. "Yes, which is why I have more distressing news to report. One of our dear brothers has received his crown of glory."

"Who?" A young mother hugged her arms around her long torso.

"Sayed Soltani."

"Sayed? Why? What did he do?"

"Nothing," the pastor said. "Our brother Sayed was killed because he refused to renounce his faith. He was picked up by the secret police, interrogated, and executed."

"Do you know for sure?" a thickset student asked.

"A Christian in the jail cells described the events to us. Our brother Sayed was dragged to a public square, where he was forced to kneel and take a bullet to the back of the head. Apparently he sang 'Amazing Grace' up until the end."

"How is Mirza taking it?" the young mother asked.

"The elders and I talked to her last night. She's devastated, as you would expect, but she's hiding in the wings of the Savior. Please keep her in your prayers."

"May we pray for her now?" the mother asked.

"Of course." Davood led them in a prayer for Mirza, asking for comfort in the hope of the heaven and strength in Christ.

"Pastor, what are we to do?" the thickset student inquired afterward.

Davood thought for a moment. "We have to find another place to meet. It's too dangerous here. Someone could be on the look-out right now."

No one uttered a word while Davood silently prayed for guidance.

"We can meet at my house," one woman said. "As long as we keep meeting on Thursday nights when my husband is playing in his soccer league."

"Are you sure, Rida?" Davood was concerned. "Do you know what you are agreeing to?"

"I had a feeling we would discuss this tonight." Rida lifted her chin a notch. "I've been praying all day, and I feel the Lord wants me to offer my home. Mohammed doesn't get home from his soccer league until 9:30 or 10 P.M."

10

Thursday, April 13
8 P.M. local time
Riyadh

That same evening, eight hundred miles to the southwest, Steve and Kim Cobb stood on the balcony of their fourth-floor apartment overlooking Riyadh's Jeddah Avenue, sipping from plastic bottles of Crystal Geyser water and watching the world pass by.

Below, evening shoppers peered into window displays teeming with DVD players, digital cameras, Palm Pilots, and watches imported from Switzerland and Japan. One woman, dressed from head to toe in black with three identically dressed daughters in tow, stared at a knickknack store's display of candelabras, vases, and household fixtures. Next door, a fashion outlet drew onlookers eyeing the Western-looking mannequins wearing stylish ankle-length dresses and embroidered blouses.

"It's our first warm evening of spring," Steve commented. "Reminds me of Bakersfield."

Kim shot her husband a glance. "Don't start with the Bakersfield jokes again."

Steve made a face like he was offended. Both knew Steve loved to tell anyone and everyone that he was born and raised in the armpit of California, a place where tumbleweeds were the cash crop and youngsters aspired to attend Bakersfield College, where students could earn their GEDs or, if they were more ambitious, their dog-walking licenses.

"Dad sent me a new one today. Have you heard what the official motto of the Bakersfield Bureau of Tourism is?"

"I don't want to know." Kim cupped her ears and returned to the living room.

"OK, be a spoilsport." Steve followed her and bear-hugged his newlywed wife, then returned with her to the balcony to people-watch.

Kim's thoughts turned twenty months earlier when they had first exchanged glances at Young Life's Malibu Club in British Columbia. They were introduced during counselor orientation at the Big Squaka, the facility's meeting room. Its picture windows overlooked the breathtaking Princess Louisa Inlet, a crystal-blue waterway resembling a Norwegian fjord.

"I see your name tag says you're from Bakersfield," she remembered saying to Steve.

"Yup, but don't hold it against me."

She laughed. "Very funny. But isn't this place beautiful?"

"I'm pretty impressed with the Malibu Club already, and I've only been here an hour."

As counselors, Steve and Kim were each assigned to a cabin that housed eight campers ranging from ages thirteen to eighteen. That summer they wore several hats: counselor, friend, disciplinarian, teacher, listener, and spiritual mentor. Many adolescents left the Malibu Club with their hearts eternally changed for Jesus Christ.

Steve and Kim fell in love that summer and maintained a long-distance relationship during their senior year of college (he was finishing up at Biola University in Los Angeles; she was attending Calvin College in Grand Rapids, Michigan). He flew back and met her family in Colorado over Christmas break, and on New Year's Eve, to the warbled strains of "Auld Lang Syne," Steve perched on bent knee and asked her to marry him at the stroke of midnight.

Kim smiled at the memory. Two weeks after college graduation, they recited their wedding vows in her hometown and honeymooned at an uncle's lake cabin thirty minutes outside of

Durango—it was all they could afford. A job in inventory procurement with a southern California defense contractor called Alliance Star awaited Steve. They moved into a small apartment in Anaheim, just a short drive from Biola University, where Steve enrolled in graduate-level Bible classes three nights a week. He wasn't sure if he was called to the ministry full-time, but he wanted to keep his options open.

Six months ago, Kim and Steve were enjoying their weekly date night at their favorite Mexican restaurant, a hole-in-the-wall called the El Ranchero.

"Here, read this." Steve pushed a company newsletter across the table. He had circled something in the Positions Available section.

Kim's eyes found the item advertising a short-term position—two years—available in Saudi Arabia.

"Alliance Star has been contracted by the Saudis to upgrade its internal communications systems with U.S. satellites," Steve explained. "I've been giving this some thought. The prospect of living in a part of the world that never hears the gospel intrigues me."

"And you're wondering if this intrigues me."

"Honey, we're footloose and fancy-free. We have nothing tying us down." Steve dipped a warm tortilla chip into the spicy salsa and looked into her eyes.

Kim was decidedly underwhelmed. "If I read this correctly, this job is in Saudi Arabia. Now why would I want to travel there and have to wear a black blanket over my face every time I'm out in public?"

Steve hadn't thought about that objection.

"I'm just asking that you have an open mind about this. Remember how we saw lives changed at the Malibu Club? I think God could really use us in Saudi Arabia. And besides, it's only for two years, and I get a nice raise. They pay for everything: transportation over there, a furnished apartment, a car, and round-trip tickets home every six months or anywhere we want to go."

"Anywhere in the world?"

"Anywhere."

The conversation had happened last October, and now Steve and Kim were ready for a little R and R. In two weeks, they would be taking their first trip—to the Maldives islands off the coast of Sri Lanka. Kim had chosen the destination, sure that the pearl-white beaches and sheltered coves teeming with tropical fish would make for a great second honeymoon.

Sunday, April 16
10 A.M. local time
Tel Aviv

Amber soaked in the beauty of a cloudless azure sky and the warmth of the morning sun as she walked from her parking space toward Tel Aviv University. She pushed aside the events of the last ten days and focused on what lay ahead. Many of her journalistic colleagues would not understand why she would take time out of her busy schedule for this, but Amber knew that what would happen in the next ninety minutes would restore her spirits and energy.

Amber approached the doors of the lecture hall and joined the flow of people. Upon seeing Amber, one of the greeters broke into a broad smile. "Amber, so good to see you. I wasn't sure you'd be able to make it today considering what has been going on lately."

Amber gleamed a relaxed smile. "Wild horses couldn't keep me away, Don. Besides, I've been looking forward to this all week. How are Linda and the kids?"

"Oh, they're doing well," Don answered. "Linda's getting the two boys settled in their Sunday school classes right now. I know what you mean about being here. It really makes a difference in my week. Uh oh, I'd better get back to work. Great to see you."

Amber entered the 500-seat lecture hall and noticed it was already half full. A banner hanging from the alcove above the stage read International Evangelical Fellowship of Tel Aviv. The church had been in existence for only three years. Amber knew of another English-speaking church in Tel Aviv, but that church was traditional in its worship and preaching style. When some baby-buster members of the international community talked about the need for a contemporary church, a call was placed back to the States. Within six months the denomination agreed to send a young pastor, Matt Morgan, so long as he had time to work on his doctorate at Tel Aviv University. It wasn't a problem to rent a lecture hall and a few classrooms on Sunday mornings.

The ethereal music of a six-piece worship band filled the modern lecture hall. Amber smiled, recognizing an instrumental version of "Breathe." She hummed the tune during the "This is the air I breathe" line and walked down the left-hand aisle. Like most people, she tended to sit in the same general area each week—force of habit. Others in her section did as well, giving her the chance to hunt for the familiar faces of her friends—other expats living in the Holy Land.

Sure enough, she spotted two friends sitting in her row.

"Got room for one more?" Amber asked rhetorically, seeing several seats free.

"Amber—nice to see you." Monique, a young woman from San Francisco, offered a warm hug. "I've been following your work on the Passover Massacre."

"Yeah, it's been a tough week."

The service started when the worship band belted out a familiar anthem—"Almighty." The band's shaggy-haired drummer, Amber noticed, seemed rather energetic as he laid down a strong beat.

Midway through the first verse, she became aware of a new arrival taking a seat on the aisle directly across from her. His familiar eyes met hers.

What are you doing here? Amber said with her eyes. Luke "Divot" Mickelson merely grinned and jumped into the chorus of "Almighty." Every few seconds, she caught him sneaking a look at her.

After four more songs—including the requisite "golden oldie" from yesteryear's hymnal—Pastor Morgan delivered the announcements: the church picnic would be at the Mount of Olives next month, a new couples Bible study was being hosted by the Arnells, and Katja Meier was still undergoing chemotherapy treatment for breast cancer. After the burgundy velvet collection bags were passed through each aisle, Pastor Morgan said, "Before the sermon today, why don't you say hello to someone next to you."

That's all the invitation Luke needed to cross the aisle and extend his hand to Amber. "Well, fancy meeting you here."

"You beat me to the punch." Amber pointed to her left. "Let me introduce you to my friends, Kelly and Monique. Kelly's climbing the corporate ladder of the Hyatt Hotel chain. She's on a two-year assignment. Monique's working for a multinational company researching technologies in water desalinization with the Israelis."

"Pleased to meet the both of you," Luke said as he shook hands. "I wish you a good morning, lovely ladies."

Amber felt disinclined to encourage his charm offensive. "Let's talk afterward," she said to Luke. She wanted to know if he was Luke on the make or just happened to attend the same church.

Pastor Morgan preached from the Gospel of John, weaving in stories from his family's European vacation last summer. It was effective, though. Amber noticed how her ears perked up every time the pastor said, "That reminds me of something that happened to us in Paris last summer . . ."

When his sermon was over, Pastor Morgan closed the service in prayer. Amber opened her eyes and saw Luke smiling at her. Together, they walked out of the lecture hall.

"So, you go to church much?" she asked.

"Yes, I do, ma'am. I came looking for a good church to attend while I'm here in Israel. I happened to see you walking in, and since you're the only face I know, I sat near you. I hope that was all right."

"Sure, it was fine." Amber relaxed. "I just wanted to be sure you're more drawn to the Lord than to me."

"Amber, it was not my intention to come just to see you." Luke paused. "But hey, since you're here, do you want to get a coffee or something?"

"Sure, if you don't mind my asking my friends to join us. We usually go to a nearby café after the service. I'm sure Monique and Kelly won't mind if you tag along." Amber grinned.

"Good, let's go," Luke said, placing a hand on her shoulder.

The olive-skinned man, dressed in a rumpled black suit, white shirt, and no tie, glanced up from a circular rack of magazines at the kiosk next to the Tel Aviv University lecture hall. He looked down at the color photo in his left hand. The grainy head shot showed a white woman with a hint of European aristocracy in her visage. She looked to be in her twenties, maybe twenty-five, with shoulder-length brunette hair, wide hazel eyes, and a hint of rouge on her cheeks. The gold earrings looked expensive.

He looked down, then up, studying it again to be sure. There she was, exiting the evangelical Christian church. Three others accompanied her, strolling briskly across the square, laughing and enjoying the bright sunshine. One of the three looked to be U.S. military, based on his haircut and erect gait.

The e-mail from al Shanoosh had directed him to find her and complete a mission.

Sunday, April 16
12:36 P.M. local time
Riyadh

At the same time Luke and three American women were walking to a sidewalk café, Steve Cobb was in the midst of his workweek in Riyadh. The "weekend" in Saudi Arabia—as in most of the Islamic world—happened on Thursdays and Fridays, so Sunday was a workday. Even after six months, Steve wondered if he would ever get used to it.

At the Alliance Star lunchroom, it wasn't hard to meet fellow workers, but none were Saudis, to Steve's regret. Instead, they were guest workers like himself: young men in their twenties and thirties from Yemen, Kuwait, Iran, Indonesia, and the

Philippines who were allowed into Fortress Saudi Arabia to perform a job. Steve knew evangelism worked best when it was relational, so he set his mind on making friends. He was the only American who chose *not* to eat lunch with other Americans. He always carried his cafeteria tray to a table where a Middle Eastern or Far East guest worker was eating alone and politely asked, "Mind if I join you?"

Steve was never refused. Why should he be? They welcomed the chance to talk to someone. These men were a long way from home, just like him, and maybe even lonelier. The Saudis didn't allow them to bring spouses or families to Saudi Arabia. Only Americans received this preferential treatment.

Employing the same skills Steve learned in the summer cabins of British Columbia, he listened, engaged in conversation, and empathized—genuinely caring about them. Soon, Steve and his newfound friends had their own table. They discussed their work, what life was like back home, and their wives and girlfriends. After a month or so, they felt comfortable enough to discuss the twin taboos—politics and religion.

Steve was genuinely interested to learn what they believed about Buddha, Allah, and the Hindu deities Shiva and Vishnu. He remained patient, knowing that sooner or later he would be asked about his religion. When the inquiry came, he surprised them by saying he didn't believe in a religion but in having a relationship with God through His Son, Jesus Christ.

Relationship? What did that mean?

Steve was careful not to go too fast or appear spiritually superior. "If you'd like, I'd love to show you some things I learned in the Bible," he said. "It's a really fascinating book." He carefully took out a leather-bound copy from his black canvas satchel. What he was doing was highly risky, but the lunchroom had emptied five minutes before.

"In comparison to all other books, the Bible is quite unique. It was written over a period of 1,600 years in sixty-six books by forty different authors from all walks of life. The Bible was written in different locations, including the thrones of kings and the dungeons of castles, on three different continents—Asia, Africa, and Europe—and in three different languages—Aramaic, Hebrew, and Greek. In spite of being written by so many different authors over such a long period of time, the Bible displays a consistency in facts as well as theology."

"But the Qur'an has one author, the prophet Muhammad, who received the words from the angel Gabriel," said Vijay, an Iranian computer programmer.

"That would be correct, Vijay, but do you know what the difference is between the God of the Bible and Allah?"

Three men shook their heads.

"The test for identifying the true God is the ability to announce what's coming—the future. The prophecies in the Bible are not right just some of the time; they are right all of the time. These prophecies foretold with certainty events that would change the destinies of entire nations like Israel, Egypt, Syria, Babylon—even Iran."

Vijay's eyes flickered with surprise.

"Yes, I know what you guys are thinking." Steve flipped open his Bible and quickly found his place. "Listen, Jesus thought this was an important difference too. In John 13:19—that's one of the four Gospels in our New Testament—Jesus said, 'I am telling you now before it happens, so that when it does happen you will believe that I am he.'"

"I have never heard this before," said a Malaysian technician.

"Most people don't in this part of the world," Steve replied. "According to biblical scholars, approximately 25 percent of the Bible consists of prophecies. But more important, the Old Testament of the Bible contains more than 300 prophecies concerning the Messiah that were fulfilled by Jesus Christ, who is the Son of God. These prophecies were written anywhere from 450 to more than 2,000 years before the birth of Jesus by men inspired to write the Word of God."

Steve looked around the table to gauge his audience's interest. *Help me, Lord,* he prayed. His hands sweated with excitement regarding this first open door to the gospel. "I'll tell you what. Kim and I would love to have you come over for dinner some night, and then we could talk further if you'd like. I think you'd really enjoy it."

Two men expressed an interest, but Steve wasn't sure if they said yes because they were more interested in eating a free American meal or learning something about Jesus. Whatever the case, that's how his clandestine Bible studies began, but he was careful to never call them that or even utter those two words together in public.

Within a few weeks, the Cobbs were hosting "dinners" two nights a week, drawing an average of three to five men. Over the months, they were blessed to see a handful of conversions.

On this Sunday morning in April, the Iranian computer programmer Vijay sat down across from Steve in the lunchroom.

"Hey, good to see you, Vijay. They working you hard?"

"Like a pregnant cow in spring, as we say in my country," replied the programmer. Vijay turned his head to the right and left to check if anyone was within earshot.

"One of the guys told me about your dinners," he said. "I would like to come sometime. Ask questions."

"Well, isn't this good news." Steve lightly thumped both open palms on the Formica table. "We're having another dinner tomorrow night. Can you make it?"

"So soon? That would be very nice. Would you mind if I ask a friend to join us? He's also Iranian, but he doesn't work at Alliance Star. He's a sales clerk at an electronics store here in Riyadh."

"Of course, please invite him. Just as long as he doesn't eat us out of house and home."

Vijay grinned. "You have nothing to worry about. I'll tell Sam to be on his best behavior."

11

Sunday, April 16
11:51 P.M. local time
Tel Aviv

The four Americans approached an outdoor café on a nearby street—nothing special—but the location was convenient for this postchurch coffee klatch. The foursome seated themselves at a glass table near the sidewalk.

"Kelly, what brings you to Israel?" Luke asked.

"I don't know. Maybe adventure." Kelly said, accepting a menu from the waiter. "The extra pay doesn't hurt since this is a fairly dangerous spot in the world."

Monique snorted. "Fairly dangerous? I'm beginning to wonder if I'm going to get a permanent crick in the neck from constantly looking over my shoulder. You never know when something's going to happen here. You could be standing in a grocery store—"

"I know what you mean," Amber put in.

Kelly took a sip of water. "Sure, it's dangerous in Israel these days, but what an exciting place to be, especially if you're a Christian."

The waiter arrived, accepted their orders for two coffees and two cappuccinos, and shifted away.

"Aren't your parents worried sick about you?" Luke asked.

Kelly bunched up the corners of her cloth napkin. "They weren't thrilled when I accepted this two-year position with Hyatt, but I want to do more with my life than work at some slip 'n' slide in Orlando."

With a lull in the conversation, Amber felt Luke's blue eyes lock onto her. "Amber, let's hear from you. Tell us about your parents."

The attention startled Amber for a moment. "My parents . . . let's see, my father is from Dallas, and my mother is Swiss. We grew up in Dallas's Highland Park area, but we spent a lot of time in Switzerland seeing Mom's family."

"Your mother is Swiss?" Kelly was clearly intrigued. "That sounds interesting. How did they meet?"

"Mom came over to the United States to teach skiing and learn English. She was teaching at Vail one winter when she met this guy on a chairlift. He turned out to be my dad." Amber beamed. "But Mom likes to tell everybody that Dad couldn't ski when she met him. Every time he tried to keep up with her on the double-black diamond runs, he had a yard sale."

"Yard sale? What's that?" Monique asked.

"I know what she means," Luke said. "Hey, I grew up in Colorado Springs, so I saw a few yard sales at Breckenridge. It's when you wipe out and all your gear—hat, gloves, goggles, skis, and poles—scatters across the ski slope. We thought you Texan skiers"—Luke looked toward Amber—"had the most yard sales. We always used to joke that if God wanted Texans to ski, he would have given them mountains."

Everyone laughed. "Not so fast," Amber interjected. "You wanna know what we said in Texas?" She paused dramatically. "We said that if God wanted Coloradoans to ski, he would have given them money!"

Luke nearly choked on his water. "You got me there," he said. "I'm not going to beat you down the mountain after that one. So tell us, how did you get to Jerusalem as a reporter?"

"Great question." Amber looked at her fingers before gazing into Luke's eyes. "I guess it's in my blood. Dad owns several newspapers, so I hung around a few newsrooms growing up. I attended the University of Missouri because everyone said they have the best journalism school in the country."

"I bet Daddy had a plum job waiting for you when you graduated," Kelly teased.

"No, not at all. I mean, I had a foot in the door, but I had to start at the bottom as a cub reporter with the *Dallas Morning News*. They put me on the city-hall beat, which sounds glamorous, but it wasn't. I attended a lot of dull hearings about sewage rates and road reconstruction. Great training ground, though. I also got to participate in the team coverage whenever the president was in Crawford, which whetted my appetite for writing more significant stories. Then one of Dad's papers, the *Washington National*, had an opening at the foreign desk in Geneva. Since I carry two passports, speak French and some Swiss-German, getting the job didn't raise many eyebrows."

"What was it like working in Geneva?" Luke asked.

"I knew Geneva well since my parents once had a home in Chêne-Bourg on the city outskirts. That was before we got the chalet in Villars. I don't know. Geneva felt like home, but I didn't like the work. I wrote a lot of frilly features about the big honchos at the World Health Organization or boring stories about OPEC meetings. Reminded me of my days back on the *Dallas Morning News*."

"And now you're in Israel," Kelly commented.

"Nothing boring about this beat."

"Think you'll ever go back to the States?" Luke wondered.

"Yup. I have my heart set on covering the White House or Congress someday. Dad says I need more seasoning before I'm ready to play in the major leagues. Besides, he's had reporters in his office offering their firstborns for the chance to cover the White House, so those jobs aren't easy to get."

Amber sipped her cappuccino, aware that Luke had nodded at the appropriate moments and followed up with sincere questions. Maybe he wasn't hustling her for a date after all—just earnest. She liked how he had carried a Bible into church with him and had been familiar with the worship songs. During the sermon he even looked up the references Pastor Matt used.

As the conversation shifted, Amber reminded herself to maintain a reporter's sense of objectivity, although she found Luke's charm becoming. *Maybe if he did ask me out—*

KA-BOOM!

A bomb detonated in a Volvo sedan parked across the street, causing a concussive explosion to rock the neighborhood. The four Americans dove underneath their table as shards of sheet metal and plastics rained down from the heavens.

"What happened?" Kelly screamed.

"I don't know!" Amber yelled over the din. "Some sort of bomb!"

Then they heard the shrieks. She looked up to see that a white-and-red Tel Aviv city bus had taken the brunt of the blast. The Plexiglas windows had shattered, and flames licked the crumpled passenger area. A dozen blood-spattered passengers—men, women, and children coping with facial cuts from the exploding glass and metal shards—spilled onto the pavement, falling into a heap.

Dear God, help us. Amber watched Luke jump up and sprint toward the bus. She scrambled right behind him, and when she reached the shattered bus, she lifted a crying preschool girl in her arms.

"We'll find your mommy," Amber soothed, wondering if the child understood English. "Everything's going to be all right." She squeezed the young girl to her chest.

The acrid smell of burning rubber and burnt hair assaulted her nostrils. Amber fought to keep her composure, knowing she had to stay strong for this frightened child. Were the child's parents alive? She could see others pulling unconscious bodies from the bus. The screams of the injured pierced the air, and in the distance, sirens wailed from approaching emergency vehicles.

Amber prayed as Luke performed CPR on an elderly woman. He kneeled next to the woman, placed his left hand atop his right, and pumped her chest three times. Then he pinched her nose, covered her mouth with his, and carefully blew for all he was worth.

She continued to rock the young child from side to side. The girl's cries turned to sniffles, but she still showed signs of distress. Amber wondered if the youngster was going into shock.

Two emergency vehicles roared into the impact zone. Several paramedics jumped out carrying small medical cases. The wounded and the unconscious were strewn on the macadam. Others sat on their haunches, waiting for someone to attend to them.

A paramedic tapped Luke on the shoulder and motioned that he could take over. The American scooted aside, gesturing the number of times he had administered CPR.

A female paramedic approached Amber, speaking Hebrew. Amber's reply was a wide-eyed look.

"Speak English?" the paramedic asked.

Amber nodded her head.

"I can take her. Thank you."

Amber let the girl's hand slip from her grasp as the uniformed paramedic escorted her away from the accident scene.

She caught Luke's eye and walked toward him. His trembling hand brushed a strand of hair from her cheek.

"That could have been us, you know," he said.

"You mean the bus—"

"That's right. If the bus hadn't driven past when the bomb exploded—"

Amber's knees weakened, and her stomach felt woozy.

"You OK?" Luke put a hand under her right elbow. "You look pale."

"I feel a little lightheaded, but I'll be OK. Maybe we should sit." She plunked down on the curb, Luke beside her. Amber rubbed her temples. "I can't believe that happened."

"It does in this part of the world. That had all the trappings of a hexogen bomb."

"Hexogen?"

"Yeah, it's a substance used by terrorist groups because of its malleability and low volatility. Hexogen has tremendous explosive power. Nasty stuff."

Amber took a breath then rose. "I better call the office." As if by rote, she pushed through the gawkers back to her curbside table. Her leather purse was still underneath her chair. She pulled out her cell phone and within ten seconds was on the horn with Evan Wesley at the *Washington National*.

"Hey, Evan, Amber here. You'll never believe what just happened."

"Are you OK? I'm hearing a lot of commotion," replied the voice from Washington.

"I was sitting at an outdoor café with some friends when a car bomb went off across the street."

"Thank God you're all right. Or are you?"

"Ah, I think so." Amber willed her knees to stop shaking.

"Sounds like you have an exclusive: 'Western journalist an eyewitness to Israeli terror attack, probably Hamas or Hezbollah.'"

"Or the Martyrs Brigade. Things have been pretty quiet since the Passover Massacre. Maybe they want to show they weren't one-hit wonders."

Any link between the Martyrs Brigade and today's car bombing would be speculation until someone representing the terrorist group phoned ITV's Channel 1 claiming responsibility.

"Could be. You keep working on it."

"I will." Amber signed off then heard the sickening screams of a little girl.

She turned around. A woman was sprawled on the pavement with a bloodstained sheet half-draped over her. The girl she had comforted clung to the lifeless body, wailing as she hugged her dead mother.

Monday, April 17
10:14 P.M. local time
Riyadh

The last of the invitees had left the Cobbs' apartment five minutes earlier.

"I'm so tired," Kim said as she handwashed the dessert dishes. Kim had been working as a civilian at the Prince Sultan Air Force Base, where the United States Air Force 4404th Provisional Wing was stationed. She was among the 1,000 civilian employees performing heroic amounts of busy work in the office pool.

The biggest hassle was carpooling: Kim, like all women in Saudi Arabia, was not allowed to drive. Two American civilian contractors—one a Christian from Detroit—had offered to carpool to work with her.

"I know. I'm pretty bushed too." Steve opened a cupboard and put the dessert dishes away. "What did you think about tonight?"

Kim pulled the drain plug and allowed the soapy hot water to empty. "I can't believe Vijay accepted Christ. He got it when you walked him down the 'Roman Road.' That was really nice when he said he saw something special in us because we're Christians."

"I know. Awesome, wasn't it? Vijay's a special person. It's not every day an Iranian converts to Christ."

"Vijay told me he's a Kurd, not an Iranian, even though he's from Iran." Kim dried another glass and put it in the cupboard.

"I thought Kurds were from Iraq. Didn't Saddam Hussein gas them after the first Gulf War?"

"You're right, but Vijay said many Kurds live in Iran as well, but they keep to their own neighborhoods and small villages. Pockets of them are Christians, including a cousin of his who smuggles people and goods out of the country."

"Interesting. What did you think when Vijay said he wanted to be baptized?"

"Yeah, that surprised me, but where are we going to do it?" Kim put the last of the glasses away. She knew they couldn't step into an outdoor pool—nor wade into the Wadi Hanifah wetlands that cut Riyadh in half—and start baptizing converts, unless they had an overwhelming desire to lose their heads the following Friday at noon.

"I know—our bathtub!" Steve jabbed the air with his fist and began pacing. "I think this is going to work."

"And who's going to clean up the mess?"

"Honey, we're going to splash some water around, that's all."

"I know, sweetheart. And guess who's going to do the mopping up?" Kim gave Steve a wink as they sauntered off to bed.

Two nights later, Kim decided to cook something truly "American" for her dinner guests—tacos. Cooking Mexican in Saudi Arabia necessitated an extra trip to the Base Exchange, but Kim didn't mind. There were no El Ranchero restaurants in Riyadh.

"Here's what you do," she explained to her wide-eyed guests after placing a plate of fried flour tortilla shells and spiced hamburger meat on the dining room table. "In the States, we put some hamburger meat in the tortilla and top it off with lettuce, tomatoes, shredded cheese, and salsa, depending on how hot you like it."

The four men—two Iranians, one fellow from Syria, and another from Singapore—looked at the array of food as if it were laced with anthrax.

Kim passed around the plate of fried tortilla shells followed by the necessary ingredients. After everyone had constructed tacos, there was an awkward pause.

"Steve, can you say the blessing?" *Hey, lunkhead, pay attention.*

"Why sure, honey." Steve forced a smile. The others grinned, especially those who were married.

"Lord, we thank you for these new friends and for the food we are about to enjoy. Amen." Steve grabbed his first taco with his right hand and took a bite while his guests reached for their forks and knives and made awkward attempts to cut their tacos into pieces.

"No, no." Steve set his taco back down on his plate and wiped his hands with a napkin. "Eat with your hands. That's the American way."

Vijay looked at his Iranian friend, Sam Teymour, and winked. "OK, Steve, is this how you do it?" Vijay reached for his taco and took a man-sized bite. "Very good," he said between chews. "I like this taco."

Soon they were all enjoying their meal with hearty servings of teasing between mouthfuls of food.

"What are we going to talk about tonight?" Vijay asked.

"I thought we'd talk about baptism, since you expressed a desire on Sunday night to be baptized," replied Steve. "Does that sound OK?"

For the next twenty minutes, Steve walked through the biblical principles of baptism before asking them to open their Bibles.

"Vijay, can you read Matthew 28:19?" Steve asked.

The Iranian Kurd fumbled through his Bible.

"You'll find Matthew in the New Testament," Steve commented. "It's the first Gospel." The last thing he wanted to do was embarrass Vijay.

"I think I got it." Vijay, however, took a few more moments to find the right chapter and verse. "Let's see. Matthew 28:19 says, 'Go, therefore, and make disciples of all nations, baptizing them in the name of the Father and of the Son and of the Holy Spirit.'"

"Thank you. Sam, could you read Acts 2:37–38?"

"Acts? I'm afraid I do not know your Bible."

"Here—I'll find it for you." Steve took the Bible he had lent to Sam and quickly found the correct passage of Scripture.

Sam peered at the words then began reading the words slowly. "'When . . . they . . . heard this . . . they were pierced to the heart . . . and said to Peter . . . and the rest of the apostles . . . "Brothers . . . what must we do?" . . . "Repent," Peter said to them . . . "and be . . . baptized . . . each of you . . . in the name of Jesus the Messiah . . . for the forgiveness of your sins, and you will . . . receive the gift . . . of the Holy Spirit."'"

Cho Mei, who was from Singapore, next read Romans 6:34: "'Or are you unaware that all of us who were baptized into Christ Jesus were baptized into his death? Therefore we were buried with him by baptism into death, in order that, just as Christ was raised from the dead by the glory of the Father, so we too may walk in a new way of life."

"Thank you, Cho Mei," Steve said. "*Baptize* is actually a Greek word taken directly into the English language. Its meaning in Greek is basically 'to dip.' Therefore, to baptize someone is to dip them into water. But it is not the physical act of dipping that was important here. Jesus told us that being baptized was the way a person declares his faith in Christ."

The four men looked at their Bibles and appeared to be thinking deeply. Finally Vijay spoke. "It seems like Romans 6 is saying that it shows a person dying with Christ and then being given a new life. So the going into the water would be like being buried and coming out of the water would be like a new life."

Steve was clearly pleased that his star pupil had gotten the picture so quickly. "Yes! That's exactly right, Vijay. When a person is baptized, he is saying that he believes in Jesus. He is saying his old life has ended and that he has a new life with Jesus—eternal life!"

There was one final item of business before the dinner was over.

"We were thinking that we would do Vijay's baptism later this week. We're off on Friday, so we could do it in the afternoon in our bathtub," Steve said.

"Bathtub?" Vijay looked skeptical.

"Yes," Kim said. "We'll fill the bathtub with some water, dunk you, and that will be it. Don't worry—you can keep your clothes on. Just bring some dry clothes to change into."

"And you are all welcome to join us," Steve said, "even if you don't think you're ready to get baptized."

"Thank you," said Vijay's friend, Sam. "It would be an honor to see this baptism."

Following the taco dinner, Vijay dropped his friend off at his run-down apartment house twenty minutes away. Vijay and Sam traveled the entire way with nary a word exchanged between them.

"See you later," Vijay said as they arrived at Sam's apartment house.

"Thanks for the ride." Sam jumped out of the car.

That Sam sure doesn't say much, Vijay thought, as he pulled back into traffic.

Sam waited until Vijay's car was out of sight. Instead of entering the lobby of his apartment building, however, he headed to the nearest bus stop. After a long ride, he stepped off and briskly walked three blocks to another weathered apartment house, where he took an elevator to the third floor.

His nerves always prickled when walking down the hallway to al-Shanoosh's apartment, but the news he carried that night would make the Hammer very pleased to see him.

Tuesday, April 18
6:21 A.M. local time
Jerusalem

The cool of the dawn's early light was certainly the best time to jog. Amber's body craved the daily endorphin rush, and a morning run always cleared her head. Her body responded well to the same cadence, the same route, and the same distance during each jog, which happened five or six mornings a week.

Which is why she continued to jog through the Harish neighborhood after the Passover Massacre. It had been part of her three-mile route long before the horrific killings, and it had remained part of her route after the tragedy. She turned a corner and jogged up Zigzo Street. The blood—red paint—that adorned the glass doorway leading into the infamous apartment building had been painted over. The Passover Massacre was starting to fade in the public consciousness, but Amber believed what happened was not simply another random act of violence but part of something bigger. Maybe the Holy Spirit was prompting her to keep probing.

Amber, dressed in her white Adidas warm-ups, came to a corner and saw a break in the light traffic. She was about to sprint across the intersection when she glanced behind her. A dusty black Honda Accord had slowed to a crawl.

Wait a minute. She had noticed the same car when she turned up Zigzo Street. It was the same car parked outside her apartment block that morning. She glanced over her shoulder at the two men in the front. The one in the shotgun seat was clean-shaven and wore a rumpled beige suit and a felt hat. His driver looked like any other guy in this region of the world—three-day-old beard and a white dress shirt.

The back of Amber's neck tingled. She didn't want the conspicuous pair to know she'd discovered they were tailing her. She accelerated across the intersection and continued on her normal route. Fifteen seconds later, she peeked over her shoulder again. The Honda maintained a respectful distance—about fifty meters.

Amber increased her cadence as her heart beat faster. Why would anyone follow her? Maybe they knew she was an American reporter and wanted to . . . Up ahead, she saw several shop owners washing the sidewalks and setting out their wares. *This would be a good spot*.

Amber made a quick left turn between two cars parked along the curb and halted in the middle of the street. She squared up and faced the Honda Accord, hands on hips. "What do you want?" she screamed, attracting the attention of the shop owners. The car jerked to a stop as the driver slammed on the brakes. For a long moment, they regarded each other. Amber tried to get a good look at the older man in the passenger's seat, but the brim of the hat shielded his eyes.

The car suddenly lurched into gear and sped toward her like a dragster leaving the starting line. His brazen act paralyzed her for a split second before Amber realized that in this game of chicken she would be the loser. She jumped back between the parked cars and let the black Accord speed by. The pair never looked back. The incident happened so quickly that she failed to get a good look at his license number.

"Are you OK, miss?" a shop owner asked, coming to her aid.

"I think so." Amber hunched over and drew deep breaths as the man patted her on the back.

"Thank God you weren't injured. What happened out there?"

"I don't know," Amber replied. "I'm trying to figure that out myself."

Friday, April 21
4:24 p.m. local time
Riyadh

Steve opened the front door to his apartment on the first knock. Vijay and his friend Sam stood there with casual grins.

"Welcome and please come in," Steve said as he pumped their hands. The sound of running water filling a tub could be heard from the bathroom. "Kim's getting ready for us."

The American waved the pair into his apartment and led them into the living room, sparsely furnished with a solitary sofa, two wooden chairs, and a modest coffee table. "Have a seat," he directed, motioning for the two men to sit on the refurbished sofa.

"Care for some peanuts?" Steve held out a palm-sized piece of glassware. "They're Spanish peanuts. They come from Georgia, which doesn't make any sense, but Kim picked them up at the base."

A couple handfuls of Planter's peanuts relaxed his guests. "So, this is a big day for us," he continued, clapping his hands. "You know, I've never done a baptism in Saudi Arabia. The last time I dunked somebody I was in British Columbia."

"Where?" Vijay inquired.

"Oh, sorry. British Columbia is part of Canada. Let me tell you, the water's frigid—a lot colder there than our bathtub. But

Kim's making sure our bathwater will be plenty warm. How are you feeling, Vijay? Excited?"

The Iranian flashed a set of white teeth. "I'm not sure. I mean, I am excited about this baptism. I want to follow Jesus because he is the true God. I know that the future will not be easy, but that verse you gave me from Philippians helped me. I can't remember where in Philippians—"

"It was Philippians 4:8. Here, let me repeat it for you: 'Finally brothers, whatever is true, whatever is honorable, whatever is just, whatever is pure, whatever is lovely, whatever is commendable—if there is any moral excellence and if there is any praise—dwell on these things.' I admire you so much, Vijay, for the step you are taking. Your courage for Christ amazes me, and I'm sure God has big plans for you."

"The tub's ready," Kim called out from the bathroom.

"That's our cue." Steve stood up and swept his hand toward the hallway. "Sam, I know you're not ready for something like this, but I want to thank you for coming."

"I would have not missed today for anything," Sam said in clipped English. "You said today is a big day, and I am sure you are right."

The cramped bathroom had just enough room for Vijay and Steve to stand up in. "You should take off your shoes and socks and empty your pockets," Steve directed.

Vijay deposited his shoes, socks, and wallet into a plastic bag that held his change of clothes. He wore black slacks and a white dress shirt. "You may step in now," Steve said.

Vijay stood in the half-full tub. "What do I do next?"

"Sit down," Steve replied. Vijay lowered his frame and sat cross-legged in the Cobb bathtub. Steve clasped his shoulders as he knelt on the tile floor.

"Ready?"

"Ready," replied the Iranian, who stared intently straight ahead.

"Do you, Vijay, believe that Jesus Christ died for your sins and rose again three days later, and that if you believe in him you shall not perish but have eternal life with him?"

"Yes, I do."

"Then I baptize you in the name of the Father, and of the Son, and of the Holy Spirit. Amen."

As Steve slowly lowered him backward, a wave of water splashed on the bathroom floor, just as Kim predicted. She burst out clapping when Vijay popped back up, gasping for air. When Steve glanced at Kim, he noticed Vijay's stone-faced friend pressing a button on a pager attached to his waistline. Sam then looked up, maintaining a poker face.

Vijay stepped out of the bathtub and accepted a towel from Kim.

Steve's ears perked up. He stepped outside the bathroom, where he could hear a crowd chanting from the sidewalk below. He hurried to the balcony, followed by the others.

"What are they saying?" Steve turned to the still-dripping Vijay. More than two dozen demonstrators—all males—were gathered on the sidewalk below their apartment, shaking their fists and chanting toward a robed man who appeared to be leading the demonstration.

Vijay cocked his head. "They are chanting in Farsi, not Arabic. The slogans are . . . 'Allah Is the Only True God' and . . ."

Vijay didn't finish the translation.

The leader's shout split the air, and the mob sprinted through the front door of the apartment building.

"What are they doing?" He reached for Kim and held her close.

"I don't know," Vijay replied. Sam shrugged his shoulders.

Steve could hear whooping and hollering from the stairwell. He thought about opening the front door for a closer look when he heard heavy pounding.

"What do I do?" he asked Kim.

Before she answered, two loud thumps busted the front door open. A dozen men stormed the apartment and seized the occupants.

Steve fought to maintain his footing as he wrestled with two men. "What's going on?" he screamed.

"Defending the cause of Islam!" the bearded mob leader yelled back. "You just baptized one of our brothers this afternoon." He pointed to Vijay with disgust. "You're still wet, *brother*."

Steve stopped struggling, and the intruders allowed Kim to rush into his arms.

"Go look at the bathroom," the leader with a facial scar instructed in Farsi.

"Water is still draining from the bathtub," came back the report.

Steve watched as the leader turned to Sam. "Very well, you may go."

The American's stomach churned as he watched Sam leave without making eye contact. He squeezed Kim's shaking frame and brought her closer to his side.

"There is only one way the three of you can live to see another sunrise," the leader said in accented English.

Steve, Kim, and Vijay listened to the proposition. *So this is it,* Steve thought. "My answer is no," he said to the mob leader. Kim nodded her agreement. They both looked to Vijay. Such a new believer—would he have the strength?

"I believe in Jesus," he said. "I declare allegiance to no other."

Steve's eyes brimmed with tears.

"Fools. I expected as much." The leader leaned toward the ear of a dark-clothed man and whispered something then exited the apartment, his robe flowing behind him.

Steve couldn't believe what he saw next. The man reached into a satchel and unsheathed a shiny hunting knife, its sharp blade a foot long.

Two men clasped his arms, while another grabbed his hair from behind and jerked his head back. He felt the sharp edge of the knife prick the side of his neck.

"I love you!" Kim screamed.

That was the last memory he had as everything went black.

12

Saturday, April 22
9:14 A.M. local time
Tehran

The Great Leader liked to keep a close eye on his enemies and an even closer eye on his friends. One of the few people he trusted happened to be seated across from him on a Persian carpet, sipping Ceylon tea from Sri Lanka—al-Shanoosh.

"My esteemed colleague, welcome back from your travels." Ayatollah Hoseni dropped a cube of brown sugar into his tea. "They were profitable, I assume." The ayatollah glanced toward his top agent from Savak—the secret police. He was one of the few people he could rely on because they thought so much alike. The Great Leader did not want to appear too congenial, however. Leadership discipline must be maintained always, especially with underlings.

"They were, Your Excellency. The situation in Saudi Arabia is coming together better than expected." The agent reached for a folder. "Yesterday, I personally initiated a new phase, taking our first action against infidel evangelists from America."

"Will the Saudis discover we are behind this?"

"I doubt they will mount much of an investigation . . . only if the American media makes a big deal about it, but dead Christian missionaries have never been of much importance. I'm still keeping an eye on that Christian journalist in Jerusalem—that American woman."

"Very good."

The two men took several sips of tea as they leaned comfortably against pillows on the carpeted floor of the Great Leader's palace, an ornate edifice "liberated" from the shah twenty-five years earlier. The calming effects of the tea caused Ayatollah Hoseni, head of the Islamic ruling council and the most powerful man in Iran, to become reflective.

"Why is the Islamic world like this?" The Great Leader often posed rhetorical questions, especially to al-Shanoosh.

"I am afraid I don't understand, Your Excellency."

"I mean why does every faction in Islam think they have a corner on the truth? Throughout the Muslim world, from Malaysia to Morocco, we have various interpretations regarding what the Holy Prophet meant in the Qur'an."

"You are a wise man, Great Leader, but others are clearly not as wise when it comes to explaining the Prophet's great thoughts or understanding the need for Islam to be united with one faith, one vision, and one future."

"Perhaps, but one future won't come a moment too soon. A united Islam will never emerge unless our enemies are rooted out. To start, renegades such as Kuwait and Turkey have allowed the bribery of American fighter planes and radar systems to cloud their judgment. They are nothing but *whores!*"

"I do not trust our brother nations any further than I could throw a camel," the Hammer said. "That's why we have wholeheartedly made it a priority to infiltrate their governments quickly and deeply."

"Just as we moved after Baghdad fell?"

"Yes, Your Excellency. It's only a matter of time before a new Islamic republic rises under our control in Iraq."

"And our friend bin Laden?" Both men knew that America's public enemy was a Saudi Arabian Sunni, which provoked mountains of mistrust within the Iranian Shiite ruling clergy.

"Our network of informants in Pakistan and Saudi Arabia are keeping tabs on this character."

"And enemies inside our borders?"

"I can report progress on that front, Your Excellency. We are exterminating underground Christian churches like vermin by decapitating their leadership and executing their followers. We are taking our time, however, so as not to attract too much attention. Christians are not our only threat. The Kurds and the spineless holdovers from the shah's regime continue to be an irritation."

The Great Leader grunted, mentally noting the irony of the last statement. His secret police—the National Intelligence and Security Organization of Iran, an acronym of Persian words forming "SAVAK"—*was* a holdover from the days of the shah. Most observers believed Savak had been disbanded following the shah's exile, but Ayatollah Khomeini had neatly folded the secret police organization into the new revolutionary government. Of course, known loyalists of the shah were rooted out and killed.

Savak's mission remained the same following the revolution—internal security and foreign intelligence. Iran's neighbors feared Savak since they couldn't be *sure* if the organization worked within their own borders. Not that Savak didn't have its hands full on the home front—assassinations and terrorist attacks on Iranian government officials were a constant source of irritation, but anyone suspected of untoward thoughts about the ayatollah was quickly dispatched to Paradise.

"I still need to be seen among the people," the Great Leader commented. "In coming months, I will need their support as we bring the Islamic world closer together."

"We can show you visiting new schools and mosques around the country," the Hammer suggested.

The Great Leader grunted. "Yes, since we control the TV, we control the images." The ayatollah looked upon the IRIB—the Islamic Republic of Iran Broadcasting Company—as the informational arm of the Iranian government. Since 1995, Iran had banned satellite reception equipment—a ban enforced with intensity. "But not all the newspapers are with us."

"You are correct, Your Excellency. We have closed down sixteen newspapers and jailed several prominent critics, but we no sooner stamp out one newspaper than another rag sheet takes its place. We must also do a better job of controlling access to the Internet, but clandestine Internet cafés are making that chore a difficult one."

"One step at a time." The Great Leader spoke with an assurance that Allah had given him strength at a unique time for a mighty purpose. "To bring the Muslim world together from the islands of Indonesia to the sands of North Africa has fired my passion ever since the Imam himself, Ayatollah Khomeini, tapped me to be his successor."

The Great Leader picked up a leather-bound folder. "To bring Islam together, I've formulated a plan."

"A plan?"

"It's called Plan Sword. Now let me tell you where the next domino should fall."

The following morning, the Hammer boarded a Royal Jordanian Airbus 310 for a nonstop flight to Amman, Jordan. As soon as the wheels retracted following takeoff, the Savak agent reached for a briefcase under his feet. He spooled the lock numbers to the right place and popped it open, revealing several file folders inside, including one handed to him by the Great Leader.

Typed atop the first page was a person's name—Hassan Hussein. A black-and-white photo had been affixed to the right-hand corner. The man with salt-and-pepper hair looked to be in his late sixties. Al-Shanoosh knew exactly who Hassan Hussein was—a Jordanian crown prince and the brother of the late King Hussein I, "the father of Modern Jordan."

Hassan Hussein, the narrative said, had been groomed as his brother's successor for nearly four decades. The king had even gone to the trouble to alter Jordan's constitution in 1965 to allow him to name his brother as his successor upon his death. In 1999, King Hussein was struck with end-stage cancer; doctors told family members he had only months to live. Two weeks before his death, the king—no doubt influenced by the American wife of his, Queen Noor—announced on his deathbed that the Hashemite kingdom would pass into the hands of his oldest son, Abdullah bin Hussein, not his brother, as promised decades earlier.

The Hammer shook his head at the memory. The betrayal! To be Jordan's crown prince for the better part of forty years and then learn at the eleventh hour and fifty-ninth minute that your nephew would receive the crown you coveted?

Al-Shanoosh continued to scan the dossier. The new King Abdullah, as his subjects addressed him, spoke English better than Fusha, the classical Arabic dialect spoken in Jordan. His father had shipped him off to British boarding schools when he was four years old, and he had attended high school in the United States. After studying international affairs at Georgetown and Oxford, the chap joined the British military academy at Sandhurst and served in the British army in West Germany and Britain. Abdullah was as Western as a pair of blue jeans, the Hammer thought, but he had the Jordanian people in his pocket.

The dossier contained a Reuters clipping, dateline Amman. The faded newsprint contained the story about the time King Abdullah donned a false white beard and pretended to be a commoner dealing with the government. He queued up at the federal income tax department, chatting up his countrymen as he waited to submit a form claiming a tax refund. Another news clipping described how the king posed as a taxi driver, navigating the capital city of Amman to get a feel for how bad the traffic was. The Hammer remembered that incident. The electronic media, who had been tipped off, filmed him cruising for fares. That footage led the news shows in the Arab world.

The Hammer's thoughts returned to his meeting the previous day with the Great Leader. The ayatollah said that he could stomach the youthful antics of a publicity-seeking junior king if his heart was in the right place with Israel, but it wasn't. "King Abdullah continues to support the 1994 peace treaty that his father signed with Israel, and he is a moderate voice on the Palestinian question," the Great Leader had said. "What galls me more, however, is the way King Abdullah cooperated with the Americans during the invasion of Iraq. Jordan handed over ten of the fifty-five most-wanted Iraqis on the Americans' infamous 'deck of cards,' and I wouldn't be surprised if they were behind the capture of that infidel Saddam."

The Hammer and the Great Leader were in agreement. The free-flying Jordanian king needed his wings clipped, and al-Shanoosh knew just the clipper to do it.

The two men met that afternoon at an intermediary's home in northern Amman. The Hammer knew that Hassan Hussein, still a crown prince, conducted business on behalf of the Hashemite kingdom. This was how al-Shanoosh was introduced—as someone to do business with in Iran, someone tightly connected with the mullahs in Tehran.

He and Hassan moved about a third-floor balcony overlooking a courtyard billowing with vines and potted olive trees. They spoke of the upcoming date harvest and whether there was enough water in the reservoirs for the coming summer—small talk. Al-Shanoosh bided his time, studying his prey before broaching the delicate subject. Then the Hammer cleared his throat. "Your Royal Highness, have you thought what the future will bring?"

"Yes, of course, many times. What particular aspect of the future do you refer to?"

"The reason I make this inquiry, Your Royal Highness, is that the people I represent are very much interested in working with a New Jordan. For this reason, we are laying a groundwork for the future."

"A New Jordan? What sort of New Jordan?" Hassan inquired stiffly. The Hammer could sense that the prince did not like the direction this conversation was taking.

The Savak agent took a glib approach. "We envision a Jordan with new visionary leadership, Your Royal Highness. We in Iran were just as surprised as you were when your brother handed the keys to the kingdom to your nephew."

That statement caught Hussein's attention. He glanced into the villa to be sure no one had overheard the remark. Satisfied that their conversation was confidential, he motioned for al-Shanoosh to continue.

Time to play his cards. "The king is more interested in being a populist than in advancing the Islamic world," the Hammer declared. "Bold leadership is necessary to advance Jordan's rightful place and strategic importance. I have chosen to speak to you because the people I represent are choosing sides, and we want to choose you."

"Choose me?" Hassan managed to maintain a mask of equanimity.

"Yes, Your Royal Highness. My superiors are most impressed with the crown prince. Of everyone in your family, you are the one with great intelligence and vision, and we see you as the obvious choice to lead Jordan into the future. More important, you are a True Believer of Islam. You have been faithful to the Five Pillars. You have made the *hajj*. You agree that Muhammad is the greatest, final, and universal prophet for humanity. Unfortunately, your nephew does not believe any of these things. He has been corrupted. King Abdullah, while not a total apostate, has become totally secularized in what is important to him. He is Islamic in a cultural sense, but not a religious one."

Hassan Hussein nodded as he considered the Hammer's statement. "Allah cannot be pleased by his actions," he allowed.

Yes! Al-Shanoosh knew he could bait the hook. "The king's antics have isolated him in the Nation of Islam and brought dishonor to our cause. This is why we need your help."

"Help?"

"May I remind you, Your Royal Highness, that there are powerful people poised to bring together the Islamic world and fulfill the Prophet's mandate of one world, one Islam. The decision has been made to take King Abdullah from the scene; his party time has passed. The question now becomes, Are you prepared to join us, or will we have to act without you? We will remember who our friends are in this jihad against apostates within our own ranks."

The Hammer paused to let his proposition sink in. Within fifteen seconds, he had his answer.

"What is it you're asking of me?" The Jordanian prince inquired in a delicate, statesmanlike tone.

Although the Hammer didn't smile, he knew as soon as Hassan asked the question that it was no longer a matter of *if* he would join the plot against his nephew but *when*—and the price. The Hammer took his time describing what Hassan's role would be, flattering the prince and coaxing him along with flowery speech.

After he put forth the proposition, he waited for a reply.

"Yes, I will do it." With a single statement, the deal was done.

"As a token of my people's esteem, we have a small gift for you." Al-Shanoosh reached within the pocket of his khaki pants and pulled out a bankbook from the Swiss National Bank.

"You'll find the bank on the Bahnhofstrasse in Zurich. It's a numbered account, all safe and secure." The Hammer's right-hand index finger pointed to a string of numbers: 64-112-84. "One entry has been made for 10 million Swiss francs, the most stable currency in the world. That's about 7 million in American dollars."

The Hammer smiled, careful to look sincere. "Once our plan is carried out, a deposit *ten times* that amount will be made. For you."

Tuesday, April 25
9:32 A.M. local time
Amman, Jordan

"How does anyone get anything done?" Prince Hassan put his hands on his hips and motioned to the head of construction. On a warm morning where the desert winds were starting to pick up, the Jordanian leader had driven to Amman's central district for a surprise inspection, but all he saw were dozens of docile workers milling about and a handful of laborers erecting wooden bleachers in front of city hall. They appeared to be working in slow motion—and it wasn't even that hot on the late-spring morning.

The foreman wiped his brow. "Your Excellency, if you bang on tables loud enough or slap heads together like coconuts, you can usually accomplish something by the end of the day."

Prince Hassan was unimpressed. "Looks like you need to do some head-slapping. We are just days away from a Grand Prix race on our streets, and we're not finished yet. Why?"

"I don't know, sir, but I have ordered temporary lighting so that we can continue working tonight. We will work around the clock until the bleachers are completed to your satisfaction."

"If I don't see significant progress by tomorrow, not only will you be fired, but your next job will be digging latrines in your own work camp."

Hassan preferred not to bully workers, but King Abdullah had put him in charge of staging a Formula 1 race on the streets of Amman. Michael Schumacher, Kimi Räikkönen, and other top Formula 1 drivers would be putting on a show, à la Monaco, with wheel-to-wheel racing on hairpin turns snaking through Jordan's capital city. Sponsoring a Formula 1 car race was further proof, in Hassan's mind, that the king—a former National Rally Racing champion—was taking his eye off the road.

Time to check on the security arrangements. Hassan turned to the local security liaison. "I'm losing my patience. Your report better please me."

The local security chief puffed out his chest. "Your Royal Highness, all buildings and residents within a two-block radius of this reviewing platform have been screened. This information is contained in my report."

"I read it earlier today. On the day of the race three days hence, I will personally inspect the platform for explosive devices or anything else suspicious. The security of King Abdullah cannot be compromised."

Saturday, April 29
11:58 A.M. local time
Amman, Jordan

King Abdullah bin Hussein was driven to the reviewing platform in a white stretch Lincoln Navigator. He arrived just two minutes before noon, wearing a navy blue suit from Ermenegildo Zegna, a white starched shirt, matching tie, and his family's trademark red-checked head scarf.

Al-Shanoosh peered through the curtains from a penthouse apartment overlooking the bleachers. A security detail had searched the apartment the day before, but they had found nothing of interest. The Hammer turned his eyes on two of the tools he would need that day—powerful binoculars and a secure cell phone.

When the Great Leader initially suggested this operation, the Hammer had blanched. Too dangerous. Then he reviewed the situation with the placid disposition of a corporate accountant. The upside, as they say, was tremendous. The downside . . . well, he didn't want to consider that. The next few minutes would be decisive. If things went according to plan, the cause of Islam would take a giant step forward. If not, his world would be set back for years—maybe a decade or more. And, of course, if things went really badly, his life would be in jeopardy.

The Hammer knew success or failure depended on one man's betrayal. Everything hinged upon the prince. Was his lust for power great enough?

Al-Shanoosh, peering through his range finder at the reviewing stand, spotted the crown prince carrying a male purse. The Savak agent, whose tobacco-stained teeth hid behind a black beard flecked with gray, worked hard at maintaining the menacing image he intentionally projected to others. On this postcard day, however, he was having a devil of a time living up to that image. He was enjoying himself immensely, but he would never allow his associates and underlings to see the satisfaction on his face.

That morning he had packed enough Semtex into Hussein's handheld purse to rocket the reviewing stand and everyone on it two hundred meters into the air. Would the crown prince go through with it? The Hammer put down his binoculars and exhaled. Yes, he decided, if Hussein believed he was doing it for the greater glory of Islam. But the Hammer had been around long enough to know that you could never tell how someone would react under pressure.

"Faster! Can't you make this taxi go any faster?"

Amber hated last-minute story assignments. The e-mail last night from one of the *Washington National* foreign desk editors told her to take the next plane to Amman. The king of Jordan had agreed to be interviewed about bringing Formula 1 racing back to the Middle East. Amber knew the storyline was thin, but perhaps she could piggyback on the interview and ask the king how the staging of major sporting events—like a car race—fit into his political goals. Early that morning, she had jumped on a Royal Jordanian puddle jumper to Amman's Queen Alia International Airport, where she hailed a taxi.

"No faster!" the bearded driver yelled back, slamming the steering wheel with his right hand for emphasis while gesturing at the hundreds of pedestrians choking the downtown boulevard.

Amber leaned back in her seat and took a deep breath. She opened a file folder and fingered an official-looking fax from Jordan's foreign press secretary, allowing her to interview King Abdullah for fifteen minutes before the race started. According to her watch, though, she was running late and getting nowhere fast.

Her file folder contained a city map of Amman. During the short flight, she had used a neon yellow highlighter to outline the race course on the city streets.

Amber leaned over the front seat and showed the map to the driver. "We are—"

"Here." The driver pointed a dirty fingernail at an intersection.

Amber saw she was a good four blocks from the reviewing stand, close enough to walk.

"Stop. I leave," she said, pulling out a crisp $20 bill from her purse. She knew taxi drivers around the world appreciated being paid in American dollars, which were useful on the black market. "Keep the change."

Amber slung a leather satchel over her shoulder and shot out of the taxi. Within five minutes, she had the royal bleachers within sight.

King Abdullah bin Hussein, two half-brothers, their wives and children, and various ministerial officers took their preferred seats above the starting line of the Grand Prix. Twenty-six speed rockets formed the starting grid. With their fire suits displaying dozens of sponsors' patches, the drivers left the pit area and paraded like walking billboards to their parked cars.

Tens of thousands of fans packed the bleachers alongside the main straightaway. The crowd fell silent when a Jordanian honor guard presented the nation's flag. Hassan stood in respect and thought of the Arab Abbasid, Umayyad, and Fatimid dynasties that were represented by the black, white, and green bands on the Jordanian flag. The crimson triangle joining the bands symbolized the Hashemite monarchy, just as the seven-pointed Islamic star set in the center of the crimson triangle represented the unity of Islamic peoples in Jordan.

Camera crews besieged the royal box. A technician handed the public address microphone to King Abdullah. With his left arm raised, he said in English, "Gentlemen, start your engines!"

A blast of noise assaulted the reviewing stand as the Formula 1 drivers revved their Cosworth three-liter engines. The pit crews hustled to safety behind the concrete barriers, and all eyes looked toward the royal box. King Abdullah slowly raised a green starting flag into the air. For five seconds, he held the flag aloft before slashing it toward his feet. Michael Schumacher, the German legend, was sitting in the pole position. His red Ferrari roared into an early lead as the fans in turn 1 roared their approval.

The race was on—in more ways than one. The crown prince reached inside his pants pocket and pulled out a small blue pill. He nonchalantly popped it into his mouth.

Al-Shanoosh had told him that the effects of ipecac, a vomit-inducing drug, would come in sixty seconds. Whoever made this ghastly potion was certainly right. A watery surge rushed up his esophagus; within seconds, Prince Hassan spewed a stream of lime green vomit. The offensive body fluids deflected off his spit-shined Italian shoes and splashed onto the clothes of several royal family members, whose scowls registered disgust. The pale green vomit was a nice touch, he thought. He had eaten a heaping bowl of broccoli soup an hour earlier.

King Abdullah jumped to his feet and covered his nose with his right hand, lest his nostrils be overwhelmed by the fetid smell.

"Oh, I feel horrible," Hassan moaned. An attaché hurried to his side to escort the crown prince off the platform. As the aide struggled to assist him, he accidentally kicked Hassan's purse, which had been placed next to his feet. Together, they watched the leather satchel drop through the wooden bleachers toward the pavement below.

The buffoon! Prince Hassan helplessly watched, certain that he and everyone would be blown out of existence, but to his relief, the purse bounced harmlessly off the ground.

"My humble pardon about your purse, sir," the panic-stricken aide said. "I'll have someone fetch it." He spoke into a lapel mike and ordered someone to retrieve the purse posthaste.

Things were not going to plan. The prince's bomb-laden purse was supposed to stay in the stands while he exited the area. Hassan wiped his brow, sure that a second bout of nausea would overwhelm him. "Take me to some facilities," he groaned.

Amber turned a corner only to be assaulted by the decibels of high-performance race engines passing the straightaway in front of the royal family reviewing stand. She had never heard anything so loud in her life—not even at a rock concert. A sinking feeling hit her stomach. Since the race had started, she was now officially late for the interview.

Amber stood in the plaza, thinking about what she should do next. She had already passed through a security cordon, where she had presented her passport and the fax from the foreign press secretary's office confirming her interview with King Abdullah. Her biggest need at the moment, though, was finding a bathroom.

She turned around and saw an impressive building with tall columns. Surely she would find a woman's toilet there.

The Hammer watched the prince's performance from the five-story apartment. The stream of vomit impressed him, but he was appalled by the clumsiness of the careless attaché.

Not that it would change the outcome. There were still plenty of explosives to send King Abdullah and his next of kin into the sky. Whether the Semtex-laden purse was five feet away or thirty feet below, the result promised to be the same.

He looked through his binoculars and watched the attaché drag the crown prince into a large stone building behind the reviewing stand. He figured it had to be city hall. Two white-gloved military guards snapped to attention. A young-looking woman dressed in Western clothes fell in behind Hussein, and he watched the two of them step inside the foyer of city hall.

Al-Shanoosh's fists clenched, however, when he watched a low-level military aide move double time across the square, holding Hassan's purse high above his head.

The crown prince was escorted to the men's bathroom in the basement and led to a stall. Typical for the region, the bathroom did not come with a toilet but a ceramic hole in the floor.

He knew there was no time to lose. Hussein fumbled through his breast pocket, where he found the wallet-sized electronic detonator.

The moment of truth had come. Hassan hesitated. The detonator felt slippery in his hand. His head began spinning, and he suddenly felt another urge to vomit. He turned to the ceramic hole in the floor, bent over, and unleashed another heave.

The Hammer's mind raced as he assessed the situation. The military aide was putting some real distance between him and the royal box. "Hurry, Hassan, if you know what's good for you."

The military aide suddenly disappeared in a fireball that issued from the middle of the square. The thundering blast caused a concussive shock wave that toppled the royal reviewing stand like a house of matchsticks.

From his perch, al-Shanoosh watched with glee as the wooden stands imploded in a cloud of dust and confusion. Screams of the injured pierced the air. Somewhere, he thought, King Abdullah and his two half-brothers lay underneath tons of wooden beams, their bodies crushed as well as their apostate spirits.

Amber had been running a brush through her hair in the basement bathroom when the blast rocked the building. Heart pounding, she hustled up the staircase only to run into a cloud of noxious dust outside city hall.

The scene was surreal—a collapsed grandstand and the sounds of high-pitched race engines whining in the distance. Another bombing?

Amber willed her shaking hands to steady as she speed-dialed the *Washington National* foreign desk. The sun was just coming up on the East Coast, so Evan Wesley wasn't in yet.

"Jack? Amber here. You can forget the article about King Abdullah bringing Formula 1 racing back to Jordan."

"What article?" The assistant news editor sounded shocked.

"The one you assigned me to last night. By e-mail."

"I never sent you an e-mail."

"Come on. You're joking."

"No, I'm not."

"So you don't know about the bomb?"

"What bomb? Amber—"

"The bomb underneath the royal box. It's total chaos here. The king is probably history."

There was an interruption on the line. "Fox News is breaking in with the story," Jack said. "My goodness. Are you OK?"

"I was in the ladies room when it went off. So who sent me that e-mail?"

"I don't know. That's spooky. Hey, are you still up to writing a story?"

"I guess so. I'm a bit shaken, though."

"Listen, you don't have to do this, but—"

"That's OK. I know the drill. I'll have something to you in a few hours."

"You stay out of trouble, you hear?"

"I'm trying."

The Great Leader took the phone call in his office.

"Hello, my friend," the ayatollah said over an encrypted line. "I trust you're calling with good news."

Ayatollah Ali Hoseni waited for his words to go through several moments of encryption.

"I had to step in, Your Excellency," the Hammer said. "Hassan did not know this, but I had a detonator as well. In the name of Islam, I pushed the button."

"Was that traitor of the True Faith killed?"

The Hammer was taken aback. He expected the Great Leader to employ a euphemism for the word *killed*, such as "sent to the next world" or "taken before judgment."

"I don't believe he survived," al-Shanoosh replied. "The blast covered King Abdullah and his brothers with a large pile of wooden beams. Rescue crews are still digging through the wreckage."

"And the American journalist?"

The Hammer recalled the e-mail that he had sent yesterday, posing as one of her foreign desk editors. Apparently, his ruse had worked.

"I think she arrived too late. A pity."

"Very well. Call me when you have an update."

13

Sunday, April 30
8:50 A.M. local time
Tel Aviv

Luke Mickelson desperately needed someone to talk to, and he hoped that someone would be Amber Robbins. He arrived early for the 9:00 A.M. church service at the International Evangelical Fellowship of Tel Aviv and took his usual seat fifteen rows up, left side.

The worship team was into the second stanza of their spirited opener, "High and Lifted Up," when Amber, obviously rushed, stepped in next to Luke.

"Glad you could make it," Luke whispered into her ear.

"You won't believe what happened yesterday," Amber said. "I'll tell you about it after church." She waved to Kelly and Monique, who stood on the other side of Luke.

The service followed its usual pattern—four songs, a few announcements, another song, the offering—until a man and a woman stepped out from the eaves and performed a skit. They were supposed to be a husband and wife, acting out a typical confrontation: she was shopping too much; he was tight with the money. The repartee was witty, and then the point was made: We all have our scripts, and we're most likely to stick to them if we're not careful to think through what's being said.

Everyone shifted in their seats when Pastor Morgan, dressed in a Hawaiian shirt and beige slacks, bounded out of his front-row seat to the stage and stepped behind the lectern. Not that he ever used it. The pastor, wired to a cordless microphone, preferred to work the stage, pacing from one side to the other as he delivered his message. The pastor read from Acts 7, which told of the stoning of Stephen, the first Christian to be martyred for his faith.

"As we worship here today, we are a very short drive from the place where that happened." The pastor had already worked his way to the right side of the stage. "That should certainly bring home to us the reality of Stephen's death. But if you think dying for your faith is something that happened only in the Bible, let me assure you we are seeing martyrs today. In fact, more Christians are being martyred today than ever before in history."

Luke nodded. He had heard Amber talk about the "suffering church" and how Christian persecution was on the rise in Islamic countries.

"The greatest number are being murdered in Sudan, where followers of Christ are systematically slaughtered by government forces in the north," the pastor continued. "Their children are taken as slaves or forced to convert to Islam. In Indonesia, Christian villages are plundered, and dozens of saints have been hacked to death because they believe in Jesus.

"Even in India, which has a centuries-old indigenous church, Christians are attacked. Militant Hindus have killed a number of Christians in the past few years. In North Korea, more than 100,000 Christians are in prison for the crime of believing in Jesus. A sizeable portion of that number will not leave those jails alive. It is happening all over the world. In Fidel Castro's Cuba, evangelical Christians are routinely thrown in prison for proclaiming their faith."

Pastor Morgan paused. "Josef Stalin once said that a single death is a tragedy and a million deaths is a statistic. I was reminded of that statement this week when I read in the *Jerusalem Times* about the young American couple martyred for their faith in Riyadh. Their offense? They had Muslim friends over to their apartment, and they shared Jesus. For this, they were found in their bathtub, stacked like cordwood, their throats slit and their blood flowing down the drain. My friends, isn't it becoming clear that we are being targeted for persecution?"

Just then, Luke choked and gasped for air. He stared at his shoes and concentrated on breathing. He did not want to make a scene. Amber turned to him and placed a hand on his right arm.

"Are you OK?"

Luke didn't answer her. He bolted out of his chair and kept his head down as he rushed up the aisle into the foyer. Amber followed him to the foyer and caught him as he pushed his way through the glass doors.

Luke lowered his head and wrapped his arms around his chest. He began bawling, and he didn't care if Amber heard him or not. Tears streamed down his face as she came around to his side.

"Luke, what's wrong?" Amber rubbed her hand in a circle on Luke's back, and he felt her love and concern.

"Amber, I wanted to tell you before church—"

"Sorry. I was running behind this morning after getting in late last night. Is something wrong?"

"That American couple in Saudi executed for their faith? Well, that was my . . . my . . . sister, Kim, and her husband."

Luke could hardly speak through his overwhelming grief and hunched over as if an emotional dam had burst. As more tears flowed, great gasping sobs wracked his body. "She was my only sister."

"Oh, Luke, I'm so sorry."

Luke managed to gather himself as the tidal wave of emotion receded.

"What's made things worse is that the Saudis have been making it difficult to get the bodies out of the country. There's so much red tape, so much bureaucracy. The U.S. embassy hasn't been much help either. It's as if they blame Steve and Kim for what happened."

Luke lifted his gaze and took a deep breath. "This makes me so mad. Thankfully, Rob Turner has managed to cut through some bureaucratic tangles. He assures me the bodies will be released, so I'm flying back to the States tomorrow."

That night, Amber felt as uneasy as she had ever been in her life. Someone had wanted her in Amman at the same time a blast killed a major Arab leader. Who could that be? And why?

Too many things were happening to her. She needed someone to talk to. Amber racked her brain for someone to call, someone who could shed light on what was behind the Passover Massacre, the assassination of King Abdullah, and the horrifying news of Luke's sister and brother-in-law having their throats slit in Saudi Arabia. The fact that someone was following her while she was jogging and got her to Amman just before that bomb exploded . . . was her investigation getting too close?

She opened her Entourage software and typed in "Christian sources." Thirty-two names were found in the database among the nine hundred and forty-two names in her electronic Rolodex.

The name Lowell Mason came to her screen.

Lowell Mason . . . Lowell Mason . . . where had she met him?

Then she remembered. He spoke at her father-daughter retreat at JH Ranch in northern California just before her senior year of high school. Dr. Mason, who chaired the Comparative Religions Department at Fuller Theological Seminary in Pasadena, wasn't in the Siskiyou Mountains to speak about the differences between an ashram and a hermitic monastery. Instead, the learned professor spoke from his heart about the value of father-daughter relationships. Amber remembered that week as a turning point in her relationship with her father.

She had called Dr. Mason several times during her college years, usually to pump him with questions about why the Orthodox Greeks split with the Roman Catholic Church or what those who subscribed to the Ba'hai faith believed in.

Now she needed another favor. Amber looked at her watch. Ten at night in Jerusalem, lunchtime in California. She reached for her cell phone and dialed Dr. Mason's home number since it was Sunday.

She recognized his voice immediately. "Dr. Mason?" she began brightly. "Amber Robbins calling from Jerusalem."

"Amber! So nice to hear from you. I had dinner with your father last month when he was in Los Angeles for some media confab. He told me you're doing well in the Holy Land. He's quite proud of you, Amber."

"Thank you, Dr. Mason, but I—"

"Please. It's Lowell."

"OK . . . Lowell," Amber said uncomfortably. "Wow, I wish he would have mentioned seeing you. Anyway, in light of all the events happening in the Middle East, I feel like I need a refresher course on Islam and how it relates to everything going on around here."

"So what is it you need to know? Don't forget that I'm not an expert on the Islamic religion. I'm a jack of all religions and master of none."

"You're being much too modest, Dr. Mason."

"Lowell."

"Dr. Lowell. Anyway, I need some background. Would you mind if I typed in some notes?"

"No, be my guest." Dr. Mason seemed eager to have a student again. "Let's see, where do I start? The essence of Islam is the belief that there is only one God, and that it is the people's duty to believe in him and serve him in the manner that is laid out in the Qur'an. In Arabic, *Islam* means submission and a *Muslim* is one who submits to God's will."

"What can you tell me about its founder, Muhammad?"

"Well, Muhammad, the Prophet of Islam, was born around A.D. 570 in Mecca, and he seems to have been some sort of wealthy trader. Have you heard of Mecca?"

"Yes, I've heard of Mecca." Amber thought about telling Dr. Mason that she wasn't *that* dumb. "The holiest city in Islam, and it happens to be situated in Saudi Arabia."

"Correct." Dr. Mason resumed his professorial stance. "Mecca is about fifty miles from the port city of Jidda, and it is located in a narrow valley overlooked by hills crowned with castles. That's what oil money will buy you these days. But let me return to Muhammad's story. When he was around forty, he must have gone through some sort of midlife crisis because he felt selected by God—whom he called Allah—to be the Arabian prophet for true religion. Muhammad claimed that he was squirreled away in a cave in Mount Hira north of Mecca when he had a vision from God and was given the command to preach. He continued to have many revelations for the rest of his life, which were later recorded in the Qur'an several centuries later. Muslims are fond of saying that the Qur'an was first written on palm leaves and flat rocks and in the hearts of men."

"What were some of these revelations?"

"That there is one God; man must submit in all to him; and in this world, nations will be amply punished for rejecting God's prophets, such as himself. He said that heaven and hell were waiting for all of us, and the world will come to an end with a great judgment. He believed in many religious duties, such as frequent prayer and giving to the poor, and he forbade usurious interest rates in loans."

"He sounds like a nice guy."

"He may have well been a likable fellow, but when his new religion failed to win many followers, he took it personally. His religion was not, shall we say, universally embraced by nomads roaming the desert sands. Many nomads were Jewish, which explains why they did not look favorably upon someone announcing that he was a holy prophet for some other God-force named Allah."

"What about in Mecca? Did the locals like him or his new religion?"

"Muhammad did not lack for enemies in those days. In the summer of 622, a plan was hatched in Mecca to murder Muhammad, but he made a dramatic escape in the middle of the night and fled to a nearby city. After that, Muhammad took a different tack. He needed numbers, so he decided he would grow his flock by *making* people believe in his new religion. The results were quite brutal. He and his warriors descended upon an encampment, and the male leaders were told to either believe in Allah and Islam that day or be slaughtered by sunset. It was called 'conversion by the sword.'

"Few tribes were any match for Muhammad and his swordsmen, so by the time of his death in 632, all of Arabia had been converted, and the Prophet's missionaries began fanning out to Persia and Ethiopia. His greatest resistance came from the Christians and the Jews, however, because Muhammad firmly believed he was the last of the prophets and was the successor to Jesus Christ. Try as they might to resist, the Christians and the Jews were no match for Muhammad's military might, however."

"So they took over."

"Right."

"What happened after Muhammad's death?"

"A fellow named Abu Bakr succeeded Muhammad by becoming the first caliph, or religious leader, but he lived only a few years after the Holy Prophet's death. Omar was Abu Bakr's closest assistant and adviser, so the powers that be decided that Omar would be the next caliph. During Omar's reign, Islam captured Arabia and built the Muslim city of Baghdad, where Babylon once stood. They also captured the rest of Persia, Egypt, and Israel, then known as Palestine, in 637. These Medinan Arabs—the so-called True Believers of Islam—continued a successful campaign of international conquests over the next thirty years, conquering parts of Europe, North Africa, and Central Asia. No religion grew as fast in its infancy, but what Islam offered was the 'carrot or the sword.' If you converted, your taxes were immediately eliminated, as well as your tithe to the Roman church. If you didn't, you were slaughtered, as I mentioned before. The choice wasn't hard for most to make, unless you had a death wish to become a martyr."

"Hang on, let me catch up." Amber typed furiously. "OK, please continue."

"Back to Muhammad and what happened after his death: Ali, a son-in-law to Muhammad by virtue of marriage to his daughter

Fatima, became the new caliph after Omar. A religious civil war broke out when a fanatical group called Kharijites claimed that Ali was not the rightful caliph and sent assassins out to kill Ali, and they succeeded. The people who revered Ali did not esteem the new caliph, and this is when the Islamic world split into Sunnis and Shiites. The Sunnis didn't believe that Ali was a martyr, while the Shiites revered him."

"I'm getting confused. All this Sunni and Shiite stuff seems like one big mishmash."

The professor chuckled. "Most Westerners can't keep this straight, so don't worry. Just remember that the gulf between the Sunnis and the Shiites has widened over the centuries. These days, the Sunnis have 90 percent of the world's one billion—let me repeat that—one billion Muslims, while the Shiites have the remaining 10 percent. The Sunnis, much to the consternation of the Shiites, believe in the separation of church and state, which is why Saudi Arabia—and Iraq when Saddam was calling the shots—has a more secular government. Meanwhile, Shiite fundamentalists believe in a religious government, which explains why various ayatollahs have ruled Iran since the shah was overthrown during the revolution."

"Do you know anything about Muhammad's personal life, if he got married, things like that?"

"Muhammad married many times, and troubles in his harem have been extensively written about. Still, most Muslims consider him sinless. He's the holy of holies."

"Thanks, Dr. Lowell. You've helped a lot."

"Are you working on a story?"

"You could say that."

14

Tuesday, May 2
5:27 P.M. local time
Jerusalem

Amber reread the e-mail that she'd already lost sleep over. It was unsigned and from an address she didn't recognize:

Tuesday afternoon

Dear Amber:

I know you never expected to hear from me again, but as I was reading about the Passover Massacre on the Internet, I noticed that you had written the story in the *Washington National*. I cannot travel to Jerusalem, but I often travel to Geneva. Would you ever be interested in another raclette meal at Les Armures? It would be for, how you say, old times' sake.

Amber stood and stepped away from her computer. Lost in thought, she paced around her 800-square-foot studio apartment, furnished with a love seat, twin bed, bookshelves, and small table for her computer. First this unexpected message, then that bogus e-mail that sent her to Amman, where she nearly got killed. But this one had to be legit because only *he* knew about their meal together at Les Armures.

She retrieved a scrapbook filled with pictures taken the summer after graduation from the University of Missouri. She thought about how she had wanted to do a European backpack-and-train thing with a couple of sorority sisters, but her father had nixed that idea, feeling that gallivanting across the Continent was too dangerous and unworthy of a Robbins.

"But I want to see the world before I start my career," Amber remembered saying.

"Let's compromise," her father had offered. "We'll find a language school in Switzerland where you can perfect your French. Mom will love that idea, and it would give you plenty of time to explore Europe. I think I know just the place: the Mont Blanc in Villars."

"Wait a minute. The Mont Blanc isn't one of those finishing schools, is it?"

Jack Robbins rocked on his heels. "Well, they don't call them 'finishing schools' anymore. Students spend six months in intensive language study but also learn social graces and how to engage others in the art of conversation, including when to ask the right question. That could help you in your chosen field, and you'll have free time to travel around Europe, soaking up the culture."

"Travel, huh . . ."

"I think you'd enjoy it."

"OK, Dad, but if I hate the Mont Blanc, can I come home?"

"You can come home, but I'm going to make you promise that you don't end up staying in Switzerland."

Amber placed the Mont Blanc scrapbook on her knees, flipped to the right page, then studied the photo of her and the handsome man standing in front of a white van marked "Institute of the Alps." As she stared at the four-by-six snapshot, which had been mailed to her by a friend from southern California, her mind drifted back to those days.

"Are you going to the Geneva Fest?" Mary Lawson waved a print-off from the Internet.

"It's coming up?" Amber reached for the flyer.

"Yeah, it's this weekend—Saturday night."

"I loved that parade when I was a kid. My parents first took me when I was, like, six years old. The Swiss always have some interesting floats."

Mary Lawson flopped onto Amber's twin bed. "A bunch of us are going. There's a free concert after the parade with country artists from Nashville, including Toby Keith. Everyone parties until the huge fireworks show at midnight."

"How's everyone getting there?"

"In a van with some students from the Institute. We're having another mixer."

Amber had attended a mixer once with the Institute of the Alps, a male-only international language school in Villars. "Yeah, those students may come from all over the world to study—but I bet they don't have classes about which fork to use."

Mary Lawson laughed. "I wouldn't say all over the world. Most of the guys are from Middle Eastern countries like Jordan and Saudi Arabia."

"Yeah, you could be right. Which means we won't have to speak French because they'll be more interested in practicing their English."

"Or flirting with us!"

Amber grinned. "Count me in. I wasn't going anywhere this weekend anyway."

Several days later, Amber felt a sense of anticipation as she stood with a half-dozen friends in front of the Mont Blanc's magnificent chalet. An Institute of the Alps van pulled into their long, half-circle driveway. Eight young men in their early twenties—all from the Middle East, as predicted—jumped out of the long van.

Quick introductions were made, but Amber didn't retain any of the strange-sounding names. Pictures were taken of the group before she and the others were directed into the van. A lanky, handsome man—probably a year or two older than she—sidled up next to her on the passenger bench. A winning smile creased his mustachioed face.

"Hello," he greeted her. "Going my way?"

Amber sighed. Did these guys learn English by watching Hollywood movies? What was next? A line from *Casablanca?*

Not that this fellow looked like Humphrey Bogart. Not even close. More like Omar Sharif from *Dr. Zhivago*.

"I believe I am going your way." Amber flashed a smile. "All the way to Geneva, right?"

"Yes, and it will be nice traveling in the company of someone as beautiful as you."

Don Juan was laying it on thick. Amber slid into her seat. A bit too thick for her taste. Time for a dash of cold water.

"Cool your jets. We barely know each other." She looked out the window as the van lurched into gear and departed the Mont Blanc premises.

The confusion on his face revealed that her American slang had missed its mark. "Jets? I do not understand. Why do you bring up airplanes? And what does it mean to cool them?"

Amber barely contained her laughter as she turned and faced him. "It's just an expression. In America, it's a girl's way of telling a guy to slow down." Somehow his innocence was already breaking down her guard.

"Ah, yes, this I understand. No problem." He shrugged his shoulders. "Please allow me to introduce myself again. My name is Mohammed Faheedi."

"Amber Robbins. Glad to meet you. Where are you from?"

"Iran. My parents sent me to Villars to perfect my English."

"Oh, really? What do your parents do?" Amber felt her body slide in Mohammed's direction as the van made a sharp turn. She grabbed the seat bench in front of her to keep from pressing against him.

"My father is in the oil business. He has been very successful."

"Good for him. And for you, I suppose."

"May I ask where you're from?"

"Dallas, Texas. That's oil country, too, but my father isn't into oil. He's into ink."

"Ink? What is this ink?"

Amber smiled again at his innocent confusion. “Ink—you use ink to print newspapers. He owns several newspapers.”

“Oh, now I see.”

“Have you ever been to Texas?”

“No, but I hear Texas is very big. What is it you say? ‘Don’t mess with Texas’?”

“Yes, we have that saying.” Amber had that bumper sticker on her first car. “It’s a slogan to keep people from littering.”

“Oh.”

An awkward silence fell. Amber was anxious to catch up with her friends. But as she noticed Mary Lawson chatting up another handsome guy, she realized the long drive to Geneva was about to get even longer.

The fifteen-passenger van descended the well-maintained two-lane road, tucked against the steep, grassy mountainside, to the floor of the Rhone Valley. With each hairpin turn, Mohammed watched Amber steady herself by holding on to the seat in front of her.

Mohammed gazed into Amber’s face. She was a beautiful girl. Beautiful enough to keep him from remembering what he was really there for. The van lurched again, and she turned her back to Mohammed. Her light brown hair fell over her shoulders, and more than anything, Mohammed wished he could see how it felt to his touch.

“Sorry,” Amber muttered. “I get sick on these alpine roads.”

“I understand.” Actually, Mohammed *did* understand. Riding in the back of a long van felt similar to the nauseating pitch and roll of the highly maneuverable fighter jets he had trained to pilot.

Despite his struggles with motion sickness, Mohammed could not take his eyes off Amber. He had noticed her at the mixer held last month for the two schools. He wondered that evening if he could arrange an introduction to this gorgeous American woman. Now that he had finally made her acquaintance, he decided the wise course would be to “cool his jets,” as he heard her say.

He didn't attempt to resurrect the conversation until the van reached the autoroute on the valley floor. Mohammed stuck to his cover story. The oldest son of a prominent Iranian family. The product of private schooling in Switzerland since his teenage years. A desire to work in the Iranian government once he left the Institute of the Alps.

What Mohammed did *not* tell her was that he had been handpicked out of flight school to enter the Iranian intelligence service or that he was being groomed for intelligence gathering against the United States. He figured that that piece of information would have created a definite cooling trend with this attractive American. Moreover, the Committee would undoubtedly frown on a novice intelligence officer spilling his real identity to the first skirt he came across.

The grand plan, after a yearlong stay in Villars, was to move to Geneva as a low-level military attaché at the Iranian embassy. Then he would hit the cafés along Embassy Row and develop contacts among the numerous foreign nationals who disliked the cultural imperialism of the Americans.

Amber was not the kind of contact he was sent to make. What possible use could a leggy Texan have for the cause of Islam? What did she say about her father? Oh, yes, he was in the newspaper business. Well, wouldn't that be useful? He knew immediately that he was kidding himself. His interest in this Amber had zero to do with intelligence and everything to do with male hormones.

Maybe she was one of those loose women he had been warned about before he left Tehran. Premarital sex was off-limits in the new Iran. You had to travel abroad and meet Western women if *that* was on your mind.

"Be careful," his instructor had warned. "The Americans are shrewd, and they think nothing of surrendering the honor of their young women if it will serve their cause. Don't forget: Monica Lewinsky got what she wanted. She pursued President Clinton, and, afterward, she didn't even call it sex. She said they were just fooling around. I can tell you that Allah knows the difference, and so do I."

Parking, as usual for Geneva, was practically impossible. Amber noticed the sidewalks were littered with cars. Some bore CD, or consular diplomatic, license plates, affording the driver complete immunity from any and all traffic violations—an exclusive perk given to Geneva's consul community.

The Institute of the Alps van inched along the Quai du Mont-Blanc, Geneva's signature boulevard that hugged the Lac Léman—the Lake of Geneva.

"What time does the parade start?" Amber asked the driver.

"Seven o'clock," he responded. "I'm dropping you off here." The driver momentarily parked the van on the sidewalk. The young men and women had arrived in plenty of time for the Geneva Fest parade.

Amber fell in with Mary Lawson and the group, but she noticed that Mohammed hustled to stay near her right shoulder. She didn't mind. He seemed kind of cute, and she had never spent any time with someone from the Middle East.

The students found seats in temporary grandstands lining the Quai Wilson, named after President Woodrow Wilson, who spearheaded the establishment of the League of Nations, formerly situated in Geneva. Precisely at 7 P.M., the parade began with two-dozen brown Swiss cows lumbering along the parade route.

"Aren't they cute?" Amber enjoyed the Swiss cows, each with oversized ceremonial cowbells slung around their necks and their heads adorned with bouquets of flowers. Farmer boys, dressed in traditional Swiss leather pants and brightly embroidered shirts, prodded the slow-moving cows with sticks to stay within the herd. The cows were followed by goats, which blissfully stepped into hubcap-sized paddies deposited by their bovine predecessors.

"Reminds me of the Texas hill country." Amber held her nose.

Mohammed winced. "Really? Then Texas must smell like Tehran!"

They both laughed. Mohammed brushed her shoulder with his right hand, a motion that did not escape Amber's notice. For the next hour, they sat back and watched flower-bedecked floats—representing various eras of Geneva's long and colorful history—stream by. Amber's favorite "drill team" was the Swiss Guard regiment, garbed in colorful costumes of Renaissance design with puffed sleeves and knickerbockers stripped in red, blue, and yellow. Every hundred meters or so, the Swiss Guard—marching in wooden clogs—performed a precision drill with their halberds, a weapon with an ax-like blade and steel spike mounted on the end of a long pole.

When the parade ended and the street sweepers cleaned up, Amber and Mohammed ambled to the water's edge for a closer view of Geneva's Jet d'Eau, which shot a geyser-like spout of water more than four hundred feet into the air. Mary told Amber that she and her friends were going into town—*wink, wink*.

"I heard once that the Jet d'Eau started as a safety valve for a hydraulic plant back in the early days of electricity," Amber said. "Now it shoots several hundred liters of water per second into the air, which is just awesome." In the warm, summer twilight, time seemed to stand still for Amber as she recalled standing at this very spot with her parents.

"Would you like to eat something?" Mohammed inquired.

"Sure. What do you feel like?"

"How about something Swiss? It seems appropriate on such a festive day. Do you like cheese fondue?"

Amber crinkled her nose at that suggestion. "Fondue is not popular with the Swiss in the summer. I have a better idea. Have you ever had raclette?"

"Raclette? What's that?"

"The Swiss take a wheel of raclette cheese, cut it in half, then place it next to a fire or under a special raclette oven. The cheese slowly bubbles, and just before the melted cheese starts to drip, the wheel is taken away and the melted cheese is scraped onto a plate containing small boiled potatoes, onions, and tiny kosher pickles. They call it raclette because the French verb *racler* means 'to scrape.'"

"I see that you know your Swiss cooking. So where do we find it?"

Amber was enjoying the role of a connoisseur. "I know just the place in Old Town. It's called Les Armures, and it's been around since John Calvin walked the streets of Geneva five hundred years ago. The place is a historical landmark and is located across the square from a medieval arsenal. The wood-beamed cellar is rustic and romantic."

"How do you know all this?"

"I've been to Geneva many times."

"It is far to walk?"

"Not at all. About three kilometers to Old Town—a half-hour walk. Even if we had a car, we couldn't find a place to park over there. What time do we have to be back for the van?"

"We have plenty of time. The van leaves at midnight, about an hour after the fireworks show."

Les Armures was packed, which was to be expected since this was the final weekend of Geneva Fest. They arrived at 8:20 P.M. and were told to expect at least a forty-five-minute wait. Amber and Mohammed were directed to the bar, where they found a small table.

The first thing Amber noticed upon entering the dark walnut-paneled bar was the overpowering stench of cigarette smoke. While smoking was definitely unpopular in the U.S.—you couldn't light up in a restaurant or public building in most states—every bistro and brasserie from Amsterdam to Zurich was filled with the blue haze of acrid cigarette smoke.

The restaurant reeked. Amber involuntarily coughed as the stench rose in her nostrils. "Excuse me. I'm not used to the smoke."

"That's all right. In Iran, everyone smokes. But I didn't like the way it made me smell, so I never started."

Mohammed offered Amber a baguette slice. “My friends tell me that Geneva’s a pretty boring place,” he said. “Nothing but a bunch of watch stores and cuckoo clocks.”

“They must not know Geneva,” she commented, as she quickly buttered a crusty wedge of bread. “This is my favorite city in Switzerland because it’s so international here. The Swiss even say that Geneva is not Swiss because one-third of the population is made up of foreigners. Geneva gets a bad rap as a city filled with gray-suited UN types and loupe-eyed watchmakers.”

“But the people are so . . . I don’t know the right word.”

“Sans joie de vivre?” she said, slipping into French.

Mohammed nodded. “My friends tell me that the Geneva people are dull.”

“People are always saying that about the Swiss in general. Which reminds me of an old joke.” She squinted her eyes in a playful grin.

“Well, go ahead.”

“What’s the difference between heaven and hell?”

“I don’t know.”

“Heaven is where the French are the cooks . . . the English are the policemen . . . the Germans are the mechanics . . . the Italians are the lovers . . . and the Swiss run the place.”

A smile surfaced on Mohammed’s coffee-toned face. “Very good.”

“But hell is where the French are the mechanics . . . the English are the cooks . . . the Germans are the policemen . . . the Swiss are the lovers . . . and the Italians run the place!”

Mohammed laughed so hard he coughed up a storm.

“Excusez-moi, madame et monsieur, but your table is ready.” The pair looked up at the maitre d’. “Follow me, if you please.”

Amber and Mohammed were led down a winding wooden staircase into the cellar dining room, where white linens and single roses in thin vases accented each table.

The maitre d’ seated them at a cozy table midway toward the back, set against the foundational wall of stone that dated back five centuries. Amber could almost feel the restaurant’s history seeping through the mortar. She accepted a leather-bound menu from a snooty waiter wearing a white apron.

"I think I know what I'm having," Amber said with anticipation.

"That would make two of us. This raclette sounds wonderful."

When the waiter returned five minutes later, they ordered two raclettes and a liter of San Pellegrino mineral water without the carbonation.

"I can't drink the bubbly stuff like Perrier," Amber explained after their waiter left.

"What about wine?"

"Oh, I haven't developed a taste for it. What about you?"

"Muslims are forbidden to drink alcohol. It's against our religion."

"Well, it's not against mine." Amber saw a curious look on Mohammed's face. "What I mean is that I believe in God and all that, but I don't go to church much. My parents took me to church every Sunday when I was growing up, but ever since I started going to college, religion hasn't been very important to me. What about you, Mohammed? Are you a good Muslim?"

He sat up straighter in his chair. "I believe in Allah and Islam."

"Do you pray to Mecca and all that?" Amber had never met a practicing Muslim.

"Five times a day."

"Hmm, that's a lot. I should pray, too, but I never have the time."

Amber looked up as the waiter arrived with a basket of boiled red potatoes, wrapped in a red-and-white checked cloth. He also carried small bowls containing cocktail onions and mini-sized kosher pickles cut in full-length slices. A second basket containing a crusty baguette completed the presentation.

The waiter pointed toward a large fireplace. "If you look over there, you can see your first raclettes being prepared."

They watched a chef in a toque and white apron lift one half-wheel of raclette cheese from the raclette oven and scrape the melted part onto a plate. Then he took the other half-wheel and scraped the gooey cheese onto a second plate. Within seconds, both plates arrived at their table.

Amber picked up the small basket of red potatoes. "Here, take a couple, as well as some onions and pickles. You eat raclette by cutting a piece of potato and scooping a glob of raclette cheese on top. The taste is heavenly."

Amber sprinkled some nutmeg over her melted raclette. "That's what the locals do. You can try some if you want."

Mohammed scattered nutmeg on his raclette cheese, then took his first bite. "You're right. This is very good."

"Hmm, it is." Amber was already into her second bite. "The whole day has been very good."

They left Les Armures shortly after 10 P.M. Since the van wasn't departing until midnight, Amber and Mohammed had a couple of hours to enjoy the evening and digest their fabulous meal before the ninety-minute ride back to Villars.

They strolled along the cobblestone streets, not walking in any particular direction until Amber looked up at the outdoor lights from La Praille Stadium, where FC Onex—FC standing for "football club"—played their games. Her ears caught the sound of a familiar song being sung by thousands of people. She couldn't make out the words, but she thought she recognized the melody. It sounded "churchy" to her.

"What do you think it is?" she asked.

"A football match? I know that people sing at matches, especially when their team is winning."

Amber knew enough about European sports to realize that the football Mohammed was talking about was soccer. "Football on a holiday evening? I don't think so. Let's take a closer look. I played a lot of football growing up."

Mohammed took her hand, and Amber didn't resist. They came upon the stadium where they encountered students handing out two-sided flyers—French on one side and English on the other—announcing that the "sensational" American evangelist J. T. Hawkins would be speaking that night.

"J. T. Hawkins is here in Geneva? You're kidding me! He was the greatest quarterback in Dallas Cowboy history. But it says here that he's going to be 'sharing the gospel.'"

"Sharing the what?"

"Gospel. How to become a Christian. You've heard about Jesus, haven't you?"

"Uh, yes, a couple of times. He's revered as a holy prophet in Islam."

"Well, then you've got nothing to worry about. I've heard this Jesus talk for years. It goes in one ear and out the other. Doesn't matter. I just want to see my hero J. T.!"

The pair strode into the 25,000-seat stadium and found two seats halfway up from the stadium floor. The west grandstands facing the stage were fairly full.

Rebecca St. James, a young Australian woman backed by a five-member band, jumped into a frenzied number called "Reborn," and the crowd leaped to its feet and cheered the infectious Christian rock music. Amber and Mohammed stood and clapped as well.

"Thank you, thank you," Rebecca said after the final number. "We have to leave now, but not before I make an introduction." The singer waited for a French speaker to produce the simultaneous translation. "Like you, I was stunned when J. T. Hawkins retired from the Dallas Cowboys at the height of his career to preach the gospel. But he wanted to win souls for Christ, not more football games."

Amber leaned closer to Mohammed and whispered, "I always thought that was the stupidest thing J. T. ever did—retiring on national TV after being handed the Lombardi Trophy for winning the Super Bowl."

They watched J. T. Hawkins bound athletically onto the stage and give Rebecca St. James a tight hug as the audience whooped and cheered.

"Thank you very much." J. T. hustled back and forth across the stage with a Bible in his left hand. A French translator tailed him and simultaneously translated his welcoming comments.

"I'm glad I'm in Switzerland with you during this great Geneva Fest. I'm also pleased that I can spend a few minutes telling my story. You see, when I was in the NFL, I chased women. Ran from women. Got high. Went to parties. I thought I was 'the Man.' I was young and single, and I liked to mingle. I was doing all those things because I thought they would make me happy. I started using cocaine and developed a full-blown drug habit."

For several minutes, the former Dallas quarterback painted a picture of an out-of-control athlete who wouldn't deny himself any pleasure or listen to anyone—including the star running back who told him that he needed Jesus, not another line of coke.

"For a long time, I thought about what my teammate said to me, how I had to get right with God and ask Jesus into my life," Hawkins said. "On May 12 four years ago, I was lying on my couch. It was two A.M. I had been doing cocaine all night, but really, I had been doing drugs ever since I started smoking marijuana in high school. I thought that playing in the NFL, being on television, and walking around like a star would make me happy, but after ten years in the pros, I was empty inside. I was the prodigal son who blew his inheritance on drugs and having sex, thinking it would make me happy. It didn't, and I knew I needed something greater—Jesus Christ. Christ came down on this earth and died a horrible death, so that I didn't have to die but could have eternal life.

"I didn't want to be eternally separated from God. I didn't want to continue living an empty life that had no meaning, so I got on my knees and simply prayed, 'Jesus, I ask you to be my Savior today, and I will surrender my whole life to you. I don't want to live for myself anymore. I will do whatever you want me to do. I will be whatever you want me to be.'

"Early that morning, Jesus Christ became my Savior, and I stopped doing cocaine that day, stopped cursing that day, stopped smoking marijuana that day, and I got right with my girlfriend,

Shana, who is now my wife and the mother of our two children. You can get right with God, too, tonight. You can accept Christ into your heart and know that you will never die but spend eternity with him."

Amber listened as she had never listened before. J. T.'s words penetrated deep into her heart, which was softened to receive them. She was forced by the hammer blows of the gospel to face the emptiness that was inside her, an emptiness she had long tried to ignore.

What was it that she had told Mohammed? That's right. She had stopped going to church in college. That's because she had never humbled herself and *accepted* Christ into her heart. She had to admit that there was Someone greater than she, Someone who loved her and wanted her to come to him. He was stretching his hand, and all she had to do was take his hand into hers.

"I want you to come forward and let us pray with you." J. T. waved his arms, signaling people to walk toward the stage. "Come, he is waiting. Come, he wants to welcome you into his kingdom."

Amber felt disconnected from her body. She saw herself stand up and walk forward to experience the same message of peace and forgiveness that J. T. had.

She didn't care who was watching. Jesus was stretching his arms to receive her, and she wanted that warm embrace more than anything in the world.

Tuesday, May 2
10:20 P.M. local time
Jerusalem

Amber seated herself at her computer and tapped out the following reply:

Mohammed:

i was shocked to receive your e-mail today. how did you get my private address? oh, well, you can answer that question in Geneva. yes, i would like to see you. what about meeting next tuesday at les armures at 8 pm?

amber

She knew it was short notice, but if he really wanted to see her, she figured he would move heaven and earth to get to Geneva in a week. Besides, she needed a break from the Middle East after that creepy incident while jogging this morning. There were some contacts she could talk to in Geneva, and maybe Mohammed knew something about all these crazy things happening in the Islamic world. She could ask him for his take on the assassination of Jordan's King Abdullah.

"Evan, I have to go to Geneva."

"You don't need to have your nails done again, do you?"

Amber ignored the dig. "No, Evan. Listen, I received an e-mail from a contact, and he's asked me to meet him in Geneva."

"Is he high level?"

"High enough," Amber replied noncommittally.

"Does he know anything about the Passover Massacre?"

"That's what I hope to find out. Can you have Rachel cover for me?"

"I don't see why not." Evan's voice grew serious. "Amber?"

"Yes?"

"After what happened in Amman, you watch your backside, you hear? Your old man told me that I'm responsible for you."

Amber grinned. She liked being talked to like one of the guys. "I appreciate the concern, Evan, but there really isn't much you can do from Washington."

"Except give you a safety reminder every now and then."

"I'm hearing you loud and clear."

15

Monday, May 8
9:32 A.M. local time
Geneva, Switzerland

Mohammed pushed through the revolving doors of the Hotel Bristol and stepped onto the busy Rue du Mont-Blanc, looking like just another tourist in Geneva. Dressed in black slacks and a fashionable black leather jacket, he strode purposefully toward the lakeshore, where two windsurfers skimmed across the normally placid lake.

When he had entered the Iranian intelligence service, Mohammed had received some perfunctory training in field operations, but his superiors weren't about to waste valuable training resources on someone certain to be tied to a desk. They discovered Mohammed was brilliant at pulling isolated threads of information together and weaving them into a coherent picture. At no time did he expect to become a clandestine field operator. He left that tradecraft to the professionals.

Mohammed's limited knowledge in espionage would come in handy on this sunny, windswept morning. His goal was to appear to be enjoying a leisurely sightseeing tour, yet he felt terribly exposed as he pounded the gray *trottoir* of the Rue du Mont-Blanc. A shudder coursed through his body at the thought of what could happen if his true motives were discovered.

His rendezvous point was just a kilometer away across the Pont du Mont-Blanc, where inline skaters stroked their way across the bridge, using pedestrians as slalom poles. Several lovebird couples leaned against the railing, their arms wrapped around each other's waists.

Once past the bridge, Mohammed regarded the imposing five-story limestone buildings that fronted Rue General Guisan—many the length of a city block. The avenue was named after a World War II Swiss army general who mobilized the country to defend Switzerland's neutrality by turning the landlocked republic into an armed fortress. Mohammed remembered attending a briefing about how the Swiss armed themselves to the teeth after Hitler unleashed his blitzkrieg upon Europe. If attacked, the Swiss army was prepared to retreat to Alpine redoubts, where weapons and matériel were cached in dozens of tunnels and underground fortifications. The clever Swiss were forewarned and forearmed, Mohammed reminded himself. He needed to have the same mind-set for what he was about to do.

The Iranian intelligence officer grunted to himself as he continued his march past several watch stores. The last time he had peered into these storefronts belonging to Patek Philippe, Bulgari, and Raymond Weil, the sweet fragrance of Amber Robbins was in the air. He let the pleasant recollection of their evening at the Geneva Fest linger as he regarded two Saudi men, each dressed in ankle-length *thobes* and wearing *ghutras* headdresses, window-shopping at Patek Philippe. It never ceased to amaze Mohammed that the only people who ever purchased the bejeweled Swiss watches costing $25,000 were the Saudis. Americans, he heard, shied away from the nameplate stores because the Swiss watchmakers never came off their posted price.

Mohammed continued sauntering until he arrived at Intersports, Geneva's largest sporting goods store. He stepped inside and walked past the clothing racks and tennis racket displays to the rear of the store, where he exited to the Rue du Rhône. He surveyed Intersports' rear entrance. Nobody had followed him.

The Iranian agent continued one block west and entered the Hotel Richmont, where he strode purposefully into the hotel restaurant, the Mille Fleurs. A hostess immediately seated him in a rear booth that allowed him to survey everyone entering or leaving the restaurant. Mohammed ordered a *petit déjeuner*—coffee and a basket of brioche and buttery croissants, which came with individual portions of Héro jam, Switzerland's most popular fruit preserves.

He rustled a copy of the *International Herald Tribune*, the English-language newspaper of Europe, giving the clear impression of a businessman reading the front page. In reality, he surreptitiously glanced around the restaurant for some sign of what to do next. All he knew was that he was supposed to have breakfast in this restaurant, and once seated at the Mille Fleurs, he would be told what the next step would be. He slowly spread Héro blueberry jam onto a soft wedge of brioche and sipped his coffee, all the while perusing the *IHT*. Time dragged on. Mohammed chatted up the efficient waitress, whose accent told him she was not a native of Switzerland but hailed from France, just over the border five kilometers away.

Mohammed felt no pressure to vacate his table since it was midmorning and the lunch crowd wouldn't arrive for another hour. Either way, he shouldn't be waiting this long. This was turning out to be a busted meet.

Mohammed allowed his peripheral vision to scan the restaurant. No one looked like a spy. How was he supposed to recognize his contact? Why didn't he have more specific instructions? The intellectual part of Mohammed's mind informed him that his flood of questions was the precursor of panic. *Remain calm.* But the tension was becoming unbearable.

Mohammed decided to abort this misadventure. He would pay the bill, scoot back to the hotel, and figure out what to do next. Yes, that would be the wise course of action. It was time to forget about this Passover Massacre business and how it related to Iran. Surely, there had to be a safer method of obtaining information without initiating such a dangerous contact as this one.

Relief flooded Mohammed when the decision was finally made. Although peeved that he had been stood up, he realized the offense was only to his ego. He waved the waitress over to pay his bill. She pulled out a bulky leather purse from her black apron. As per Swiss custom, she doubled as the cashier.

"Douze francs, cinquante, s'il vous plâit," she said. Mohammed produced a red ten-franc note from his billfold and the necessary coinage.

"Merci, mademoiselle."

"Je vous en prie." She slapped a receipt on the table and spun on her heels to the next table.

He gave the receipt a glance. Written across it in large black ink was "Room 404." Mohammed's calm disappeared, replaced again by tension. So, this was not going to be a wasted endeavor after all.

Now what? The waitress obviously knew about room 404, which troubled him. He shrugged and wondered if he should slip out of the restaurant when she wasn't looking. But would that be the safest thing to do in the long run?

I have come this far, he thought with a resigned air. Mohammed gathered his male purse and exited the restaurant to the hotel lobby, reminding himself with each step that everything was still under control.

Mohammed stepped off the elevator on the third floor and immediately walked to the stairwell. Satisfied that he was not being followed, he bounded up the stairs two at a time to the fourth floor. Arriving at room 404, he knocked twice lightly.

After a brief pause, the door slowly opened to reveal Lev Goldman, the only Mossad agent Mohammed had ever met. Several years earlier, they'd become acquainted while stationed at their respective embassies in Paris. For one moment in time, the best interests of their nations aligned themselves to oppose Iraq before Saddam's downfall. Since then, on rare occasions, they had consulted one another with extreme caution.

For this rendezvous, the Iranian could barely believe he'd contacted someone working for Israel's famed espionage and counterterrorism organization: a man sworn to serve Iran's oldest and most passionately hated enemy. Yet the questions regarding his country's future were too great. Sure, it would be safer to let them go, but if change was ever to come to Iran, the truth must be told. If the Great Leader was putting Iran at risk, what else could Mohammed do?

Goldman extended his hand. "Mr. Faheedi, here, here. Come in, quickly."

Mohammed regarded his counterpart, who exuded the patrician air of an English headmaster. Late fifties. Strands of gray hair slicked back across a speckled cranium. A crisp navy blue pinstripe suit from Armani or Versace. The faint odor of cologne hung in the air of the well-appointed hotel suite. Mohammed recalled the pertinent details from Goldman's dossier: born in London following World War II, immigrated with his Jewish parents to Israel following the Suez War of 1956, educated at Eton, and recruited by Mossad during postgraduate studies at Cambridge.

"I cannot honestly say it is good to see you, Mr. Goldman." Mohammed shook the proffered hand. "Meetings like this cause me to lose sleep, but I do appreciate your seeing me. I have some questions of great concern."

"Please, take a seat." The Israeli indicated a love seat next to a coffee table. "I'll lay five quid that it has to do with the appalling attack on the apartment dwellers."

Mohammed folded his hands. He noticed all the drapes had been closed.

"You have a good nose, Mr. Goldman. It seems too many facts don't fit. Chief among them is that this action was not characteristic of al-Aqsa Martyrs Brigade, and your country knows that."

"What gives you that impression, old boy?"

"I live in the same region of the world as you Israelis. I know how you respond when someone slaps you in the face. You don't just slap back—you cut their heads off. But with this . . . nothing. The worst terrorist action in years, and no retaliation from Israel. Your people are howling for revenge, and yet you do nothing. There can be only one reason: You don't know whose head to cut off."

For several moments, Goldman stared intently at Faheedi, seemingly deciding whether to trust him. Mohammed waited, confident that Goldman knew significant information.

"Tea?" Goldman asked.

"Thank you," Mohammed replied, reaching for a cup and a saucer.

The Mossad agent inhaled deeply as he poured from a pot of tea. "My instincts permit me to take you into my confidence, though I may live to regret it. Something is not cricket, but I don't think you're part of it. But first, cards on the table: I would never expect you to work against the best interests of your country, whilst I could not work against the best interests of mine."

"Of course." Mohammed nodded, urging him to continue.

"Here's my go at it: your leaders are queuing up to something not in the best interests of your people."

The Iranian leaned forward and met his counterpart's gaze.

Goldman shifted in his seat and adjusted his tie. "Allow me to unwrap this enigma to your satisfaction. Our investigators believe that Barzin Shirazi was pinched by your Savak before the massacre. We are convinced that your superiors were behind the massacre and ordered Shirazi's body to be planted at the crime scene. They are trying to fasten the blame on the Martyrs Brigade, but that would never pass the smell test at Scotland Yard."

"You mean—"

"Yes. Your government was behind the Passover Massacre. A shocker, I know."

Mohammed realized his lack of field craft was failing him. Surely his face betrayed him. *Why,* he wondered, *would Ayatollah Hoseni condone such an action? What could the Great Leader possibly hope to gain?* Mohammed did not doubt Goldman's words. They explained everyone's unusual behavior at the briefing, which raised another question for Mohammed.

"If you know that Iran was behind the action, why have you not retaliated?"

"Before we retaliate, we must proceed with caution. That is all I am at liberty to say."

"What do you mean? Isn't it enough to know that my superiors sent a team into your country to murder seventy-four civilians in cold blood? I am no friend of Israel, but this kind of action is the type of thing we should be trying to stop."

Goldman unbuttoned his double-breasted pinstripe jacket, and Mohammed wondered if he was signaling his intentions as to the *real* reason behind the meeting. "This action makes no sense to us either," the Israeli offered. "We have concluded that it must be part of some larger operation. Since we do not know what that operation is, we will wait and see how the other boot drops. We are concerned that anything done in ignorance or haste might worsen the situation. Seeking confirmation will help us piece together who exactly was behind the Passover Massacre."

"Any ideas?" Mohammed's appetite was thoroughly whetted.

Goldman paused, sipping his tea. "Have you ever heard the name Jamsheed Nasser?"

Mohammed searched his memory. "No, that name is unfamiliar."

The Israeli spymaster rose out of his chair and peeked through the drapes. "We are not absolutely certain that Nasser is his real name. He has two aliases we are familiar with, but there are undoubtedly more. Perhaps you've heard of his nickname—al-Shanoosh."

Mohammed froze. He knew about the Hammer! From what he knew of al-Shanoosh, he had no interest in pursuing this topic with Goldman. It was difficult to separate legend from fact when it came to the Hammer's reputation. Even if a quarter of what he had heard was true, this was one man Mohammed would prefer not to cross. His cunning, courage, and, most of all, cruelty ranged from awe-inspiring to appalling. If al-Shanoosh should somehow discover that Mohammed had discussed his name in a conversation with a Mossad agent, his days of exchanging oxygen for carbon dioxide were over.

Mohammed opened his mouth to disavow any knowledge of the name when Goldman held up his hand. "Don't bother denying it. I can see from your reaction that you are familiar with the bloke. We have an unconditional directive to our operatives to report any sightings, no matter how insignificant the information might seem. But here's where it gets interesting. One of our agents in Jordan reported that Nasser, assuming that is his real name, was observed in Amman the day King Abdullah was mucked up by that bomb."

Mohammed shifted in his seat and ran a hand through his black hair. If true, the presence of the Hammer in Amman meant his government *could* be involved in the assassination of Jordan's ruling monarch. And he had not heard a whisper of it! He felt his face flush from the revelation.

"I see you've finished your cup. Would you like another spot of tea before we continue?"

"Continue? There's more? I'm not sure I want to hear it." Of course, this was not true. Mohammed knew it was imperative to obtain whatever information he could from Goldman. "Please, go on."

The Israeli dropped his athletic frame into his chair. "We have pieces of intelligence that the Americans have passed along that may have some bearing. The first is that American reconnaissance satellites have been keeping tabs on a major construction project in the port of Bandar Abbas."

Mohammed shrugged, relieved to be in the loop on something. "I know about that one. Our government has rebuilt the dock and loading facilities for tankers."

"That is what has been released for public consumption, but what actually has been constructed is rather puzzling." Goldman lowered his voice. "It seems the largest phase was a massive covered dock, accompanied by significant dredging of the channel. Its purpose is to both dock and hide major vessels."

Mohammed was also aware of this but didn't let on.

Goldman rose up and circled Mohammed, who remained seated. "The Americans have provided what we believe to be the key to this complicated puzzle. An American Los Angeles-class attack submarine lurking off the Russian coast near Vladivostok picked up sonar traces of a Russian sub leaving the navy base there. Due to the miserable financial condition of the Russian navy, their subs haven't been active these days. In fact, many of them are rusting at their moorings. The Americans considered this a grand opportunity to practice tracking a live Russian submarine. It was just like the good old days of the Cold War, they said. Apparently the Russians never knew they had a shadow, and the American sonar was so superior they could hear the Russians clinking their glasses of vodka. They followed the sub south past Japan, Taiwan, and into the South China Sea. They tracked it all the way through the Singapore Straits, into the Indian Ocean, and eventually to the Arabian Sea and the Gulf of Oman."

He stopped and leaned toward Mohammed. "Do you know where they ported the bloody U-boat?"

Mohammed shook his head.

"In Bandar Abbas."

Mohammed's pulse raced. So the new building at Bandar Abbas was for a Russian nuclear submarine? Iran had no designs on building a powerful ocean-ready navy. His country operated several diesel subs, which were well suited for maneuvering in the shallow waters of the Persian Gulf region. What possible use could they have for a deep-water nuclear sub?

Then Goldman added the final blow. "The sub was a Typhoon-class."

Mohammed sensed icy fingers moving up his spine. A missile sub! Though his expertise wasn't in Western military hardware, any intelligence analyst with minimal training would know about this monstrous weapon. The world's largest submarine. One hundred and seventy-five meters with a displacement of 33,800 tons. Twenty SS-N-20 Sturgeon sea-launched ballistic missiles tipped with nuclear warheads. A Typhoon-class was built for only one purpose—to wipe cities off the face of the Earth. Now this potential lay in the hands of those who ruled his nation.

With his mind swirling, Mohammed stammered, "Do you know whether . . . is it . . . does it contain a full complement of . . ."

"Spit it out, my dear boy. You mean are there missiles on board?"

Mohammed nodded.

"We have no solid evidence one way or the other. However, it is hard to imagine what possible reason your nation could have for purchasing a ballistic missile submarine without the missiles. I'm afraid we can only assume the worst."

Goldman clasped his hands then shrugged, signaling the meeting was over.

Mohammed could draw no other conclusion himself. As he stood, one thought dominated his consciousness. The land of his birth, the Iranian people—his people—were in danger.

She was known on the street as Guinevere, but Corinna Pietroud was too high-class a prostitute to work a street corner in Geneva's red-light district—the Paquis—waiting for some john to proposition her. She plied the convention traffic and relied on repeat clientele. Lev Goldman had been a steady customer for the past year.

That morning when she woke up next to Goldman, she received a hundred-franc tip and a request: ask the Mille Fleurs waitress in the downstairs restaurant to write "Room 404" on the bill and deliver it when a certain Iranian ordered a petit déjeuner.

That part had been easy. Now that Goldman's meeting was breaking up with the Iranian, it was time to unplug her listening device—a plastic cup called Sonic Ears—from the wall outside Goldman's room. The "take" had been captured on a micro-cassette recorder. Better yet, there were no interruptions since no one had come down the hallway.

Guinevere allowed a thin smile as she sauntered to the stairwell. The Hammer tipped well—a lot better than a hundred-franc note.

As he retraced his steps to the Hotel Bristol, Mohammed's brain stirred with confusion. *Why would the ayatollah order the massacre in Israel? Why would he approve an attempt on King*

Abdullah's life and risk alienating the entire Arab world? What was this submarine business all about? Where was the ayatollah taking his country?

But then a new idea entered his head. *Can you trust Goldman? Is it possible that a Russian Typhoon-class slipping into Bandar Abbas is nothing more than a ruse?* On the face of it, the story sounded preposterous. What credible proof did Goldman offer regarding his "information"? Could they both be unwilling pawns in a new Mossad game? The questions pounded with every step. Where did the Great Leader come up with several billion dollars to purchase a fully equipped Typhoon-class sub?

Even as these thoughts rolled through his brain, Mohammed tried to convince himself that everything was fine, but the icy fear racing through his veins proved contrary. He would put nothing past the man known as the Great Leader, not after witnessing Colonel Heen's demise. If Ayatollah Hoseni believed that launching a few nukes would serve the Islamic revolution, it meant nothing to him that tens of millions would die as a result.

As for the Russians, the bottom line was that there were plenty of powerful people who had never gotten over their Cold War animosity toward the Americans. With the passage of more than fifteen years since the breakup of the Soviet Union—and the Russian economy teetering as store shelves lay bare—there were plenty of Russians eager to lash back at the U.S.A., especially after the Yankees bullied their way into Iraq. The Americans had been vainly calling themselves the world's lone superpower for years and smugly believed capitalism should rule the earth.

Yes, many in Russia believed the Americans deserved to be knocked down a peg or two. Turning Iraq into nothing more than a three-week demonstration of their superior firepower and military irritated many of Russia's ministers, who, along with the French and Germans, had bitterly opposed U.S. military intervention against Saddam. That's why the idea of selling a fearsome weapon to a nation that hated America appealed to those in the land of the north. Undoubtedly, the infusion of a huge sum of Iranian cash made the deal even more attractive.

Mohammed knew the Russians had put a Typhoon-class sub into a Vladivostok dry dock for a refit, but the project had run out of money. Wasn't there a report that work had resumed on the beast? Yes, and the retrofit was nearing completion. He remembered a colleague wondering how they managed to scrape up the money to finish the job—or why the Russians would bother, since they could barely afford to gas up the thing for a test dive.

How could he be sure this wasn't another Mossad subterfuge? Mohammed couldn't ask the Russians how sub sales had been lately. And he knew of no sources that he could trust, no one he could confide in with his doubts regarding his country's direction.

Mohammed detoured to the Jardin d'Anglais along the quai of Lac Léman, where a pair of gardeners in blue overalls pruned prickly stems of rose bushes. All his questions were leading to a prickly conclusion: forces greater than he were sweeping Iran toward events that could isolate the storied Persian culture from the West *and* the Arab world. If Goldman's disclosure about the nuclear submarine was true, then Iran was destined to become the next North Korea. Ostracized. Isolated. Another rogue nation.

He gazed at the inky water and the medieval chateaus that hugged the coastline of the Swiss Riviera. *What was I thinking when I contacted that Mossad agent? Those Israelis aren't to be trusted. No, I'm not getting involved. I'm forgetting everything I've learned so far.* He quickened his pace to his hotel, each step making him more certain that the prudent course would be to walk away from this mess.

As his mind churned, though, he realized he hadn't taken any precautions against surveillance during his walk back to his hotel. Immediately he stopped to look in a shop window, checking his reflection to gauge whether anyone had suddenly halted in a similar fashion. He forced himself to think about a safer, more thorough approach to the remainder of his walk back to the hotel.

Mohammed exhaled a sigh of relief when the Hotel Bristol came into view. He walked into the marble lobby and inquired if he had any messages.

"No, monsieur, but you have a visitor."

"A visitor?"

"Nice to see you, Mohammed."

Mohammed turned, shocked to hear Amber's voice. "I thought we were supposed to meet tomorrow night at Les Armures," he said.

"When you mentioned in your e-mail that you were staying at the Hotel Bristol, I thought I would surprise you. How many years has it been?" she asked.

"Why . . . five or six years, right?"

She moved closer. "I think we have some catching up to do."

16

Monday, May 8
3:12 P.M. local time
Geneva

"Amber! This is quite a surprise."

Mohammed leaned over and bussed her once on each cheek while placing his right hand on her left shoulder.

Amber warmly received his embrace. She knew this type of physical contact, although characteristically European, would have earned them a flogging in Tehran. "I got into Geneva early and figured, why wait?" She stepped back to size up her old friend from Villars days. "The passage of time has been kind to you."

"And the passage of time has made you more beautiful."

Amber felt her cheeks slightly redden. "Thank you, but I don't make it a habit to flirt with married men, though I see that you are still spouting those corny lines."

"Corn lines?"

Amber relaxed. "Corny. It means—never mind. It's just another saying we have. But listen, you're married, right?"

Mohammed looked down at the simple silver band on the ring finger of his left hand. "Yes, I am married, and I have a lovely wife. Her name is Rida."

"Congratulations. I'm happy for you." And she was. Genuinely. She had sensed a vibe between Mohammed and her during her semester at Mont Blanc, but after rededicating her life to Christ in Geneva, she knew she couldn't be yoked with a Muslim in any serious relationship.

"Do you have any pictures?"

Mohammed laughed. "I'm afraid that is a uniquely American custom." He peered at her left hand. "Ah, I see that you remain a single woman."

"Yes, but I'm wearing a special ring on my right hand."

Amber extended her right hand toward Mohammed, where an eighteen-karat gold band sprinkled with diamond chips rested on her ring finger.

"Is this like an engagement ring?" Mohammed looked confused. "I thought American women wore their engagement rings on their left hand."

"No, it's a promise ring. It symbolizes a promise, or covenant, that I have made with God to wait until marriage."

"Wait?"

Amber figured that the nuances of English were failing Mohammed again. "Wait to have sex," she said rather bluntly. "God has reserved physical relations for married couples."

"Oh, I see." Mohammed figured this had something to do with becoming a Christian when that American football player spoke. "Well, thank you for coming to Geneva. Where are you staying?"

"At the Noga Hilton. My room has a great view of the Jet d'Eau."

"I know it was a shock to hear from me after such a long silence."

"I *was* surprised." Amber became aware that the two of them had been standing in the Hotel Bristol lobby for several minutes. "Perhaps we should sit?"

"Oh, yes, but of course." Mohammed pointed the way to a small sitting area off the main lobby. The hotel had furnished the meeting nook with a large beige couch and matching love seat, along with two railback carver chairs and a round English George IV breakfast table.

"I also was surprised you wrote to my private e-mail address. How did you do that?" she asked, as she straightened a fashionable black pantsuit she had purchased on a recent trip to Geneva.

"Actually, that's a secret." He mustered a large grin.

Amber tsked-tsked. "You know that answer will not satisfy an intrepid reporter."

"OK." He tilted his head in acquiescence. "I have friends in the Iranian government good at finding out information."

"I see." Amber let the matter drop. "So what brings you to Geneva, other than to see me?"

"I work for the Iranian government in a variety of areas. Right now, I have responsibilities with OPEC—coordinating deliveries and making sure oil tankers end up in the right spot."

Amber knew about OPEC from her stint in Geneva. OPEC stood for "Oil Producing Export Countries," and its eleven members—Algeria, Indonesia, Iran, Iraq, Kuwait, Libya, Nigeria, Qatar, Saudi Arabia, United Arab Emirates, and Venezuela—viewed themselves as developing countries whose economies were heavily dependent on oil export revenues. That was the image spinning. The reality was that OPEC was a cartel of oil-rich countries that controlled 40 percent of the world's oil output with an iron grip.

"Don't those oil sheiks meet at the Hotel Inter-Continental?"

"That's why I'm staying here at the Bristol. I didn't want anyone seeing us at the Inter-Continental."

"Makes sense."

Amber noticed Mohammed shift his weight, and she sensed Mohammed wanted to exit the chitchat and move right into the reason behind their reunion. He appeared vulnerable, if she read him right.

"Listen," he began. "I contacted you because I thought you could help me—and perhaps I can help you."

"Oh, really?"

"I know how interested you are in the Passover Massacre. I've been following your writings on the Internet."

Amber reminded herself to maintain an impassive expression. "And—"

"I may know some information that could help you—how you say—break this story. But I hoped we could do a little trading. You tell me what you've heard, and I'll tell you what I've heard."

"That's an interesting proposition, but I never say yes right away. I would like to give it some thought." Amber stalled for time because she anticipated learning more information that afternoon—from an excellent source.

Mohammed let his arms fall off the chair railings. "Why must American women always make men wait?" He smiled, as if to take the sting out of his statement. "So, shall we continue this conversation tomorrow night at Les Armures?"

Amber liked keeping Mohammed off balance. "What about tonight instead of tomorrow?"

"You mean you're available?"

"Sure. As long as we don't call it a date."

"Don't worry. I'm a married man."

Amber departed the Hotel Bristol and turned up Rue Rousseau, where she slipped into a sandwich shop and ordered Parma-style prosciutto with tomatoes on a Parisian baguette. She carried her tray to a wooden table. A combination of fatigue and hunger had taken its toll, but after sinking her first bite into the hardshell bread, she felt energy returning. With each chew, Amber reflected on the amazing pace of events occurring in the Middle East. It had begun with the Passover Massacre, followed by the bold assassination of King Abdullah. It looked like Abdullah's uncle would be crowned the ruling monarch in the Hashemite kingdom. What was his name? Hassan Hussein.

What would be next? Increasingly militant and violent demonstrations in Riyadh, Saudi Arabia, may have been relegated to the back of section A and ignored by the twenty-four-hour news networks, but those reports had to be indicative of escalating tensions in the royal kingdom. From a professional standpoint, these three news stories were like hitting the mother lode. The common thread running through all three storylines was violence perpetrated in the name of religion.

In thirty minutes, she was due to arrive at the Saudi Arabia embassy on the Route de Pre-Bois, where a meeting with Prince Fahd al-Aziz, she hoped, would yield additional insights into the events taking place in the Middle East. Prince al-Aziz, about the same age as her father, was an acquaintance from her childhood vacation times in Geneva. The prince had invited media mogul Jack Robbins and the family to his estate in ritzy Cologny, and a budding friendship between the two resulted in several shared ski holidays at Prince al-Aziz's chalet in Gstaad.

Amber reviewed what she knew regarding Prince al-Aziz. Of course, he was a member of Saudi Arabia's royal family, but it seemed like half of Riyadh could claim kinship to some branch of the Saudi royal tree. Amber could never figure out who was who in Saudi Arabia. She figured the prince had to be one of the movers and shakers since he was a consultant to the Saudi army.

Several years ago while riding a ski lift in Gstaad with her, the prince told Amber that royal family members usually gravitated toward the Saudi air force whenever they tried their hands at military affairs. The wild blue yonder was much more glamorous than dealing with the great unwashed who populated the desert ground forces. Prince al-Aziz, however, was one of the more analytically minded royals who understood that while a superior air force could turn the tide in any regional conflict, there was still no substitute for boots on the ground. Operation Iraqi Freedom had underscored that wartime doctrine.

Consequently, Prince al-Aziz had made it his life mission to strengthen the Saudi army. He was in Geneva as part of an arms procurement team, looking into the latest generation of German-made armored personnel carriers being tested by the Swiss army. After making a formal request to speak with him, she received an affirmative reply. Amber looked forward to hearing the prince expound on current events in his country.

Amber gathered her belongings and took a taxi to the Saudi consulate. Upon arrival, she presented her press credentials and informed the receptionist she had an appointment with Prince Fahd al-Aziz.

"If you will please take a seat," the receptionist said. "I will inform the prince that you are here."

Within five minutes, Prince al-Aziz arrived from the hallway beyond the receptionist's desk. Amber could not help but smile as soon as their eyes met. Fahd al-Aziz was not Hollywood's idea of what a prince should look like, especially since the Saudi royal family tended to produce handsome, medium-built men with plenty of black hair. The prince was rather short, standing a mere five-feet-six, and his roly-poly physique suggested "couch potato" rather than "dashing." Prince al-Aziz's rapidly receding hairline threatened to become no hairline at all. His eyes, however, sparkled with good humor, and an enormous grin accented his kind face. Whatever the prince might look like, Amber knew that his rumpled appearance was balanced by a gentle wit, an honest and compassionate soul, and a first-class intellect.

"Miss Robbins, what a delight to see you again! How long has it been?"

"Three years? I'm not sure. It's wonderful to see you, Your Highness."

"Enough of this 'Your Highness' business. Our families have been friends far too long for such formality. Please, you should just call me . . . Major!"

This brought a peal of laughter from Amber. "Major? I think I would prefer to call you Prince al-Aziz."

"As you wish, Miss Robbins. Let's return to my office, where some tea has been prepared."

Amber followed Prince al-Aziz down the hallway. They stepped into a nicely furnished office appointed in English antiques and accented by red tulips, golden daffodils, and purple crocus from the Netherlands. Next to a large cherry wood desk was a small sitting area with three leather chairs and a love seat grouped around a coffee table. A British-made sterling silver tea service, as promised, was waiting.

Amber settled into one of the supple burgundy chairs while Prince al-Aziz poured tea. She took a sip of the smooth yet bitter beverage and wondered how Middle Easterners, who lived in such a raging-hot climate, could consume so much of the stuff.

After exchanging the latest news regarding their families, she reached into her satchel and pulled out a Slim Line reporter's notebook. She doubted he would agree to be tape-recorded, so she didn't even bring up the possibility.

"As delightful as it is for us to renew our friendship, I assume you probably have some particular reason for contacting me," the prince said, clinking his teacup back into its saucer. "How can I help you?"

Amber consulted her notes as she collected her thoughts. "First, I want to ask about the state of affairs in your country. I'm interested in your thoughts regarding the recent wildcat strikes, bombings in public squares, and scattered demonstrations in the streets. Where do you think these things are leading?"

"I could not be more concerned for my nation." Prince al-Aziz folded his arms across his ample midsection. "But what I'm about to tell you is not for publication."

"Background?" That meant Amber could use the information—even quotes—but she would have to attribute them to a "highly placed source" or "a Saudi official speaking on condition of anonymity."

"Deep background," the prince replied, meaning she could use the information but not link it to any Saudi official.

"Understood."

Prince al-Aziz began anew. "It is no secret that many in my family have given the Saudi Arabian citizenry reason to despise them. Their profligate lifestyle is an affront to the common people. Much of the oil money coming into the kingdom has been squandered and misappropriated by the royal family. While the princes fly around the world in private jets and relax on lavish yachts, the average Saudi continues to struggle at poverty level. I think we, the royal family, have put ourselves in a situation ripe for rebellion. When appropriate, I have made my concerns known."

Amber nodded. "That's what I thought. The people are getting tired of the way they are treated. They're ready to do something about it."

The prince shook his head. "It's true they grow impatient, but what is happening in my country is far more sinister than a simple uprising."

Amber took comprehensive notes, close to word for word since she had taught herself Quickscript—a poor man's version of shorthand. The last statement left her puzzled. "I don't understand. You just made a pretty good case for the people taking to the streets against the royals. Why do you think something more sinister is going on?"

Prince al-Aziz wiped a dab of perspiration from above his lip with the butt of his thumb. "First of all, lest you take me for being disloyal, I think the best chance for Saudi Arabia to function in the twenty-first century lies within the power of the royal family. Some of us think more progressively than the playboys whose pictures appear in the scandal sheets. As long as I, along with others of my generation, are appointed to more influential positions, you will see small, incremental steps taken without violent revolution. That is our goal. Change without violence, change without bloodshed." He sighed and ran a hand over his balding head. "Yet, there are some who would wish otherwise . . ."

"But your ideals of peaceful change don't seem to be working." Amber drummed her pen on her notepad. "Why the sudden protests? How many have been killed? Isn't the number up to two hundred?"

"Yes, at least that many." He sat forward in his chair and spoke softly. "In recent days, we have received intelligence that much money is being spent to organize unauthorized demonstrations not approved by my government."

Amber stopped writing and looked at him. "Hired demonstrators?"

The prince nodded. "Paid instigators get it going, and the crowd and noise attract the rest. I don't deny there's genuine anger at the extravagance of the princes, but it has been fanned by an orchestrated smear campaign. Someone is behind this."

"But how do you know that?" Amber pushed.

Prince al-Aziz pursed his lips. "I am telling you this as a friend, and because I would like someone in the media to know the truth. Perhaps this will cause you to look in a different direction and turn up something you can write about."

"You can trust me," she said. "I kept my word when, after 9/11, you told me that your armed services were operating at half strength because they were poorly equipped. I corroborated that information elsewhere. And when I interviewed you about Osama bin Laden and his childhood growing up in Saudi Arabia, I did not quote you as a source."

"I remember, Miss Robbins. Don't get me started on that renegade."

Amber scribbled a few notes then looked up, signaling that she was ready to continue.

"OK, one of my uncles is in intelligence. He and I speak often since we hold similar views. He believes a large, well-financed organization is behind the unrest in Saudi Arabia."

"Al-Qaeda?" Amber's pulse raced.

"Our agents have deeply penetrated this organization, but it has turned out *not* to be al-Qaeda." The man's normally jovial eyes narrowed. "It's Iran."

"Iran? What do you mean? Why?"

"We are not sure what Tehran is up to, although anyone can put two and two together: those in control are radical Shiites, and we are Sunnis. They harbor great disdain because they think we have compromised our faith. Their ayatollah believes if he can start a Shiite revolution, then the Islamic world will eventually fall under his dominion."

"You have proof that Iranians are involved?"

"We know an agent with Iran's intelligence services periodically meets with those fomenting unrest in the royal kingdom. For sure, he gives them orders. We haven't identified him yet, but our undercover agents know he exists. We even have a composite picture of him. We are considering circulating it to Western intelligence groups, but we are reluctant. If this information leaked, it would put our agents inside at mortal risk. I can assure you if you write anything about this, you also will put their lives in jeopardy."

Amber wasn't sure how she should handle this thunderbolt from the sky, but what the prince was telling her fit. Something or someone had to be underneath the unprecedented events occurring in the Middle East.

"What are you going to do?"

"That is, how you Americans like to put it, the million-dollar question. The temptation is to crack down on the demonstrations and round up the ringleaders."

"I was thinking the same thing."

"The royal family is playing for time. They are receiving favorable reports from the Western press for being temperate in their response. Eventually, though, they will crack down hard. I personally believe this will be a huge mistake."

"Why?"

The prince gulped the final sip of his tea and poured himself another cup. "I've seen these demonstrations, Amber. They're not peaceful freedom marches." His looked pained. "While we know Iranian militants are behind them, the main crowd is made up of Saudi citizens. They're frustrated, angry, passionate. If our government ends up killing our own people, we will be throwing kerosene on the very fire we wish to extinguish."

A shiver raced down Amber's spine. She had received another glimpse into the Middle East's deep political and religious turmoil, and the vision was frightening.

"What do you think will happen next?"

"Frankly, I am not sure. The Iranians can be ruthless. Our people have never trusted Tehran, even when the shah or Ayatollah Khomeini was in power."

Amber let that thought hang in the air, but she could tell by the way the prince leaned in his chair that it was time to wrap things up. "Prince al-Aziz, thank you for your time. I will honor my pledge to you, but I will be digging for clues regarding Iran's intentions."

"Miss Robbins, nothing would make me happier than if you unearthed their activities and exposed them for the world to see."

"I'll do my best." With that, Amber shut her notebook. Her mind swirled with the ramifications of what the prince had shared.

"Do you need a ride back to your hotel?" the prince asked. "Where are you staying?"

"The Noga Hilton, but I can manage."

"That's right on my way. I'm leaving for my weekly tennis game at Parc des Eaux-Vives. Allow me the pleasure of dropping you off at your hotel."

"No, that won't be necessary."

"I insist. Your father would do the same thing for one of my daughters."

Amber knew he had a point.

"Then it's done," the prince said. "I'll inform my driver."

Amber gathered her belongings and followed the prince through the marble lobby to the front of the embassy, where a black Mercedes limousine was waiting. A Saudi national—Amber figured he was the bodyguard—snapped to attention and opened the rear door. Prince al-Aziz stepped back and motioned for Amber to enter first.

"This thing is built like a tank," Amber noted as she strapped on her seat belt.

"It should be. The Mercedes factory installed plated armor and bulletproof glass. A necessary precaution these days, but it does cut down on the gas mileage."

Amber smiled. Like the prince was really worried about miles per gallon.

Their small talk turned to skiing. "You must visit us in Gstaad again," Prince al-Aziz said. "Are your parents going to be in the chalet next Christmas?"

"I'm sure we'll be in Villars for the holidays. Perhaps we can ski a day in Gstaad."

"Let's count on it."

Within ten minutes, the Mercedes stopped in front of the Noga Hilton. The bodyguard riding shotgun jumped out and opened the prince's curbside door. He stepped out and offered his hand to Amber.

"Thank you, and thanks for the interview," she said, exiting the car. "Have a good tennis game."

After a light embrace, Amber passed through the revolving door. She looked back to wave a final good-bye when she noticed that a gray Citroen had double-parked next to the Mercedes. A woman dressed in a black abbaya alighted from the car and waved to the prince. *Must be one of his constituents,* Amber thought.

She watched the woman shake the prince's hand. Suddenly, the woman stepped back and tugged at her midsection. The bodyguard quickly reached into his shoulder holster and pulled out a handgun. The last thing Amber heard before the explosion was the high-pitched scream of a suicide bomber knowing that she was about to die.

The deafening detonation rocked the hotel façade, collapsing the plate glass window into small pieces and tripping all sorts of chaos. The explosive force threw Amber to the marble floor, as the sulfur-like smell of burning flesh assaulted her senses. Adrenaline kicked in. Amber swam across the marble floor and took cover behind a couch as hotel personnel sprinted to the entrance.

With an involuntary shiver, Amber knew she would never see the prince—her friend—again.

Mohammed lifted the hotel room phone on the second ring.

"Oh, Mohammed," cried out the female voice. "We lost him!" she wailed, as the crying intensified.

"Rida, calm down. What happened?" Mohammed knew it had to be serious for his wife to call him at the hotel, especially since it was closing in on 10 P.M. in Iran.

"They . . . they took Ata away!" The statement prompted more sobbing from his wife.

"Wha—what?" Mohammed knew that Ata was Rida's favorite cousin, probably because they were born in the same month.

"My aunt said the secret police picked him up as he was leaving a gathering of Christians. Happened just a half hour ago."

"Did you say Christians?" Mohammed suddenly felt very uncomfortable, although Rida couldn't know that he had found that Bible in their dirty clothes hamper. He wouldn't divulge that information quite yet.

"Aunt Lima said that Ata had become a Christian a few months ago. Apparently, his church met on Monday nights in someone's apartment. Why would the government arrest him for going to a Christian meeting? Is that suddenly against sharian law?"

Mohammed didn't know what to say. If his wife was attending the same "Christian meeting" as her cousin, then . . . he didn't want to go there. "This is horrible news," he offered. "I'm not sure what—"

"I was hoping you could call someone," Rida said brightly, putting her tears momentarily behind her.

"I don't know . . . certainly not at this hour. Maybe I can do something when I come back."

"Ata's not the first Christian to be picked up by the secret police."

Mohammed wondered how she heard about that bit of information but knew better than to ask and raise her suspicions.

"Oh?"

"There are all sorts of rumors going around. Some people are saying that if they don't recant their beliefs in Christianity, they get shot."

Again, Mohammed wanted to know how she knew that but resisted the urge to interrogate her.

"This is terrible news. Listen, as soon as I get back, I'll make a few phone calls. Promise."

"Thank you, love."

Mohammed returned the phone to its cradle. Seeing Amber that day—and now this distressing phone call from Rida—instigated memories of the evening he attended that Christian evangelistic event with the American during Geneva Fest. He had listened to that football player talk about Jesus, but he didn't understand the new vocabulary: words like *salvation* and *grace.* He recalled remaining behind when Amber stood up and walked down the stadium steps toward the stage. Yes, he was deeply moved by this preacher's message, but Mohammed viewed himself as a man of reason, a man who deliberated before taking action. What J. T. Hawkins said about Jesus Christ being the Son of God made sense that evening, but Mohammed knew that in Iran, Christians often were estranged from family members and not allowed to hold any government positions.

Besides, he was a Muslim. Always had been, always would be. While he had some ambivalent feelings about the faith in which he had been raised, Mohammed was certainly not ready to throw it overboard because of one speech by an overpaid athlete from the land of the Great Satan.

Yet this phone call from Rida rocked his world. If what she had said was true, it was more confirmation that the Great Leader and his cabinet were persecuting Christians. The killing of Colonel Heen had not been an aberration.

Wait a minute. What had Goldman said about al-Shanoosh as he departed his hotel room? Right—he had a nasty scar on his left cheek. *It was the Hammer who murdered Heen in cold blood!*

Now he wondered what would happen to Rida if she were picked up. What would happen to *him?* Mohammed realized that he could not walk away, not when his wife's life was at risk—or his as well.

He was in too deep to turn back now.

After police finished taking her statement, Amber returned to her room, threw herself on her bed, and stared at the ceiling. She replayed the terrifying event in front of the Noga Hilton—

hugging the prince, watching the gray Citroen pull up alongside them, the Saudi woman—almost propelled out of the rear door of her car. The American couldn't go any further. She buried her head in a pillow and released a deep wail, then reached for a box of tissues next to the nightstand to blow her nose.

Amber pulled herself up and walked across the room to open the curtains, where the Jet d'Eau whistled a plume of freshwater high into the air. She thought about taking the next flight to Tel Aviv, but then she remembered her dinner with Mohammed later that evening and his proposal to swap information. Amber knew she had every reason to be scared since the prince could have been assassinated for the very things they had talked about. Was their association putting her in harm's way? Deep down, though, she knew she could depend on God to protect her. Wasn't that her purpose in life—to report on Middle East events from a perspective no one else was giving in the mainstream media?

She lay back down on the bed and turned her head on a fluffy pillow. Delightful—and necessary—rest seized her within five minutes.

One hour later, Amber's eyes fluttered open. She stretched and meandered to her desk, where her Apple laptop had been in sleep mode. She checked her e-mail and perused her iCal, which contained notes she had written to herself. One was regarding her promise to several office colleagues back in Jerusalem that she would return with arms full of Swiss chocolate bars and Tex-Mex cans of enchilada sauce—foodstuffs available at the Grand Passage, an everything-under-one-roof department store on the Rue de Rive, Geneva's main shopping district.

Amber called the concierge for a taxi, which deposited her ten minutes later in front of Switzerland's answer to Nordstrom's, her favorite store in Dallas.

Amber admired the Grand Passage's magnificent window displays. Shapely mannequins draped with off-the-rack outfits in summery hues stood against an Alpine background. The scene said, *Summer elegance in your mountain chalet.*

Amber felt a sharp bump on her shoulder. She turned to her right, where a well-dressed, middle-aged man—definitely Middle Eastern—stepped back after stumbling into her.

"Oh, pardon me." The man spoke crisp English. He reached for the tip of his felt hat. "I hope you are OK."

"How did you know I'm American?"

He ignored the question and made a slight bow. "I wish you a pleasant day." Then he turned on his heels and lost himself in the crush of shoppers crowding the sidewalk.

Wait a minute! That was the passenger in the car that nearly ran her down in Jerusalem! And now he was on her trail in Geneva. Why? What had she done? She needed help. Amber's eyes darted toward the front entrance, where she saw a graying uniformed security man glancing at shoppers as they stepped into the revolving door.

"Mister, I need your help," Amber pleaded in French. She didn't exhale as she described the man in the felt hat and how he had been following her. "I saw him go right past you!"

"Can you point him out?"

"I think so."

The pair charged through the revolving door, but Amber stumbled into a Z-rack of spring dresses and fell in a heap. The security man reached for her arm and helped her regain her footing.

"The escalator!" she shouted, gathering up her purse.

The pair raced past the racks of women's summer fashions and arrived at the escalators. *Up or down?*

"The parking garage." Amber bounded down the moving stairs, nearly tumbling into a young mother with a stroller. "Pardon-moi," she said, as she and the security guard sprinted into the men's section. She scanned the large sales floor—nothing. Her patience was rewarded, however, when she spotted the man's hat bobbing up and down among shoppers at the far end of the floor.

"That's him!" she pointed. "He's headed for the parking garage."

The security guard spoke rapidly into his field mike. Amber jumped up to get a better look only to see him exit through a door marked with a blue sign and a white P.

This time the security guard took the lead, zigzagging his way through the Z-racks like an NFL running back. Amber followed as best she could until they reached an exit door leading to the underground parking garage.

The security guard leaned on the panic bar and pushed open the door, revealing a covered garage filled with cars but devoid of people. Once in the parking garage, the guard crouched past several parked cars while Amber followed him.

Tires squealed and the bright lights of a two-door Mini Cooper bore down on them. Just as in Jerusalem, the man in the felt hat sat shotgun as the pint-sized two-door revved in their direction. Amber and the guard sidestepped between two parked cars, but she got another good look at the man in the felt hat, who stared straight ahead.

At the end of the row, the Mini Cooper jerked to the left toward the exit, its tiny tires protesting. Amber ran three futile steps before stopping. The man in the felt hat and his accomplice were gone. Amber hunched over and closed her eyes then ran both hands through her hair.

She looked at the security guard with a resigned air. "I'm being followed, and someone wants me to know it."

Monday, May 8
7:08 P.M. local time
Tel Aviv

Pizza Fino, a charming hangout in Tel Aviv's affluent north quarter, was known for its outdoor terrace overlooking Dizengoff Road, Israel's answer to the Champs-Elysées. Each wooden table was decked with a red-and-white checkered tablecloth and a faded red Cinzano umbrella, establishing Pizza Fino as *the* place to eat al fresco as the sun dipped below Tel Aviv's pastel-painted roofline.

Luke Mickelson was a regular customer.

"Ah, Mister Divot, I see-a that you are in the company of two beautiful ladies," exclaimed the expressive owner, Bruno Bertolini. "Would you like-a your usual table?"

"Bruno, you are too kind. Is it available?"

"For you, my friend, everything is-a possible." The Italian owner gave Luke a wink.

Luke smiled.

"How do you know the owner?" Kelly asked, once the threesome was seated.

"A friend of mine introduced me to Bruno shortly after I arrived for my tour of duty. Nobody makes pizza like Bruno."

The trio scanned their menus before the owner arrived a few minutes later to take their orders.

"The usual, Mr. Divot?"

"Sure, the Pizza Quattro Stagioni."

"What's that again?" Monique asked.

"That's-a pizza with tomatoes, mozzarella cheese, olives, mushrooms, artichoke hearts, and-a ham."

Kelly and Monique looked at each other. "I guess I'll have the Pizza Quattro Stagioni, with a small salad and a mineral water," Kelly said.

"Same for me," Monique said.

"I'll have a *salade mixte* and a San Pellegrino too," Luke chipped in.

"Very good." The owner accepted their menus with a slight bow.

Kelly wasted no time turning the discussion to Amber. "I guess our intrepid reporter finally met up with Mohammed in Geneva." She put on a pair of sunglasses against the low-lying sun. "Did you get the e-mail?"

Monique dipped a wedge of Tuscan bread into a saucer of olive oil and pepper. "Yeah, I guess her schoolgirl crush is over since he's married."

"Amber was never serious about Mohammed," Kelly said. "She knew it could never work for the simple fact that he is a Muslim and all that. That probably makes you happy, Luke."

The fighter pilot feigned hurt. "Take it easy, guys. We're just getting to know each other, that's all."

"Fair enough," Monique conceded. "So what's happening at work?"

"I think you two already know I'm here on a super-secret mission that I'm not at liberty to talk about." He grinned. "I could, though, but then I'd have to kill ya."

"OK, Captain Tight Lips, then tell us something about you," Kelly interjected. "Or is that top secret as well?"

Luke hemmed and hawed, smiling at the attention he was receiving. "Well, since you are dying to find out everything about me, I grew up in Colorado Springs, where Dad was a civilian counselor at the Air Force Academy and Mom was a—mom."

"You mean she didn't work?" Kelly wondered.

"Not outside the home, if that's what you mean. She taught some piano lessons in our basement, so she was always around. Since I hung out at the Air Force Academy a lot, I wanted to become a pilot. Something about those exciting flyovers during their football games stuck with me. Anyway, I received a congressional nomination to get in and a commission when I got out."

"Any brothers or sisters?" Monique asked. "Oh, I'm sorry, Luke. I forgot about Kim."

Luke paused and pursed his lips. "Thank you. I can't believe she's gone. She was my role model, someone I really looked up to." Luke appeared to be lost in thought. "Did I tell you that I received the nicest letter of condolence from Amber?"

"No," Kelly said.

"She was so sweet. I have it in my jacket."

"Can you read it to us?" Monique asked. "I mean, if it's not too private."

"I don't see why not." Luke reached into his light uniform jacket and pulled out an opened card. He held it for a moment before he began reading:

Dear Luke,

I'm so sorry about the death of your sister, Kim. Even though I didn't know her, I find comfort that she's in glory with Jesus Christ—that she is a new creation in heaven, where Jesus has wiped away her tears, and she will never know pain again. And just think: your courageous sister is wearing a martyr's crown right now. She gave up her life for Jesus and didn't deny her faith. What an inspiration that is to me. Each day I'm reminded that we live in a time when any of us may be called upon to make the ultimate sacrifice for Him.

I know that doesn't make you miss her less. I wish I could understand the grief you must be feeling. I know I can't possibly . . . but I'm praying for you. I pray that the Lord will grant you a peace that passes all understanding. Please let me know if I can be of help in any other way. May God bless you during these difficult days.

In Him,
Amber

For several moments, neither woman could speak as tears welled in their eyes. "Leave it to a writer to know just the right words to say," Kelly said.

"Was Kim your only sibling?" Monique asked.

"I have a younger brother, Pete, who graduated last year from the University of Colorado at Boulder. He's working for a high-tech company in Denver."

"How's he doing?" Kelly asked.

"He took Kim's death pretty hard, too, but he's a workaholic. I think he's been immersing himself at the office. My parents have been doing better, but it's been really hard for them. Dad doesn't like to talk about it, and Mom cries a lot when I talk to her on the phone. All of us kids were into sports growing up, and on weekends, we would run from one event to another. I guess you could call us a close-knit family."

A silence fell over the table after Bruno delivered the salads and pizza. After Luke said the blessing, he began eating his pizza European style—with a knife and fork. "How did you two get to know Amber?"

"You're taking us out to dinner to interrogate us about our friend—hmm?" Kelly asked.

"Well, yes, I am curious how you know each other." Luke tried to appear innocent.

"Amber and I met on a church-sponsored tour to Elah Valley, where David supposedly fought Goliath," Kelly said. "It was a day-long bus excursion along the Bet Shemesh-Qiryat Gat Highway—I think I got the name right—and we sat next to each other the entire trip. We hit it off right away and have been friends ever since."

"What about you, Monique?"

"I met Amber through Kelly. The three of us started hanging out together. We seem to think alike, and we're signed up for the same book club because we love to read. Amber is the smart one in the group. Nothing goes past her."

"Where did you two meet?" Monique asked.

"I met Amber at an embassy reception a couple of weeks ago. The assistant cultural attaché at the American embassy invited me to attend. She definitely caught my eye that evening."

"Do you like her?" Monique asked.

"Yeah, we want to hear you dish," Kelly interjected.

"Of course, I like her. Who wouldn't? She seems to be quite the journalist, and much, much more." Luke blushed lightly. This conversation was starting to make him uncomfortable.

"It's OK, Luke, you can relax," Kelly said. "We all like Amber. But Monique and I have a little bet going. We think you're interested in Amber."

"Well, I guess you could say I am. But she seems to be too busy for anything serious these days."

"Are you going to ask her out?"

"Maybe I will when she comes back from Geneva. But she better like pizza."

Shortly after 8:00 P.M., a Geneva taxi driver negotiated the windy cobblestones of Old Town and deposited Amber at Les Armures. Her hands trembled slightly as she stepped out of the car.

Not even a steamy bath at the Noga Hilton had taken the edge off her anxiety. Why was that man in the felt hat tailing her? Was he connected to Prince al-Aziz's death? So much was happening, and now instead of simply reporting the story, she felt like a part of it. After toweling off, she had stepped into a bathrobe and knelt next to her bed. "Lord, I don't know what's happening, but I do know that I'm scared," she'd prayed. "Please build a hedge of protection around me. Please protect me from those who wish to harm me. I only want to write the truth, Lord—your truth."

Outside Les Armures, Amber adjusted her scarf while her eyes swept the courtyard square. She halfway expected the creepy guy in the felt hat to be standing in the shadows, illuminated by a cigarette. What was his game? If harm was his intention, he had had plenty of opportunities. Maybe he had backed off because he was waiting for a better moment. *That* thought caused a shiver.

She found Mohammed waiting just inside the door, holding a single red rose surrounded by greenery and wrapped in a chiffon ribbon.

"For old time's sake—"

The moment overwhelmed Amber, who dissolved into tears.

"Amber, it's just a simple rose. I don't understand—"

Amber opened her purse and found a Kleenex. "I'm sorry," she said. She dabbed her moist eyes and regarded her old friend. "It's just that some things have happened . . ."

"Amber, perhaps I can help you. Are you in trouble?"

"I'm not sure, but I can't talk about it. I'm sorry I brought it up."

Mohammed stayed quiet and handed her the simple arrangement. "Let's start all over. It's good to see you tonight." Mohammed leaned forward to buss each cheek with a Swiss-type greeting.

Amber smiled as normalcy returned. She appreciated that his tone of voice sounded more like a concerned brother than an amorous suitor. After today, she didn't need anymore complications in her life.

She straightened the front of her peach cashmere cardigan. "Did you check on our reservation?"

"We can be seated as soon as we present ourselves."

A hostess led the couple down the limestone staircase to the cellar dining room where they were seated at the exact same table they had graced years earlier.

"I'm not sure I like coincidences," Mohammed remarked.

"Me neither, but this will probably take the guesswork out of what we're ordering."

"I was thinking the same."

Amber pretended to scan the menu. "Raclette again?"

"And their finest bottle of San Pellegrino," Mohammed quipped.

Amber laughed, reviving her flagging spirits. After placing their orders, a basket filled with hunks of heavenly baguette and a tub of butter arrived at their table. Mohammed offered her the first piece.

"Thanks, Mohammed." She placed the warm bread on her plate. "Since you don't have any pictures of Rida, tell me about her."

"She's a wonderful wife."

"Surely you can tell me more. How did you meet?"

"Actually, our two families have known each other for a long time. My parents and her parents thought we would be a good match, so they encouraged us."

"Encouraged you? Was this some sort of arranged marriage?"

"Our parents thought we would be good for each other, but we were free to choose whether we wanted to marry each other."

"But I thought arranged marriages were common in your part of the world."

"Parents take the first step in suggesting the match, but we have a saying: 'First you marry, and then you fall in love.' Who can know for sure that you're really in love before you get married?"

"You may have a point there," she conceded. "What's she like?"

"I don't know—modern, open to ideas. Perhaps that's because she studied abroad like me."

"In Switzerland?"

"No, she spent two years at the University of Michigan after your Clinton loosened up student visa restrictions. So her English is pretty good."

"I see—any kids?"

Mohammed shook his head while tearing a piece of bread in half.

"I bet the grandparents are wondering when the first grandchild will arrive," Amber offered brightly.

Mohammed swallowed a piece of baguette and spoke. "We started trying in earnest two years ago, but so far, Allah has closed the womb. We hope for a more positive result in the coming year."

A look of concern came over Amber. "I'll pray for you, Mohammed. I've heard that infertility can be very hard on a couple."

"This has been a stressful time," he allowed. "You know, speaking about praying has me thinking . . ."

"What?"

"I don't know. Well, actually I do know, but I'm not sure you'd understand. Then again, maybe you would be just the person to understand."

"I'm listening." Amber leaned toward him.

"I haven't told this to anyone, but I think Rida might be a Christian."

Amber stopped chewing her baguette and quickly swallowed. This was the last thing she expected. "How . . . when?"

"I'm not sure. I found a Bible hidden in our laundry hamper.

Inside the Bible were notes she had taken. Apparently, she has been attending some sort of Christian classes."

"Probably a Bible study at someone's house."

"How would you know?"

"Just an educated guess. I don't think you'll find too many Bible studies advertised under 'Christian Churches' in the Tehran Yellow Pages these days. What are you going to do? You're a Muslim, aren't you?"

"Yes." Mohammed puffed his chest out. "I pray five times a day."

So? Amber thought. "Why are you telling me about Rida?"

"I guess it's because I can't tell anyone in Iran. It's becoming dangerous to be a Christian in my country. Officially, the Iranian constitution recognizes Christianity as well as Judaism, but unofficially . . ."

"I'll fill in the blanks. The government makes it tough to be a Christian."

"Correct."

Amber felt sorry for Mohammed's wife, but her thoughts were interrupted by the arrival of dinner.

"Bon appetit." The waiter set the numbered plates with the first scrape of melted raclette cheese before them.

"Merci," the pair replied in unison.

When the dessert cups, which formerly housed an out-of-this-world chocolate mousse, were cleared away, Amber probed some more.

"Now, who did you say you're working for? I'm confused about this OPEC position."

"It's just a position in the Iranian government. I'm an aide to some of the big shots. It's like working in the White House. The people in power like to know what's going on."

"So you know what's going on?" Her voice held a hint of curiosity.

"I know a few things."

"That's good," she continued, "because earlier today you said maybe we could swap information. I thought about your proposal, and I think we can work together. You may know a lot about who's behind the Passover Massacre."

"And you may have the one piece to the puzzle I'm looking for. What do you say?"

"OK, Mohammed, you have a deal." Amber thrust out her hand for him to shake. "Why don't we begin with you? Go ahead, spill your guts."

"What do you mean, 'spill my—'"

"Never mind, Mohammed. Let's talk."

17

Tuesday, May 9
6:32 A.M. local time
Geneva

Mohammed sat up in bed at the Hotel Bristol and studied the sunrise through the curtained window. He glanced at the clock on the nightstand—too early to get up. Mohammed's mind was tired from a long stretch of late-night European television.

The stupor lifted and his mind clicked into gear, sending thoughts zipping through his head like the sleek BMWs streaking the nearby N1 autoroute. He recalled the stressful meeting with Lev Goldman, the Mossad field agent. He wasn't even close to sorting out the ominous load of information that Goldman had burdened him with. Then there was the dinner with Amber Robbins a day ahead of schedule. Seeing her again after all those years raised personal issues that he thought he had put away a long time ago, issues he certainly didn't need to be dealing with right now.

How should he evaluate their "swap" of information? He could clearly tell that Amber had not revealed everything she knew, but perhaps she was holding back to protect a source. His interest was piqued, however, when she relayed information regarding Iran's involvement in civic unrest in Saudi Arabia—a report that hit him like a truckload of Iranian crude oil. Was there any validity to her claim? Could be. The nightly news had reported the mysterious assassination of a Saudi minister in downtown Geneva. Police suspected a suicide bomber—a first for Switzerland, said a local news anchor.

Mohammed lined up the pieces of information in his head: a hideous terrorist attack in Israel, the assassination of Jordan's ruling monarch, the activities of al-Shanoosh, a Russian ballistic missile submarine—and now serious unrest in Saudi Arabia. What was this leading to?

Then again, in his exchange of information with Amber, Mohammed hadn't shared all his cards either, particularly the revelation about the Russian nuke sub. The fact was that his country's leaders, unbeknownst to him and nearly everyone else, were dirtying their hands in more places than he cared to think about. What was next? Overthrowing the Iraqi provisional government in Baghdad? Choking off the Straits of Hormuz so that oil tankers couldn't pass? At this point, he wouldn't be surprised by anything.

The Iranian took his time showering and shaving in preparation for a breakfast meeting in Goldman's room at his hotel. He stepped outside the Hotel Bristol to a soft, springtime breeze that portended pleasant temperatures later in the day.

Instead of crossing the Pont du Mont Blanc across the Rhone River, however, Mohammed walked parallel to the river before crossing the Pont du Berges Bridge. Every few minutes he stopped walking to check for anyone following him.

His mind spun with all the information he'd gathered, but could any of it be verified? What if everything he had learned was hearsay leading him down the wrong path? He knew—if he had designs of seeing his children born some day—there was no way he could make the slightest attempt to verify the activities of al-Shanoosh.

He might be able to find out if Shirazi was kidnapped prior to the massacre, but he'd need a lucky break to learn more about who was behind the insurrection on Saudi soil. Ferreting out information about the Russian sub seemed impossible.

This time when Mohammed stepped into Goldman's room, he immediately spotted someone he didn't recognize. The Mossad agent beckoned him into the room.

"Mr. Faheedi, greetings on a fine morning. I've asked a colleague to join us—Harold Salomon."

"Zeh pleasure is mine," Salomon said, revealing his Swiss-German origin.

Mohammed warily took the extended hand. He quickly sized up Salomon, who was slight of frame with a bush of brown curls. He wore rimless glasses that perched on a broad nose.

Goldman noticed Mohammed's cautiousness. "Harold lives here in Geneva, but he's a Swiss-German who knows the inner workings of the Swiss banking world, a Johnny-on-the-spot who works for us on special projects," Goldman explained. "You have my word that he's not Mossad, but I've brought him in because I think he can help us."

"Help us?" Mohammed wasn't pleased to hear the insinuation in Goldman's voice.

"Excuse the choice of words, my dear boy. I meant help *you* find out more information about that Russian sub parked on your coast. But first, a bite to eat. I ordered room service."

The threesome sat down, where a petit déjeuner had been set on a white tablecloth: croissants, brioche, and several chocolate éclairs.

"Croissant, Mr. Faheedi?"

"Thank you." Mohammed retrieved a croissant from the proffered basket then spread some boysenberry preserves on one end of the horn-shaped buttery treat.

"I've briefed my colleague on the situation. What's your take, Harold?"

Harold took off his glasses and cleaned them with his linen napkin. "In order for WMD like a Typhoon to change hands, billions uf dollars vould've been exchanged," Salomon declared in an unctuous manner, as if he was belaboring the obvious. "My advice: Follow zeh money."

A quizzical look came across Mohammed's face.

"Let me amplify what my friend is saying," Goldman offered. "Harold is—how you say—a computer nerd, but one with a special talent for the financial world. He worked many years on Zurich's Bahnhofstrasse, although I'm not at liberty to say where. Harold understands the serpentine ways of the New World economy, but it's his unique ability to hack into computers that sets him apart."

"'Hack'?" Mohammed inquired.

"*Hack* means 'to break into.' Harold can eavesdrop on the world's banking system. Monitor transactions. Track wire transfers. Even capture a stray e-mail or two. The Americans asked him to help sort out the Enron scandal, but my friend is much too modest to boast about achievements like that."

Salomon jumped in. "If a great deal of money has been ziphoned from Iranian resources and vired to Russia, I vill have no problem tracking zat down."

"I see that you're not lacking in confidence," Mohammed mused. "But why are you so eager to help me?

"Money. I *love* money. Dollars. Euros. Not zat tissue paper your country issues."

"Wait a—"

Goldman stepped in. "Harold, this is no time to insult our guest. You know our Iranian friend cannot invoice his superiors for this type of information. That could get him killed! Just put it on our tab."

Wait a minute, Mohammed thought. *Since he's offering to pay so quickly, Lev Goldman and Mossad must be anxious for this information as well, which they could use against Iran.* Although this meant working jointly with an Israeli intelligence organization that he didn't trust to carry a bag of groceries across the street, he saw no other alternative. Mohammed needed to put his hands on undeniable evidence linking his government to the procurement of a Russian missile sub, and that information could be the catalyst to propel his countrymen to force positive change. He'd simply have to risk it, even though if someone in his sector discovered his co-venture, his life would last as long as a snowman in a Saudi summer.

Mohammed finished swallowing his bite of croissant. "I'm in, but how can I trust you, Mr. Salomon?" he heard himself say. He *had* to ask that obvious question.

"You can't, Mr. Faheedi, but we find ourselves in the same boat, so is it not in our interests to row together, even if it's just for a short time?"

"I suppose . . ."

"Listen, Harold is anxious to get started. If it's OK with you, I'll contact you in the usual manner."

"Time frame?"

"Harold?" Goldman cocked an eyebrow.

"With transactions as large as zees, I don't think it vill be difficult to discover vere Eee-ran sent $80 billion. No more zan a day, at most."

"Thanks for the ride, Jen," Amber said. "We'll do this again on my next trip."

"When are you coming back?" asked her old friend from their Mont Blanc days.

"Next month for sure. Mom's coming over to spend some time in the chalet. Maybe you can come up to Villars for the weekend."

"I'd like that. Give me a call. You have my cell."

"Sure do. Thanks again for the lift."

Amber stepped away from the Renault two-door and watched her friend rejoin the quick-paced Geneva traffic. Yellow tape and plywood prevented her from using the main entrance of the Noga Hilton where the revolving door had once been. The smells of sawdust and ash sent the image of the Saudi woman blowing herself and the prince into a thousand pieces rushing back into her mind. Amber shuddered and crossed her arms, gathering her light sweater closer. She followed a new path to an auxiliary entrance adjoining the hotel lobby.

She exited the elevator on the third floor and turned right to her room—number 314—four doors to the left. After swiping the white computer card to open her door, she stepped inside, flicked on a light, and gasped. A man was huddled over her computer.

"What are you—"

The man slowly turned and touched the tip of his felt hat with his right forefinger.

"It's you!" Amber turned and sprinted for the fire escape, certain he would chase after her. She hustled down the concrete steps one by one as a concession to wearing heels, then burst through the lobby door and hustled to the front desk, pushing aside three businessmen in line, including one signing a credit card receipt.

"Attention! Il y a un voleur dans ma chambre!" she screamed. "Chambre trois cent quatorze. Allez!"

The young front desk manager phoned security and then placed a call to the police. Two burly hotel security men arrived within thirty seconds, and a frantic Amber described what had happened.

Hands on their gun belts, each took a stairwell, leaving Amber in the lobby. Five minutes later—the police still hadn't arrived—the two guards leisurely alighted from the hotel elevator.

"The door was open, but he was gone," one guard announced. "Did you leave any valuables in the room?"

"No, everything's right here," she said, patting her chartreuse Louis Vuitton leather purse.

"Well, it's your lucky day because he didn't even take the computer. It's still on the desk, all turned on."

"Really?" Amber breathed a sigh of relief. Then a dark cloud came over her. She was sure the computer had been turned off when Jen picked her up for a girl's day out.

Absolutely sure.

18

Wednesday, May 10
9:13 A.M. local time
Geneva

"I'm afraid that Miss Robbins is no longer staying at this hotel," the front desk clerk pontificated in a no-nonsense manner. "She checked out yesterday afternoon."

"You don't know what her plans were?"

"Sir, I wouldn't release that information even if I knew it. I wish you a pleasant day."

Mohammed returned the hotel phone to its cradle. He certainly recalled Amber saying that she would call before she left. Had he said something to offend her? Was she in danger?

The Iranian intelligence analyst willed himself to focus on the present. In forty-five minutes, he had another breakfast meeting with Goldman and the Swiss computer nerd at the Mille Fleurs. If Salomon was as good as Goldman claimed he was, the information would be handed to him like a bar of chocolate. The question then became, *How do I use the knowledge that my country has a secret attack sub tipped with nukes to steer my country closer toward reform?*

Mohammed retraced his steps to the Hotel Richmont, this time losing himself among scores of office workers streaming across the Pont du Mont Blanc. He wore a midnight-black trench coat and carried a tan leather attaché case to fit in with the business crowd. He turned up his lapels and slumped his shoulders, taking on the persona of just another salaryman about to put in his eight hours that day.

Goldman and Salomon were waiting at the same table. The scent of strong coffee wafted by as Mohammed took a seat across from them and quickly got down to business. Directing his gaze toward Salomon, he asked, “Have you been able to discover anything? You said yesterday it shouldn’t take too long.”

Salomon set his café crème onto its saucer and glanced at Goldman, as if seeking permission to begin. Goldman nodded.

“I had big fun hacking deeper into your outmoded federal banking system,” the Swiss-German began. “You ought to tell zomeone in Tehran that they’re only two hundred upgrades behind.” He rubbed the handle of his ceramic cup with his thumb, a smirk rising in the corners of his mouth.

“And?” Mohammed wondered, sloughing off the insult.

“Your government’s been shifting funds around like gypsies on street corners with zere shell games. I found a significant movement of American dollars from your great nation’s oil accounts into Zwitzerland.”

“Just how significant are we talking about?” Mohammed queried.

“Multiple billions of dollars, enough to pick up a used submarine on zeh black market.”

Mohammed blew out a breath. “Do you have any idea where the money is going?”

“Of course,” he replied. “Zat is why I’m here, ja? It began two months ago when the National Iranian Oil Company deposited $4 billion into a Zwiss account.”

“NIOC and the federal government are one and the same,” Mohammed commented.

“Right,” Goldman interjected. “One hand washes the other.”

“Too bad zere transactions veren’t cleaner,” Salomon said. “I hacked into five main accounts: zeh Cayman Islands, zeh Bahamas, Hong Kong, zeh Channel Islands, and Macao. Zeh money in each account vas divided into two and transferred again into other foreign offshore banks. From zees ten accounts, zeh funds vere vired to a branch office of Zürcher Kantonalbank in Zug. Zeh entire $4 billion, minus transfer fees and minor administrative costs, was then electronically delivered to zeh Central Bank of Russia." His lips twisted in a grin. "Nice try, but truly, zey could have been more careful."

Russia. It looked like Goldman and Salomon were trafficking in veracities after all.

"We're telling the truth," Goldman said, as if reading Mohammed's mind, "but I wouldn't take our word for it, just as we wouldn't accept your word on face value."

"So what can be done?" Mohammed asked.

Goldman flicked a croissant crumb from the front of his white dress shirt. "My colleague has prepared a dossier containing all the information we have disclosed here—copies of wire transfers, bank statements, and routing orders. It takes someone with banking expertise to piece it together, but you're a resourceful man, I presume."

"The dossier—"

"—isn't quite finished. How much longer do you need, Harold?"

"Not long. Zeh rest of the morning, maybe over zeh lunch hour," the hacker said.

"Good." The Mossad agent turned toward Mohammed. "Where shall we meet? I know—the Parc des Bastions."

"Next to Old Town?"

"Correct. There's a vendor who sells roasted chestnuts at the entrance. To the right of the vendor will be a series of park benches. Count seven park benches to the right, and Harold and I will be there with the necessary information."

"Don't you zink zat's a little dangerous, Lev?" Salomon asked.

"You're right. Listen," Goldman continued, "I have a better idea. Before you arrive, we will tape the dossier to the bottom of the park bench. Then we will move to a discreet area so that we can observe whether the packet is picked up by someone other than yourself."

"When should I arrive?"

"Precisely at three o'clock. Remember, it's the seventh bench to the right. You can sit down, drop something to the ground, look under the bench, and spirit the dossier away. You'll find it on the left side of the bench."

"We'll only be a few minutes, so keep the meter running," Lev Goldman instructed the taxi driver. The Israeli peeled off a fifty-franc note from a money clip and handed it over to the driver.

The two men strode casually into the Parc des Bastions, barely acknowledging the chestnut vendor they passed. Inside the lapel of Salomon's business jacket was a small packet containing a half-dozen pages, each one a fingerprint of a nation seeking a weapon of mass destruction. Goldman had seen to it that photocopies were sent by diplomatic pouch to Tel Aviv; this information was much too sensitive to be transmitted electronically, which would have been easy pickings for the National Security Agency eavesdroppers back in Washington.

Goldman wasn't sure what a second-tier analyst like Faheedi could do with such sensitive information, but if he gummed up the works back in Tehran, wouldn't that be to Israel's advantage?

The seventh park bench, as Goldman knew, was nearly a quarter of a kilometer into the park and situated under a massive oak tree, which was coming to life with a springtime canopy of green leaves. He and Salomon sat down and spent several minutes surveying the surroundings. A young mother pushed her towheaded toddler in a stroller, while two older ladies' leather slippers gently slapped the sidewalk as they walked arm in arm. School wasn't out yet, so the park was uncrowded. When Goldman saw no one in the vicinity, he coughed. Salomon reached into his lapel pocket and pulled out the small packet. In one motion, he pulled off a strip covering a band of adhesive, bent over, and slapped the packet against the bottom of the wooden bench.

"Nicely done, gentlemen," said a feminine voice.

"Guinevere—what are you doing here?" Goldman's nervous voice pitched two octaves higher.

The prostitute stretched out her right hand, which contained a small bottle. She sprayed the contents directly into their faces while she covered her mouth with a handkerchief. She kept spraying until Goldman and Salomon lay in a heap at her feet.

She collected the packet and deposited it into her purse. "It was a pleasure," she said as she turned on her stiletto heels.

The man in the felt hat opened his leather satchel, where the packet safely rested. He reached for his passport and boarding card, which he handed to the Crossair Airlines boarding agent. She glanced at the black-and-white picture before slapping the official document back in his hand.

"Have a pleasant flight, sir."

"Merci," he replied. The Iranian stepped through a doorway onto the tarmac of Geneva's Cointrin Airport, where a double-length bus waited to ferry passengers to a Crossair commuter flight to Zurich. After a fifty-minute wait in the transit lounge, the man would board a Swiss International Airlines overnight nonstop to Tehran.

Once in Zurich, though, he planned to find an airport Internet kiosk. Al-Shanoosh had an insatiable appetite for information from the field, which meant he must be fed regularly. The man in the felt hat knew exactly what kind of report the Hammer was looking for.

Mohammed alighted from the No. 4 bus across the street from the Parc des Bastions. He could smell the roasting chestnuts before he spotted the vendor stirring them in a black kettle perched on a wood-fired drum.

"Combien?" he asked the vendor.

"Cinq francs suisse ou trois Euros, monsieur," the mustachioed vendor with a dirty apron answered. Five Swiss francs or three Euros.

He purchased one bag and turned to his right. The first park bench was occupied by a pair of Swiss teens dressed predominantly in black. One had dyed her hair a garish red; the other looked as though he had swiped his hair with a bottle of black shoe polish. Each sported an array of piercings.

The next park bench was home to another gothic-looking adolescent couple. A fog of cigarette smoke permeated the air, causing Mohammed to involuntarily cough while he ambled past the pair. He popped a warm chestnut into his mouth and began chewing. The seventh park bench was probably two hundred meters away.

He mentally counted each park bench until . . . he saw flashing red lights up ahead. Wait a minute. What was an ambulance doing in the park?

Mohammed broke into a jog. He arrived to discover two bodies lying next to a park bench, covered with white sheets. Their feet and legs stuck out from under the shroud. Recognizing the business suits, Mohammed knew Goldman and Salomon's bodies were fast approaching room temperature.

Mohammed stared off into space, panic rising in his constricted chest. He willed himself to calm down. Then he noticed a policeman interviewing a park gardener, who wore blue overalls and leaned against a fan rake. The gardener gestured with his free hand, trying to impress something upon the gendarme taking the eyewitness statement.

The policeman closed his notebook, and the gardener slipped away. Mohammed hustled after him. "Excusez-moi, monsieur," he called. "J'ai une question pour vous."

The gardener stopped and faced Mohammed, and from the look he received, Mohammed knew he had to think of something plausible.

"Are the police taking statements from eyewitnesses?" he asked.

"Of course. What do you think I was doing?" The gardener tossed a half-smoked cigarette onto the dirt and ground the butt.

"I wasn't sure, but I wanted to know. I think I might have seen something."

"You better tell the cops. They were only talking to me because I discovered the bodies."

"So you didn't see how they were killed?"

"No. Did you?"

"Not really, but I saw them when I entered the park," Mohammed lied. "Everything looked normal."

The gardener reached into a side pocket for a pack of Gauloises. "Not for long. Drug overdose. Least, that's what the *flics* said. I tell you, I see it all the time in this park."

Goldman and Salomon died from taking drugs? Right, and my mother is Jewish. "They don't look like junkies," Mohammed offered.

"You kidding me? We get all kinds here, even the businessmen. Open and shut case, if you ask me."

Mohammed thanked the gardener for his time and turned away, suddenly feeling cold in a brisk breeze that blew off Lac Léman. It certainly wasn't any coincidence that Goldman and Salomon had been murdered after they began looking into Iran's finances. But how would somebody have found out? Mohammed knew that coincidences in the intelligence game were as rare as finding a pork sandwich in a Tehran delicatessen.

Mohammed had never felt more exposed, and with each step, his personal paranoia inched up one more degree.

Thursday, May 11
8:49 A.M. local time
Tehran

Rida Faheedi used a towel to lift a hot pan of *nan-e barbari*, a crusty flat bread, from the propane oven and set it on a wooden table. The scent of fresh bread quickly spread through their home.

Rida looked at her watch; her husband should be arriving any minute from the airport. He had sounded tired when he called a half-hour earlier from the baggage claim, but that was probably because he didn't sleep well on the flight. The red-eye was a long one, he said, around six hours.

She heard a car pull up and voices in the street. Rida opened the door to see two men walking toward her—her husband with a slept-in-his-clothes look and a taxi driver schlepping his luggage and overnight bag.

"Nice to see you again, my love," Mohammed said, giving her an enthusiastic kiss and embracing hug. He sniffed the morning air. "Are you baking something?"

"Your favorite bread just came out of the oven."

"Nan-e barbari?"

"Yes, my love."

"You amaze me."

"Come, I have breakfast ready for you."

Rida had scattered fragrant jasmine on the *sofreh,* a cotton tablecloth embroidered with poems and prayers, which she had stretched out atop the living room rug. Rida had set out the oven-fresh nan-e barbari, blackberry jam and honey on saucers, and a small bowl of feta cheese. After putting aside his travel belongings, she and Mohammed sat cross-legged on the floor around the sofreh, per their dining custom.

"You're being too good to me," her husband said, surveying the breakfast meal. "Don't think that men don't notice these things."

Rida knew she'd changed after she accepted Christ, but she didn't realize that it was *that* obvious. She heard herself saying, "Then I shall treat you even more special tonight after you come home from your football match. I'll prepare some *kaleh patcheh*—your favorite soup."

"Fantastic! I was getting tired of all that cheese in Switzerland."

Mohammed's enthusiasm for her cooking confirmed her thankful heart for having grown up in a home where meals were held in high esteem. Whenever her mother had filled the sofreh with lamb brochettes, rice with yellow split peas, and a dizzying assortment of side dishes, she repeated an old saying: "Feasting our eyes is the first pleasure of a good meal."

After breakfast, Rida wrote herself a shopping list: tripe and the head and feet of a lamb for the kaleh patcheh, along with leek and onions. "Is there anything special you'd like with your soup?" she called out to Mohammed, who was shaving in the bathroom. "I'm going to the market later this morning."

"No, I can't think of anything," he answered over the din.

Her husband's even-tempered reply told Rida that he wasn't suspecting anything. *He still has no clue that Christians are meeting in our home every Thursday evening while he plays his weekly football match.*

Although she was sick with worry about Ata, she decided now was not the right time to push Mohammed about making phone calls on her cousin's behalf. *One thing at a time.*

Following the light breakfast, Mohammed found an open seat on the Route 40 bus into downtown Tehran. He was thankful that Rida had not pressed him for more details about his trip to Geneva—or brought up her cousin's situation. She had carefully stuck to bland questions. How did the trip go? Did you stay in a nice place? What did you eat? No way would he tell Rida about Amber.

He figured his superiors wouldn't be so accommodating. His travel excuse to Geneva had been sketchy from the start—something about making contact with a disgruntled American reporter, so he was worried that his departure might have tripped unwanted attention his way. Paranoia remained his travel companion during his commute; he saw shadowy figures everywhere. The old man sitting across from him kept glancing over his copy of the *Tehran Times*. Why was he doing that? The well-dressed businessman cleaning his nails looked twice too often in his direction.

When Mohammed disembarked, he was sure that the traffic officer stationed at a busy street corner reported his movements to local authorities. He fought the impulse to glance over his shoulder during his short walk to the office, but a tickling sensation ran up his spine all the same.

Mohammed wearily trudged to his office cubicle, reminding himself that he was not a field agent but was having to operate as one. Carrying the burden of what his nation was up to was taking a toll on his nerves. At least all he had to work on today was reading through a backlog of informants' reports labeled "Suspicious Activities." Usually it was nothing more than a neighbor keeping on his lights all night or someone flashing a lot of cash in the market.

Mohammed leaned forward in his chair and took the first folder from a tall stack. Each manila folder was stamped with the words "Top Secret" in bold, red letters across the front. *What a joke*, he thought. *What could possibly be secret in these reports?* Mohammed put the first folder back and began sorting through the rest in search of reports from informants who occasionally passed along valuable information. Mohammed noticed a yellow Post-it note stuck to the front of one of them. The words *aqab gashtan naqshe shamshir*—"Look for Plan Sword"—had been scribbled on the paper. The bottom of the note was signed "J."

Some idiot clerk wrote himself a note and then stuck it to this folder by mistake. He tossed the crumpled note into the wastebasket and settled down to his pile of mundane reading material. The hours dragged by as Mohammed flipped through the endless pages. The analyst increasingly found himself distracted. *What did that note say again?* He reached for the balled-up Post-it in the wastebasket. After rereading it, his nagging subconscious told him to consider its message—"Look for Plan Sword"—from a completely different angle. When he did so, Mohammed felt a jolt of excitement.

Could it be that someone in intelligence knows of an operation named "Sword" and wants me to find out? The implications stirred fascination within Mohammed. Could Plan Sword be related to the attack in Israel, the Jordanian assassination, the crackdown on the Christians—even the missile sub?

This nameless person must have been quite frightened by this discovery, but what could he do with the information? He could not report what he had learned to his superiors. That would be professional suicide. To try to contact someone outside the agency would be even more unthinkable. *If it were me,* Mohammed thought, *I would try to cryptically and anonymously pass that information on to someone I could trust, someone who would be appalled at the potential dangers and implications of this information, someone with sufficient authority who could investigate further. Yes, that is exactly what I would do.*

Mohammed's priorities suddenly changed. His need to discover what Plan Sword was all about leaped to the top of his clandestine to-do list. He had a strong hunch that if he could manage that, he would simultaneously confirm what he had heard from Lev Goldman and Harold Salomon in Geneva.

Thursday, May 11
7:04 P.M. local time
Tehran

Pastor Davood Rashee knocked on Rida's door with a tinge of nervousness since he wasn't sure what to expect. His wife, Mrna, stood at his side.

He relaxed when a cheerful Rida opened the front door. "I saw the yellow scarf, so I guess our meeting is on," he said. They had devised a little system: if Rida tied a yellow scarf around the decorative iron light fixture next to her front door, that meant Mohammed was playing his soccer match and the Bible study was on. The absence of the scarf meant something had come up and the Bible study was cancelled.

Pastor Rashee was thankful that his budding underground church had remained intact. He had another reason for optimism: three more people had asked to join the Thursday night

Bible studies to learn more about Jesus. Sadly, there would come a point when they couldn't take anymore. As Davood mentally counted who might show up that night, he realized with some concern that twenty could arrive. That would be three or four too many.

Growth was a nice problem to have, and the pastor was hearing similar stories from other underground churches in Tehran. The government's oppressive policies against Christians were not succeeding in extinguishing the gospel. Instead, the effect was propelling even *more* interest in the religion of the enemies of Allah. All of this was fueled by word-of-mouth testimonies given by people—usually a family member—whose lives had been changed and had received freedom in Christ. In Iran, you only shared your Christian faith with someone you could *really* trust, and nine times out of ten, that was another family member. You didn't chat about Jesus Christ with casual acquaintances when you hung your laundry out to dry.

"Thank you, again, for offering your home." Davood knew that Rida Faheedi's willingness was a sign that she was truly committed to Christ.

"You're welcome, Pastor. I know that it's not the safest thing, but I feel this is something God wants me to do."

"He will protect us, but simultaneously, we must be extremely cautious."

"I understand. Our neighbors generally leave us alone."

"You have a beautiful home. We are much more comfortable here than in the cramped surroundings of our modest apartment." The pastor smiled.

There was a knock on the door from the first arrivals. By 7:20, eighteen people had quietly made their way through Rida's front door, which fronted a busy thoroughfare. Under the natural camouflage of foot traffic, anyone seen walking in the neighborhood would not invite unwanted attention. A quick knock, the door opened, and another saint was whisked into the sanctuary of the Lord.

Davood began strumming his guitar, signaling for everyone

to find a seat on Persian rugs or one of the two couches in the living area. Once his flock looked settled, the pastor handed out their "songbooks"—spiral-bound pages with lyrics to a dozen praise songs.

Iran, Davood noted, did not have a strong Christian music tradition, which is why most songs came from the West and were translated into Farsi. He hoped that would change someday, and he also wished that he could write a song or two himself. Davood struggled to finger chords beyond E, A, G, C, and D on his guitar, so for the moment, he had to content himself with strumming simple melodies.

The pastor/worship leader led the group through five songs and finished up with "Be Exalted," which stirred emotions and carried the group into a mood of worship.

Davood stood up and cleared his throat. "Thank you again for coming tonight. Before we begin the Bible study, I thought we'd begin by having someone share her testimony. I asked my wife, Mrna, to be the first one, but I made sure I finished all the dishes and gave her a big slice of baklava first."

The group laughed and everyone loosened up.

Mrna rolled her eyes at her husband's joke. "Actually, when my husband brought home baklava from Azadeh's Bakery, I knew he was sugaring me up for something," she teased, prompting more merriment around the room.

"Anyway," she began, turning more serious, "what I'm about to tell you is very difficult for me to talk about, as it would be for any Shiite women. I don't want to speak ill of my parents, especially my father. I believe he simply behaved as he was taught."

"I can assure you, Mrna, that everyone in this room knows what you are feeling," her husband said.

"I hope so. Anyway, Father's authority in our family was absolute, so when I was sixteen, he decided that I would marry a thirty-year-old business acquaintance of his. Fewer and fewer marriages were being arranged back then, but Father was traditional in that way."

Mrna paused as she thought what to say next. "I really think that Father was more interested in how much the dowry would cost him than in arranging a marriage of happiness for me. Thankfully, I was this man's first marriage, and he did not take another wife. He was a good Muslim who practiced the Five Pillars essential to Islam. He prayed five times a day, fasted during Ramadan, gave alms to the poor, and strongly believed the main tenets of Islam. He desperately wanted to make the hajj pilgrimage to Mecca, and we dreamed of one day being able to afford the journey, but it never happened because his bicycle shop didn't do great business.

"After two years of marriage, I was very unhappy. I had not grown to love this man like my mother foretold. To my dismay, he preferred to smoke with his friends than stay home with me. Many nights I spent alone in our meager home. God used this time to send an Indian woman, whose husband did computer work for the government, to befriend me. She listened to my frustration and offered to do whatever she could to relieve my unhappiness. Then once when we were having tea at her home, she took a great risk. My friend asked me whether she could show me her Bible. I had never seen one before, so I was curious what this devil religion was all about.

"Over the next few weeks she patiently and lovingly explained to me that Christianity is a relationship with God. A person is accepted by God, not because of anything we can do, but because we are each a child of God. She said that instead of man seeking God, as in Islam and other religions, God is looking to have a relationship with us, kind of like a parent searching for a runaway child.

"I learned that I was born a sinner, but God still loved me anyway, and proof of that love came when he sent his only Son, Jesus, to die for my sins on the cross. The only thing I had to do to reach heaven was accept Jesus as my Savior, and I would have eternal life with him. This is so different from what I was taught! Don't you remember? Salvation is based on doing good deeds in the Muslim world. If you can implement the Five Pillars of Islam in your life, you are supposed to go to heaven, although there are no guarantees. I guess it depends on Allah's mood that day, no matter how good you've been. That always troubled me. What made Christianity attractive was that salvation was not based on good works or doing nice things. Salvation was a free gift.

"My former husband eventually found out that I had become a Christian. He was scandalized and furious. He used the information to divorce me. Then I met Davood, but that's a story I'll save for another day."

"No, please tell us about Davood!" pleaded one of the women.

They were interrupted by a phone that rang once and then stopped ringing.

All froze.

Davood stood up. "That was a signal from a Christian brother who's a volunteer lookout. We are in danger. Perhaps there is a patrol in the neighborhood or a brother or sister was picked up nearby. We must leave immediately."

The Hammer sat in the lead van parked outside the apartment block situated in one of Tehran's ordinary neighborhoods. He relished stakeouts, the *tick, tick, tick* passage of minutes, sometimes hours, as the tension built. For now, the Hammer and his team were biding their time. Their quarry had returned from their evening Bible study an hour ago, so it was just a matter of time before al-Shanoosh delivered the "go" signal. The Hammer preferred to tarry until the marks were in bed and fast asleep. That way, when his black-hooded agents knocked the front door off its hinges and burst into the house, the residents would be too shocked to offer resistance.

The Hammer called over to his top lieutenant. "Is everything in order?"

"Yes sir. They don't come much easier than this. The apartment is located on the ground floor with front and rear entrances. We will be coming through the back, but I've stationed three men in the front to guard against a possible escape. Not that I expect them to make a try. These Christians are as meek as lambs."

"Yes, I noticed."

"But they never give up their beliefs."

"That's because they're stupid."

Three men dressed in black from head to toe and wielding submachine guns moved briskly along the alleyway. One shined a light on the back door, which suddenly opened.

Davood Rashee stood in the doorway, shielding his eyes from the bright light. "I'm ready. I've been expecting you."

The Hammer's men closed the short distance to the door entrance with their weapons drawn. Davood held his hands high. "I am not armed," he said.

Handcuffs were slapped on him. "Please leave my wife here. She has nothing to do with this. I forced her to come with me to the Bible study meetings. Please, she's asleep, as well as our three children. It's me whom you want."

The group leader spoke into a lapel mike and described what had transpired.

"I'll be right there," a gruff voice replied.

Within a minute, the Hammer emerged out of the darkness.

"Sir, this man says he knew we were coming, and that he forced his wife to go with him to the Bible study meetings."

"Really?" The Hammer spoke with heavy sarcasm. "And how did you know we were coming?"

"Sir, when I came home this evening, I felt like the Lord Jesus Christ wanted to speak to me. I began praying and reading my Bible. I was given this overwhelming urge to read chapter 18 in the Gospel of John, in which Jesus was betrayed and taken prisoner by the Roman authorities. As I read and reread this chapter, I believe he revealed to me that I was to be taken away tonight, just like him."

"Interesting."

"Sir, you apparently are the man in authority here. In the name of Jesus, I beg you to leave my wife and children here. They have nothing to do with this."

The Hammer didn't like being put into this position, especially in front of subordinates. Then a thought came to him. Since he had curried a reputation as being the toughest of the tough, the chance to show a measure of Islamic mercy might elevate his stature in their eyes.

"Take him away. You can leave the others here." With that, the Hammer turned on his heels, disappointed that the man had not put up more of a fight to save himself.

19

Saturday, May 13
1:13 P.M. local time
Riyadh

Sam Teymour had been waiting for this moment for a long time.

Perched in a corner office four stories above Prince Faisal Square, Sam watched thousands of Saudi nationals and foreign workers stream toward a hastily constructed wooden platform in the center of the square, where a demonstration would begin in twelve minutes.

Saudi police dressed like SWAT commandos in black body armor and helmets with clear plastic faceguards waited behind barricades that circled the protestors. The riot police carried a variety of weapons, including MP-5 automatics armed with rubber bullets and pepper spray.

Reporters and cameramen from al-Jazeera and the Western news media could sense a pulsating undercurrent of unrest. Normally three persons wouldn't be allowed to gather in a phone booth if the intent was to protest against the Saudi Arabian government, but this demonstration had received official approval from the local authorities. Reason? Sam's operatives had filed for a permit to protest *against* Christian missionaries such as Steve and Kim Cobb.

Sam's group had produced a forty-eight-page report detailing the proselytizing activities of the Cobbs, which he backed up with a press release from the ad-hoc "Keep Saudi Arabia Pure" movement. The Saudi media widely disseminated the message that the American couple had been working underground to convert loyal Muslims to their perverted Christian religion. Since the finger of blame pointed at the Great Satan—not the Saudi government—Sam's group received the necessary permits to demonstrate in downtown Riyadh.

From his observation post, Sam peered at the increasingly belligerent crowd pressed against the speaker's platform. His corner office, leased with monies allocated by al-Shanoosh, allowed Sam to observe—and direct—the demonstration below. Within forty-five minutes the office space would be vacated, if everything happened as planned. Sam scanned the crowd with his binoculars then brought a radio transmitter close to his mouth. He carefully considered what he should communicate to his operatives dotting the plaza.

After several introductions, the main speaker—a trusted Saudi freelancer whom Sam had paid $10,000 for this engagement—began whipping the crowd into a frenzy with his rhetoric. Instead of blaming the United States, however, the speaker rebuked the Saudi government, just as Sam told him to do.

"My friends, the royal family *knew* the subversive Cobbs were Christians, but the Americans opened up their fat wallets and bought their way into this country!" The speaker slammed his clenched fist onto the platform to dramatize his point. "Our leaders have been thoroughly compromised, both morally and religiously, by their close connection with the infidel Americans. It saddens me to say this, but the royal family is secretly hoping to turn the kingdom into a 'Christian' nation like America, so that the royal princes can freely pursue their immoral lifestyles. Do you know what this means, my people? The most holy site of all Islam, Mecca itself, is in jeopardy of being contaminated by the Great Satan!"

Sam scanned the perimeter, where the Saudi policemen exchanged looks of bewilderment. Cameramen jostled toward the stage to capture the speaker's next pronouncements. Sam could barely contain his glee since he knew what would happen next.

"I have proof!" the speaker cried. On cue, dozens of Sam's operatives passed out thousands of copies of *Stern, France*

Dimanche, *Bild*, the *Daily Star*, and the *National Enquirer* that had been smuggled into Saudi Arabia just for this moment. "Just open one of these filthy magazines, and you will see the truth of what our royal princes do when they are on 'vacation.' Their acts are despicable." The speaker ripped open one of the magazines and started riffling through the embarrassing photo spreads.

Sam grunted his approval as the Western magazines spread through the vast crowd like an oil refinery fire. One didn't have to be able to read French, German, or English to catch the gist of what the tabloids were dishing: photo features of randy Saudi princes frolicking with nearly nude Western women. Double-truck pictorials managed to fill in the blanks quite well on that score. It seemed that the European paparazzi—tipped off by the Hammer—had their long lenses ready when the Saudi playboys engaged in immoral escapades in the backyards of their French estates or atop the decks of their luxury yachts while they plied the Mediterranean.

The false accusation that Saudi Arabia had allowed the Cobbs to enter the kingdom and the shocking photo spreads of members of the royal family shook the demonstrators like an 8.0 earthquake. The speaker led the fevered crowd in chants and sloganeering. After a few minutes, dozens of demonstrators—also on Sam's payroll—"spontaneously" lifted handmade signs into the air.

"No More Infidels in Our Midst," one sign in Arabic read. "Holiness Is Our Mecca, Not Money" and "God Is Great, Our Royal Family Isn't" others said. Sam had some of the protest signs written in English with the American media in mind. One pictured the American president with horns and a pitchfork, along with the age-old cliché, "Yankee, Go Home." Others said, "Follow the Prophet, Not the Profit" and "Religious Autonomy for Arabs." Many holding the English signs had no idea what they said—or who had prepared them. All they knew was that someone had shoved them into their hands and directed them to thrust their signs at the Sony Betacams.

The speaker kept the crowd under tight control. As they chanted "Allahu Akbar, Allahu Akbar"—"God is great, God is great"—Sam consulted his watch. The prearranged time drew near. When his cell chirped, one of his agents informed him that four princes would be arriving at the Saudi Central Bank building in two limousines within seven minutes. Located two blocks away, the Saudi Central Bank smelled of oil money and Old Guard class. The Central Bank acted as the government's bank, regulating and monitoring all commercial banks within Saudi Arabia, while also managing the kingdom's foreign assets.

Sam hung up and spoke several coded words into his transmitter. Within a few seconds, he watched an operative on the platform whisper something into the ear of the speaker, who nodded in understanding.

The speaker raised his hands. "I need your attention. Quiet! Quiet, please!" The boisterous crowd quickly settled down.

"Are you satisfied with the way things are?" he shouted.

"No!" came back the thunderous response.

"Do you approve of our leaders and their decadent lives?"

"No!"

"Do you want the infidels and Christians ruling our land and corrupting your children?"

Now he had lit a fuse. The crowd erupted in anger at the very thought. "No! No! No!"

"Do you want change?"

"Yes!"

"Do you want a pure kingdom?"

"Yes!"

"Brothers, we must march over to the Central Bank and let the money changers know that we are not going to stand for it anymore! Allahu Akbar!"

He jumped off the platform to lead the way to the Central Bank building with the bloodthirsty crowd surging after him. The police at the barricades could not hold back such a massive mob. They frantically pushed against the lead elements while radioing for backup. Some officers shot tear gas into the crowd. Others pepper-sprayed the demonstrators. This only incited the testosterone-enriched crowd to sprint faster toward the Central Bank.

Officers in riot gear stationed around the perimeter of Prince Faisal Square attempted to stem the tide by screaming into megaphones: "This demonstration is authorized for Prince Faisal Square only! If you leave this plaza, you will be arrested. Do not head toward the Central Bank. We repeat: Do not go in the direction of the Central Bank or you will suffer the consequences."

No one paid them heed. The clash between the police and the demonstrators escalated when the latter hurled rocks and bottles into the air. The crowd surged onto Makkad Road, knocking down several barricades. Policemen clubbed rioters with American-made PR-24 nightsticks and kicked demonstrators with hobnailed boots. The anger level on both sides escalated exponentially as blood flowed on the sidewalks. In the midst of the shouting and yelling, the hundreds trampled in the streets screamed out in pain as the first ambulance sirens wailed. Chaos, noise, and ferocity built to a crescendo, causing many of the rank-and-file police officers, poorly trained and poorly paid, to break ranks and abandon their posts. This act further incited the crowd, spurring them to fight all the harder.

From his vantage point, Sam could see several police sergeants beyond the front lines preparing a counteroffensive. The retreating policemen regrouped into a phalanx of officers brandishing riot shields. Sam knew the time to act was now. He shouted into his transmitter. Three operatives pulled out Heckler & Koch USP pistols and fired at the police. A predictable response ensued. Hearing shots and seeing fellow officers go down, the police immediately returned fire on the hostile crowd.

Sam had planned it so that his people would push the masses from behind to prevent the crowd from retreating when panic broke out. Amid screams and shouts of rage in the ensuing crossfire, the crowd surged, overwhelming the front line of police and blowing right through the phalanx. Many clubbed the officers with their own nightsticks. The demonstration had turned into exactly what Sam wanted—a full-fledged riot.

The enraged mob gathered momentum as they raced through the streets of Riyadh, smashing shop windows, looting displays, and throwing burning torches into buildings. They reached the Central Bank Building as two limousines carrying the Saudi royal princes pulled up to the front entrance—just as Sam had planned it. The crowd pounded on the long, black cars, rocking them from side to side. "Infidels! Infidels!" they screamed. Meanwhile, rioters hurled rocks through the windows of the bank building and flooded through the doors. They destroyed the Louis XIV furniture in the atrium's sitting areas, pitched office papers into the air, overturned trash cans, and slammed uprooted tropical plants against the fine European art gracing the walls.

Out on the street, someone heaved a brick into the window of one of the limousines, which gave way in a shower of shattered fragments. Several burly men dragged the terrified occupants onto the pavement. All they could do was cover their heads as rioters savagely beat them.

For twenty minutes, the riot continued unabated until Saudi troop carriers dispatched from a nearby base arrived. An accomplice alerted Sam, who radioed for his people to seek safety.

Left behind were the dead: three-dozen rioters, eighteen policemen, and four Saudi princes beaten to death. Millions of dollars worth of destruction to buildings and expensive automobiles had been inflicted in the downtown area. Disturbing images televised to the rest of the world demonstrated the horrific damage inflicted upon the Saudi kingdom. The headline beneath the CNN Breaking Exclusive: "Saudi Arabia in Flames."

Back in his Tehran office, al-Shanoosh opened an armoire to reveal a Panasonic twenty-one-inch flat screen TV. What he saw on CNN pleased him immensely. The Western press constantly assumed things—he heard it once described as "working from a template"—and in this case, the worldwide media assumed that Saudi Arabians had risen up and spilled the blood of four Saudi princes in the ensuing riot.

Nothing of the sort had happened. The tame Saudi populace was not capable of such insurrection, which is why the Hammer had planted his best men to complete the job. Once word got around that this was a chance for an Iranian Shiite to plug four Saudi Sunnis—royals at that—dozens of volunteers stepped forward. Al-Shanoosh had to disappoint a few people, but he reminded them that their time would come.

Amber Robbins watched the same CNN feed from the *Washington National* office in Jerusalem. Just as Prince al-Aziz had predicted, the Western news media blamed the riots on anti-royal sentiment, noting that never before had the Saudi citizens risen up against their rulers. Experts on the Middle East expressed amazement and surprise.

That makes sense if you think the Saudis are behind this, Amber thought. Prince al-Aziz had predicted that Iranian elements would mastermind an operation to fuel unrest in Saudi Arabia. She didn't go to print with that theory for two reasons: (1) she needed to corroborate breaking news from another source, and (2) she had received the information on deep background from a family friend who paid for his political views with his life.

Amber rubbed her eyes in the privacy of her cubicle. She needed to call Dr. Lowell Mason again. Maybe a conversation with the chairman of the Comparative Religions Department at Fuller Theological Seminary out in California could ease her growing headache.

Amber looked at her watch. Six A.M. on the West Coast—too early to reach him at his office. During their last conversation, Dr. Mason had given her his cell number and casually mentioned his big-league commute—an hour-long drive from Claremont to Pasadena along the 210 Freeway. She could catch him on the road now. He picked up the line on the second ring.

"Dr. Mason? Amber Robbins here."

"Amber! Where are you?"

"Jerusalem."

"Thanks for brightening my day as I sit here in stop-and-go traffic. What's up? Must be important for you to reach me at this time of day."

"I believe it is. I have a little theory going about the events of the last few weeks in the Middle East, and I want to run it by you. Is now a good time?"

"Seeing that I'm not going anywhere in this traffic, sure."

Amber and Dr. Mason spent the next twenty minutes discussing the plausibility of Iran being behind current events.

"The one aspect about this story that greatly interests me is the martyr angle," Amber said. "Something deep within me wants to write about the 'suffering church' and modern-day persecutions of Christians."

"Christians are being persecuted in horrible ways," Dr. Mason agreed. "You never hear about it over here. Not newsworthy, I guess."

"That's why I have to go to Iran. I have this contact over there. She says that followers of Jesus have been forced to go underground because their members are being picked up and given an ultimatum: convert to Islam or die."

"That's happening elsewhere in the world, you know."

"But never as part of official government policy. I believe the ruling clergy have been picking off Christians as part of some grand plan. I'm not sure what that plan is, but perhaps if I report about the plight of the Iranian Christians, that will spur others to ask questions."

"But by going to Iran? You cannot be serious. Does your father know about this?"

"No, I haven't told Dad, but I don't have to ask his permission. I have been on my own for quite some time."

"Excuse me," the theological expert said. "What I meant to say is that it's dangerous for an American to travel to that part of the world these days."

"Anymore dangerous than living in Jerusalem?" Amber knew she had him there.

"Ah . . . good point. So I can't talk you out of going to Tehran."

"Thank you for thinking about my welfare, but not this time. I need to see for myself if half of what I've heard is true. If so, the world needs to know."

Saturday, May 13
11:49 P.M. local time
Ouvda Airbase, Israel

Luke Mickelson arrived at Ouvda Airbase shortly before midnight in preparation for a nighttime training mission. Ouvda Airbase, built in 1981 for Israel by U.S. taxpayers, was located near the Jordanian border. Two parallel runways serviced the military outpost. Ouvda was currently home to several Israeli air force squadrons—and two F-22 Raptors, the new stealth fighter plane secretly shipped to the Israelis from the U.S. Luke was in the midst of training several IAF pilots to master its mission-ready capabilities. Training flights could only be done at night, of course, since the plane was still under wraps.

Luke Mickelson, dressed in his flight suit, performed a walk-around inspection of the F-22, which was shielded from prying eyes inside a large hangar located at the rear of the air base. An Air Force bird colonel accompanied him, along with a Lockheed Martin technician, on hand in case there were any questions from the brass or the driver.

Luke knew the F-22 as well as any pilot in the world since he had tested the first prototype out of Edwards Air Force base in California's Mojave Desert.

"She sure is purty." Luke whistled as the three of them stopped to admire the $173-million plane.

"Makes me wish I was thirty years younger, Divot," the bird colonel agreed. "I thought I rode in high-tech stuff in my day. . . ."

"Look at the way the sides slope on the fuselage and canopy." Luke pointed. "And the way they canted the vertical tails and sweeping angles on the trailing edges of the wings is just awesome."

"I can't believe what they've done with the weapons systems," the colonel noted. "They're hidden. What's the payload, Jim?"

The Lockheed Martin tech cleared his throat. "The -22 comes with an M-61 20-millimeter cannon with 480 rounds, plus AIM-120 AMRAAM and JDAM missiles. She's racked with fire-and-forget."

"That'll smoke the competition," Luke said.

"But that's nothing compared to the Raptor's ability to evade radar," the tech continued. "You'll be able to sneak up on an enemy plane and shoot it down without the pilot ever knowing what blew him out of the sky."

"I call that winning decisively," the colonel said.

"Right," the Lockheed Martin man interjected. "Whoever said fights should be fair?"

When the inspection was over, Luke greeted the Israeli fighter jock accompanying him that evening. Luke thought about telling his IAF counterpart that flying the F-22 was like a Chevy owner test-driving a BMW—once your ride around the neighborhood was over, it was pretty hard to go back to your ten-year-old Beretta—but that analogy would probably be lost on the Israeli. Still, Luke had been impressed with the gymnastic maneuverability of what was being called the world's most deadly fighter—the ultimate flying machine.

The ninety-minute training flight couldn't have been smoother. While an AWACS "command and control" plane took notes, Luke showed the Israeli pilot how to test the Raptor's advanced radar capabilities. The F-22, he explained, gave the pilot "beyond visual range" capability in air-to-air combat to track, target, and shoot at multiple enemy aircraft while remaining invisible. To demonstrate the Raptor's aerial prowess, several Israeli F-15s became "bogeymen" as the onboard computers simulated an encounter. Luke took down all three planes.

Following the training exercise, Luke returned the F-22 to the garage and hopped into a UH-1N Iroquois Huey, a twin-turbine utility helicopter for the return trip to the Palmachim Air Base southeast of Tel Aviv. When he touched down, he switched on his cell phone, which contained a text message from Amber.

His heart leaped, but not in ways he had hoped it would. Didn't she realize how perilous it was for an American to slip into Iran these days? Maybe he still had time to talk her out of making the trip.

20

Sunday, May 14
8:15 A.M. local time
Tehran

Laying in his prison bunk bed, Pastor Davood Rashee closed his eyes and tried to blank out the squalor and misery that had been his environment since Thursday evening. He turned and faced the masonry wall in an abortive attempt to rid his assaulted senses of the stench of unwashed bodies and human waste filling the yellow plastic pail in the corner. He cried out to God, asking how his soul could survive this hell on earth. After a long reflection, it seemed to Davood that his best chance to get through another day would be to focus his thoughts on Christ and his family.

With his eyes closed and his heart turned toward heaven, Davood brought to mind snapshots of happier days. He recalled the smiling face of his loving wife, Mrna. He pictured his three children frolicking joyfully in the park near their home. He remembered the last time his parents came over for dinner and the delicious lamb kebob Mrna had cooked. He thought of the wonderful people who attended his Bible study at Rida's house. Those memories of his beloved family and Christian brothers and sisters brought moments of joy to his heart. Still, there were unanswered questions: *What have they done to my wife and children? Will I see them soon? What is going to happen?*

Davood had once heard a Christian brother say that you can live three weeks without food, three days without water, and three minutes without air, but only three seconds without hope. He put his full trust in Psalm 33:20: "We wait in hope for the Lord; he is our help and our shield." He drew on that Scripture to give him strength for whatever lay ahead.

"Davood?" A voice from the bunk above spoke to him.

"Yes, Muammar." Muammar was the most recent inhabitant of the cell, having only joined their sad band last night.

"Do you think there is any hope?"

Davood thought for a moment, knowing that his words would be received by five cell mates contemplating the threshold of eternity. "That depends, Muammar, on what kind of hope you are looking for. If you mean hope that we will be released and allowed to return to our families, I cannot say. Sadly, I do not have much confidence in the 'justice' our leaders claim to stand for."

"But won't they let some of us out of here?" Muammar asked, desperation tingeing his voice.

"It depends on what your crimes against Islam are, but it is also possible that they will forget we even exist." Davood's face brightened. "Whatever they decide, I have hope nonetheless. It is a hope greater than anything in this world, a hope that passes all understanding. My hope in Jesus Christ is greater than the hope of getting out of here."

Davood looked around the dimly lit four-by-six-meter cell. The grimy walls, constructed of cement blocks, had turned an ugly brown, stained by years of dirt, blood, grime, and human waste. A solitary sixty-watt bulb hanging from the ceiling provided the only artificial illumination. He had no idea which prison they had locked him in. During the revolution in the late 1970s, so many older buildings in Tehran had been "appropriated" for makeshift jails that the authorities didn't even bother naming them.

Davood's cell faced the courtyard and had a small window that allowed a little fresh air and daylight. The constant drip-drip from a baseboard water pipe running along the courtyard wall only added to the torment. The water collected in a puddle before draining through the floor to some wretch's cell below.

The cell was furnished with two sets of bunk beds. The pastor called the middle bunk on the left side his home, although he wasn't content to live in it all day long. Davood straightened up his frame and hopped off his bed.

"Where are you going?" Muammar asked.

"I think I'm going for a walk."

"Don't go too far." Muammar and his cell mates shared in the joke.

"Don't worry. I won't."

Davood smiled. He was determined to get some exercise every day, even if that meant pacing back and forth between the bunk beds. For this walk, he took seven steps in one direction, turned around, and took seven steps back. He usually counted off fifty laps during each exercise period.

After completing twenty-five laps, he asked Hootan, another cell mate, "When's the next time we go outside?"

"Tomorrow," he answered. "We're allowed into the courtyard for thirty minutes of fresh air every third day." When Davood had completed his fifty-lap tour, he bent over a clay jug in a corner and dipped his cupped hands for a slurp of water. He wondered what organisms were swimming in the water, but since he needed to drink to stay alive, it was better not to know.

The sound of heavy boots caused Davood to stiffen. The ill-tempered guards arrived several times a day, usually to escort a prisoner to the interrogation room or to deliver a meal. Twice a day they were served a watered-down gruel—usually consisting of cardoon or celery—and pieces of nan-e barbari.

Muammar looked up. "Breakfast?"

Before anyone could answer, a guard slammed a key into the steel door and swung it open. "Who has toilet duty?"

Four prisoners dropped their gaze. The yellow pail used to collect the human waste had to be emptied into a prison toilet each day.

Davood raised his hand. Ever since his arrival, Davood had volunteered for this odorous chore. Toilet duty provided an opportunity to serve his fellow prisoners—and a chance to leave the stinking cell for at least a few minutes.

Davood reached for the slop bucket and grabbed its wire handle. He stepped out of the cell while the two guards followed at a distance as he approached a prison toilet at the end of the hall. He dumped the contents into a ceramic hole in the floor and then turned on a nearby hose to rinse out the plastic pail. Davood suppressed a gag reflex.

"Why do you do this every day?" asked one of the guards as they walked back to his cell. "We usually have to force somebody to do it."

"Jesus said whenever we do something for the least of our brothers, we do it for him. That's what I'm trying to do—serve Jesus by serving those in the prison cell, so they can see Christ in me."

No sooner had Davood uttered those words than he felt a sharp thwack to the small of his back, a direct blow from the butt end of the guard's AK-47, sending him sprawling to the stone floor.

A stunned Davood stared at his captors.

"Next time, try your sermon on someone else," the guard snarled, moments before delivering a swift kick into Davood's buttocks. "Now get up."

Davood silently did as he was told.

Sunday, May 14
12:19 P.M. local time
Tel Aviv

"Mister Divot, I see-a you are in the company of a beautiful woman," exuded the owner of Pizza Fino. "Would you like-a your usual table?"

Luke played along with the running gag as he shot a knowing smirk to Amber. "Bruno, you are too kind. Is it available?"

"For you, my friend, everyting is-a possible." The owner gave Luke a wink as he escorted them to a patio table overlooking Dizengoff Road, home to Tel Aviv's happening scene.

"So this is the famous Pizza Fino that I've heard so much

about." Amber set her purse on the stone patio floor and adjusted her sunglasses against the noonday sun.

"This is the place. Best pizza this side of Napoli. I'm partial to the Quattro Stagioni myself."

Amber picked up her menu and glanced over the offerings. "Thanks for inviting me to lunch."

Luke grinned. "It seemed like the natural thing to do after church. Plus I wanted to hear more about your trip to Geneva."

Amber's mood darkened.

"What's wrong?"

Amber was instantly transported to the front of the Noga Hilton. She waved good-bye to the prince as the woman in the black abbaya stepped out of the gray Citroen. And then the explosion.

Amber felt her eyes tearing up, and she was thankful they were shielded by her sunglasses. "There's something I need to tell you about," she said, and for the first time since the horrible event, she unburdened herself to Luke—sparing nothing in details and the emotions inside her.

When Luke reached over and placed his right hand on top of hers, she felt better. His crystal blue eyes locked on her. "I'm so sorry," she heard him say, followed by a gentle squeeze of her hand.

"Thank you," she sniffled. "That means a lot to me. But there's one more thing I need to talk to you about—something I'm struggling with."

Luke gave her hand another squeeze. "Take your time. We have all afternoon."

Sunday, May 14
2:12 P.M. local time
Tehran

"You'd better stop right there. I don't want you saving my soul. I have enough problems."

"Listen, Ibrahim, Jesus Christ died so that you can have eternal life," Davood gazed at Ibrahim sitting on his moldy top bunk.

"All you have to do is believe in him, and he will touch your life in incredible ways."

"I don't care," Ibrahim replied.

Davood knew Ibrahim was easily the most secular of the group. A lapsed Muslim and a Tehranian journalist, Ibrahim had written one too many thinly veiled articles criticizing the clerical leadership. He was one of those calling for a new, more secular Iran—a stance that had landed him in this cell.

Davood looked around. He and his cell mate Adel were in prison for the hideous crime of believing in Jesus Christ. The others in cell 22 had run afoul of the *sharia*, the strict code of Islamic laws. One of those caught in a sharia dragnet was Farid.

"Why are you here?" the pastor inquired.

"The Mutawa picked me up," Farid replied.

"I'm sorry to hear that our morals police picked you up. What happened?"

A look of pain came across Farid's face. "I was with my Malaysian girlfriend. We had gotten a hotel room. We were awakened at four A.M. by an insistent knocking on the door. A woman said, 'Housekeeping,' so I opened it. The Mutawa swarmed me. They handcuffed me and arrested me for violating the Islamic law of *khalwat*—being alone with a woman who was not my wife."

The men in cell 22, transfixed by Farid's story, beckoned him to continue.

"Lili drew up the bedsheet and put her hands out to protect herself," he continued, "but two of the religious policemen beat her with nightsticks. She screamed out in pain. There was nothing I could do to save her."

"Where is she now?" Davood asked with empathy.

"I don't know. That was the last I saw of Lili. When I arrived here, they interrogated me. They told me that I would be in jail for the next three years unless I 'cooperated.' When I asked them what that meant, I received a beating. Then they showed me a copy of the *Tehran Times*. My picture was on the front page, and the article called me an adulterer. The lead interrogator told me things could get much worse if I didn't name any friends who were sleeping around. Then they threw me in here."

"That sounds like my story, but a little different." All eyes turned to Muammar, who sat on the bunk next to Davood. He had been there the longest, and his bony knees poked through holes in his ragged slacks.

"What's different?" Davood asked, pleased that these men were opening up. From what he learned about Muammar, his story was far from ordinary as well. He was an Islamic cleric who had grown disgusted with the brutality and power politics of the religious leaders of Iran.

"The Great Leader thinks he has his finger on the truth, but he wants to take this country back to the days when we beheaded anyone who didn't convert to Islam by sundown," Muammar grumbled as he leaned back against the concrete block wall.

Davood was shocked. "You said this in front of others?"

"No, just a few close friends. People I thought I could trust. I was arrested, and now I find myself in this filthy place." He turned his gaze to the pastor in their midst. "But you. You are worse than all of us. How could you betray your country by turning to the religion of infidels?"

Davood smiled. "I'm sure I am worse than all of you. That's why I need Jesus. So what do you think of Jesus Christ?"

"He is a historical prophet as the Islamic tradition has taught," Muammar parroted. "God has spoken through numerous prophets down through the centuries. The six greatest are Adam, Noah, Abraham, Moses, Jesus, and Muhammad. Muhammad is the last and greatest of God's messengers."

Davood listened, asking the Lord to give him the right words. "My dear Muammar, you obviously know our country's faith well, but you are sadly mistaken. Jesus Christ is not a mere prophet, but the Son of God. He said, 'I am the way, the truth, and the life. No one comes to the Father except through me.' Jesus proved that he was God by dying on a cross and then rising from the dead three days later."

Muammar didn't concede any ground. "The Qur'an says, 'There is only one God and his name is Allah, and there is only one prophet and his name is Muhammad.' Jesus was not God."

"I believe differently," Davood said, "so I will leave you with this thought. Are you sure you're going to Paradise when you die?"

"Allah is just and merciful."

"But how can you know for sure that you have followed the Five Pillars to the letter? I was once like you, striving fervently to follow the teachings of the Prophet with all my heart. But I never had peace. I could see things in my own heart, things that I know are in the hearts of others, even the mullahs and imams. Ugly things that surely cannot be acceptable to Allah. But try as I might, I could not change my heart. Then an uncle took a risk and told me about Jesus. In Jesus I found forgiveness for all the ugliness. I found hope that is real and a peace that is profound."

A silence fell over the jail cell—interrupted by the sound of boots walking toward their hallway corridor. Rattling keys warned that guards would soon be standing at their cell door—and it wasn't mealtime. This could be either very good or very bad news. The door opened with the screech of metal on concrete. Two guards with drawn automatic pistols stood outside in the corridor.

A uniformed guard clicked his heels and announced, "Prisoner Rashee, present yourself." The other guard held a set of chains.

Davood knew he was headed for the interrogation room. He didn't have to use his imagination to know what awaited him. If things went well, he would be roughed up a bit. If not, heavyset guards would be called in to deliver brutal beatings with rubber truncheons and then . . .

Davood uncoiled himself from his bed and stood up. He saw tears in the eyes of several of his cell mates, even in those of the cynical Ibrahim. They murmured words of support and reached out to touch him as he headed for the door.

"Trust in the Lord's strength, Davood," Adel said. "Jesus is walking with you every step of the way."

As the guard placed manacles around his wrists and ankles, Davood looked at the prisoners and quoted the words of another man unjustly imprisoned, the apostle Paul. "Philippians 1 says, 'I know this will lead to my deliverance through your prayers and help from the spirit of Jesus Christ. My eager expectation and hope is that I will not be ashamed about anything, but that now as always, with all boldness, Christ will be highly honored in my body, whether by life or by death. For me, living is Christ and dying is gain.'"

A guard gave him a shove to move him along. As he shuffled down the corridor, Davood knew fully the horror of what lay ahead, for he had already been interrogated twice since he was arrested. The authorities had tried to beat information they wanted out of him, demanding he reveal the identities of other believers in Jesus. So far he had resisted. *Dear Lord,* he prayed, *please give me strength. I don't know how much more of this I can take. And Lord, I tremble with fear of what they are going to do to me. I fear the pain, Lord. Please, let me not bring shame to your name.*

Davood steeled himself as they approached the interrogation room at the end of the corridor. To his surprise, the guards pushed him right past the room and continued to march him toward a different cell block door. *Are they going to release me at last? Or are they taking me to be tortured elsewhere?*

His guards did not escort him to a different torture chamber. Instead, they accompanied him out of the prison and across the courtyard to what looked like offices adjacent to the jail. What glory it was to be out in the fresh air!

Unfortunately, the feeling did not last long. The guards led him to an office building then pushed him into a small anteroom. He was slammed into a seat and told to wait. Several moments later, the door opened, and the guards dragged in his wife, Mrna, and roughly deposited her in another wooden chair. For a long moment, he stared at Mrna, dressed in prison garb with chains around her feet and hands. She looked as though she had aged ten years. He immediately rushed into her arms, embracing and kissing and hugging his wife so tightly that he nearly squeezed the breath out of her.

"How I have longed to see you and hold you! But my love, why have they brought you here?"

"I was taken away the morning after you were picked up," Mrna cried through her sobs. "I love you so much, Davood. I was afraid I would never see you again. Oh, Davood, please don't let them ever separate us again."

"Oh, if I could only promise this to you. I would die before letting them take you from me again. But what about the children? Are they all right?"

"I thought you would know. But perhaps we are going to be released since they have finally let us see each other. Perhaps they will bring the children to us shortly."

The door to the anteroom opened. Two new guards indicated they were to follow them to a makeshift courtroom adjacent to the anteroom. *Could this be it?* Davood wondered. *Are we finally going to be able to go home?* He looked at Mrna and could see the same questions in her eyes. All he could do was shrug his shoulders and put his hands together as if to say to her, *Pray!* Mrna nodded.

Davood and Mrna were ushered before a robed Islamic cleric who was serving as a judge. A court clerk read out the charges against them.

"The Islamic Republic of Iran versus Davood Rashee and Mrna Rashee. The Rashees are charged with blasphemy against the Prophet and treason against the Islamic Revolution."

The judge peered at the couple. "How do you plead?"

Davood's head spun. They had no attorney to represent them. They had been given no warning, no time to prepare for their appearance in court. But maybe this was just a formality before they would be set free. Davood spoke for both of the accused. "We are not guilty, Your Honor."

"Is it not true that you have spoken against the Holy Prophet and proclaimed heretical doctrines, seeking to convert others to your heresies, thereby undermining the Islamic revolution?" the judge asked.

"Your Honor. We have no desire to speak against Muhammad, and we love our country. We would never commit treason against it."

"Enough of your lies!" the judge shouted. "We have witnesses that testify that you have said that the Prophet is *wrong!* You deny his divine revelation! You claim that Jesus is greater than Muhammad. Do you deny that you have said such things?"

"No, Your Honor. But if you permit me to explain—"

The judge cut him off with a dismissive wave of his hand. "Your own words condemn you. I pronounce you guilty. The sentence for your crimes is death." With that pronouncement, he slammed his gavel on the wooden desk with finality.

Time stood still for Davood. He looked at Mrna. Her mournful eyes said, *This can't be happening to us*. But it was. His mind raced with thoughts, but he didn't know what to say.

The judge broke the silence. "Allah exhorts kindness, so I have decided to grant you leniency." He shuffled his papers and looked at the two people he had just condemned to die.

"I will give you another chance. Your sentence will be commuted to time served if you will repent of your crimes. I will give you each a chance to recant your heresies and proclaim your faithfulness to the Prophet Muhammad. We will begin with you, Mrs. Rashee. Will you repent of your heresies and commit yourself to follow the teachings of the Holy Prophet, and his teachings alone?"

Davood saw Mrna's face drain of color. Her eyes widened as they filled with fear. Her mouth opened and closed several times, but no words were uttered. Finally she managed to whisper a few words. "Please, Your Honor. We have never harmed anyone. We only want to live in peace—"

The judge slammed his fist down on his desk. "Silence! The question is simple. Will you obey the Prophet? Will you deny this Jesus? Yes or no?"

Mrna was completely overcome. She could not speak. All she could do was shake her head from side to side. Davood squeezed her tight as she buried her sobbing face into her husband's chest.

"Then I sentence you to die. Sentence to be carried out immediately. Now it is your turn, Prisoner Rashee. Because we know that women are of little value, we will give you a chance to save not only yourself, but your wife as well. If you will repent and follow the Prophet, then not only will you be set free, but your wife also will be pardoned. You can save her life as well as your own and live to see your children and your children's children. I ask you now. Will you, Prisoner Rashee, save your life and the life of your wife by honoring only the Prophet Muhammad and his Holy Truth?"

For several moments Davood could not respond. After a brief silent prayer, he gathered strength from the Holy Spirit. "As the apostle Paul once said, 'For me, living is Christ and dying is gain.'"

The judge exploded in fury. "Then you shall die! Get them out of my sight and kill them immediately."

The guards grabbed the couple and dragged them toward the door. "Please, Your Honor, what about our children?" Davood asked. "Can we not request that they be taken care of by members of our family?"

At this, the judge regained his composure. A thin smile appeared on his face. "Your children will be taken to an Islamic orphanage in the holy city of Qom. They will be taught the ways of the Prophet. If they do not subject themselves to his teaching within three months, they will follow you to perdition."

"You can't!" Mrna screamed. "Our children!"

"Mrna—"

The room spun as Davood attempted to compute the events of the last five minutes. Mrna was ashen-faced and looked like she would throw up at any moment. Davood felt a rifle barrel in the small of his lower back.

"Move on!" the guard barked. "Courtyard!"

Davood struggled to put one foot in front of another, but he knew it was his duty to lead Mrna on this final walk. He loved her with all his heart. He wished their time together did not have to end this way.

The pastor had heard people say that their lives flashed before their eyes when the end was near. That wasn't happening to him. All he could think was that he had failed to save his wife and that their three children were about to become orphans. They would probably be brainwashed to believe that Muhammad was the True Prophet. There was nothing he could do about it. *Lord, you know that. Please protect their hearts. Let them always believe in you!*

"To the wall!" one of the guards shouted.

Davood looked up and his heart sank. The stone wall had several splatters—like someone had tossed watermelons at it.

"Kneel down!" a guard commanded.

Davood helped Mrna to the ground before kneeling himself. He placed his right arm around her waist and held her as close as he could.

"Jesus, I love you," he whispered.

Mrna's body trembled slightly. "Yes, I love you, Lord," she whispered.

Davood felt someone come from behind and jam a rifle muzzle against the back of his head. He turned slightly and met Mrna's soulful eyes.

"Jesus—"

21

Monday, May 15
9:30 A.M. local time
Tehran

Rida Faheedi bounded off the bus that led to the open-air market in Tehran's southern sector. In the distance, a muezzin standing in the spire of a nearby mosque rang a cast-iron bell for late-afternoon prayers. Most of the customers in the crowded market ignored the call to prayer, which suited Rida. She had received the expected phone call shortly after Mohammed left to work.

"We grieve for our brother and sister, Davood and Mrna, who received their martyrs' crowns yesterday," a church "elder" had informed her.

Rida closed her eyes for a moment. "How did you find out?"

"Omeed got us word from inside the prison."

"What can we do? Aren't we next?"

"We're asking those who are hosting Bible studies to meet with Pastor Youssef to discuss our options. Can you meet later this morning? We cannot wait for the lion to devour us."

Rida scribbled down directions. How she wished she could ask Mohammed for his advice. He would know the best way to move around clandestinely. Rida had taken two different buses and scooted through another flea market to lose anyone shadowing her. She doubted anyone could have kept up with her darting moves through the claustrophobic mass of shoppers.

In this open-air market, Rida had enough shopping to legitimize her trip to this part of town. She purchased half a kilo of boneless lamb, 200 grams of onions, and a small bag of tomatoes for that evening's kebab, along with a ripe melon and table grapes. With her meat, vegetables, and fruit tucked away in a burlap bag, Rida departed the market for a street leading in a southerly direction. She walked one block and glanced into the window of a second-floor apartment. Good. The shades were up and a crescent moon hung in the window. The all-clear sign.

Confident that she was alone, Rida entered the apartment block, taking the stairs to the second floor. She knocked three times on an apartment door. After a brief pause while her identity was checked through a peephole, the door opened and a plump, middle-aged woman with a pleasant smile greeted her. "Rida, I'm so glad you could make it," she said, wrapping her guest in her arms.

"Vira, it always does my heart good to see your smiling face." Rida warmly embraced her friend.

"Please come in. Everyone is waiting for you. We feared that something might have happened."

"I'm OK. I was just being careful."

Vira led Rida to the main room where eight others sat cross-legged on the floor in rapt conversation.

"Rida, welcome!" the leader said. "My name is Youssef Nouri, and I would like you to meet my friends."

Rida breathed a sigh of relief. "You are the pastor?"

"Yes, I am," he replied, "although I don't go around town yelling it from the rooftops, not in Iran at this moment of history." The pastor grinned.

Rida nodded her head in affirmation. Mrna had told her that there were dozens of "cell" or house churches across Tehran—churches with no name, no constitution, no buildings, no youth program, and no children's ministry. Some even gathered in grassy parks under the guise of picnic outings.

"We have gathered with other Bible study hosts to talk about how to keep safe. We've invited you to discuss what will happen to your cell group after losing Davood and Mrna," the pastor said in a gravelly voice.

"Who were Davood and Mrna?" one person asked.

"Davood was the shepherd of a small flock of believers, but I have sad news to report. It seems that our brother and sister in Christ have gone home to be with the Lord. The authorities picked them up and had them executed, which was bad, but for them, it is good. As Paul said in 2 Corinthians 5:8, 'We are confident and satisfied to be out of the body and at home with the Lord.' Davood and Mrna are there now, and they are rejoicing in his presence."

"Amen," another believer said.

The pastor tugged on his black beard, which was long enough to touch his chest. "We grieve because three children no longer have a mother and father. The execution of Davood and Mrna makes nineteen members in the past two weeks who have followed in the footsteps of the martyrs. Our government has significantly stepped up its efforts to eradicate Christians. And things are going to get even worse. As diligent as we have been about taking precautions, we must now become even more careful."

Several women could be heard softly weeping, which made the horrifying events of the past few days all too real to Rida. She wondered how long it would take for the cloud of grief to lift from her.

"Brother Youssef, we know God loves us," one of the men—his beard was neatly trimmed—stated before the group. "We know he loves us enough to die for us. But . . . then why doesn't he do something to protect his children?"

Rida noticed the pastor considering how he could answer this very real and human question. "Brother, why does God do some things? Why does he allow others? Ultimately the answer is 'For God's thoughts are not my thoughts. The secret things belong to the Lord.' We must continue to look to the Lord Jesus for guidance. The world certainly hated and persecuted Jesus. They tortured and executed him. So it should not come as a surprise that they seek to do the same to us."

A petite woman blew her nose before speaking. "I believe what you are saying, Brother Youssef, but I don't know how much longer I can take it. I'm fearing for my children, my husband, myself. Every day I'm waking up with a gripping sense of foreboding. I'm breaking into tears every time someone knocks on the door. I am afraid even to go shopping. How can I go on?"

"I know exactly how you feel," the pastor replied. "Every time I leave my house, I wonder if it will be the last time I see my wife and children. I can hardly bear to leave them. When my fears become overwhelming, I take my anxiety to the Lord. He quiets my soul. He gives me strength. He reminds me that this world is not all there is."

A gruff, heavyset man whose beard squiggled out in wild curls spoke up. "I appreciate your words, brother, but I'm a practical man. If what you say about the government's campaign is true, I say we quit meeting together. No sense asking for trouble."

"On this matter, each of us must make a personal decision." Youssef paced around the living room, furnished with two large beige sofas and several wooden chairs. "You may decide that it's too dangerous to meet, and I, for one, certainly would not blame you for that. However, Hebrews 10:25 says, 'Let us not give up meeting together, as some are in the habit of doing, but let us encourage one another—and all the more as you see the day approaching.' My friends, what day is the Lord talking about?"

"Paradise?" the petite woman squeaked.

The crow's-feet around Youssef's eyes creased in a smile. "Yes, sister. Our hope is there, isn't it?"

She and the others slowly nodded while the burly man lowered his head.

"Perhaps with the increasing danger we'll need the encouragement and strength we draw from each other even more," Rida put in. "I don't know if I could stay strong without all of you."

The pastor tugged on his long beard. "I believe our meetings are worth the risk."

"My wife says they're too dangerous," the big man said.

"Then you shouldn't come," the pastor said. "But for those who decide to continue meeting in cell groups, we recommend you do not meet more than once a week, and that your groups meet on different evenings and locations, although I know that might not be possible for everyone."

"Those are good ideas," nodded one of the men.

"Allow me to leave you one last suggestion. If you feel so led, and it's within your means, you should consider sending your children out of the country. We can help you find Christian families in Europe and America who will look after your children until you can be reunited again. Where Western governments would not give your asylum request the minimum regard, they are apparently more lenient in cases of children."

Rida dabbed at her eyes again. All she could think about were Davood and Mrna's three orphaned children. She had baby-sat them once a week or whenever the pastor and his wife had an important meeting to attend. They were such cute kids. Too bad they didn't get out in time.

Monday, May 15
3:30 P.M. local time
Jerusalem

"How was your trip?"

"Very difficult, Evan. How come you haven't gotten back to me? I left you a couple of messages." Amber was grateful to finally get her Washington editor on the horn, but steaming inside because she had sent two e-mails and left one message asking him to call.

"Busy, Amber. I've been busy."

No, you weren't. Amber prided herself on returning phone calls and answering her e-mail in a timely manner; she treated others as she wanted to be treated. "Never mind. I was tracking you down to talk to you about something."

"What would that be?"

"Going to Iran."

"Iran? Are you crazy? We can't get an American in there. Every Western news organization from the BBC to ABC News has to hire local freelancers to cover the news inside that country. It's impossible, Amber. Not even your father can pull this string."

"I don't need my father's help. In fact, I already have my plane ticket and visa."

"Plane ticket? Where are you flying from? Certainly not Tel Aviv. And how did you manage to secure a visa?"

"I'm flying from Tel Aviv to Zurich tomorrow afternoon and connecting with a Swiss International nonstop from Zurich to Mehrabad International. The visa was no problem after I showed Iranian authorities my Swiss passport."

A long silence ensued.

"Evan? Are you still there?"

"Yes, yes, I am. I had forgotten that you have dual citizenship. When did you get your visa?"

"I dropped by the Iranian consulate just before I left Geneva."

"Tell me again why you're going to Iran?"

"I have an excellent contact who may help me break the Passover Massacre story."

"Do you know how dangerous this is?"

"There are risks, but I've been praying about it, and the Lord has given me a sense of peace. He will protect me."

Amber thought he'd make a snide comment, but he let the moment pass.

22

Tuesday, May 16
9:30 A.M. local time
Jerusalem

Amber awoke in her studio apartment, aware that the coming day would be a busy one. First things first: she packed her suitcase for her afternoon flight to Zurich. Satisfied that she wasn't forgetting anything, she switched on her Apple laptop. She zipped through several online news services, anxious to access any breaking news that might have occurred while she slept.

Every day, she thought, something significant happened in an area of the world that Christian evangelistic groups called the "10/40 Window"—a region of land located between ten and forty degrees north of the equator. The 10/40 Window stretches from Indonesia and Malaysia to the vast expanses of China, India, and the Middle East, continuing all the way to the top half of the African continent. Amber knew that the 10/40 Window contained the largest population of non-Christians, or, looked at another way, the world's highest concentration of Muslims.

As she sipped on a strawberry-banana power shake, Amber visited the *Washington National* Web site to see how Evan Wesley had played her most recent story. She had filed 1,500 words on another suicide bombing in Israel; this time, a Palestinian male in his twenties had rammed his explosives-laden car through the glass doors of a McDonald's restaurant in Tel Aviv. Fourteen Israeli teenagers, two employees, and one suicide bomber had been blown to smithereens during the after-school incident.

Amber scrolled halfway down her story and reread a few paragraphs:

> Bernard Arvitan, a Hebrew religion professor from Tel Aviv University, says that the Qur'an could be interpreted as promising Islamic "martyrs" the company of seventy-two virgins upon entering eternity. "It's my strong contention that some—but not all—suicide bombers are motivated by the sensational image of a sexual paradise in the hereafter," Arvitan says.
>
> When pressed why, Arvitan explains, "More than 1,400 years of Islamic tradition emphasizes the eternal rewards of martyrdom; the belief that dying a martyr automatically punches a ticket to Paradise. This explains why Islamic terrorist organizations can recruit timid, introverted young men for suicide missions. They get them to say yes through working on their minds, telling them that Allah has picked them for a very special mission. By glorifying suicide bombers, pasting up their posters on alley walls, and exalting those who said yes to killing themselves and others, these terror groups can strike a blow for Islam."
>
> Those remarks touched off heated criticism from a Palestinian Liberation Organization spokesman, who complained that the Israelis were painting a false picture of the motivation behind the "freedom fighters" striving to liberate Islamic believers from oppressive Israeli rule.

Amber noticed that underneath her bylined article was a link to a related story. Ayatollah Hoseni, leader of the Islamic Revolutionary Council of Iran, had railed against Western influences during a ninety-minute speech before 100,000 witnesses at Ayra-Mehr Stadium in Tehran. Hoseni's oration detailed the shortcomings and sins of Western Europe and the United States.

> "The infidels are exporting their social ills upon Islam," the ayatollah thundered from the podium. "For them, freedom means huge drug and alcohol problems, rampant crime and lawlessness, general vulgarity and crudity of culture, rising rates of couples living together, the resulting breakdown of the family, and the search for their Mecca of materialism. We do not want these freedoms foisted upon us! Allah has called us down a different path, a path that leads away from Western culture, away from Hollywood films, away from their licentious music, and away from their perverted views of sex. Have you seen the photos of those homosexuals marrying in Boston, kissing each other on the lips for all the world to see? If we're not careful, their decadent culture will infect and degrade Islamic countries from Indonesia to Morocco!"

Actually, the infidels already had, the article said, quoting the Great Leader when he pointed out that Islamic nations "in our midst" had been seriously corrupted and compromised by "infidel hedonism." Amber figured he was talking about Saudi Arabia, although the correspondent did not speculate on that.

The ayatollah wrapped up his speech by declaring that Islam must not surrender to Western perversion. "We will fight until death with any means possible. Muhammad warned us long ago that our enemies must be eradicated before it's too late."

Amber shut down her laptop and checked her suitcase once more. She had a flight to Zurich to catch.

Tuesday, May 16
10:44 P.M. local time
Zurich

Amber reminded herself that she was Swiss when she boarded Swiss International Airlines Flight 494, an MD-11 with a distinctive red tail and white cross parked at Zurich's Kloten Airport. That meant no speaking English, no reading English books, and no using her Apple laptop, where she would be tapping away in English. Amber couldn't wait to use her new toy, though—a battery-powered satellite modem that would allow her to bounce e-mail messages from anywhere in Iran without being hooked up to a phone line or cable modem. She had purchased the satellite modem at a high-end electronics store in Geneva.

Amber had made another purchase that evening—several French magazines at the airport gift shop, including a copy of *France Dimanche*, which promised another shocking exposé of several Saudi princes caught in flagrante delicto atop their prized yachts off Monaco. She wondered how those princes could be so bold and so breathlessly ignorant simultaneously. Amber didn't expect to accomplish much reading on this overnight flight, however; she had set her mind on getting horizontal as quickly as possible in her business class seat. That was following the late dinner, of course.

For Swiss International, airline food was never a culinary catastrophe. She smacked her lips when she learned of the night's entrée: medallions of veal cooked "Zurich style" in a white-cream sauce and served with buttery panfried potatoes. The delicious meal worked like a charm. Amber nodded off minutes after her tray had been taken away and slept soundly until a flight attendant touched her gently on the shoulder thirty minutes before landing at Mehrabad International.

Amber visited the lavatory to wash her face, brush her teeth, and freshen up her makeup. She also put on a *rusari,* a black scarf, over her head and tied it underneath her chin. Amber spent several minutes looking in the mirror, tucking the folds of the rusari to ensure that her hair, ears, and neck were covered. A black long-sleeved, loose coat called a *rupush* was waiting for her in the overhead storage bin. Every time she stepped out in public, Amber had to be clothed in a rusari and a rupush as it was against the sharia to wear "exciting clothes" that inflamed the desires of men.

She had no desire to inflame any male's desires. Instead,

she hoped to fly under the radar as low as possible. From what Rida said in her e-mail, Amber faced the real possibility that the authorities could pick her up, which caused her stomach to sour. While she knew God had given her nothing but green lights to go to Iran, she wondered how much grave personal danger she would face in coming days.

Wednesday, May 17
7:38 A.M. local time
Tehran

The passport officer with a pencil-thin mustache waited in his glass booth for the next set of weary travelers to arrive at his station in Mehrabad International Airport. Anyone deplaning at this hour had flown half the night from a European capital. Passport Control was located in the bowels of Customs Hall, which had seen brighter days, but that was to be expected. The Iranians had been building a new airport, Khomeini International, for the better part of ten years, so maintaining Mehrabad International didn't make sense.

Customs Hall suddenly teemed with activity as the passengers from Swiss International 494 disembarked from the transfer bus that had picked them up on the tarmac. The fifth person in his line slid her Swiss passport and visa under the glass partition.

He fingered the fire-engine-red passport before opening it and studying the photo. "Do you speak English?"

He noticed that she affected a quizzical look. "Eu . . . a leetle bit," she replied, holding her right thumb and forefinger an inch apart.

"Business or pleasure?"

"Eu, how you say, plaisir?"

The conversation bored the passport officer. While white European women seldom passed by his post, the customs officer knew that well-heeled Swiss had "discovered" Iran, probably after reading those travelogue articles in *Vacances*. TRCO, the Tourism and

Recreational Centers Organization and ombudsman of Iranian tourist efforts, had been luring more visitors to Tehran—tourists from hard currency countries like Switzerland—to visit the city's fine Archaeological and Islamic Art Museum and Saadabad Palace. Many Western visitors signed up for a package trip that included the Nomad Tour—a one-day bus ride to Shiraz, where they spent two nights in the desert camping out with Kurdish nomads. *Perhaps this infidel is looking for another eco-jaunt in some third-world country,* the customs agent thought. *Well, I hope she spends a lot of money.*

"Have a nice stay," the passport officer said, something he had already uttered ninety-four times that morning.

A recent directive from Savak required him to write her name on a separate form and forward that to the proper authorities.

Again, he thought, *all in a day's work.*

Wednesday, May 17
10:14 A.M. local time
Tehran

The Tesco motor coach—the shiniest vehicle on Keshavarz Boulevard that morning—rumbled into downtown Tehran. From her window seat midway back, Amber regarded the other European tourists—predominantly women—on the half-empty tour bus. They were clumsily dressed in chadors, rusaris, and whatever else was deemed proper Islamic dress. The bus ride was proving to be an adventure in itself. Donkeys and camels, carrying heavy loads of lumber and wheat, roamed the streets, tethered to their owners. Horse-drawn taxicabs vied for room with bicyclists. Dusty trucks and dented sedans of various vintages fought each other for a moving traffic lane. To describe the traffic circulation as chaotic would have meant a relaxation of the term. From what she witnessed that morning, Iranian drivers made their own lanes, took huge risks in passing others, and drove much too aggressively for the crowded conditions. Signals and street signs that normally served as suggestions of proper traffic etiquette were virtually ignored.

The chaos astounded one of the French tourists sitting in the front. "Can you explain this traffic to me?" he demanded to the guide in French. "C'est incroyable!"

The local tour guide shrugged her shoulders. "What can I say? The drivers like to lean on their horns."

"But where are the traffic policemen?" the Frenchman inquired.

"They concentrate on less dangerous pursuits, like illegal parkers!"

The bus dropped off the guide and the tourists several blocks away from Tehran's famous On the Bridge Bazaar, where the guide promised open-air markets lining both sides of a major bridge.

The group passed several stores painted in red and white that offered chicken looking suspiciously like a certain colonel's from Kentucky. Delis and sandwich shops also were prevalent, probably because they were so close to the bazaar.

A display case caught the eyes of several hungry tourists. "Let's have a closer look," the guide said, leading the pack inside. A sly grin spread across her face as she pointed at several sandwiches. "Our most popular snack is a brain sandwich made from sheep brains, which you can eat with some barbecued lamb's testicles," she announced. "They are very flavorful."

On cue, the proprietor offered samples to the assembled group. The guide smacked her lips and devoured a small square of brain sandwich, which elicited squeamish looks from the Europeans.

When they stepped back out into the crowds, two men pinched Amber on the bum. That ticked her off. Getting pinched had never happened, not even on the Via Veneto in Rome.

Amber looked at her watch. Her rendezvous was less than a half hour away.

Rida Faheedi, like her mother and her mother's mother, enjoyed shopping every day for food. Though she and Mohammed could afford a box-sized refrigerator, Rida preferred fresh-from-the-farm vegetables and freshly slaughtered meat. She could taste when something had been refrigerated.

At 11:45 A.M., Rida departed on foot for On the Bridge Bazaar, just a fifteen-minute walk from her home. On this midweek morning, the streets leading to the open-air markets seemed especially busy. A dozen city buses, stuffed with passengers, inched along the boulevard as cars honked and drivers' patience wore thin.

Near the entrance to the bazaar, she made her first stop at a stall selling exotic spices from India and Pakistan. A special curry powder from East Bombay Co. topped her shopping list.

The spice seller recognized one of his regular customers. "I'm sorry, Mrs. Faheedi, but I'm afraid we're out of your favorite curry powder. Maybe tomorrow we'll have some. But your friend is here." He jerked his head with a conspiratorial air.

"Rida?"

"Amber? You made it!" she said in English.

The women resisted the urge to hug in such a public place. Amber turned to her guide. "Vous etiez gentille," she said, thanking her for her flexibility. "Merci mille fois." She slipped her guide a twenty-Euro note as a tangible expression of her thanks. "I'll be fine from here. I can take a taxi back to the hotel."

"Au revoir," said the female guide with a wave as she rejoined her group.

Amber turned to Rida. "Your directions were perfect, and what a fascinating place to meet."

"You must be tired after a long flight. Shall we go have a coffee?"

"Great idea, but I have to say that your English isn't as rusty as you let on in your e-mails to me. Where should we go?"

"I think I know a place just off Darband Square, not far from here."

They snaked their way among the thousands of shoppers crowding the sidewalks along Varzesh Avenue, which was choked with traffic and drivers who punctuated their frustration by blasting their horns. "Is it always this busy?" Amber asked.

"The spice seller told me there's a noontime rally in Darband Square. He said the government is paying people to show up."

"Really? What for?"

"I'm not sure, but it could be for a public hitting."

"Hitting?"

"Your English word escapes me. You know, when people get hit with a stick?"

"Oh. I think we call it a flogging."

"That must be it. I read in the *Tehran Times* this morning that some young men were caught drinking alcohol. So they will get a hitting—I mean flogging."

Amber blanched. Maybe this was like those canings in Singapore. "What do they hit them with?

"A whip called a *tarizi.* An imam holds a Qur'an under his right arm while he swings the whip with his left. This is supposed to demonstrate the mercy of Islam because it softens the punishment since he can't swing as hard."

"It still must hurt . . ."

"I'm sure it does. I saw one of these floggings. They got twenty-five hits, so the pain had to be excruciating."

"All because they were caught drinking."

"If you're a Muslim, you can't drink in Iran, although non-Muslims can. The article in the *Tehran Times* said alcoholic consumption had been on the rise in Tehran and other major cities. It's a forbidden fruit. That must be why the authorities are cracking down."

"Can we take a look? Might be something interesting to see." Already, Amber had her reporter's hat on.

"Sure."

Amber trailed Rida, who followed the herd of people into Darband Square, which was ringed with Iranian military men in their fatigues. The first thing Amber noticed was a soldier yelling into a megaphone.

"What's he saying?"

Rida listened for a moment. "He's calling people to witness this important event for the future of Islam."

As hundreds streamed into Darband Square, soldiers handed out paper money, just as the spice seller had said. The women turned their attention to two platforms erected in the square's center. One looked to be a reviewing stand with chairs and a podium. The second platform was an empty stage, where Amber figured the guilty parties would receive their punishment.

"Look over there." Rida pointed to a riser where a dozen video cameras on tripods had been set up. "They usually broadcast these beatings on Channel 1, our news channel."

Amber regarded several soldiers from the Revolutionary army, dressed in combat fatigues, circling the punishment platform. Each brandished submachine guns and holstered pistols on their belts. She wondered where the clerics were since the seats on the VIP platform remained empty.

The proceedings commenced several minutes later when five robed clerics marched on the stage. One after another, they took turns making their opening remarks. Rida translated snatches, saying that each cleric was expounding on the importance of obeying every letter of the sharia, for the Holy Prophet had said this was the path to Paradise.

"This is practically word for word Ayatollah Hoseni's speech from several days ago," Rida said. "Do they think we are so stupid that we didn't get it the first time?"

"Talking points," Amber declared. "They want everyone singing from the same song sheet."

Rida listened as the final speaker, a gray-bearded cleric, thumped the podium for emphasis, which riled the thousands of young males in Darband Square.

Amber looked to Rida for help.

"He abruptly changed the subject," she said. "He's saying that our Great Leader wants us to fight with any means possible against the forces aligning themselves against Islam. Today, we will see a public demonstration of this new policy. We will witness the first step toward a new, purified Islamic nation."

Amber watched the robed cleric turn to his left and nod to someone. Within seconds, soldiers herded eight men, dressed in beige prison garb, from an open flatbed truck and paraded them onto the second platform. Any time a prisoner looked up, he received a brusque shove from a guard.

The prisoner in front of the line began singing, prompting the other prisoners to join in the worshipful melody.

"I recognize that song," Amber said. "'Awesome God' by Rich Mullins!"

"That was one of Pastor Davood's favorites—"

Amber looked at Rida, whose face had visibly paled. "Is something wrong?"

Suddenly, Rida sunk to her knees, while Amber grabbed her arm to keep Rida from falling over.

"Let me sit for a moment."

"We'll find a place."

"No, right here."

Rida shielded her eyes and then rubbed her forehead as she sat on the pavement.

"I only need a moment."

"Rida, are you OK? What happened?" Amber felt great concern for her new friend.

"The first prisoner—it's Ata," she whispered.

Amber remembered the e-mail. Rida's cousin was the one picked up last week after attending a Bible study. A bad feeling and sour bile rose in her throat. She hoped against hope that this wasn't what she thought it would be.

Amber looked toward the punishment platform. Ata and his cohorts had sung no longer than ten seconds when he received the butt end of an M-2 carbine against the back of his neck. The blow knocked him to the ground, causing the other prisoners to hesitate, but only for a split second as they took up the melody again with renewed boldness.

The cleric screamed into the microphone, causing the singing to stop immediately. The disoriented prisoners milled about the platform, surrounded by guards, until another robed cleric took the microphone.

"Ata Kanuni . . ." Amber couldn't make out the rest.

One of the guards shoved the prisoner to the front of the platform.

"What's he saying?"

Rida found her legs as she accepted Amber's lift. She cupped her ear and listened. "He's saying that Ata Kanuni, you have been found guilty of heresy and treason against the Islamic revolution."

She cupped her ear again. "He's saying that you have denied the truth of the teachings of the True Prophet, claiming the teachings of the man Jesus are superior to those of Muhammad. I will now give you one last opportunity to redeem yourself. Will you deny this Jesus and accept the true teachings of the Prophet Muhammad?"

Amber could not understand Ata Kanuni's reply, but from the response of the cleric, he had given the wrong answer. She reached into her purse for her digital camera and snapped five photos of the bound prisoners on the punishment platform before depositing the camera back where she found it.

"What's he saying now?"

Rida's brow furrowed as she listened. "He's saying that for the protection of others and for the good of all Islamic peoples, Ata Kanuni must be removed from our midst." The cleric nodded to Iranian soldiers standing next to the prisoner.

Two soldiers ordered Ata Kanuni to kneel, facing the rear of the stage. One dressed in fatigue pants and a dirty white T-shirt stood behind him and drew a Browning pistol from his belt. He raised the sidearm into the air and demonstrated that he was taking off the safety. Slowly . . . slowly . . . he brought the point of the pistol down to the middle of the prisoner's head. He allowed the tension to heighten while he rested the gun against Ata's skull for several seconds. The kneeling prisoner bowed his head slightly, and then he cried out, "Yasus Christus!" The executioner pulled the trigger, causing a huge gasp to arise from the assembly.

Amber closed her eyes, willing her trembling body to stop shaking. Rida had slumped to the ground again. The raw scene elicited a divided response from the large noontime crowd. The younger men jumped up and down and screamed for more bloodshed, while older men and women became sickened by what they had just witnessed. Two soldiers grabbed the lifeless body and dragged it onto the flatbed truck.

Another cleric took the microphone and read the same script to the next prisoner. Amber felt horribly ill. All eight prisoners would be executed before her eyes. This time, she could not bear to watch as the muted pop of the pistol caused her stomach to constrict into knots. As tears stung her eyes, Amber desperately longed for the horror to stop, beseeching the Lord to keep each one brave.

The clerics asked the prisoners one by one to renounce their faith or receive the consequences. Each believer declined and was summarily shot in the head. After the eighth prisoner received his fate, the leading cleric, his large, dark eyes blazing hatred and satisfaction, took the podium.

Rida translated for Amber's benefit. "He's saying let today serve as a reminder that there is but one true Allah." The youthful crowd roared their approval. "That's not all. He's saying that those who've been eliminated today are just a start. At this very hour in our prison courtyards, they have dispensed justice to three hundred others who deny that Muhammad is the messenger of God. Allahu Akbar!"

With that, the crowd dispersed—not a moment too soon for Amber. She barely put one foot in front of the other until she found a nearby storm drain, where her distressed stomach heaved the contents of a PowerBar eaten on the tour bus. Then she sat down on the curb and placed her head between her knees.

Amber closed her eyes and silently prayed for Rida and all the brave Christians in Iran, asking God to give them his strength at their moment of decision.

And then she prayed for her protection.

23

Wednesday, May 17
7:38 P.M. local time
Tehran

Seven hours later, the official blew the whistle, prompting the captain of each team to jog onto the soccer pitch of Revolution of the Saints Field for the ceremonial coin toss. Mohammed Faheedi, captain of the Holy Warriors, shook hands with his counterpart at midfield.

"May the best team win," Mohammed said, extending his right hand.

"The same to you, sir," the opposing captain said, accepting his handshake.

Tonight's match pitted the Holy Warriors against All Roads Lead to Mecca. Normally, Mohammed played on Thursday nights, but this was the first round of the city championship play-offs for teams in Tehran's Premier League. Mohammed had reminded his team that they needed to win to maintain their chances for advancing in the city championships. If the Holy Warriors advanced to the Khomeini Cup finals, they would play to a capacity crowd in the 20,000-seat Martyrs Field, a big deal for these amateur players.

Mohammed's adversaries drew first blood when one of their strikers redirected a corner kick with an adroit head-butt into the goal.

"Come on!" Mohammed yelled to his dispirited teammates as the All Roads Lead to Mecca squad celebrated the unlikely goal. "How did their man get open?"

The goal energized their opponents, but when they couldn't produce a second knockout effort, the momentum shifted slightly to Mohammed's team. The Holy Warriors mounted an offensive attack, controlling the ball and attacking the goal. Mohammed no longer had the young legs to streak up the sidelines, but his feet could still work magic. One of his swift forwards centered the ball to Mohammed, who fed the ball right back, leading his man perfectly. The goalie rushed out to cut off the angle, but the Holy Warrior striker blew the ball by him.

Goal! The teams were tied 1 to 1.

Wednesday, May 17
7:52 P.M. local time
Tehran

At the same time Mohammed was engaged in a soccer match at Khomeini Field, Amber exited the elevator and stepped onto the gleaming marble floor in the Tehran "Hyatt" lobby. Twenty-five years ago, the hotel had been affiliated with the American chain, but the twenty-story edifice had been nationalized after the Revolution and renamed the Azadi Grand. It didn't seem to matter. Everyone in Tehran still referred to the hotel as "the Hyatt," including Amber's cab driver.

Two things about the Hyatt surprised Amber upon inspection of her room. The toilets were Western—old-school American Standard toilets that flushed nearly four gallons of water down the drain, not like those frustrating 1.6-gallon tanks back in the States that you had to flush twice to get the job done. The other interesting discovery was the red arrows painted on the white ceiling, pointing Islamic believers toward Mecca. *I won't be needing those,* she thought.

Amber strolled through the lobby, careful not to make eye contact and draw attention to her pale skin. The rusari covering her facial features itched like crazy, and the rupush felt like an oversized trench coat. At least she wasn't wearing a chador, which had all the charm of wearing a pup tent. As Amber exited the hotel, she handed the doorman a slip of paper with an address.

The uniformed doorman straightened up and blew a whistle. "Taxi!" Now there was a word that was the same in every language.

A dusty, beige Mercedes roared toward the hotel entrance and pulled to a stop. The doorman opened the rear door for Amber, and she listened while he and the taxi driver conducted an animated discussion, probably haggling over the price. Amber's intuition proved correct as she noticed the doorman hand over a wad of bills from his own pocket.

"Taxi say feefty-dowsend reeals," the doorman said.

Amber remembered that she was supposed to be Swiss. "Eere," she said, reaching into her purse and pulling out five 10,000 rial notes. She forgot how much this amounted to, but it couldn't be more than ten dollars. Having already paid the driver, the doorman pocketed the cash.

The doorman watched the beige Mercedes belch blue smoke as it noisily pulled away from the entrance. He looked across the large driveway and made eye contact with two men sitting in a turquoise Honda Accord. He jerked his head toward the Mercedes taxi, and the Honda's engine roared to life.

For that little work, he had received a 50,000-rial tip. That and the 30,000 rials he had ripped off from the European tourist was the start of a great evening.

Her taxi approached a residence, interrupting Amber's recollections of Darband Square, for which she was thankful. When the taxi came to a stop, she thanked the driver and walked to the front door, where she tapped twice.

The door swung slowly open. Rida's face lit up. "Welcome! Please come in," she said.

"Thank you, Rida. By the way, your directions were perfect."

"I guess that was a good idea to e-mail them to you in Arabic. I figured the taxi driver had a better chance of getting you here that way. May I offer you something?"

"Do you have any bottled water?"

"Yes, we do. I bought some yesterday because I know you have a Western stomach."

Rida set out a bottle of Amolo mineral water from the nearby Alborz Mountains along with a plate of homemade rice cookies.

"Thank you."

Amber noticed that Rida seemed to be on emotional tenterhooks.

"How are you doing?"

Amber's question nearly prompted tears. Rida pursed her lips and exhaled. "Not good. Not good at all. Losing Pastor Davood and Mrna was a blow, but this . . ."

"I'm so sorry. I'm in shock as well."

"I called Aunt Lida, but she was in so much distress that she couldn't come to the phone. Oh, Amber! What are we going to do?" Rida covered her face as tears streamed down her cheeks and wet her cotton dress shirt. "I can't get Davood and Mrna's children out of my mind either."

"Did you find out what happened to them?"

"A contact inside the jail told us that the three children were transported to an orphanage in Qom, where I'm sure the efforts to 're-educate' them in Islam are taking place as we speak."

"Can anything be done?"

"I don't think so. There are probably a hundred orphanages in Qom, and for all we know, they split up the children. I think we've lost them."

Amber touched Rida's hand. "I can't imagine what the kids are going through. First losing their parents, then . . ."

"They were such happy, beautiful children."

"This is just the sort of injustice that I want to report about," Amber declared. She took out a notebook and scribbled several sentences. "Is it still OK for me to attend your Bible study tomorrow night?"

"Yes, it will be fine, but I'm not sure where we're meeting because Mohammed doesn't have a game tomorrow night. I still don't know what I will say to my husband about where I'm going." Rida glanced out the window at the busy street.

"You know what?" Rida continued, strengthened by a thought. "The Lord's doing some mighty work. It's hard to believe, but some very strong Muslims who see these brothers die with such peace find themselves curious about Jesus. Our underground church is growing incredibly. It seems like the more we are oppressed, the more we grow."

"That's amazing," Amber reflected. *We have it so soft back in the States.* "I can't wait to meet these brave people."

Wednesday, May 17
8:15 P.M. local time
Tehran

The second half of the football game between Mohammed's team, the Holy Warriors, and All Roads Lead to Mecca began with the teams tied 1 to 1. Mohammed knew that whichever team scored first in the second half would probably win, since that team would pull back its defenders, making it much more difficult to square the game. At this moment, the two sides were attacking and taking bold chances, although neither team had made a goal.

Ten minutes into the second half, the lights ringing Khomeini Field suddenly extinguished, plunging the football pitch into total darkness. Another power failure! Mohammed remembered that greater Tehran had been subjected to rolling blackouts, and it looked like tonight was this neighborhood's turn.

Soccer action stopped immediately to the groans and frustration of the players, and it took a minute or two for everyone's eyes to adapt to the resulting darkness. A three-quarter moon provided some illumination as people bunched up to discuss their options.

The All Roads captain wasn't concerned. "Don't worry, the lights will be on again soon."

The goalie didn't sound as optimistic. "The newspaper said the electrical outages have been lasting up to two hours."

"Let's wait ten minutes to see whether anything happens," Mohammed said.

Twenty minutes later, the referee officially postponed the game. Mohammed looked at his watch and pressed a small button at the one o'clock location. The face illuminated the time: 8:35. If everything went well, he would be home in fifteen minutes—a good hour early.

Amber sipped from the plastic bottle of water in Rida's living room. "Do you really think the mullahs will kill every Christian they can?"

Rida nodded affirmatively. "I believe so. They justify it by telling themselves they are doing it on behalf of Islam."

"But . . . why?"

"I don't know, Amber. Why do men do these things? War, politics, religion? They get it in their heads that to make Islam stronger they must kill, torture, imprison . . . so they kill good people like my pastor and his wife. Good people who loved their country and only wanted to live peaceful lives." She directed her almond eyes back to Amber. "There's no sense in it."

Amber shuddered to think how cruel those in power could be to their own people—including Christians.

Suddenly, Amber heard footsteps on the landing, but before she or Rida could move, Mohammed entered the residence.

His eyes blinked in surprise as he recognized the American. "Amber! What are you doing here? How do you know my wife?"

Before she could answer, Mohammed exploded, directing his wrath at Rida. "I can't believe what you've done," he hissed in English, which Amber figured was for her benefit. "Do you know how much danger you're putting us in?"

"You weren't supposed to come home from your game this early."

"We had a power blackout."

"Amber, if someone saw you enter my home, I would have some serious explaining to do."

"I'm sorry to surprise you like this, but I thought coming to Tehran would be the only way to get my story. The world needs to know that the ruling clergy are killing followers of Jesus unless they convert to Islam."

"You're going to get us all killed." He shoved his soccer bag onto the sofa. "How could you be so thoughtless and stupid?"

Her friend's words hurt. She paused, trying to get a take on his thinking. "I'm not stupid, Mohammed. I prayed and fasted before I came. I felt God leading me to come here. He gave me nothing but green lights."

"I wish I had heard the same message from your God, but he conveniently didn't send me an e-mail, which is just as well, because I'm sure someone is reading all my personal e-mails anyway. You must leave." He pointed to the door.

"Mohammed, please." Rida placed a hand on her husband's arm, but he shook it off.

Amber softened her voice. "Mohammed, we are friends. I'm sorry if what I've done seems inconsiderate. I didn't mean to—"

"There's no time for this," Mohammed said. "People are getting executed. And for less than this. Please leave."

Amber tried to think clearly. "Don't you think that if somebody followed you home, I should stay here for an hour or so until he leaves?"

"That's not what I meant. There's no one following me."

"How can you be so sure?"

"I'm not suspected of anything. Everything I've done, including visiting you in Geneva, was done for Allah and country. That I can swear to. No one is following me."

"But someone has been following me."

Mohammed's eyes bulged in shock for the second time that evening. "What did you say?"

"Somebody has been following me. I first saw him in Jerusalem, and then in Geneva—several times, including when he bumped into me at the Grand Passage. He wished me a pleasant day in English and then disappeared. I think he wanted me to know of his presence."

"What did he look like?"

"Middle Eastern. I'd say late forties, early fifties, in relatively good shape. Hair still black. He struck me as a businessman, probably because he wore a dark suit and overcoat when he bumped into me."

"Are you sure he spoke English with you and not French?"

"Absolutely. I'm sure of it."

Amber could see Mohammed thinking. After a long moment, he asked her, "Where are you staying?"

"The Hyatt."

"Can you make your way back?"

"Sure. I have the name of the hotel and address written on this piece of paper. I can hand it to the taxicab driver."

"You can pick up a taxi on the main boulevard just a block from here."

"Actually, my driver spoke a little English, and after he dropped me off, he said he would pick me up here at nine o'clock."

"That's in a few minutes."

"I know."

"Amber, listen to me. I want you to take the first flight out of Iran in the morning. It's much too dangerous to be here, even to get a story. The people in power don't care that you are a Western journalist. They will make you disappear."

"I will think about your advice and pray about what I should do."

The sound of a car driving up interrupted their conversation. As Amber fumbled for her purse, there was a knock.

It was the taxi driver.

Amber gathered her belongings and stepped out of the living room. She regarded the taxi driver. "Wait a minute." She froze. *That's not the guy who dropped me off.* "You're—you're the man who's been following me!"

"I certainly am," he replied in English as he tipped the bill of his felt hat. With that cue, four armed men slipped out of the shadows and stormed the Faheedi apartment. With surprising swiftness, they surrounded Mohammed, Rida, and Amber, guns drawn.

"What's the meaning of this?" Mohammed demanded.

The man in the felt hat assumed control. "For you, I hope nothing at all. It's just that we would like to ask you a few questions. Nothing out of the ordinary, I can assure you."

Amber could see the fear in Mohammed's eyes. Was she being arrested for spying? Something she wrote? For being a Christian? One of his henchmen grabbed her left arm in a vise-like grip and jerked her out the front door. She, Mohammed, and Rida were led outside, where a second car had quietly pulled up.

"I suggest that you not make a scene," the man in the felt hat said.

Two men escorted them to the rear seat of the second car, while the other two occupied the front bench. The man in the felt hat sat shotgun in the taxi. Within a few seconds, they were on their way.

Amber allowed her head to slump, wondering for the first time if she would leave Iran alive.

24

Wednesday, May 17
9:38 P.M. local time
Tehran

The taxi swerved in and out of traffic as though the driver were playing a Gran Turismo arcade game. Mohammed recognized Boulevard Keshavarz, a three-to-five-lane thoroughfare, noting that they were headed in the general direction of downtown.

"Where are we going?" Amber asked.

Mohammed looked to the guard sitting in the front seat. "Is it OK for me to speak to her?" he asked in Farsi.

The guard nodded.

"Into Tehran, but I'm not sure where we're going," Mohammed said.

They had passed ten-story apartment blocks and commercial areas for thirty minutes when the car left the relative smoothness of the main thoroughfare for bumpier secondary roads. After a series of turns, the taxi rolled to a stop next to a nondescript four-story office building, illuminated by a solitary street lamp.

Mohammed stepped out of the car and regarded his new surroundings. No signs had been posted identifying the businesses established there. He noted the presence of two armed guards, each with cigarettes dangling from their mouths, walking in their direction. Equipped with AK-47s, the guards were not wearing official uniforms, an observation that caused Mohammed to wonder if this was a Savak satellite building. If so, no one would ever know that they had been picked up by the secret police—or what their fate would be.

One of the armed guards waved his AK-47, directing the trio toward a rear entrance. The fact that they had been transported together surprised Mohammed. Under conventional interrogation protocol, the prisoners would have been separated to determine discrepancies in their stories. But since it didn't matter if they talked to each other . . . the thought caused the hair on the back of Mohammed's neck to bristle. *Our destiny has already been decided.*

The entourage marched up a staircase to the second floor where they entered a drab room furnished with a rough-hewn mahogany table and six wooden chairs.

"Sit here," directed one of the guards. An orderly approached them with a tea service. "May I?" he asked, and all three nodded.

Mohammed soothed his parched throat with a hot cup of sweet Indian tea as he regarded his wife and Amber. The ever-present machine guns squelched his desire to make small talk.

After ten minutes passed, the man in the felt hat entered the interrogation room.

"Good evening," he said in English as he doffed his hat onto an empty chair. He directed his gaze toward Mohammed and Rida. "Do you mind if I speak in English since Miss Robbins has yet to learn our beautiful language?"

"Of course not," Mohammed replied. The man took a wooden chair and sat across from the huddled group.

"I am your Joseph."

The statement drew blank looks from the three prisoners.

"Are you aware of the story of Joseph from Genesis in the Bible?"

Amber lifted her hand. "I am."

"I've heard the name, but no, I don't know his story," Rida said.

Mohammed refused to say anything.

"Allow me the privilege to enlighten you." The man lit up a cigarette and drew a long draft. "Joseph was the eleventh and youngest son of Jacob, but he was also the favored son. Jacob gave Joseph a special gift--a brightly colored coat—and showed partiality to him. His older brothers became jealous, and they conspired to sell him into slavery. Joseph was eventually taken to Egypt, and after eleven years of slavery, his master's wife had him tossed into prison because he refused her sexual advances. Can you imagine? Joseph might have thought that being a slave was bad, but that was nothing compared to being a prisoner in the pharaoh's jails."

"Why are you telling us this story?" Amber asked.

"You shall soon understand, Miss Robbins. Please, indulge me for just a few more moments, if you will. What happened to Joseph shows the handiwork of God. Through a series of incredible miracles, he was placed in a position of leadership in the pharaoh's kingdom." The man in the felt hat stood and walked behind the threesome as he continued speaking. "During a period of strong harvests, Joseph said that Egypt should store as much grain as it could for a coming seven-year famine. When the famine arrived, Joseph's brothers traveled from faraway Canaan to buy grain. They did not recognize their younger brother, but he recognized them. Can you only imagine how startled they were when they heard him say, 'I am Joseph'?"

Amber, Mohammed, and Rida shook their heads.

"No, you can't, but his brothers feared that Joseph would throw them into prison for what they had done to him. Instead, Joseph explained that God had sent him to Egypt to keep them and their families alive. In a similar vein, God has placed me in my position with Savak. Now I am able to save lives, including yours."

A long silence ensued.

"You mean—you're a Christian?" Amber stammered.

"Yes, I am, and I have been keeping tabs on all of you. My real name is not Joseph, but you can call me that to simplify matters. It's better that you do not know my name or which department I work for."

Mohammed wondered if Joseph was connected with al-Shanoosh. If so, this agent would be boiled in a vat of frying oil if the Hammer ever found out what he was doing.

"Why were you watching me?" Mohammed questioned him in the Farsi tongue. "Excuse me, Amber," he said, slipping back into English.

"Fine with me, Mohammed."

"I repeat, why were you watching me?" Mohammed demanded in Farsi.

"Your name came to us after your wife was observed attending a Bible study at the Rashee residence," Joseph replied.

"Rida, is that true? Have you been meeting with Christians behind my back?" Mohammed acted indignant, although this was confirmation of something he had suspected all along.

"Yes, Mohammed. These people introduced me to the one true God, Jesus Christ."

A silence fell as Mohammed processed his wife's confession.

"When you flew to Geneva," Joseph said, "that sent an alarm through the department."

"But I used to be stationed there!"

"We knew that from your file, but an informant noticed that you had, shall we say, doubts about who was behind the Passover Massacre."

Mohammed wondered if it was Ganji from the Western Europe section, whom he'd chatted with at the Sepahsalar Mosque meeting over the garlicky boulani so long ago. "But I never voiced those doubts to anyone."

"Ah, but your facial expressions gave you away, and none of your work in the last few weeks has advanced the official government position. When you traveled to Geneva and made contact with this beautiful woman next to you"—Joseph cocked an eyebrow toward Amber—"and Lev Goldman at the Hotel Richmont—"

"You know that I met with Goldman?" Mohammed's heart recoiled in his chest.

"That is not all. We also have a recording of your conversation—and a small packet that was left for you at a certain park bench." Joseph allowed a thin smile to crease his lips. "You have a keen mind, Mr. Faheedi—you even ran with the clue about Plan Sword I left on that file folder."

"Unbelievable!" Mohammed cupped his head in despair. "I'm as good as dead."

"Maybe so. Since Savak was planning to pick you up very soon, I suggest you and your lovely wife leave the country. The reporter too."

The suggestion stunned Mohammed. He took a moment to translate Joseph's revelations and plan of action. Why was this happening? He was a good Muslim who loved his country. He had merely questioned the course of action that his government might take—the way the Great Leader seemed set on isolating Iran from the community of nations. The more he thought about it, though, the more he realized he was simply a pawn, a minor irritant—expendable. If Savak knew how much he had discovered about Plan Sword, they would surely view him as a security threat to be eliminated.

Joseph took a step closer to Mohammed. "You remain a good Muslim," he said. "But Savak will probably believe that you are cooperating with the Western media or with Mossad. They will view these acts with, shall we say, great suspicion. The burden will be on you to prove your innocence."

Mohammed didn't reply.

"We can help you relocate," Joseph continued, "possibly even to the United States, but I can't promise you what the future holds. With your English skills and consideration for political asylum, though, I believe we could successfully assist you."

Mohammed looked at Rida, whose eyes pleaded with him to say yes.

After discussing the plan, Joseph returned to his office and flipped through a Rolodex until he found the right name. He dialed the phone number, confident the party would pick up since he was calling a satellite phone.

"Hello, my friend," a voice said.

"Hello, Jaml. I kept forgetting you have caller ID on that fancy cell phone of yours."

"Ah, my friend, but my phone is not as special as yours. Your calls cannot be traced, correct?"

"Of course not. Listen, I have three special packages that need a pick up and delivery. You Kurds are still in the human smuggling business, are you not?" Joseph enjoyed tweaking his friend. He knew the Kurds were the greatest smugglers in the world, as well as the largest group of people in the world without a homeland, even larger than the Palestinians. When Saddam Hussein's regime leveled 4,000 Kurdish settlements and butchered 200,000 Kurds in the 1980s and early 1990s, several missionary-based relief organizations, such as the Conservative Baptist Mission, flooded their refugee camps in the no-fly zone of northern Iraq. More than a few came to know Jesus as their personal savior, including the Kahn family.

Some of the displaced Kurds slipped into neighboring Iran and lived in small villages along the Turkish-Iranian border, raising sheep, goats, and cattle. The Kahn family also made the move, but Jaml's father discovered that smuggling black-market goods and people into Turkey were profitable "tent making" businesses that allowed the family to spread the gospel in a region hostile to Christianity.

"Where should I pick them up?" Kahn asked.

"Number 4," the Savak agent replied, referring to one of Kahn's safe houses in Tehran's northern district. "There's something else you need to know."

"What would that be?" Kahn asked.

"One of the packages is an American woman, a newspaper reporter."

"American? Now that's surprising. Not too many Americans—and female at that—in this part of the world."

"Agreed, but I've talked to her, and she has money. Lots of money."

"Oh?"

"But her father isn't as rich as Ross Perot," he said. Jaml's father had collected nearly $500,000 for ferrying three of Ross Perot's Control Data executives to freedom after they were rescued from a Tehran prison during the revolution in 1979. Mr. Perot's half-million dollars had been sunk into an extensive and disciplined smuggling network that included black-market goods like global positioning equipment, night-vision goggles, an array of armaments, and a set of safe houses in the Tehran suburbs—six in all. "It looks like this job should be a profitable one since a Yankee woman is involved."

"I take it the American reporter is the Christian in the group," Kahn asked.

"You're half right. The wife of the Iranian couple is also a believer."

Kahn didn't sound surprised. "I've noticed more Christians wanting out of Iran these days, my friend. And you know my cousin Vijay was martyred in Saudi Arabia."

"I'm sorry. A sign of the dangerous times we live in," Joseph commented. "Have you noticed anyone monitoring your Bible studies or church activities?"

"No, not in the mountains, but my contact in Tehran says he and his friends are being very careful. Do they have passports?"

"Yes," Joseph replied. "All the papers are in order."

"Good. That'll keep the overhead down. It seems that our friends in Turkish customs demand bribes in dollars or Euros to overlook the glaring lack of paperwork."

"So when do you want me to do the pick up?"

"Can you get here tonight?"

"That might be tricky, but I'll see what I can do. If all goes well, I'll meet you in one hour."

"House number 4?"

"House number 4."

When Amber was introduced to the handsome, rugged Jaml Khan, her fears dissolved into a luxury of confidence. Maybe it was because Kahn looked the part. The bronzed Kurdish nomad, who appeared to be in his mid-thirties, was dressed in baggy trousers, a billowy white shirt that opened at the chest, a light cotton jacket accented with brightly colored sashes, and a burgundy turban.

"A pleasure to meet you." Amber waited for Mohammed to translate her greeting. They stood in the living room of a ground-story apartment somewhere in northern Tehran.

"He assures me that the pleasure is his as well. He says that it is not often that he meets a Western woman as beautiful as you," Mohammed said.

Amber blushed. As she usually did when someone complimented her, she steered the conversation in another direction. "I don't understand why we had to pull the plug so quickly," she said, instantly realizing that she had employed a colloquialism that mystified her companions. "What I meant to say was, were our lives really in danger?"

Joseph, wearing his felt hat again, coughed to signal his intention to speak. "Miss Robbins, I can assure you that you were within hours, maybe minutes, of being intercepted and questioned by our Savak police."

"But what did I do?"

"For starters, they would ask you why you came into this country."

"I arrived on a tourist visa, to learn more about this mysterious country that I have read so much about."

"So why were you having contact with an Iranian intelligence officer and his wife?"

Amber's eyes widened. "Mohammed . . . did I hear right? You work in intelligence?" Her voice quivered at this new revelation.

Mohammed shifted his stance. "It's not what you think. I'm not a spy. I just read a lot of reports and report on my findings to the Iranian government."

"Which is why we must get you, your wife, and Miss Robbins out of the country." Joseph appeared rather insistent to Amber.

"I understand."

When Joseph and Kahn began speaking in Farsi—Amber figured they were talking about logistics—she pulled her Apple laptop out of her backpack. She booted up the computer, not taking for granted her new satellite modem as she typed out e-mail messages to her parents, Evan Wesley back at the *Washington National*, and one to the home office in Jerusalem, each containing a lengthy description of the events of the last forty-eight hours. Amber also notified her father that Jaml Khan's services did not come cheap, nor did he guarantee success. If the escape into Turkey ran into problems, he said, it was entirely possible that the bill could reach $100,000.

When she finished with her housekeeping e-mails, Amber sent one more electronic missive. She typed "Insurance policy" on the subject line and spent fifteen minutes writing a three-page letter.

She hoped he could help.

From Amber's geopolitical understandings, departing Iran did not leave a wide range of options. Directly east of Iran lay Afghanistan, where al-Qaeda still menaced the populace from its mountain redoubts. Pakistan, to the southeast, was another place where Americans were not welcome. Directly west was Iraq; Operation Iraqi Freedom may have freed the country from Saddam's clutches, but lingering lawlessness and the unsettled political situation made it too dangerous for an American to step into the country unannounced. She shuddered for a moment when she pictured herself falling into the wrong hands and being personally beheaded by Abu Musab al-Zarqawi while a camcorder purred. *Nope, we better not go that way,* she thought, or to Iran's northern border, which brushed up against several unfriendly and unstable Islamic republics that had split off from the old Soviet Union—Turkmenistan, Armenia, and Azerbaijan. All road signs pointed toward Turkey.

When she asked Joseph about other possible avenues of escape, he replied that they could try an ocean departure from the Persian Gulf, but that approach began with a demanding overland journey from the northern end of Iran to its southern coastline. Then there was the problem of finding the right "coyote" ship and slipping out of Iran's harbors undetected, which was only the start of an uncertain, costly, and very long voyage around the African continent to Europe.

"It's better to stay on land, which means the best available escape route is somewhere along the Turkey-Iran border," Joseph said.

So it would be Turkey. "How far is that from here?"

"A good eight hundred kilometers to the northwest corner of our country," he replied. Amber listened as Joseph explained that everyone connected with the smuggling trade knew this—including the Islamic Republic of Iran. "Patrols along the Iranian-Turkish border—as well as the Iraqi frontier—have been stepped up in the last month," he said. "Furthermore, the entire northwest region between Tabriz and Maku is flooded with secret police and border guards keeping vigil."

"So how do we get out?" This was sounding more dangerous by the minute to Amber.

"You can't take the main highway between Tehran and Tabriz. Instead, Jaml's going to detour directly north of Tehran through the Alborz Mountains. Once you reach the Caspian Sea, you'll turn west and hug the coastline before slipping into Tabriz on a series of back roads. It'll take all day," Joseph concluded. "That's why you need some good rest."

Thursday, May 18
6:04 A.M. local time
Tehran

The next morning at dawn, Amber walked into the living room of the apartment and saw that a typical Middle Eastern breakfast of pita bread, feta cheese, tomatoes, cucumbers, and fresh cantaloupe slices had been prepared.

"This looks very good." Having only snacked on dates and bread for dinner, she suddenly felt famished. The American had heard that Iranians eat on the floor, so she wasn't surprised to observe Kahn and his men taking their seats on the Persian carpet. Kahn, she noticed, was no longer wearing traditional Kurdish garb. That morning he had changed into blue jeans and a long-sleeved shirt to pass himself off as just another city boy going home to see his parents in the Old Country.

After breakfast, Amber washed her hands and face in a bowl, careful not to drink the local water. She used a bottle of Perrier to brush her teeth—the carbonated water creating the foamiest mouth she had ever experienced. Thankful for the little pleasures of civilization, she placed her toothbrush and toothpaste back into her backpack, which contained her Swiss passport, red leather wallet, and Apple laptop.

When they were ready to go, they walked single-file out of the apartment. Fifty meters to the left, Kahn had parked his car—a specially equipped two-year-old black Toyota Forerunner with just enough dents so as not to attract undue attention. Parked behind the SUV was a late-model Mercedes driven by trusted lieutenants.

Amber noticed that Mohammed took the shotgun seat without asking, but then again, she was in Tehran—women sat in the back. Amber and Rida took the rear seats while the American tried to cover up her Caucasian face as much as she could.

The engines roared to life, and they were on their way. The caravan proceeded without incident through northern Tehran before converging on the headway of the Tehran-Cholus road, which fed into the heart of the Alborz Mountains. Several peaks topping 13,000 feet still had snow, even on this late spring day.

The shah had built the two-lane road when times were better. Mohammed explained that European engineers had carved Swiss-like switchbacks into the hump of the Alborz Mountains to create a pass between the two valleys. Nearing the crest of the impressive mountain range, Amber spotted a sign posted on the road: Dizin, 5 km. The international sign for a downhill skier was also shown.

Amber leaned forward. "I've heard of this place! Years ago in a Warren Miller ski film, they showed men and women skiing on different slopes—separated by a rope and enforced by Islamic Revolutionary Guards."

"The slopes are segregated still, but now they have snowboarders," Mohammed said.

"Snowboarders?" Amber couldn't imagine boarders shredding these slopes. Instead, she pictured Iranian women dressed in voluminous black chadors over their ski pants and parkas. Now that would be a sight to see.

They left the breathtaking Alpine-like scenery behind as the car descended to a coastal road abutting the Caspian Sea. Simple farming villages passed by—sights of Iranian rural life that captivated Amber until they arrived under the cover of twilight in Tabriz.

Mohammed turned around and looked at Amber in the backseat. "Jaml says we will sleep in a safe house, but he adds that from here to the border won't be as easy as today's drive."

The weary travelers exchanged greetings with their "host family" before being directed to the pillows on the living room floor of the Tabriz safe house.

"We can sit down," Mohammed said. He and Amber were getting settled when they looked up from the carpeted floor and noticed Rida engaged with Kahn. He said something that caused Rida to sob. As Kahn comforted her, Mohammed stood, looking surprised. He reached for Rida and embraced her.

Amber rose and approached the couple. "Jaml has informed me that we have some surprise visitors waiting for us in the other room," Rida said.

"Visitors? Who even knows we're here?" Amber wondered if she should be concerned, but the Faheedis—especially Rida—looked happy.

"Jaml assures me that they are good visitors. Shall we have a look?"

Rida and Amber walked into the room, where three small children were playing quietly with toys.

"Who are they?" Amber asked.

"Maree, Caleb, Ruthina!" Rida fell to her knees and hugged the frightened children, wetting their black hair with tears.

A lump rose in Amber's throat as she realized these must be the orphaned children of Davood and Mrna Rashee. Her eyes moistened as she witnessed the reunion.

"How did they get here?" she asked Rida.

Rida's voice was shaky. "Jaml, he . . . I can't believe it." She cupped her hands around the oldest girl's sweet face. "He had them rescued. It's a miracle!" She hugged all three to her chest again. "I never want to let them go."

Mohammed walked into the bedroom. Rida gathered the toddler Ruthina into her arms and spoke to him. From what Amber could discern, Rida was explaining the presence of these three orphaned children and the sad fate of their parents.

For the next five minutes, Rida pleaded with Mohammed, quietly urging him to have compassion. Amber didn't need a translator to follow the conversation. After hemming and hawing, Mohammed smiled at Rida. The three orphans had new parents.

"I guess we're going to have a family after all," she said softly, wiping her damp eyes with the back of her hands.

After dinner, Amber excused herself to check her e-mail. She was hoping to hear from a certain person, and when she did, she returned to Mohammed. "I need to tell Mr. Kahn that some friends want to help out. Can you translate for me?"

"Sure. But who are these 'friends'?"

"You'll find out when you translate what I have to tell him."

25

Thursday, May 18
5:12 P.M. local time
Adana, Turkey

"You're saying I can't go, right?"

Inside an aging Quonset hut at Incirlik Air Force Base, Luke "Divot" Mickelson stood before Sergeant Pete MacMillan, staring a hole into the forehead of the Special Forces jarhead. MacMillan could have been an Air Commando poster boy. His wiry frame, standing five-feet-seven and packing one hundred and sixty pounds of lean muscle, was certainly the spark-plug type. Like most Air Commandos, he wore his brown hair considerably longer than normal, as there was always the possibility he might have to infiltrate the general population.

"You fighter jocks think you can do anything, even real-time insert and extraction missions," MacMillan retorted. "Just because some big-shot newspaper guy in Washington rattled some cages to get his girl out of a tough spot doesn't mean you can come in here and declare yourself mission ready."

"You know it's more than that. We have a chance to bring a real live intelligence agent over to our side. We don't get too many defectors from this part of the world."

"You're still not going."

Luke was undeterred. "How tough can it be hitching a ride on a Pave Hawk and landing at some LZ over there?" The air force pilot was under the impression that the extraction would involve taking an Air Force Special Operations MH-60 helicopter—the Pave Hawk—to a rendezvous site, where they would wait for Amber and her party to show up.

"Well, Captain, that would be a right nice way to go about this, all things being equal. Unfortunately, our president has an aversion to us flying his expensive air force helicopters into hostile countries and sitting around on the ground indefinitely. Seems to think that might prompt the natives to do something not so nice to those pricey choppers, not to mention what they would do to the men who fly them. That's why we're going with a HAHO insertion."

So the mission would begin with a HAHO—a high-altitude, high-opening jump. Luke knew about those from his pilot training—just enough to know that a HAHO jump was well outside his area of expertise.

"Couldn't we do a LALO incursion?" Luke asked, understanding that a low-altitude, low-opening jump presented its own set of challenges.

"No, Divot. We can't slip a 130 beneath radar coverage into Iranian territory. Even if we managed to escape detection, those 'Ranians have shoulder-armed missiles that would drop our guys in nothing flat. And sooner than you could say 'call CNN,' they'd have camera crews on the scene making hay out of the latest American 'attack.' Then we'd really have a mess on our hands."

"I suppose so."

"Besides, if you became part of this LALO insertion, I'm sure there'd be an office pool going on whether you'd survive the jump. You're only five hundred off the deck when the go light comes on. You'd be drilling a hole in the ground before you even got a hand on that ripcord. Nope, this mission calls for a HAHO jump, which automatically DQs you, sir."

Luke resigned himself to not going. "What's the mission plan?"

"Here's what command and control has cooked up. We're going to take off in a C-130. Routine training mission. We fly east toward the Iranian border, careful not to cross into 'Ranian air space. We skirt along the border, measure the upper air currents, and when we think we're in the right spot, we green-light our seven-man team to jump out at 30,000 feet. They paraglide into the Iranian LZ, where they meet up with the escaping party."

"What happens next?"

"With the Kurds' supplying on-the-ground muscle, coupled with our weaponry, they should be able to waltz across the border without a scratch. We pick up the Donner Party just inside the Turkish border with two Pave Hawks, and then we get out of Dodge as fast as we can."

Luke felt confident that this mission was in good hands. The Air Commandos shared the distinction as the most highly trained soldiers in the United States military, along with the Green Berets, Navy SEALs, and the Army's counterterrorism Delta Forces.

"Hope she's worth it."

"Pardon me?"

"I said I hope she's worth it," MacMillan repeated. "The defector too."

"Why are you saying this?"

"Deduction, since you're here and orders have come from way, way up."

"I don't know about the Iranian, but let's just say that she's a close friend."

Friday, May 19
1:31 A.M. local time
Turkey

Lieutenant Kenyon Thomas of the U.S. Air Commando Forces resembled a young, muscular Denzel Washington. But it wasn't just his WWF-like physique that impressed those under his command. Thomas's incisive mind and matching charisma inspired men to follow his lead.

Just this afternoon he had been briefed about the extraction exercise. The Faheedi defector could be the real deal, he had learned. Thomas had raised his eyebrows, though, when he heard that an American woman was involved. Apparently she was some newsie whose daddy hobnobbed with the Washington power crowd. At least that's what his CO said.

Lt. Thomas regarded the six men resting their eyelids in the bare bones MC-130H Combat Talon II, leveling out at 35,000 feet above eastern Turkey. No creature comforts on this milk run, unless you considered Army java something special. The C-130 loadmaster sidled up to Thomas and yelled over the engine noise. "The flight deck says fifteen minutes to jump."

Thomas stood up from his canvas seat and walked the aisle, tapping shoulders along the way. His handpicked unit knew that was the signal to visit the head one last time, strap on their chutes, and make the requisite last-minute checks. Ten minutes later, Thomas nodded to the loadmaster that the mission team was ready to roll, prompting the air crew member to slowly lower the rear hatch. The room temperature immediately descended from 65 degrees to a frosty minus-15.

The Air Commandos were dressed for the sub-zero cold as they duck-walked toward the rear of the plane, complete with flash hood, respirator, and night-vision goggles. Thomas looked up at the "Christmas tree" signal hanging inside the fuselage. The Christmas tree turned yellow.

Ten seconds later, they received the green light. Thomas and his men never hesitated as they bounded into the dark abyss.

Friday, May 19
2:02 A.M. local time
Near the Iran-Turkey border

Jaml Khan concentrated on keeping his Toyota Forerunner on the rutted track posing as a road. On this moonlit night, they were traveling from the north end of Lake Urmia toward the village of Khoi. His backup maintained a two-minute separation since late-night caravans in this part of the country drew unwanted attention.

While maintaining one hand on the steering wheel, Jaml pressed a button on his cell phone. "Everything OK back there?" he asked the driver of the Mercedes.

"We're fine, but can't we make better time?" They had been traveling at fifty kilometers per hour in the bumpy terrain.

"Only if we want to bend a front axle. Listen, the important thing is adhering to the schedule. Within the hour, we'll reach K12, and from there, it should be all downhill, God willing."

As traveling on K12—the main thoroughfare to the Turkish border—threatened to be their most vulnerable stretch of the trip, Jaml decided to pass through around two-thirty in the morning, a time when there would be little or no traffic, and, hopefully, the patrols had slacked off. His contacts had told him that the border patrol had erected a checkpoint a kilometer outside of Qutor, but Jaml had no plans to get *near* that checkpoint.

Amber sat in the rear bench seat, stroking the feet of little Ruthina, who quietly slept in the lap of her new mother. Rida was conked out as well. Amber turned her head toward Maree and Caleb, also sleeping peacefully in fetal positions. *They've been through so much*, she thought. *Lord, keep them safe.*

Covered from head to toe in a black rupush and scarf, Amber felt too nervous to rest. She realized how spoiled she was to have grown up in Dallas, where freeways and expressways allowed people to travel great distances in leather-upholstered comfort and a short amount of time. Not here in Iran, where traveling from point A to B was proving to be an arduous adventure. The well-worn road map in the Toyota Forerunner glove compartment revealed that the distance from Tehran to the northwest border region was around eight hundred kilometers, or five hundred miles, as the crow flies. In Texas, you could hop on a tabletop freeway and speed along at eighty miles per hour, which translated into traveling five hundred miles in less than seven hours—and you would still have time for two pit stops. Not in Iran, where this journey was heading into its second day.

Amber's stomach was filled with tension, and she had a splitting headache. She wished she could take two Tylenol to take the edge off.

"I can't believe how far it is to the border. Are we making good time?" Amber was seeking assurance from Mohammed.

"I think so," Mohammed replied from the front seat.

"Have you and Rida talked about her being a Christian?" she asked softly.

Mohammed blinked and turned to her. "Just a little bit since we were picked up."

"What do you think?" Amber's heart filled with compassion as she glanced at her old friend. She'd prayed for him after their "date" in Geneva. Now she wished she'd prayed more.

"I don't know," he whispered. "A month or so ago, I found her Bible in our bedroom. I didn't say anything, but I watched her closely. She has changed in recent months. Her kindness and love surprises me."

"You shouldn't be surprised. She wants to love you because Jesus loves her despite her imperfections."

"That is much different from Islam."

"How's that?"

"In Islam, we're taught to fear and obey Allah, but we're never told that he loves us. As for our enemies, we're to kill them if a jihad has been issued against them. Even bin Laden says that killing innocent civilians is permissible under Islamic law."

"Interesting. Do you believe in an afterlife?"

"I wonder sometimes. We are taught about Paradise and how that is the goal of every Muslim believer, but I just don't see how anyone can be good enough to get there. I used to strive to follow the Five Pillars . . . now I don't even try."

"Me either."

"What?"

Amber smiled. "I mean, I don't try to get to heaven. That's why Jesus came. I'm not perfect, but Jesus is. And he loved me so much that he died as a sacrifice for my sins. It's true, Mohammed."

"That doesn't seem possible to me."

"All you have to do is believe."

When Mohammed didn't respond, Amber decided not to press the issue. She closed her eyes and felt the Forerunner rise and fall with each bump. Her greatest fear was being pulled over by gun-toting border guards more anxious to shoot than ask questions. Whether her red passport of Switzerland would provide safe harbor was a toss-up, but being found in the company of Mohammed Faheedi would not help her cause. The rulers of Iran had surely decided that her friend was a rogue Intelligence agent. The border patrol must have been notified to keep a lookout.

Amber opened her eyes again. "Do you think we'll get stopped?"

"Don't worry. If that happens, Jaml will do all the talking, and he knows what to say to these people."

Friday, May 19
2:22 A.M. local time
Above the Iran-Turkey border

Paragliding above the high desert landscape, Lt. Kenyon Thomas held up his left forearm and looked at the GPS coordinates pulsating from an LCD display: 165 degrees north by 138 degrees west. He scanned the horizon, counting his chicks like a mother hen.

Lieutenant Thomas spoke into his helmet mike. "Everyone OK?"

"Affirmative, One," the first chutist said.

"Affirmative, Two," the second announced, and so on down the line. Everyone was accounted for.

With camo paint on their faces and their night-vision goggles in place, the paragliding soldiers looked more like robotic creatures from a Star Wars movie than human beings. Each was dressed in a black camouflage jumpsuit, combat boots, and Kevlar-lined gloves. Their protective helmets or "flash hoods" were filled with sophisticated communications headgear. Each member of the team carried Heckler & Koch MP5s, silenced automatic pistols, plus a few stun grenades. The one exception was Martinez, the team's sharpshooter, who was armed with a Walther WA2000 Bullpup, a lightweight but powerful sniper weapon.

Lieutenant Thomas could not believe their good fortune. They were sailing five thousand feet above Qutor with plenty of altitude to enact a pinpoint landing at the designated LZ. "OK, guys. We are about two miles southwest of the rendezvous point. Continue your easterly descent."

When the seven men reached one thousand feet off the deck, they began making huge circles in the sky. They swooped until they completed their two-point landings in the Iranian scrub brush. The Air Commandos immediately gathered their chutes, and within three minutes, Thomas's team huddled up at a rally point.

"Where are we?" asked one of his men.

"No more than six hundred yards from our rendezvous point." The team leader was following a reading of his GPS finder.

"When are we supposed to make the UPS pickup?"

"In forty-five minutes. Let's get those chutes buried in the meantime."

Friday, May 19
2:47 A.M. local time
Near the Iran-Turkey border

Jaml could see a solitary light illuminating the intersection one kilometer ahead. He wasn't alarmed until he noticed an olive-colored troop truck and several white sawhorses blocking the pavement.

"We have a checkpoint." Jaml quickly phoned the trailing car with instructions. "When you get within a few hundred meters, I want you to pull by the side of the road, turn off your lights, and listen to what happens. I'll keep the phone on."

Jaml pulled up to the roadblock, where a cast-off Soviet utility vehicle was parked on the left shoulder with its lights shining toward Jaml's Forerunner. Four white sawhorses blocked traffic in each direction. Only three guards maintained the site during this graveyard shift. One hopped out of the driver's seat while the other two slowly departed from the passenger side. None of the soldiers looked especially alert.

"I'll try to bluff our way through."

Jaml glanced in the rearview mirror and read the fear in Amber's eyes. Rida looked just as concerned. Mohammed, he noticed, stared straight ahead and concentrated on keeping a poker face.

"Tell her to cover up and not say anything."

Mohammed translated. Amber closed her scarf and pretended to sleep.

Jaml rolled down the window as the guard arrived. "Good evening, officer. I guess I should say 'good night' since it is no longer evening, but good night sounds like we are leaving instead of arriving."

The guard grunted. "Enough yapping. Papers."

Jaml handed over a fresh set of false identification papers that his outfit had produced the previous evening in Tabriz. His men had even listed Maree, Caleb, and Ruthina as belonging to Mohammed and Rida Faheedi.

"Don't you men ever get to rest?" Jaml was hoping to distract the guard. "Must be lonely duty this time of night."

The lead guard stuck to business. "Where are you going so late at night?"

"That is my wife in the backseat sleeping, along with her brother and his wife. My mother-in-law has taken seriously ill. She lives in Qutor, and we are traveling as fast as we can to see her."

Without comment the guard walked away. Unfortunately, he kept their papers, which meant he wasn't through with them yet. He jumped up into the cab and took a seat, while the other two men stood outside and shared a cigarette. The head guard pulled out a sheaf of papers and began rifling through them. Jaml watched intensely. Slowly Jaml reached under his seat with his right hand for a German-made sidearm.

The lead guard sat in the cab, flipping through papers. When he apparently found what he was looking for, he picked up the false set of identity papers and compared them to the directive in his possession. He shined a flashlight to be sure.

"He knows!" Jaml shouted.

He jammed the accelerator pedal to the floorboard, and the Forerunner exploded through the wooden sawhorses, splaying whitewashed shards of wood high into the air. The two guards dropped to one knee and readied themselves to shoot at the runaway car, but before they could level their rifles, both guards took headshots from Jaml's sharpshooters two hundred meters away. A dozen more bullets raked the front of the checkpoint's utility vehicle, shattering the front glass and killing the lead guard. Jaml's men jumped back in their Mercedes and roared through the deserted roadblock, squealing after the lead vehicle.

Up ahead, Jaml almost lost control of his Forerunner as the SUV fishtailed down K12, but when he saw the two guards drop in his side mirror, he steadied the gas.

"We got the third one!" the Mercedes driver reported. "We're right behind you."

The Kurd knew it was only a question of time, though, before the border patrol figured out that they had lost three of their own. At least they had a head start. Would it be enough?

Jaml slowed to check his GPS finder. "We have another seven kilometers. Those Americans better be there."

Friday, May 19
2:53 A.M. local time
Near the Iran-Turkey border

Lt. Kenyon Thomas saw the four houses, which put the start of a smile on his face. The American flag was right where they said it would be—hanging in a window as a coast-is-clear sign.

He led the men into the middle of the cluster, when a voice boomed, "Welcome to Iran." The voice had a British accent.

"Whose hand can I shake?" Thomas asked.

"Mine. I'm Haci, the unit commander," said the Brit as he pumped Thomas's hand. On cue, a dozen men with AK-47s stepped out of the shadows.

One of Haci's men interrupted the introductions. "It's for you," he said, handing the unit commander a radiophone. "Jaml."

"Are the Americans there?" Jaml asked.

"Yes, they just arrived."

"Good, because we just had to break through a checkpoint. Our mission has been compromised. They'll be searching every vehicle they run into for sure. Tell them we can't escort them over the border. They have to call for a pickup if they have plans of leaving Iran alive."

Haci translated the situation to Thomas. Lt. Thomas knew that the original plan called for the Kurds to drive his group in a sheep transport truck within a few klicks, or kilometers, of the border, after which they would trek through the foothills into Turkey, arriving just after dawn. U.S. helicopters out of Incirlik would be waiting at a new DLZ—designated landing zone—on Turkish soil. Now all those plans were out the window. Any vehicle getting within ten kilometers of the border would surely be stopped and searched.

"Can you request a pickup?" Haci asked.

Lt. Thomas reached for his encrypted field telephone. "They're not going to like this in Incirlik, but I don't think we have a choice."

As predicted, the Air Commando lieutenant received an earful from the on-duty dispatch officer at Incirlik Air Force Base.

Friday, May 19
3:00 A.M. local time
Near the Iran-Turkey border

When Checkpoint 24 didn't call in on the half-hour, the attending sergeant at the Qutor command post of the Iranian Border Patrol attempted to radio a connection.

Nothing.

With that, he picked up the phone and placed two phone calls.

26

Friday, May 19
3:04 A.M. local time
Near the Iran-Turkey border

Even Amber's cinematic familiarity with bullets flying through the air and chaotic car chases hadn't prepared her for what happened at the checkpoint.

Just minutes before, she had bent forward as much as possible—assuming the "crash position" while still harnessed to a seat belt—and imagined a bullet striking the rear glass, passing through the upholstery, and tearing into her back. It wasn't until Mohammed voiced the all-clear that she straightened up—and breathed. She did her best to keep her nerves in check while Jaml deftly handled the sandy track at 100 kph.

"What's going to happen?" Amber asked Mohammed as the Forerunner jolted through the rugged landscape.

"I'm not sure," came the reply from the front seat. "Our friend has learned that the Americans have arrived, but with our unfortunate incident back at the checkpoint, this area will be crawling with air and land patrols. The only thing in our favor is that the checkpoint guards weren't able to call in a description of our cars."

Two minutes passed, and a cluster of lights could be seen in the distance. "Looks like we're there," Mohammed said.

The Toyota Forerunner and Mercedes skidded to dusty stops and were directed to carports next to two homes. Several Kurds waited to drape the cars with camouflage netting.

The choreographed movements impressed Amber as she stepped out of the Forerunner. Her attention turned to Rida, who was fussing over the three children. Their group was led inside Haci's residence, where Amber quickly regarded the clad-in-black Air Commando men waiting to greet her.

"Amber Robbins, I presume." Lt. Kenyon Thomas extended his hand.

Amber felt immense relief that she was now in the good hands of the U.S. military. Maybe she would get out of Iran alive.

"I'm pleased to meet you, Lieutenant," Amber replied evenly. She removed her scarf and ran her fingers through her hair. "Are you at liberty to tell me your name?"

"Yes, I am Lieutenant Kenyon Thomas. We have been asked by the United States military to escort you and the Faheedis to safety."

"Do you know the Faheedis are bringing three children they are planning to adopt?"

The lieutenant blanched. "No, I wasn't given that information. But that's the least of my problems right now."

Amber suddenly became concerned. "Is something wrong?"

"Apparently your little episode back at the checkpoint lit a fire under the border patrol. We can't chance sneaking out of Iran on foot. We don't have the firepower to match helicopters or a large search party, so we're calling in the cavalry."

"Cavalry?"

"Yes. Two Pave Hawks, but they can't get here until 0500. We'll have to hightail it out of here before the sun comes up. Helicopters become sitting ducks in the daylight."

"Isn't this dangerous, flying American helicopters into Iran?"

"Yes, but it's a brand new world out there. Apparently, there's a two-fold reason for this mission. Political pressure was brought to bear in your case, but as regards Mr. Faheedi, the military is quite interested in talking to him since he could share his insights regarding Muslim factions in the Middle East. You don't get an intelligence defector very often from this part of the world."

As soon as Amber felt her shoulders being shaken by Rida, she knew that a ninety-minute nap wasn't enough.

"Where are we?" she groaned.

"The helicopters are coming soon."

"Helicopters?" Amber, groggy from little sleep, struggled with the concept of helicopters. Then the fog lifted. "OK. I'm getting up." She exited the house, walking to the women's opulent latrine—a muddy trench behind one of the houses. She reproached herself for having taken Western toilets for granted.

When she returned, the half-dozen Air Commandos and heavily armed Kurds had gathered at a makeshift command post about two hundred meters from the cluster of homes. She had impeccable timing, arriving as Lt. Thomas' radio crackled to life.

"Bronco, this is Cowboy. Do you copy?"

Thomas immediately snatched the mike from his field radio and pressed the transmit button. "Cowboy, this is Bronco. Read you loud and clear. LZ is clear."

"Cowboy copies LZ is clear. ETA is eight minutes."

"Roger."

Thomas barked a command, prompting four Air Commandos to walk out into the sandy terrain.

"What are they doing?" Amber asked.

"Setting out infrared strobes to identify the LZ for the pilots."

"Won't blinking lights attract some attention out in this isolated area?"

"They are *infrared* strobe lights, invisible to the naked eye. But they show up real fine on the FLIR—forward-looking infrared radar—that the choppers have."

Moments later the radio crackled to life again. "Cowboy has visual on the LZ. Say wind speed and direction."

Thomas consulted a compass hanging from his belt. "Wind 060 at ten. Say again, 060 at ten. LZ is cold."

"Cowboy copies ten knot wind from 060 degrees. No Indians at LZ."

Amber could hear the definitive sound of rotor blades beating the air. When she looked in the direction of the chop-chop, however, she could see nothing—just the blackness of an overcast pre-dawn. Then her eyes glimpsed two black silhouettes darting across an inky background. The sound crescendoed into a deafening roar as a pair of black shapes feathered onto the makeshift landing zone and made three-point landings.

It was time for her to say good-bye to her new friends. "Thank you!" she gushed to Jaml Kahn and the Kurds. She wanted to shake hands, but that gesture was far too intimate in their culture, so she pressed her hands together and made a slight bow.

The American reporter returned her gaze to the impromptu landing strip. She expected to see landing lights on the helicopters, but then she figured the pilots were peering at the landscape through the eerie green backlight of night-vision goggles. She marveled at their operational daring and navigation skill. A small U.S. Air Force insignia on the fuselage door identified this aircraft as American, but Amber saw something more: the freedom and safety offered by the greatest nation on earth.

"Amber, can you take Maree?" The three children, crying out in fear, clung to Rida, but Mohammed appeared to be at a loss at what to do.

Amber picked up the older daughter, while Rida hugged Ruthina. Mohammed lifted a petrified Caleb into his arms as they approached the bay doors.

A blast of gusty wind whipped Amber's clothing in every direction. *I can't wait to get rid of this rupush,* she thought. Amber was wearing Levis and a light white sweater underneath in preparation for the moment she could return to Western dress.

First, though, everyone had to board. Swirling dust caused her eyes to sting while dirt in her lungs produced coughing spasms. She felt relief when the crew chief reached for Maree and boosted her into the chopper. "Welcome aboard, ma'am," the chopper pilot shouted over the engine's roar in a honey-and-grits Southern accent that had never sounded better to Amber. "Y'all doing fine?"

"I'm sure glad to see you, soldier."

Amber and the Faheedi family, plus Lt. Thomas, were deposited in one Pave Hawk; the remaining members of the Air Commando team hopped into the second chopper. They had barely strapped themselves in when their helicopter lifted into the still-dark sky.

Lt. Thomas sat next to her, wearing a headset with an attached microphone.

"You want to listen in?" he yelled over the din.

Amber nodded. Thomas leaned over and found a headset under her seat. He plugged the jack into the wall behind her. The first thing she heard was the pilot chattering with the pilot of the other chopper.

"Mustang, this is Cowboy lead," she heard one pilot say. "Time to head back to the corral."

"Mustang copies."

They had barely reached an altitude of one hundred feet when an excited voice came back on the air. "Cowboy, Mustang sees two fast movers at six o'clock! Course 270 at 20,000, approximate speed 500 knots."

Lt. Thomas leaned over to translate. "Two Iranian fighter jets are heading our way. We're in for it now."

Friday, May 19
4:58 A.M. local time
Near the Iran-Turkey border

Lt. Kenyon Thomas peered into the darkness and wondered what kind of jets they were. If they were old Soviet MiG-23s with outdated avionics, the helicopters stood a chance by staying down in the weeds. The aging MiG-23's radar had difficulty locating a low-level target. But he remembered that Iran had purchased some Russian-made Su-34s with advanced look-down, shoot-down radar. If these two jets were the modern Sukhois, they were in for a world of hurt. Their highly maneuverable helicopters would be easy prey for modern air-to-air missiles.

He figured their best defense was to fly the nap of the Earth and hope for success. All they had to do was get across the border; the Iranians would not invade Turkish air space because an incursion could result in an altercation with trigger-happy U.S. Air Force F-15 Eagles. If they could successfully evade the Iranian fighters for a few more minutes, they could slip out of Iran unscathed.

Suddenly, the chopper's RHAWS—the radar homing and warning system—warbled in Thomas's headset—they were being painted by the enemy's advanced fighter jets.

"Cowboy, this is Mustang. Take combat spacing and begin evasive maneuvers." Thomas gripped his armrests as the Pave Hawk pilot juked and dodged the helicopter to present a more evasive target to the fighters. The textbook maneuver did not work: the warbling changed to a steady tone, signaling a radar lock by one of the Iranian fighters.

"Cowboy, bogies have launched. Say again, missile launch."

Thomas knew that the air-to-air missile would arrive in a matter of seconds. The pilot jerked the craft left and up in the most violent maneuver the lieutenant had probably ever experienced. The children screamed under the strain of the g-forces as their new parents clasped them to their chests. The lieutenant lowered his head and gripped his seat belt as the helicopter gyrated wildly to break the radar lock.

"Chaff, now!" the Pave Hawk pilot shouted. His co-pilot launched bundles of chaff in an effort to decoy the missile off their signal. Their timing could not have been better. Thomas looked out the window and saw the fiery contrails of an air-to-air missile speed by their Pave Hawk—

—and explode into the other American helicopter.

Cowboy disintegrated in a ball of flames. Thomas looked out the window and watched the mangled chopper fall silently to earth, knowing that three crew members and six Air Commandos had perished. He allowed himself a moment's grief for his friends. At any moment, Thomas expected a second wave of missiles to finish them off.

Without warning, their Pave Hawk lurched and lost altitude.

"Shrapnel must have hit us!" the pilot screamed. "We're losing power!" The engine skipped several beats, and the Pave Hawk plunged farther into the darkness. The chopper pilot fought the controls to maintain altitude.

Thomas looked over and noticed that Amber appeared to be praying. He touched her on the shoulder.

"Can you pray for me?" he asked.

"Sure."

Amber bowed her head again and prayed out loud: "Dear Lord, you know exactly the situation we're in. I pray, Lord, that you will somehow protect us. If it is your will to take us, then we rest on your promise that you will be there for us when we enter eternity. Lord, I pray that everyone in this helicopter believes in you."

Lt. Thomas overheard the pilot say to his co-pilot, "We're not going to make it to Turkey. We have to find a place to set down quickly."

"How far are we from the border?" his co-pilot asked.

"A couple of miles—if we can stay in one piece."

"What's happening down there? Your screen looks like a forest fire!"

The on-duty AWACs tech considered what he should say to his commanding officer.

"From what I can determine, sir, we got ambushed. Two Su-34s came out of nowhere and splashed one of the Paves. I think the other one is flying, but my radar is failing to register a solid lock. He could be down in the weeds. If so, he never reached Turkey."

"Where are the bogeys?"

"Right here." The tech pointed to two small triangles on the green radar screen, heading east.

Suddenly, the two Iranian triangles turned into starbursts and flickered off the screen.

"What happened?" the CO screamed.

"I don't know, sir, but somebody just splashed them. It couldn't have been our Pave. They're equipped with air-to-surface missiles, not air-to-airs. We don't have any assets in the air above the Turkish border."

"That means . . ."

"You're not thinking what I'm thinking."

"Yes, sir, I'm afraid so."

The Pave Hawk pilot struggled to maintain altitude, but the force of gravity would not yield its grip on the chopper.

"We're going in!" he yelled as he worked the stick to keep the battered chopper level.

The Pave Hawk roared into a small valley, where the pilot saw a patch of grazing land. It looked level enough. Could they get there in time?

"Prepare for a crash landing!"

The Pave Hawk yawed and pitched forward, nearly somersaulting in the air. The first streaks of daylight played havoc with the pilot's night-vision glasses. The pilot fought the stick, swearing out loud as he worked it back and forth. The whine of the chopper blades grew tornado-loud as the pilot throttled up for maximum power.

"We're going in!" he screamed.

The helicopter threatened to go in nose first, but the pilot yanked back on the stick, leveling the craft for a moment. Then the Pave Hawk—out of air speed—dropped like a stone as it made the sweetest crash landing this side of— They had survived.

"Thomas, do you have a reading on where we are?" the pilot yelled back at the Air Commando officer.

The lieutenant consulted his GPS. "I got us . . . holy cow! We're still in Iran!"

"That's what I figured. By how much?"

"Less than three klicks."

"What do we do now?"

"Hoof it over the border as quickly as we can and order a pick-up in friendly territory. We don't have a minute to lose, not with the sun rising. We're completely exposed."

27

Friday, May 19
5:35 A.M. local time
On the Iran-Turkey border

Amber stood on the summit and gazed eastward. "I don't think a sunrise has ever meant so much to me."

Mohammed and Rida, along with the three children, were steps behind her, followed by the two helicopter pilots and Lieutenant Kenyon Thomas.

The sun's orange light peaked over the eastern horizon, a series of arid escarpments and green valleys suitable for farming and grazing.

"Miss Robbins, we're not on some nature walk," Lt. Thomas said. "In fact, I'm feeling rather exposed up here, so if you don't mind, I'm in a big hurry to get off this here hill and into Turkey."

"Try hiking with a canvas tent and an itchy scarf cinched around your head."

Amber realized she sounded like a grump. "I'm sorry, Lieutenant. I'll shut my mouth and get moving."

It took a half-hour to descend one thousand vertical feet. When they reached the valley floor, the vegetation turned to grasslands and a few leafy trees.

"Who's that?" Amber pointed to a shepherd on the next hill, standing on the peak with a staff in his hand and a sheep dog at his side.

"Just a shepherd," the commando replied. "He's not going to bother us."

As the sun rose in the southeast, the shepherd scanned the horizon. He made more money keeping an eye out for people escaping Iran than he did raising sheep. Fifteen minutes earlier, he had received a call on a radiophone given to him by local authorities. The shepherd was told he'd receive a six-month bonus if he spotted a certain party leaving the country.

The shepherd found a rock to sit down on and shielded his eyes. Half a kilometer away in the valley below was the group he had been told about. The black guy in combat dress was a dead giveaway, as were the two women holding hands with three small children.

The shepherd looked down at the radiophone at his feet. When he was confident they were out of sight, he lifted up the receiver, hoping the bonus would be his.

They reached the border at 6:30 A.M. Amber regarded the dividing line between Iran and Turkey, which was marked by bales of razor wire stacked three to four feet high, creating a barrier that prevented man or beast from trespassing.

Lt. Thomas reached for a pair of wire clippers attached to his belt clip. Within ten minutes, the Air Commando had cut a hole two meters wide in the razor fencing.

"Would you like to lead us?" he asked Amber.

"Wow, this feels like the Promised Land," she replied. "Now I know why Joshua ordered the Israelites to build a monument of twelve stones to commemorate their crossing into Canaan."

"Thank you for that Bible lesson," Lt. Thomas said with a hint of sarcasm. "Let's keep it moving, everybody."

Rida swept two-year-old Ruthina into her arms and motioned to Mohammed to carry Maree, the nine-year-old girl. Amber reached for six-year-old Caleb and scooted him up into her arms, tickling him at the same time. The three adults picked their way through the clearing, careful not to catch their clothing on the barbed wire.

Once they were safely through, Amber lowered Caleb to the ground and crouched before him. "Gimme five," she said, holding up the palm of her hand.

The boy looked confused.

Rida translated Amber's command for the young boy. Caleb puckered his lips and slapped Amber's hand with all his strength.

"Way to go!" Amber exclaimed as she straightened up and eyed the American commando. "Give me a high five, too, lieutenant."

Thomas broke out laughing and slapped her hand with gusto. Amber knew the sight of a black Special Forces officer high-fiving a rupush-clad American woman had to be incongruous to any onlookers, but she didn't care.

"It won't be long now," he grinned. "Which reminds me. I have to call Incirlik to see where our pickup is."

The lieutenant opened a field map and pushed several buttons on his field radio. "You have three choppers on their way now? Good." He looked down at his map. "Tell them we'll meet them at RZ 33 in twenty minutes."

Thomas switched off the radio. "C'mon, everybody. We're almost there." The motley group, huffing from exertion, followed the Air Commando through a small valley until they reached a clearing designated as RZ 33.

Amber walked over to a chair-sized boulder and sat down. Her ears detected a distinct noise in the air—the steady thump-thump of helicopter blades in the distance. Amber relaxed. In a few minutes, they would be in the good hands of U.S. Special Forces.

"There they are." The Hammer sat in the co-pilot's seat as the helicopter crossed the ridgeline and hovered over the valley. The fact that his helicopter and three other attack choppers belonging to the Iranian air force were presently in Turkish air space did not matter a twit to al-Shanoosh.

The Hammer held up his binoculars. The entire group had gathered on the valley floor—the traitor Faheedi, his apostate wife, the missing children, and the American journalist he'd last seen in Amman. Everything was perfect, although the presence of those American GIs complicated things. They would be no match for his firepower, though.

The Savak agent, sitting in the right jump seat of the glassed-in cockpit, allowed a satisfied look to come over his bearded face. He and his command helicopter maintained altitude above the fray while three Iranian military helicopters swooped in for the kill.

"Why are our guys coming in so fast?" Amber asked.

Lt. Thomas' jaw dropped. "Those aren't American choppers! Everyone take cover!"

In the midst of screams and panic, Amber's first concern was the children, but Rida had already scooped up the two youngest, Ruthina and Caleb, and ducked behind the nearest boulder. Mohammed, with catlike quickness, grabbed Maree around the waist and hustled her to safety behind the wide trunk of an oak tree. Amber, certain that the bullets would start flying at any second, realized that her nearest point of safety was behind the oak tree with Mohammed and Maree.

"Keep down!" Lt. Thomas yelled as the trio of helicopters bore down on them. The lead helicopter fired its gun pods, prompting the second and third helicopters to unleash their weapons racks. Four missiles sailed over their heads and exploded in the foothills behind them as Thomas sprayed the fast-moving helicopters with automatic fire.

"Mayday, mayday, we're being attacked!" Lt. Thomas barked into his radio headset.

"Where are you?" came the reply from the female tech back at Incirlik.

"RZ 33, right where we're supposed to be! Where's our pickup?"

"They are three minutes out. Hang on."

The olive helicopters circled for another low pass. Suddenly, Ruthina slipped from Rida's grasp and broke for the clearing, where she waddled toward the bug-like fuselage of the lead helicopter, her right arm pointing at the aerial gunship.

"Ruthina!" Rida screamed, lunging after her.

"Get her!" yelled Thomas, thirty feet away. He reflexively fired his machine gun as cover toward the helicopters, which were holding their fire as they bore down on the group.

In her haste, Rida tripped over her rupush, which sent her sprawling in the tawny dirt. Amber, paralyzed with fear, didn't know what to do—or what she could do. The Iranian helicopters would be making their second sweep in a matter of seconds . . . then Rida sprang toward the wayward child and tackled her with Caleb fast on her heels.

"Watch Maree," Mohammed said. He sprinted toward the threesome in the dirt clearing just as the lead helicopter began firing its machine gun on the exposed family. Like a flame following a fuse to the detonator, a zip line of exploding dirt appeared to be right on track toward Rida, Caleb, and Ruthina.

"Cover! Cover!" yelled Thomas, who fired his machine gun wildly against the approaching helicopters.

Amber held her breath—she could see they didn't have time to get to safety. Rida must have had the same split-second realization as well because she wrestled Caleb to the ground and fell on top of him and her sister. Mohammed, on the run, leaped on top of the pile just as the lines of machine-gun fire made their deadly arrival.

Amber looked away and held Maree close, who buried her head in her chest. While Thomas and the chopper pilots directed their automatic weapons at the attacking helicopters, an overwhelming sense of dread filled her: a young family who deserved better had just been wiped out.

"The American cowboys have arrived, sir," said the radar technician aboard the Hammer's Russian-made Mi-8.

"What?" al-Shanoosh demanded.

"Looks like three Pave Hawks coming out of Incirlik."

"Get us to the border now!"

The hovering helicopter dipped and charged toward the border while the other three Iranian helicopters continued their second pass. After one more offensive foray against the Americans, the Hammer's chopper hightailed it out of the valley.

"Target lock," said the weapons tech in the rear seat of the Pave Hawk.

"How many?" the captain asked.

"I can take out the three, but it looks like the fourth has crossed the line."

"Splash the three then."

The weapons tech typed several commands into the onboard computer and instantaneously received a confirmed target lock. He clicked his mouse on a red target circle, and five seconds later, the helicopter rocked as three Aim-120 AMRAAM missiles leaped into the air, each programmed to strike separate targets.

The weapons tech followed the vapor trail as the missiles closed in on the slower-moving helicopters. Each tried to spin and dive, but they were no match for the AMRAAMs. In a little more than ten seconds, each was reduced to a huge fireball.

"Got 'em!" screamed the weapons tech.

"Excellent, Lieutenant!"

"Thanks, Captain. They were shooting at the good guys, and we take that kinda personal around here."

Amber rushed to the blood-streaked bodies lying prostrate in the dirt. She turned over Rida, whose expressive mouth was wide open as if she had been surprised by something. Her lifeless eyes stared off to space. Amber reached for her left wrist and felt for a pulse. Her skin was still warm, but she could not detect a heartbeat.

Then she saw why. Three massive wounds in the chest area had torn her vital organs to shreds. Death, thankfully, had been instantaneous.

Amber couldn't bear to look at the two children Rida had been protecting. Ruthina and Caleb were mortally wounded as well, but thankfully their eyes were closed. They appeared to be sleeping peacefully.

Next to Rida, Mohammed lay face down and spread-eagled in the dirt. It looked like he had taken a hit in the lower back and legs.

Amber glanced up at the three American Pave Hawks circling in for a landing then was distracted by a motion in the sand near her—Mohammed's hand moved.

"If Mohammed can hang on for sixty more minutes, we can get him to some American doctors."

Amber, who was on her knees tending to Mohammed, looked up. "Luke . . . is that you?"

"Yes, it's me, Amber."

She leaped into Luke's arms and felt his powerful squeeze. "It's horrible," she cried. "Why? Why did it have to happen to them?"

"We don't know," Luke soothed. "We just don't know."

Amber composed herself. "If we're going to save Mohammed, we have to get out of here as quickly as possible."

An Air Commando medic attended to Mohammed while other personnel began the grim task of wrapping Rida and the two children into black body bags. After checking Mohammed's vital signs, the medic directed three Air Commandos to lift him onto a litter and ferry him to the Pave Hawk. Amber, with her arm around an inconsolable Maree, assisted the young girl to the helicopter, where, with a boost from Luke, she hopped in and knelt next to her new father.

"Is he going to make it?" Amber asked the medic.

"Fifty-fifty," the medic replied as the chopper blades began spooling in preparation for takeoff. "His legs were badly shot up, but the bullet that tore through his lower abdomen is the one that's life-threatening. Lots of internal bleeding."

Mohammed groaned as the medic hooked up an IV to the crook of his left arm, delivering much-needed fluids and the salve of pain medication. Amber came to his side and stroked his forehead.

Mohammed turned his gaze toward her. "Wha—"

"You've been hit bad, but you can make it." Amber's throat tightened.

"Ree-da?"

Stinging tears flowed from Amber's eyes, dotting Mohammed's dirty face. "I'm so sorry."

Mohammed grasped his chest with his right arm. Heartbreak streaked his eyes. "Children?"

She stroked his matted hair. "Maree made it. You have to hang in there for your daughter."

Amber pressed a cool compress to his forehead as Mohammed struggled to take in the life-changing events of the last fifteen minutes. She leaned close to his ear. "Hang on, my friend. We're going as fast as we can."

"I'm dying."

Amber's forehead creased with compassion. "Mohammed, I don't know what's going to happen." She closed her eyes and opened them. "You're standing on the edge of eternity. We all are, really. But you may not have time . . . I know that you have always been taught that Allah is the one true God, but you have to trust me on this. Jesus is God, not Allah."

Mohammed, whose eyes remained closed, nodded in understanding.

Amber gently gripped his shoulders as her words flooded. "I don't want you to die without going to heaven. Believe in Jesus, I beg you. Everything they say about him is true. He was born two thousand years ago and nailed to a cross to die for our sins. Dozens of witnesses saw him come back to life. Historians have never been able to refute that. Only God could resurrect himself back to life, Mohammed, and Jesus did that to prove that he was who he said he was."

In his semi-conscious state, Mohammed wasn't sure what to

believe. He knew in his heart that he had never *really* believed in Allah, but what about this Jesus? And then it struck him: Rida believed in Jesus. She must have asked questions and searched her heart before making such an important decision. She was a very intelligent woman, and she never would have become a Christian unless she knew it was true. If he died now without Jesus, he would be eternally separated from her. He did not want that to happen. But even more, he didn't want to be separated from Jesus—the name so despised in his culture. He felt like his heart longed for Jesus. The love that Amber spoke of. His love. But could someone like him receive such love? "I don't deserve it," he whispered.

"Nobody does!" she pleaded.

But Mohammed knew this was the time and place to believe in Jesus Christ. He recalled that evening with Amber when they listened to J. T. Hawkins speak in Geneva. He had said no back then, but now he was being given a second chance. He opened his dark eyes and turned his gaze upon his friend: *Go ahead, Amber. Do what you're supposed to do.*

Amber leaned over and whispered into his ear. "Mohammed, would you like to ask Jesus Christ into your heart? Then you can know for sure that you're going to heaven."

Mohammed mouthed a yes.

Amber's face filled with joy. "Then pray after me: Dear Jesus, I come to you right now . . ."

Mohammed repeated the opening sentence.

"I admit that I'm a sinner. I believe you came on this Earth and died on a cross for me. I ask you to forgive me for my sins and come into my heart now."

Amber bent over and kissed Mohammed on his dirt-streaked cheek. "Mohammed, I don't know what's going to happen, but I do know that nothing will ever separate you from Jesus Christ."

Mohammed labored to breathe. "There's one more thing you should know. In my shirt pocket is a Flash drive containing Plan Sword. Tell the world about it . . . before it's too late."

Mohammed's eyes flickered twice before shutting off the world.

28

Sunday, May 28
10:11 A.M.
Villars, Switzerland

The midmorning sun beat down on the four hikers as they trekked along a dirt trail overlooking the charming alpine village of Villars, more than a thousand feet below.

"Every time I see this view, Daddy, I just want to frame it and take it with me wherever I go." Amber paused to drink in the bucolic surroundings: green hills dotted with tan Swiss cows wearing bells that tinkled each time the bovines dipped their heads to bite off another helping of dewy Alpine grass; chalet rooftops made of slate that glistened in the sun; and all was enclosed by the craggy, snow-dusted peaks of the Haute Savoie known as "Europe's rooftop." Little cloud puffs nestled into the mountain crevices like cotton balls stuffed into the ears of giants.

"I know what you mean," Jack Robbins said. "I never tire of this view either."

The hiking trail passed magnificent chalets constructed out of varnished Norwegian pinewood and accented with window boxes that overflowed with blood-red and pearl-white geraniums. On the terraces, vacationing families enjoyed brunches of croissants and jam. Everyone waved, while some offered a hearty bonjour.

"Bonjour," Suzanne Robbins sang out, returning the greeting.

A few moments later, the group stopped to fully admire the view overlooking Villars. "I've been hiking this trail since I was a little girl," Amber said, "and it hasn't changed a bit."

She had always loved this hike to the Col de Bretaye, where a mountaintop restaurant awaited them for lunch. "Thinking about coming back to Villars was one of the things that kept me going in Iran."

"I'm sure it did. What are you going to do now?" her mother asked.

"I'm not sure. The world has changed so much in the last couple of years. One thing I've learned is to not take moments like this for granted. We really don't know if we have tomorrow, do we?"

"No, and I don't think your series of stories and photos about Plan Sword will change the plans of the ruling mullahs at all," her father said, "but there's a buzz in Washington. Evan even thinks your series is Pulitzer Prize material."

Amber looked incredulous. "We're talking about our Evan, right?" she teased.

"Afraid so. But listen to this. I was cc'd on a special White House briefing this week, and they say that Iran's indiscriminate killings of Christians and Jews have increased upon your return."

"Really?"

"Yes, I'm afraid so, and Christians will continue to be martyred unless your friend here can do something about it."

"Mr. Robbins, you're giving me too much credit—or placing too much pressure on my shoulders," Luke said.

"Don't underestimate yourself, Divot. Any person that saves my daughter from harm's way is capable of a great deal."

"I appreciate that, but in terms of Amber's rescue, the Israelis deserve much of the credit."

"The Israelis?" Jack questioned.

"Yes, what about the Israelis?" Amber asked.

"Well, remember how you and the other Pave Hawk were attacked by Iranian fighters before you crossed the border?"

"I'll never forget it. Nor will I ever forget those brave men who were killed trying to rescue us."

Luke grunted in agreement. "Yes, an incredible sacrifice, but no one would have made it out of Iran without the help of the Israelis. You see, just before the two Iranian fighters could launch another round of missiles, they were taken out by an Israeli F-22 Raptor that happened to be in the area. The bad guys never saw what hit them. At least that is what I was told unofficially."

"The Raptor?" Jack said. "I didn't know we sold the Israelis one."

"You don't," Luke declared.

"So how did they know to be in the area?" Amber wondered.

"Let's just say a little bird told them. And you never heard that from me, right?"

"No, no, of course not," Amber grinned, looking for agreement from her parents.

"While we're passing around the credit," Luke continued, "let's not forget the Kurds. They helped Amber escape from Tehran and make it to the border."

"They were amazing, Dad," Amber said.

"Oh, I heard from Jaml Khan," Luke interjected. "He said he appreciated the deposit your father made into his Swiss account."

"It was the best check I've ever written," Jack said.

"I'm sure it was, and it was sure nice of you to invite me to come to Switzerland for the weekend. I haven't seen Amber since we left Turkey. She was lucky, you know. Well, not lucky, but fortunate because God was really looking out for her."

"Yes, he was," Suzanne said, "and it looks like God was looking after Mohammed and that cute little girl. What a terrible thing that the rest of the family didn't survive. I felt so sad when Amber told me about Rida and those poor children. What's going to happen to Mohammed and Maree?"

"I hear that they are being relocated somewhere in the Washington, D.C., area," Luke said. "I can only imagine the difficulties he is experiencing—being a single-parent dad in a strange new land. I'm sure the company is taking good care of him, though."

"The company?"

"Our friends at Langley. Mohammed was quite a catch for the debriefing folks. The public will never hear about Mohammed, of course, but maybe things will change when people read Amber's story about Christians losing their lives just because they refused to convert."

"Let's hope so."

The foursome continued to hike in the late-morning sun.

"It doesn't look like this converting people 'by the sword' stuff is going to change, does it?" Jack said.

Amber agreed with her father. "The Iranian mullahs have decided that in their jihad against the West, they are going back to the basics, and if that means killing Christians and Jews unless they convert, that's what they'll do."

"Then I wonder . . ."

"What, Dad?"

"You remember how the White House asked you not to include the information about the Russian sub falling into Iranian hands?"

"Yes. They cited national security concerns."

"Well, I heard some ominous news coming out of Washington last night. A highly placed source told one of our reporters that the Iranian missile sub left Bandar Abbas two weeks ago and began steaming toward the Cape of Good Hope. We tracked the *Holy Prophet*—that's what the Iranians christened it—as it rounded Cape Town and made its way up into the Atlantic. The sub made no effort to escape detection until it made a left turn off the Azores that put it on a path for the United States. That's when the *Holy Prophet* disappeared—total silence. With everything that's been happening in the world, those in Homeland Security are in a total panic."

"When did you hear this?" Amber asked.

"This morning in an e-mail message."

"God help us!"

Acknowledgments

By the Sword began as a casual discussion between my church pastor, Rick Myatt, and me (Mike Yorkey) more than a year before September 11, 2001. One thing led to another, and we started developing characters and weaving a comprehensive plotline. Then we put words and scenes on the screen and were more than halfway done on that fateful day when al-Qaeda members commandeered four commercial airplanes over American soil.

Overnight, the American public became interested in Islam and where the United States fit into the picture. We finished the novel by early 2002, certain that we had the right message at the right time. Even one of our Iranian readers, a native of Tehran, thought we were telling a true story, even though we insisted that our work was a piece of fiction. After holding high hopes, however, we received rejection after rejection from publishers. We thought our dream was dead.

Then another budding novelist, Tricia Goyer *(Dust and Ashes, Night Song,* and *Dawn of a Thousand Nights)* introduced herself and offered to take a look. She read and reread chapters, suggested substantive edits, and showed us where we could improve our manuscript. Without her generous help, *By the Sword* would never have seen the light of a publishing day.

A talented editor, Ocieanna Fleiss, came in behind Tricia to improve the manuscript. We also received welcome aid from Denise Harbison, June Wilkens, Karen Olin, Peter Frey, Jeannette Herring, and John Goyer. Trent Gaites was especially helpful with his comments.

With a revised manuscript, our literary agent approached a dozen publishing houses. After reading Oliver North's first novel, *Mission Compromised,* I believed that Broadman & Holman would be the best publisher for *By the Sword*. Rick and I thought *By the Sword* was cut from the same techno-thriller cloth. We are thrilled to be part of the B & H team.

Finally, we wish to acknowledge our time with a former Iranian ambassador who shared how he narrowly escaped the revolutionary forces unleashed by Ayatollah Khomeini in early 1979. His harrowing story left Rick and me grateful that we live in a country with religious freedom and cognizant of how fragile that freedom really is.